# Broken Echoes

# Broken Echoes

## An Antholgy of Teen Issues

Normandy D. Piccolo

**NBI**
**Normandy's Bright Ideas**
**Florida**

# Contents

# Bug

book 1

My name's Tobi Jackson, but most people call me *Bug*. This is my story told through my eyes and heart. It is straightforward. You will sense you are there with me. I was born in June and got my name *Bug* because my Momma used to call me her little *June Bug*.

You know, in June, there are the Fireflies that fly in the night and glow with a light then go dark — off and on. That has been my life for as long as I can remember, like the Firefly - Light and Dark, but mostly dark until that day.

The Darkness began when my Momma's "J's" took advantage of me in my youth and continued until Momma died. I became homeless on the streets at the age of 14 and began my own life of the "J's". The darkness was only briefly relieved by a false sense of light supplied by the momentary euphoria from the use of *dirt*. That and my friendship with Chloe, my street sister. Though diverse in personality, we found kinship and friendship living with the darkness and sharing those false moments of light brought on by *dirt*.

Then came a chance encounter that unbeknownst to me would begin contact with another "J", but one of Light, not darkness. Though I shunned it at first, a dramatic tragedy occurred that flattened me. My struggles with the dark aftermath and the false light eventually lead me to another encounter with the "J" of Light.

Your heart and mind will be captured as you immerse yourself into the story of *BUG*.

# Bug

Normandy D. Piccolo

**NBI**
**Normandy's Bright Ideas**
**Florida**

Bug
Printed in the United States of America
Copyright ©2025 by Normandy's Bright Ideas
ISBN: 979-8-9855654-7-8

Unsplash.com Photo Credits: Eric Ward
iStock, Clker-Free-Vector-Images at Pixabay.com

www.normandydpiccolo.com

*Yesterday was a long time ago.*

# Fireflies

*Light.*

*Dark.*

*Light.*

*Dark.*

*Light.*

*Dark.*

It is what I saw at night while I lay on my back in the soft, dewy grass and watched the fireflies dance up above in the sky on warm summer nights.

Momma used to say the ones who made the letter *J* were boys who tried to get a girl to like them. But sometimes, she warned, it could be a girl pretending to be a boy to devour her competition.

"Always gotta keep your eye out for that whore tryin' to swoop in and steal your man, Bug," she sternly warned me.

I did not even know what a *whore* was back then. Only someone momma hated. Someone I eventually and unwillingly evolved into. Just like her. Just like those tricky female fireflies.

Fireflies were my escape when I was a young child. I was mesmerized by their soft, enticing glow. It seemed so warm. Safe. Like the comfort one found in the loving arms of their momma.

Being bathed in comfort and love had become foreign to me, the older I got. My nightly routine changed from fireflies in the field with momma to picking up numerous empty bottles of Jack Daniels cradled in her passed-out arms.

I swear momma loved that damn bottle of whiskey more than me. It made me mad. I often took those empty whiskey bottles and smashed them. One by one, they broke up against the side of our trailer, until the shards laid splayed out like a sea of shiny little diamonds.

But there was nothing shiny or beautiful about those shattered fragments of smelly glass. It always amazed me how, despite being destroyed, each individual piece of glass held onto the distinct putrid aroma of chaos and pain it caused. The unmistakable scent of whiskey. Almost as tightly as momma's stranglehold of memories she tried in vain to drink away but never could.

Momma never once noticed the piles of busted glass I had created. She never awoken from drunken slumbers while the bottles hit the side of the trailer. She just staggered over the shards as if they were a crystal carpet laid out especially for her. Momma staggered over everything in life, including me.

I often wondered about my daddy while I stared upwards at the darkened sky full of lit bums from the fireflies.

*'Did my daddy leave momma and me because he wanted a boy instead of a girl? Did we ever pass each other by on the street? Did he like double-scooped mint chocolate chip ice cream, too? Did I have half-brothers or sisters? Did he ever think about me? Did he miss me?'*

Questions about my daddy bounced daily inside my little wispy blonde-haired coated brain matter like a 1970's pinball machine. I always seemed to have an endless supply of metaphoric quarters to keep those thoughts banging and clanging for hours on end.

*Ping-ting-bonk-zonk-thwapp!*

At the end of the day, I tilted and drifted off to sleep until the next morning where more pinball quarters, more thoughts and endless wonders resumed.

I never knew anything about my daddy. The color of his eyes. The color of his hair. If he was tall? Short? Did he smell like an expensive cologne? Or reek of cheap whiskey and cigarettes like momma?

I never knew his last name. Momma refused to speak it. She made certain the hospital etched her family name, *Jackson*, on my birth certificate when I was born so I could never find him.

I thought, '*Was my daddy even the man you thought was my daddy, momma?*'

Before things got worse for me, whenever I saw fireflies twinkling, I embraced feelings of warmth and love from the glow of their projected light. I desperately craved for momma to love me. But she drifted further away, on purpose, the older I got. Fireflies had soon taken her place and became the closest I ever got to knowing that type of loving, motherly warmth.

I noticed when their lights vanished, horrible, empty feelings of abandonment immediately took root. My soul felt strangled by an old witch's withered, decrepit hand whose bones were brittle and yet, strong enough to inflict pain and drain the breath straight out of your body simultaneously.

I was so starved for love and affection. Unfortunately, I failed to understand back then the difference between right love and affection, and wrong love and affection. I was just a kid. How could I have known? Sadly, I would come to realize the difference.

I despised the loneliness. Momma knew my feelings but did not care or she would have changed. I would have taken priority in her life over her precious whiskey. But her precious Jack was the favored child. There was nothing I could do about it.

I often begged momma to stay with me in our rundown trailer and not leave me alone. *Nope.* Momma loved three things. Well, four. But the fourth one she dared not admit. Not even in a drunken whisper to God.

Momma loved: whiskey, the company of men, herself, and my daddy. She always acted as if she hated my daddy. But she never fooled me. I might have been young. I might have been naïve and a bit uneducated. But observations and common sense were my keen traits. I was convinced momma never got over my daddy who walked out on us when I was still in diapers.

My daddy's abrupt departure was the reason why she drank herself into a nightly stupor. It was the reason why she chose to run around with so many men. It was a deception to try and forget something that could not be forgotten.

Over time, I learned you cannot forget things embedded so deep inside the heart. It will forever remain until you acknowledge its existence.

Momma never could deal with anything. She held onto her heartache caused by my daddy until the day she kissed Jack goodbye with a hearty exhale of her alcohol-riddled breath.

Eventually, I got accustomed to momma disappearing for days at a time on drunken benders. I stopped begging her to stay. I knew sooner or later she would return with a new guy in tow. Some low life she picked up at a bar. Her flirting with so many men was how we kept bills paid and food on the table. Even *Jack's* rent in her liver was paid for.

During her drunken benders, I was left alone, locked inside a rented, roach-infested trailer with nothing but stale generic brand cereal, cold water, broken crayons, a stack of old newspapers to color on and a half-busted television to watch on days it decided to work.

Our fridge was always empty. Momma did not like to cook. We ordered a lot of pizzas. Two cans of expired sweet peas covered in dust sat in the cupboards since we had moved into the trailer two years ago. They had been abandoned by the previous tenant. I felt everything in common with those unwanted cans of peas.

My loneliness was palpable. I begged momma relentlessly to stay whenever she tried to leave without me. But my complaints and hot tears repeatedly fell upon deaf ears.

I despised loneliness. What I despised even more was the male company she chose to entertain at our trailer. To me, those men were bandits who stole momma's attention away from where it should have been.

I loathed the heavy drinking she shared with those men. The drugs, too. Our trailer filled with so much cigarette smoke; I felt like a ship lost in the fog, as I navigated my way from my bedroom across the hall to our one and only bathroom.

Before long, drunken yells between momma and whatever man she brought home started up. Next, a door slam, followed by loud grunting and mattress spring squeaking sounds from the back bedroom.

Soon after, the front door opened, then slammed shut.

I always whispered, *"Good riddance, creep!"* when the man of the night exited.

Another night of hell, over. I finally rested my head on my stained pillow and curled up with a teddy bear I had fashioned together with newspaper, then stuffed with more newspaper, and held together with various sized rubber bands. I drifted off to sleep, just as the cockroaches had awoken to try and pry those old cans of peas open.

I loathed momma for not wanting to spend time with me. I believed it stemmed from my daddy who had left us. I reminded her of him. I never knew the man, so why did I care so much, too? I still care.

I further resented how momma acted as if she gave two shits if I existed or not. She treated me like I was some burden thrust into her life on purpose. She was the one who thrusted with my daddy and nine months later birthed me.

I never asked to be born. Why was I blamed for something I had no control over? Momma should have controlled that wandering vagina of hers the night she met my daddy. That's what she should have done. Then, I never would have existed, and she and *Jack* could have ridden off into the whiskey sunset together. Mouth to bottle just as she always wanted it to be.

Momma made no secret in later years about how much she resented my existence. Especially the years I blossomed like a pure, white gardenia, while the drinking she had done, turned her into an old, ugly, weed.

I never resented my existence, despite the horrible way momma rejected me, until my seventh birthday.

From that day forward, I struggled to navigate through life.

My seventh birthday was a personal introduction into the world of dirty, nasty-minded men who were unwillingly and repeatedly thrusted into my mind, body, and soul… without my permission.

The same men momma entertained inside our trailer. The same men she used for money to pay our rent, cigarettes and her precious *Jack*. The same men who used her in return, only for their own specific needs.

The same legion of men who decided on my seventh birthday was my turn to reimburse their dues.

My self-hatred grew with each passing rotation of the sun, each inappropriate touch and each forced drag down the hallway to the back bedroom.

I tried to make sense of the new dark feelings which moved into my heart and evicted what small amount of light which had remained throughout momma's rejection and abuse. Dark feelings which festered from within until the third trimester when they were born on my seventh birthday.

Dark feelings that scratched and clawed up my insides something awful. Dark feelings that tore my soul apart piece by piece. Dark feelings that yearned to be unleashed with a retaliation cocooned within an unspeakable wrath.

I never allowed those feelings to escape.     I fought to hold them inside. I feared what or who I would become should they have ever broken free.

# Happy Hellish Birthday to Me!

*Light.*

*Dark.*

*Light.*

*Dark.*

*Light.*

*Dark.*

I sat in a three-legged dining room chair, captivated by the flickered glow of seven birthday candles momma had lit with her classic Bic lighter. The blue and white striped candles had been thoughtlessly jammed through the creamy chocolate frosting of the store-bought vanilla cake. Some candles leaned left. Some leaned right. Some had nearly fallen off with loose frosting still attached.

I watched as momma lit the candles in the kitchen and then carried the lopsided cake into the dining room.

I thought, 'She *loves me and really wants me to have a Happy Birthday, after all.*'

The cake was the most beautiful cake my eyes had ever seen. It had big pink roses and green vines swirled all around it. The imperfect cake was still beautiful until momma dropped it hard onto the tabletop before me on purpose.

The organized roses slanted, same as the candles. I knew what the dropped cake meant. Momma was furious with me.

"Well go on. What the hell are you waiting for?" She bent forward and crudely hissed into my ear, *"Your daddy?"*

I said nothing. I feared an undeserved slap to the face. Great birthday, huh.

"Make a wish before you turn eight." She then kicked my three-legged chair hard enough I grabbed onto the edge of the table or risked falling.

I was dumbfounded as I watched momma empty the rest of *Jack* down her throat. I had not extended an invitation to Mr. Daniels nor momma's latest slimeball man, to my birthday party. I was upset and disappointed.

Momma met the burly biker at one of her regular watering holes. The mountain man looking dirtbag, smelled of an alcohol, motor oil and stale cigarette combo. He stayed in our trailer for the past week and leered at me every chance he had. Momma caught him staring at me a few times but said nothing. She did not want to spoil what she believed was 'a good thing'.

*'Another drunken loser that smelled worse than the loser before him. Perfect.'*

I knew his lustful looks tossed in my direction fueled momma's anger. But it was not my fault. I did nothing to entice him. If anything, she should have been angry at him, not me. I wanted him to leave after the first night. I begged her to make him go. But she would not kick him out. So now I paid the price for her poor choice. We had even fought about it the night before my birthday party while he was in the shower.

"Dammit, Tobi! I'm entitled to some happiness in my life! Just shut up and mind your business and leave him be. Ya hear?" She then grabbed my face hard with her right hand. I thought my chipmunked cheeks were going to explode from the pressure.

"You understand what I am telling you? Don't look at him. Don't prance your tiny ass around him with them little green terrycloth shorts of yours on neither. Ya hear me. You steer clear out of his sight."

*"Yes, momma,"* I whispered back. I felt defeated.

Since our discussion, I had done everything momma asked of me. I stayed out of his sight as best I could. I spent most of my time hidden away in my bedroom where I drew pictures on top of old newspapers. I even peed in an old whiskey jar to avoid running into him on my way to the bathroom.

*'Piss on you, Jack. Take that!'*

My attempts to avoid him were apparently not enough for momma. I landed in her crosshairs based on how she treated my cake. And me, with that hard, unprovoked kick to the chair.

I had been bored for days prior while locked away inside my bedroom alone. And yet, it was not enough. I had laid on my ancient, stained mattress momma and I had fetched from a dumpster and colored on top of things I had already colored. I had no mirror to talk back to myself for company. No dresser for my clothes to rearrange. No real toys. Nothing a girl my age should have. She always spent any money gained on booze, cigarettes., occasionally bills, pizza and men. Hardly anything on me.

One time when momma had left for days with another man she had met, I went down to the dumpster and found a pile of romance books near a trash bag riddled with flies. I snuck those raunchy books into my room. I tried to read the books, but I failed to understand most of the words. So, I made up stories as I turned the pages. When I grew bored of reading, I removed the covers and made a set of cardboard dolls to play with.

For the past three days I had done my best to avoid her biker dirtbag. But I noticed if I left my room, even for a glass of water, there he was. He would just stare at me like a starving snake to a cute bunny rabbit. I wished he had slithered out of our trailer for good before my birthday.

I longed to spend my seventh birthday with only momma. I missed the time we once spent together when I was younger. I had even dreamt of doing fun things mothers and daughters do. Shopping. Going to the zoo. Stuff I had seen on our half-working television and also from pictures in the magazines I had colored over. I would have especially loved to go in the field with the fireflies.

*'To see the warm glow of the fireflies and feel the warmth of momma's desire to spend time with me...the perfect birthday. But it was not to be.'*

I remained frozen in the three-legged chair with my ruined cake before me. I tried to conjure up a wish before blowing out the candles. I was deep in thought when I felt the hairs of the motorcycle dirtbag's brown beard brush up against my right cheek.

He whispered into my ear, *"You sure are pretty. Even prettier than your momma."* He then kissed my cheek. *"Don't tell her what I said. It's our special secret."* I shivered and hoped momma had not seen him close to me. If so, the blame would have landed square on my shoulders.

I closed my eyes and wished with all my might for the motorcycle dirtbag to have disappeared so I could spend my birthday with momma, only. My grape scented *Kool-Aid* breath blew forth and extinguished each of the seven candles. When I opened my eyes, much to my horror, momma was passed out face down on the table next to the chocolate ice cream box.

*'Happy Hellish Birthday, Tobi!'*

I will forever detest my seventh birthday. I will never forget one single detail about the very day I fell into a pit of darkness and despair. No hope in sight.

I recalled, *To this day, I still see the bright yellow paper tablecloth covered with giant painted green, red, and blue balloons. My lopsided rose chocolate iced cake with the seven half-melted blue and white striped candles nestled on top. A container of chocolate ice cream melted over the sides of its cardboard container and headed towards momma's right arm. And three presents wrapped in paper towels sat in a chair, yet to be opened. I don't believe they ever were. Momma threw them away in a heated rage once she found out about the motorcycle dirtbag and me.'*

At seven years old, I became an internal prisoner trapped inside a jail constructed of pure pain, stuck in a repetitive, endless cycle of abuse propagated by momma's turnstile of degenerate boyfriends. Men who desired to assault me once momma was passed out drunk.

My seventh birthday was when the nightmare had begun. A nightmare I feared would never end. Sometimes I did not want it to end. Sometimes I felt like I deserved it. All of it. I now thought of myself as the very trash she had always said I was to the world. And maybe she had been right about me all along. Facts do not lie. Momma did not want me. My daddy did not want me. Both had thrown me away.

But the drunken men momma brought around. They yearned for me. Even if, they too, disposed of me like trash afterwards. Despite the revulsion of their touches, I experienced what it felt like to be wanted by someone. But I knew it was all wrong. I continually contradicted myself. When momma's men were done with me, I held myself tight, rocked back and forth and whispered, *'Why? Why? Why? Why did they want to hurt me? Why didn't momma stop them from hurting me? Why didn't momma take my side when I told her what they had done to me while she was passed out drunk?'*

The *'whys'* always hit my heart like sharp darts.

Bullseye.

Bullseye.

Bullseye.

And, yet never got answered.

Momma never spoke a word to me after the first *'incident'* with her dirtbag biker man happened. Not one word. Not one apology. She never offered a lame reason or pathetic excuse for his rotten behavior. She acted like it never took place until he was gone. Instead of comfort or protection from further harm, she instead glared at me and then coated her esophagus with as much whiskey as possible to swim in a sea of denial that her man wanted me more than he wanted her.

*'Why?'*

There were countless times I cupped my tiny hands tightly over my ears to silence out the sound of the screams which emanated from within me while momma's creepy men touched me. My inner cries were so loud, and yet, they went unheard, as much as my outer cries did.

I wanted momma to help me, but she never would. She heard only the soft croons of *Jack Daniels* as he tickled sweet words into her ears to continue drinking.

Sometimes I sang a song inside my head to drown out the sounds of my inner screams. One of my favorites was a song I heard from one of momma's records:

California Dreamin'
by the Mamas & the Papas

*All the leaves are brown (all the leaves are brown)*
*And the sky is gray (and the sky is gray)*
*I've been for a walk (I've been for a walk)*
*On a winter's day (on a winter's day)*
*I'd be safe and warm (I'd be safe and warm)*
*If I was in L.A. (if I was in L.A.)*
*California dreamin' (California dreamin')*
*On such a winter's day*

One day, after another of her men had done me over, I worked up the nerve and asked her, "Why do you let your men do those things to me?"

Momma stared at me, then said, "Ya must have asked for it," before she poured herself another drink, with a shot of added look of disgust aimed in my direction.

"Quit your cryin' and blubberin' and go get cleaned up. He didin't mean nothin' by it. And even if he did, that's just what men do. Get used to it."

*"Get used to it?"* I would whisper under my breath while I washed their unwanted touches off using stolen gas station soap. 'Never!'

Regardless of how I felt, I always did as momma asked. But I struggled with the *why* of it all. Mothers protected their children from hungry wolves. They did not chuck them straight into their snarled jaws like raw meat.

I often pondered, *'What had I done to make momma willingly hand me over to those ravenous wolves without care? What happened to the days when we used to lie in the field together looking at fireflies? Maybe momma allowed her men to do what they did to me because my loud cries helped drown out her own silent ones.'*

I also thought, *'Maybe momma missed my daddy. Maybe she still loved him and because of that, would change her mind and not want those men messing with her more than they already had done. So, she let them mess with me instead so that way she could still get their money to pay bills and buy booze, pizza and cigarettes. You know, the things which mattered most to her. Or maybe she was flat jealous because those men used her to get to me. To them she was the trash. I was the treasure they hunted for. I never felt like a real gold treasure. More like fools' gold. A fool for putting up with it.'*

I often prayed my daddy would return home where he belonged. I did not really know how to pray, so maybe that is why it never came true. I tried to mimic what I had heard the television preachers speak about on our half-working television and made the rest up as the wheels inside my head sputtered, backfired, and turned.

I prayed my daddy would burst through the front door and rescue me each time I was dragged to the master bedroom. While I kicked and screamed at the top of my lungs, my eyes always locked hard on momma. Messy haired. Her arms clutched around an empty whiskey bottle. The one and only thing she loved most in the world. Besides my daddy.

She would occasionally yell out in a drunken slur, "*Worf-less pisssss of shit. Go on then. Leave. We don' need you. We don' want you. Jusssss go!*"

My tiny fingers grabbed in vain at pieces of old, faded wallpaper already peeled from the wall of our dilapidated trailer. The paper was too weak to stop me from being dragged to the back bedroom by those men. But I tried my best to stop them anyway I could think of.

Meanwhile, as my horror began, there was momma, passed out drunk. Her limp body sprawled about on our floral, liquid-stained second-hand couch. Both legs gapped wide apart. Soiled, urine-stained panties wrapped loosely 'round her boney ankles. Open for business. Yet, no customers were interested in entering through her crusty, unkempt door.

I would yell at the top of my lungs, "Momma! Help! Please! Make him let me go!" Only to be met with, "*Shuuuuu up you little brat! Stop your whining! I'm tryinnnn' to sleep!*"

Soon, a loud slam of the bedroom door sounded off, "BAM!"

My eyes remained fixated on the doorknob. *"Please turn. Please. Please,"* I routinely begged in a faint whisper. But the knob only turned when the assault was over. Never before.

Afterwards, I staggered back down the hallway and into my bedroom where I tried to pretend nothing happened. I vomited sometimes in the corner of my room before I then crawled into my own bed, sore and broken.

Meanwhile, momma remained passed out on the couch with a man who had just violated her daughter sleeping like a demented version of *Goldilocks* in her bed in the back bedroom. A smile of satisfaction smeared across his face.

I dreamt about my daddy. I imagined he kicked down the bedroom door, pulled that rotten man off me and beat him into a pile of nothing but bones and bloody guts. I gleefully jumped up and down on his busted-up bones and screamed, "I hate you! I hate you! I hate you!".     But it never happened. My daddy never rescued me, except in my dreams. And momma never stopped them. Always in reality.

I was trapped inside a bad dream only hell was constructed of. I was alone. I was scared. I was confused. And I lacked a map of hope to escape from the burning flames which sizzled and cracked and hissed right beneath my feet. I soon realized no one was going to rescue me from this horrendous life. No one.

I was trapped inside a jar like a captured firefly who longed to be free to fly again. Only its captor was so entranced by their own desires the flickering insect offered, they selfishly tossed aside the insect's needs, where the insect eventually quit blinking. It's light extinguished forever.

The older I got the more men wanted to make the letter J for me instead of with momma. I never wanted their disgusting J's. But what I wanted mattered not to anyone. I despised the letter J. I refused to pronounce it in school when we had to recite our ABC's. I would cough or burp if I had to. Anything to avoid speaking it.

As I lay on my back in a darkened field covered in fireflies and attempted to recapture childhood solace, I shouted out the alphabet, letter by letter. "ABCDEFGHI..." When it came to the letter J, I stuck my middle finger up towards the sky instead. *"Screw you letter J. I hate you!"*

I continued to blossom into a teenager. By then, I accepted my daddy would never return to save me. I accepted momma was a drunken whore whose men would never leave me be. All I wanted to do was finish school, leave momma and her nasty men, and never look back. But things do not always work out the way we planned.

The warmth and comfort I once sought in the firefly's soft glow had all but disappeared. They no longer provided me with comfort or safety. I had grown cold. Hard-hearted. Hateful. Withdrawn. Empty. I felt absolutely nothing ...until the day I fell into the *dirt*.

# Blue-collared Times

Nothing felt freer than a ride in a pickup truck with the windows down. My shag-cut, dirty blonde hair whipping wildly about in the wind. My puffy cheeks, rosy with color. The taste of the cool breeze as it playfully danced across my protruding pink tongue. *"Hmmm…sweet."* I loved to open my mouth wide and shout, *"Woohoo!"* at the top of my lungs.

On a crisp early morning, I enjoyed that simple pleasure from the past. All thanks to a blue-collared John I tricked before his shift at the local garage started. He was a regular and a mechanic, but never great with his hands. After our business transaction was completed, I had asked to hitch a ride to North Nebraska Avenue.

North Nebraska Avenue was a cesspool back when I was a child of the streets. The road was peppered with car washes, strip joints, auto-repair stores, used appliance stores, a greasy-spoon diner, and several second-hand furniture stores. It was also a street where the occasional meat pole surprise was discovered hidden underneath certain ladies' skirts by the untrained eye of amorous tourists. North Nebraska Avenue was a well-known area where twenty dollars got any filthy desires fulfilled.

Once the mechanic's truck engine turned over, my ears tuned into the sound of a familiar song which played in static waves from a set of old speakers nestled behind the front bench seat. The Outlaws. I only knew it because momma used to play their records.

Green Grass and High Tides
By the Outlaws

*In a place you only dream of*
*Where your soul is always free*
*Silver stages, golden curtains*
*Filled my head, plain as can be*
*As a rainbow grew around the sun*
*All my stars of love who died*
*Came from somewhere beyond the scene you see*
*These lovely people played just for me*

I mumbled to myself, *"Momma and good old Jack Daniels were outlaws same as Bonnie and Clyde. Inseparable and insufferable."*

"You say something, sweetheart?" the blue-collared John asked.

I pointed forward with my right index finger. "Nope. Let's go."

That raise of my right arm immediately told me I needed a shower. I realized I had worn the same white crop top, cut-off jean shorts and busted down flipflops for two days in a row.

My hair was greasy.

My make-up smeared.

My skin felt grungy.

I basically stunk.

Deodorant was a long-forgotten luxury since those nice church ladies handed out bags of personal hygiene items to the working girls on North Nebraska Avenue over two weeks ago. Most times money earned went towards drugs and food. Deodorant and soap rarely made the list because, *dirt* always came first.

I truly cared less how I looked or smelled. I struggled to manage with good personal hygiene since childhood. I remained nasty back then on purpose to deter momma's boyfriends so they would leave me be. It never worked. They never seemed to mind. But I continued to do it regardless.

If I could not afford a motel room or find a John willing to let me use their shower, I got creative. I used gas station sinks and cold watered garden hoses I found in yards. I despised the cold water, but it got the job done so I was presentable enough to work for the sole purpose to score *dirt*. My only true objective.

I hung my head out the window and yelled, *"Woohoo!"* as the truck zoomed down the road towards North Nebraska Avenue.

I rustled my hair with my right hand before I pulled myself back inside the truck's cab.

The morning sun comforted my soul as I watched it glisten off the blonde hairs of my right arm, which I had rested on the door frame. I closed my eyes and enjoyed the sensation of the wind as it playfully rushed between my fingers.

My mind wandered.

I had dreamt of being a nurse. When I was a kid, I would cover my newspaper teddy bear in bandages made from perfume sample cards I found in magazines folks in our trailer park threw out. I made them stick with gum I stole from the gas station. Sometimes I made arm or leg splints from cut up cereal boxes. I used whatever I could find.

Unfortunately, my dreams were put on hold and then for a while, forgotten altogether. I had to quit school during my sophomore year to take care of momma. Her true love, *Mr. Daniels*, had beaten her liver something awful. She got sick. In the blink of a firefly's glow, overnight, momma had become the child. I, the parent.

Momna now wetted the bed. Vomited on herself. But not because she had been sexually assaulted like me. It was because of cirrhosis. Despite all I sacrificed, she remained the same evil, cruel witch who never apologized for what her disgusting men had done to me.

I used to think, '*Life's cruel to some more than others, I suppose. But life also evens the score, I suppose sometimes, too.*'

*"Checkmate, huh, momma,"* I spitefully hissed into her ear, when I yanked Jack from her grasp.

I controlled when she and *Jack* spent time with one another. She had become too weak to hold on to *Jack* like in the past. But there were times, even as the disease took a stronger hold, momma managed enough strength to land slaps across my face.

She would shout, "Whore! You made those men want you more than they ever wanted me."

I never dared utter a response. I allowed her to hit, spit, yell, curse at me. I granted permission for her to treat me like the shit she always believed I was. She was often in and out of delusions. It was pointless to fight back with words or hands. She was never going to be sorry. I had to accept it. So, I took her abuse, not just with a grain of salt, but the whole damn block.

I resented giving up my dream and sacrificing more of my life for her. She never wanted me. Maybe my life and her love for me would have differed had my daddy stuck around. But I would never know. It was pointless to wonder further, so I stopped and accepted my fate. And hers, too.

Sometimes I secretly enjoyed those contentious moments between momma and me. I loved to piss her off on purpose. The same way she loved to hurt me from past to present for no reason.

I relished watching those flames of hatred erupt and flicker inside her blue pupils like a forest fire out of control. Those hearty slaps she landed across my cheeks, despite being feeble.

Things always came to a head when I denied her the opportunity to wrap her lips around *Mr. Daniels* and drink him down.

"I should do it you know. Let you and *Jack* be together around the clock. The sooner you're both gone from my life, the better."

"You bitch! Give him to me!" She would then lunge for the bottle, which I always yanked just out of her reach in time.

I watched her struggle to grab the bottle as a form of payback for each man she had allowed to touch me. I knew it was wrong, but the anger I carried inside somehow made it alright. No guilt.

Momma was dying. She became even more delusional as time marched on. Her liver was shutting down. Inside her mind, *Jack Daniels* was all she had left in the world. The only one who understood her. The only one who loved her. The only one who never left her. Yet, she failed to realize that in the end he was the one who killed her.

I never counted. Nor did my efforts to do right by her, either. I hoped we would heal from those old, festered wounds before she passed on. The closer she got to death, the more I wanted to savor every moment with momma I had left. Sounds odd, I know. I failed to understand it all myself. She never protected me, showed no love or compassion, treated me like a burden and never wanted me. I hated her for everything, but I loved her, too. It was unavoidable. She was my mother.

The endless arguments that took place inside my head.

*'Man! Fuck her!'*

*'No! Do right by her even though she did wrong by you.'*

Back and forth.

Back and forth.

Over and again ad nauseum.

There were no more men since momma had become bedridden. Only *Mr. Daniels*, the apple of her eye. And I, the worm.

I thought, *'Shame she was not a fan of Tequila. Maybe then I would have had a shot at being in her good graces.'*

Because the men had stopped, so, too, had the money. It was not long before I was the one forced to hit the streets and seduce men for their money just like momma had done. I had no choice. Momma's medical bills had to be paid. I was not old enough to get a normal paying job. Welfare never paid enough to keep a roof over our heads and food in the fridge. I resented momma even more for I had evolved into a carbon copy of her. I never wanted that for my life. Ever!

In her final months on earth, I took what abuse I could from momma; verbally, emotionally, and even physically. I took both the bitter and the sweet. The sweet being the one and only time she said the word *"please"* when she asked for *Jack's* company while watching a game show on our half-working television set.

*"Screw you, Jack!"* I mumbled.

"What was that you said, sweetheart?" the mechanic asked.

I immediately snapped out of my past at the sound of his voice.

"Nothing. Keep driving."

The mechanic reached over and casually placed his right hand on top of my left knee. I cringed and shot him a look that implied, *'Take your damn hand off my thigh or I swear you aren't getting it back!'*

He ignored my look and kept his hand rested firmly on my knee, as if it were a stick shift. I turned my gaze away from his lustful stare and looked out the window.

I fought the urge to punch him in the face. Honest I did. I wanted to punch him so hard his head broke the glass on his side of the window from the velocity and power of my fist. It was an automatic reflex from what I had gone through growing-up. I felt helpless for so long, but not anymore. I now felt powerful in my own twisted imagination.

So strange how I felt violated by the touch of his hand on my knee, especially after the naughty things we did fifteen minutes prior. But the ride he had offered me to North Nebraska Avenue was not included as part of our business. That was over. Services rendered. I allowed his hand to stay put only because I really needed the ride. Otherwise, I would have bent his fingers backward until he pulled the truck over and let me out.

I compartmentalized events that took place in my life. Work. Getting high. Being alone. It became my knack from childhood experience. I learned to develop different coping mechanisms for each situation.

The life I lived on North Nebraska Avenue to support my habit of *dirt* and my failed attempts at erasing my past literally caused me to vomit. I had to do what I loathed doing since I turned seven years old. But there was no other way I could endure the streets or life in general without doing it. So, I did what I had to do to survive.

Business was business.

Nothing personal about it.

I got paid.

They got service.

I literally checked out during a job.

I knelt for Johns.

I laid down for Johns.

I got down on all fours for Johns.

I did a lot of odd and repulsive things for Johns.

The men had their fun.

I shivered the entire time.

I forever fought the urge to barf during it.

Release would finally happen.

They'd get dressed.

Sometimes I earned extra cash.

So long asshole!

Next.

After enough dates, enough money, quitting time.

Off to meet my dealer.

Score some *dirt*.

Next stop?

Somewhere secluded to bang the newly purchased *dirt* into my body and forget all of it.

My torments erased until my next needed fix.

Lather.

Rinse.

Repeat.

Day after day.

I had it all under control.

Or so I thought.

But who was I kidding?

Only me – that's who.

The blue-collared John mistakenly thought I owed him free touches for the ride. I strongly disagreed, but kept my mouth shut. It was very important I reached North Nebraska. I fought the urge to punch the side of his semi-gray, whiskery face and instead, wished for a steady stream of green lights for the remainder of the ride.

*'Dammit!'*

Red light.

I shook my head side to side. I was disappointed.

*'Why does the universe hate me so much?'*

His greasy, lecherous hand crept up my bare leg like a drunken beach crab. I shuddered, but dared not look down. My eyes bore a hole through that retched red light. I was pissed. Nothing in life was free. Everything came with a price. A lesson momma and *Mr. Daniels* taught me all too well. How in the hell could I forget?

Now that I was older, I mistakenly believed the tables had mystically turned in my favor. I had the power. I continued to loath men. They still longed to make the letter 'J' with me. Nevertheless, I took their money after they got what they wanted just to stay buried in *dirt*.

The truth?

The only difference between the men in the past versus current was where the money got spent. In the past I needed money for momma's care and bills. I needed it now for my drug habit. I was in the same spot. Nothing changed. I just fooled myself into believing otherwise. But when I was a child, the exchange between us was different.

I thought to myself, *'You wanted to make the letter 'J' with me? Well, it now came at a hefty price. No more freebies in the back bedroom like in the past.'*

"Finally," I blurted out, as the light turned green, and the classic truck lurched forward.

"Sorry, darlin'. Need to have a mechanic look at this old gal's clutch. She sticks sometimes." He then winked. I suppose he thought his lame joke *(because he was a mechanic)* would win him a bonus.

"Whatever," was all I replied.

I did what I had to do to survive on the streets and support my drug habit. Still, it never made what Johns' did to me in cars, alleyways, and motels seem right.

Sometimes I thought about their women during our encounters. At home. Clueless. I thought about how they would feel if they found out how nasty their men truly were both the dark and the light. I never should have wondered or cared. Somewhere in the back of my mind, it always gnawed at my conscience for unknown reasons.

Maybe because of my daddy. How momma's broken heart over him leaving caused her to drink herself to death and go through men like toilet paper. I often wondered if my daddy was a John to a girl like me. If that was the reason momma forbade his name to be spoken while breath remained in her body. She never told me anything about him. To this day, I still do not know his name or if I have his nose or ears.

I glanced at the blue-collared John. He returned my glance with a coy grin. His fingers had begun to trace tiny circles, round and around on my inner left thigh. I looked away. Repulsed.

Funny thing. In that very moment it dawned on me the word 'John' started with the letter 'J'.

I shook my head and whispered, *"Well, shit Bug. How come you never connected the dots on that one before? Idiot!"*

Countless horrible things happened to me before momma died. And even worse afterwards. I gave up my dream of going back to school to get my GED so I could then go to college and become a nurse.

*Dirt* had me firm within its filthy clutches. And I had *dirt* firm within my grimy soul. The same as momma and *Jack Daniels*. Perhaps the rotten apple had not fallen so far from the polluted tree after all.

By my late teens, I was buried deep in the *dirt*. A bonafide junky and whore who relied on men to take care of her, but only if she 'took care of them' first. I had, without question, nor reservation or even hesitation, become my momma.

*'Holy Hell!'*

The only difference between momma and me though, I preferred the sweet kiss of heroin over whiskey.

During times when I raged with anger over momma's love for booze over me, I stole mini bottles of *Jack Daniels* from a low-rent liquor store and threw them hard against an abandoned building.

"Fuck you, *Jack*! I hope the two of you are happy partying the night away with Satan! She's all yours! Always was! Always will be!"

As the ground got drunk from the countless shattered whiskey bottles, I banged *dirt* into my arm. I had to numb up the repetitive cycle of childhood heartache. The past voices. The smells. The sounds. My cries for help when no one listened. All of it.

There were others like me on the streets. We were a dime a dozen. Ones who had been abused and even worse. Then there were those who somehow escaped the abuse, the drugs, the alcoholism before it consumed them. They were sober, healed and free.

*'Why couldn't that be me, too?'*

I already knew the answer before the question was even asked.

*'Because you're weak.'*

I found it easier to get wasted and avoid the torment, than to fight back. I was never told I had strength by anyone in my life. Therefore, I believed myself to be weak as a result. Too weak to abandon whatever horrific life I was born into. Too weak to walk away from poor life choices. Too weak period.

The thing about being a junky, I never felt responsible for most of the crappy stuff I did to myself or to others. It was much easier to point the finger of blame outward than inward.

I knew I was not strong. Momma made sure to shower me with continual, venomous affirmations about being weak and pathetic. "You were so weak while inside me, you couldn't even muster the guts to give me the morning sickness."

Most women appreciated an easy pregnancy without puking. But not momma. She resented me for not making her sick.

*'What?'*

I missed her presence in my life sometimes. But only sometimes. Odd right? To miss the one who was supposed to love and take care of you. But instead, turned into the one who abused you. The one who allowed others to abuse you, too.

How was it even possible to miss things about her? To care? To cry over her not being around anymore? But I did. I hated it when my heart got sentimental for her.

You want to know something? It had been a long time since I saw a firefly. And if I were honest, for the first time in my life I did not give one flying shit about it.

*'Screw the light!'*

# Two Droplets Meet

To survive life on the streets you either kept to yourself or joined a *family*. A group of folks from different walks of life who looked out for one another. They were the ones who got treated like lepers by society and loved ones. A street family that was comprised of people who either chose the wrong road or were forced to live it due to unforeseen circumstances.

I did not have a street family for a long time. My real family, momma, had died in my eyes long before she took her last breath. The only other blood relative was my daddy. But I did not know his name and therefore had no idea where to find him. For all I knew, he was dead, too.

*'Where are you at daddy? I wish I could find you.'*

In the beginning, I kept to myself. I trusted no one. Other whores. Johns. Scraggly alley cats. Scurrying cockroaches. No one. The only exception, my dealer, Tiny. And only because he provided an escape from my excruciating mental and emotional pain. I never feared buying bad *dirt* from Tiny. If I did, the worst that would have happened was death. Pain exterminated. Effective immediately.

*'Who would care if I died anyways? No one.'*

I felt so laid back about death, practically welcomed it, until an unexpected encounter with a wannabe flowerchild named Chloe happened.

*'That damn hippie!'*

My mind, my heart, everything changed the moment I looked into those brown doe-shaped eyes of hers. I saw trust for the first time. I saw something I desired my whole life. A sister. Family. I was home.

The rain poured down from the skies, something fierce the day we met. I thought, *'God, you sure are doing your darndest to wash away all the filth polluting Nebraska Avenue, huh?'*

It was crowded underneath the small bridge sandwiched between East Hollywood Street and Grant Avenue, where eleven of us had gathered for shelter during the unexpected thunderous storm.

The air beneath the bridge was stagnant and hung heavy with various scents of *dirt*, crack, marijuana, cigarettes, and methamphetamine. The combined smoke from them all danced about in the atmosphere like a cryptic fog. Other aromas dodged their way between the smoke. Alcohol. Urine. Feces. Dried vomit on clothing. Bad breath. And loads of rancid body odor.

We were crammed together like an expired swollen tin can of sardines about to erupt at any moment. United momentarily for shelter from the rain and varied fixes for our private individual pain.

I could hardly breathe underneath the bridge without an achieved contact high from the haze generated by the heavy drug use by everyone.

I heard the whooshing sound of tires as cars passed by up above. To me, each car was a potential John and a lost chance to earn dough for *dirt*.

It was pointless to pout over opportunities lost. I accepted the clouds were going to piddle down rain until they decided to quit. Based on the booming thunder, it was going to be a while.

*'Just make the best of it, Bug,'* I whispered underneath my breath.

I positioned myself close to the edge of the concrete floor. I was nearly shoulder to shoulder with the steady stream of wetness that cascaded over the side of the bridge. Even though I periodically got battered by dirty street water, it beat sitting shoulder to shoulder with the other strung-out, foul-smelling sardines.

All I could think was *'Man, some of ya'll need to get out in the rain and clean up. You stink.'* But who was I to judge. I stank, too.

Endless droplets of water splashed hard to the ground and then sprayed onto my face like gentle kisses from up above. My mind trailed off.

I tried to convince myself in a moment of weakness that God cared about me, and I was being baptized. All of my sins forgiven. Despite never having caused most of them. But I quickly shook my head side to side and muttered, "*If He cared, He never would have let those men…Ah, forget it.*"

The smell under the bridge soon became too much. I prepared some *dirt* and then searched for a good vein. Due to frequent usage, a good vein was hard to find.

I normally refrained usage around others. If I were caught holding, people would beg, bargain, or if desperate enough, try and kill me for my stash. The dependence on the drug normally determined the outcome.

I was in pain; mentally, physically, and emotionally. The usual. I was also bored. Plus, the trapped stench underneath the bridge was not doing my stomach or nostrils any favors, either. I needed to check out for a while. I chose to take the risk and soon thereafter, a hit of *dirt*.

The needle penetrated a vein between my ring and pinky finger. The dirt descended into my heart, mind, and soul. Within seconds any bad vibes churning around inside my body were silenced. I whispered, *"Finally."*

I laid down on my back, turned my head to the right and watched mud slide down the hillside before it spilled into the Hillsborough River below.

I thought about those individual raindrops. How they dropped from a cloud in the sky like tiny paratroopers, ready to work together with their squad once watery boots hit the ground. Upon touchdown, they temporarily joined together and pulled mud into the river where they were forever separated due to the river's rough current. Never reunited again. Only a carved path of destruction; uprooted plants, bits of trash and pebbles left scattered behind marked their once existence. Mission accomplished.

I thought how much the water droplets mirrored my life. Then I thought, *'Man. I'm so high...I feel low. What the hell did Tiny sell me?'*

My deep thoughts were unexpectedly interrupted when a fifteen-year-old girl tripped over my scabbed-up legs. I reached out my hand outward and grabbed her left hand before she joined the paratrooper droplets in the river.

"Whoa! You, okay?" I asked.

The tipsy girl regained her balance and replied, "Thanks for the save. I'm Chloe." She continued to hold onto my hand and stared into my soulless eyes.

I noticed two things about Chloe straight away. A tattoo of a peace sign on her middle finger. I thought, *'Ironic, predictable and lame'.* A clear attempt to piss off her parents.

I also noticed both of her rail-thin arms were peppered with track marks. The sound of her twenty-plus, silver bangled bracelets on her left arm jingled like wind chimes when she finally released my hand.

"Bug," I casually replied, then lit a cigarette.

Chloe pointed at an area of empty graffitied concrete next to me. "Cool?"

I nodded.

From that day forward, Chloe and I were inseparable. Two paratrooper droplets, dropped onto the planet from different clouds, now merged underneath a smelly bridge during a storm. Only our mission was a path paved with a revolving door of justified self-destruction. Our meeting was a long-lost family reunion.

# Chloe

Chloe was a skinny, peace-loving, hippy. She wore her straight mousey brown hair long and parted down the middle with five scattered medium-sized braids. A threaded hairband decorated with feathers dropped by wild blue jays, crows, and trinkets *(mostly pop tops linked with string)* hugged her head like a crown.

"So many feathers," she said and shook her head side to side. "Now I can fly high, Bug! Just like that song we heard outside the strip club the other night." She then spun in circles with her arms outstretched.

"What song are you talking about?"

*"Fly robin fly! Up! Up! To the Sssssssky!"*

"You remember that song? Seriously?"

"It's a great song."

"You're high. Come sit down, Chloe before you crash to the ground like a plane that's run out of gas," I said.

She stuck her bottom lip out and pouted. "I don't care what you say, Bug. I'm a robin! I can't sit. I must fly!" She resumed making circles.

Chloe and I took the day off from hustling to spend it at the park. I needed a break. Between the two of us, we earned enough money to score dirt for the next twenty-four hours.

We purposefully chose a small park where people rarely visited. No risk of hassles from Johns, cops, or families. The grass felt soft and serene underneath my feet, like an avocado-colored shag rug. I always wondered what shag carpet felt like after watching game shows on our half-working television set when I was a kid. The grass in the park was the closest I would ever come to knowing the answer.

The sun shone brightly, but with a gentle warmth, instead of its usual harsh heat. For once it was nice not to feel like an overcooked egg in a frying pan.

I playfully wiggled my toes in the grass. It felt amazing to be off my feet. Hell, even my knees. Even if only for one day. I could just be and enjoy those little things most take for granted. Simple, long forgotten things.

Chloe's repetitive spins started to make me ill.

"Hey, robin. You do realize you're only flying high thanks to the shit I scored from Tiny, right. It's not the feathers stuck on your bird-brained head or the song, either."

"I can be a robin if I want to, Bug. I can be anything I want to be. You're not my mom. You're not even my pimp. You can't tell me what to do." She spun around again out of pure spite.

"Whatever. But if you keep spinning like that, you're going to puke," I snapped back.

Chloe grinned and fell to the ground in a fit of dizziness wrapped in a blanket of laughter. "Doesn't matter what bird the feathers come from, Bug. Don't you get it?"

"Get what?" I was simultaneously intrigued and puzzled.

Chloe rolled onto her stomach, "Feathers are always able to fly."

"Not if they're not attached to, oh, I don't know, say a bird." I then tilted my head to the side and added a smirk.

Chloe shook her head side to side. "Not true." She sat up.

"Is that so? Then how is it possible, huh?"

"The wind, silly, Bug." Chloe reached over and rustled my hair.

I hated to be touched. Chloe knew it, too. But in that moment, I did not know if it was because of the softness of the grass beneath my feet. The comforting warmth of the sun which was like a mother's hug I had ached for my whole life. Or Tiny's grade a *dirt* which coursed through my veins. I welcomed Chloe's playful affection.

"Where do you come up with this 'feather's always fly crap', Chloe? I mean, I get the whole wind cradling a light feather and carrying it for a while before it falls back to the ground. But not heavy wings or tail feathers. Impossible without strong winds."

Chloe became flustered by my inability to unravel her twisted theory. In an exasperated tone, she semi-shouted, "Ugh! Bug!"

"Ugh, what, Chloe?"

She crawled over and got so close to my face; our noses made contact. "Doesn't matter what type of feather it is, Bug. They come from birds. Birds are free. Like you. Like me." She then screamed out at the top of her longs, "WE ARE FREE!"

"Free?" I took a drag off a cigarette I had lit, then exhaled. I was skeptical over her nonsense.

"Like feathers, we are free and will always fly. Whether we're attached to a bird or not."

I snickered. "I ain't for free. Sorry girl. And I'm too big for a bird to carry me, so…"

"Emu."

"Emu? Emu what?"

"An emu bird could carry you." She smiled as if she had been crowned the winner of a fight.

I reached my right hand outward and gently pushed Chloe on her face. She fell backwards like a bowling pin and remained flat on her back. She then reached over and placed her hand on my stomach. "I'm talking about your spirit, Bug."

I sarcastically nodded my head. "Okay. So now you're saying my spirit is like a feather, too? Got it." I wanted to shut her up. Less talking, more enjoying my high in silence.

"That's right!" Chloe clutched her own stomach tightly. "Feathers are like our spirits, Bug. Always free to fly wherever they want. Never being weighed down. You're got it, Bug! You've got it!"

I thought, *'Chloe's so naïve. I did not know whether to feel pity or anger towards her ignorance.'*

Truth was, Chloe and I were weighed down: oppression, depression, sexual assaults, molestation, battery, abandonment, starvation, addiction. The list was endless. So many boulders had been piled upon our 'free-flying feathered spirits' we may as well have resided in Bedrock, A.D. next to the *Rubbles* and the *Flintstones*.

*'Note to self; find out what this shit was Tiny sold me and never give it to Chole again.'*

"I think we need to get you something to eat, Chole."

Chloe jumped up and straddled over top of me and shook her feathered coated, semi-braided hair all over my face in a teasing manner. "Be free, Bug! Be free!"

"Get off me! That shit tickles hippy nutjob. You better not bust the cherry off my cigarette." She rolled off of me and laughed. I placed my cigarette between my teeth and attempted to recompose myself. I stood up. She did, too.

I noticed Chloe continuously dressed in two ways; a very tight T shirt with bell bottom jeans or a sundress with either vanilla-colored Go-Go boots or a pair of 1970's red Dr. Scholl's clogs she found at a Salvation Army store. How those clogs remained in better condition than my 2008 flipflops was a mystery Chloe and I debated countless times.

A warped Led Zeppelin IV cassette tape repeatedly played on a Walkman some trick gave to Chloe as payment for services rendered. She always had the *Walkman* turned on, the headphones slung around her neck.

I was pissed when I discovered she got played by a cheap John. We argued about it.

"Geez, Chloe! You're so clueless. It drives me insane sometimes. That jerk trick totally screwed you and then screwed you over. Don't you get it?" I pointed at the retro hunk of junk which blasted forth sound from the warped tape.

Chloe scoffed and turned up the volume. "I don't care what you say or think about my *Walkman*, Bug. *La, la, la, la!* One day, you'll see, Bug. I am going to go to California with flowers in my hair. Just like the song says."

I nearly choked on my cigarette, bewildered by her response to having been taken advantage of by someone. "You wear feathers in your hair birdbrain, not flowers."

With both hands placed firmly on her bony hips, Chloe glared at me with a look of loathing. "Flowers? Feathers? What's the difference? I'M. STILL. GOING."

"How? You can't even catch a ride for more than two blocks without getting carsick. California is like three thousand miles away."

"I'll take a bus."

"A bus?" I sarcastically pondered. "Right, because riding in a bus won't make you carsick, too."

She grew flustered. "Maybe I'll ride in a train or fly in a plane or ride a horse or a unicorn or a…" she trailed off. "Or maybe I'll just open up my arms and fly myself to California, like a bird."

Chloe dropped to the ground and pulled me down with her in the process. We both landed flat on our backs in the grass. It reminded me of those days when I used to lay out in the fields with momma watching the fireflies.

Chloe had closed her eyes and begun to sing the song, *Going to California* loudly and deliberately out of tune to irritate me in that sisterly way.

Before long, we acted like farm hogs, snorting with laughter and rolling around on our backs on the soft grass. We were tainted head to toe in the beautiful blissful trance *dirt* afforded us to feel. We equally shrieked out our own version of the song, *"with feathers in her hair…La, la, la, la! Not flowers!"*

Chloe believed in reincarnation. I never did. I was convinced once you died you turned to worm food. She also believed there was good in everyone. I disagreed there, too.

*'Can you blame me after what I had been through since I was seven years old?'*

Chloe thought she had currently been born in the wrong era. I never bought into Chloe's kooky reincarnation idea. I secretly feared coming back as a dung beetle.

*'Just my luck to live, yet another life of shoveling shit up a treacherous hill. No thanks!'*

Hell was where I belonged and what I deserved. No time jump adventures for me. I already knew my life was destined to be one of endless twists, turns and inappropriate touches.

Every day brought with it a new place or time era Chloe yammered on about with her reincarnation theory. I never knew what period to expect. But I did expect a headache by the end of each story.

"I think. No wait. I know I was once a pretty songbird in a past life," Chloe said in a melancholy tone.

"A songbird."

"Yeah, like a parrot. Maybe I was a parrot on a pirate's shoulder. *Arrrrrrrgh!*" She bobbed her head up and down in self-agreement. "Cool, right?"

I dismissed her notion with a nonchalant wave of my hand. "Impossible."

"Why impossible, Bug?" she replied, confused.

I snickered, "Because you can't carry a tune to save your ass. No way you could ever be a songbird of any kind. Besides, parrots are not songbirds."

"Yes, they are. I heard one whistling to the radio in a pet store once."

"Is that so?" I said with doubt and unbelief in my voice.

Chloe remained silent. I panicked because I had forgotten how sensitive she could be.

*'Oh shit! Way to go, Bug.'*

Instead of tears, much to my relief, Chloe released a snort-fueled laugh. "*Squawk!* Chloe wants some *dirt. Squawk!*"

"Well, Bug isn't holding anymore." I got up in her face and shouted back, "*Squawk!*"

Chloe pouted.

I planted a kiss on her dirty hippy-decorated forehead. I then reached into my shorts pocket and retrieved a smushed package of crackers from the Beans & Jellies Café.

"How about some stale, mashed-up crackers, instead?"

She responded with a quizzical look.

"Parrots like crackers. Right?" I taunted, waving a cracker back and forth in her face. "Chloe wants a cracker. You know she does."

Chloe opened her mouth wide like a baby bird. We both laughed as I tossed pieces of cracker at her mouth.

"*Squawk!* Bug missed. Try again! *Squawk!*"

The following week, Chloe imagined she was a red poppy flower in the fields of Afghanistan in another life. The flower in this kooky scenario was her – *of course.* I resisted the urge to roll my eyes while she spoke of being a poppy flower.

Chloe was harvested, made into *dirt*, and then smuggled into the United States to bring peace to someone who was in a lot of pain.

"You are so stupid high right now, Chloe."

"It's true, Bug. It's true. I swear it." She made the letter 'X' across her heart. "I swear. I was once a poppy flower."

51

"You were never a poppy flower, Chloe. What you are right now is stupid high."

Chloe looked at me peculiarly, then busted out laughing. "I am, aren't I?"

"Come on. Let's go get some real food to eat."

"*Squawk!*"

# Petal head (part 1)

**I** considered Chloe to be a bonafide 'petal head'. A lover of flowers and all of the hippy loving peace crap which came along with it. Her entire existence revolved around flowers, feathers, and love.

Dandelions in particular.

Not roses.

Not carnations.

Not daffodils.

Nope.

For Chloe it was a damn weed.

*'As if I should have been surprised by yet, another one of her notorious kooky ideas.'*

"What makes a dandelion so special, huh, Chloe? Enlighten me," I asked as we leaned against a rusted chain link fence that surrounded the front of a recently abandoned crack house.

The front yard was overgrown with dandelions and who knows what else. Dirty needles? Used condoms? Empty liquor bottles? Beer cans? Crack pipes? Baggies? Old clothes? Soiled underpants? The possibilities were endless.

Rummaging through that nasty yard would be like a treasure hunt for desperate addicts. Imagine a discovered used baggie of drugs. One could still get a tiny buzz with a lick of the finger, a quick rub inside the baggie to retrieve any granules left behind, then into the mouth the finger went. Instant micro-high. Thankfully, I was not that desperate that day.

Chloe turned and looked at me like an innocent child does towards their loving parent. "People always see dandelions as ugly weeds. Useless, you know."

"They're right," I said. I lit a cigarette and took a heavy drag.

She grabbed my left shoulder. "It's just not true what they say about them, Bug. It's just not true."

I responded with another deep drag off my cigarette and three perfectly blown smoke rings.

"The world sprays poison junk to try and kill them, but they don't know, Bug. They don't know," she whined.

"Who in this theory of yours doesn't know?"

"People, Bug."

"What don't these", I sarcastically used air-quotations, 'people' know about how special dandelions are to the world, Chloe? Why are you the only one with this," I then leaned in and whispered, "secret information?"

She pushed me away. "Stop it. I'm serious."

I replied with more smoke rings. "I can see that."

"Dandelions are just like us, Bug."

I palmed my forehead in utter disbelief and wondered '*How are two drugged out whores like a weed?*'

I could hardly wait for Chloe's explanation, despite the risk of a migraine. "I ain't like no damn dandelion. Besides, a few weeks ago you said we were like feathers or some crap, floating here and there free. So, which is it, Chloe? Are we weeds or feathers?"

Chloe immediately sulked with hurt feelings.

I reached out and took hold of her right hand. "I'm sorry, Chloe. I'm listening. Go on. Tell me about dandelions and the people. I'm listening."

She stared at me.

"I promise. All ears. Right here. Continue."

As punishment, Chloe made me wait a whole two minutes before her explanation was provided.

'*Theatrical little twit.*'

"Dandelions are beautiful and good for the planet, Bug."

I glanced at the overgrown yard. "Where did you hear that load of malarkey from? A documentary on TV in some John's hotel room?" I snickered.

"Stop," she begged.

"In case you haven't noticed, we're whores and whores aren't beautiful. We're disgusting. They're disgusting."

She shook her head side to side. "Not true."

I countered, "You and I. Disssss…gussssss…tiiiiiiing. Dandelions, same thing. Disssss…gussssss…tiiiiiiing"

Chole tried to cover my mouth with her hand. "Shut up. Don't say that. It's not true." She forced my head towards the weeded yard. "Look at them."

I jerked her hand away from my mouth. "Not seeing it, kid. Sorry."

"You're not looking hard enough, Bug. Look harder."

I squinted my eyes. I appeared more constipated than intrigued. "Sorry, still don't see what you do."

"Dandelions have so much good to offer to the world, Bug. Most people can't see their beauty or their goodness because bad people have convinced them they are worthless with nothing to offer. And it's not true. It's just not." She slammed her palms hard against the rusted fence. It rattled loudly and violently shook.

"Careful or you'll get tetanus."

"What's that?" she asked. I often forgot how young and uneducated she was.

"Nothing. Just be careful with the rusted fence. I don't feel like spending the day in the ER."

I wondered, with Chloe's strong insistence about the dandelions, '… *was Chloe really talking about the flower or herself for once?*'

"All I see are ugly weeds that look better than I do right

now."

"You look pretty, Bug."

"You're full of shit."

"I'm not."

"You are. I saw how much cheese you ate last night," I teased.

She laughed.

I laughed, too, until she grew serious again.

"Listen, listen," she said, excited while waving her hands all up in my face.

"I'm listening. I'm not deaf, so get your hands out of my face." I smacked them away.

"Dandelions are like us, Bug."

"Let's give this flower talk a rest. What do you say? Let's go get a soda or something." I found I could always distract Chloe with promises of food, drink or *dirt*.

Chloe refused to move from the spot until I saw the dandelions her way. So, I caved and asked, "What do we have in common with a stupid weed, Chloe? Enlighten me. Please."

She smiled and joyfully replied, "Beauty."

"Beauty? From a weed? *A-hmm.*"

"Exactly! You're getting it. I can tell."

"How can you tell?"

"It's written all over your face."

"Kid, what's written all over my face is a bad hangover not a floral revelation."

*'I plan to talk to Tiny about the dirt he's been selling to us lately. Chloe's been flaking a little too much lately.'*

"Nuh-uh."

"Okay. That's it. You've officially lost your damn mind, girl."

"No, I haven't. My mind's expanded. Free. I have chosen to see beauty in all things. You don't. Why?"

"Because I don't want to." I tucked a loose piece of her mousey brown hair behind her left ear. "It's my choice, right?"

"True, but…"

"But nothing."

"But…but…people never see *our* true beauty, Bug. Don't you get it?"

I scoffed, "Our true beauty? You haven't looked in a mirror lately have you, Chloe. We're junky whores. There is nothing beautiful about us. In fact, while we're on topic, I don't want anyone to see the real me. Ever. They haven't in all these years. Why start now? It's all so pointless. And not to mention, a complete buzzkill."

"No, it's not."

"Yes, it is."

"No."

"Yes."

"No. Stop it."

"Why are you so afraid for people to see the real you, Bug? I see the real you."

"You only see what I want you to see."

"I don't believe you."

"I don't care what you believe."

"I think you're beautiful on the inside, Bug." She hugged herself, and then leaned over and squeezed me until I felt as if my bones might break, and we would both lose our balance and fall through the eroded fence.

*'Just what I needed. A lockjaw shot. Bad enough I was waiting for a Gonorrhea test result. Courtesy of a John who assaulted me without using protection.'*

I shoved Chloe off me. "If you say so, petal head. I don't see any beauty in myself inside or out." I then took a drag off my cigarette and exhaled.

"Bug?" she quietly asked.

I rubbed at my itching nose, "What?"

Chloe stared into my eyes with those doe-shaped brown eyes of hers. I felt the wall I had fought so hard to keep up over the years, buckle.

*'Damn your soft eyes, Chloe!'*

"I think you're beautiful. Just like that dandelion right there," she pointed her index finger at a flower in the middle of the patch.

"Where?" I asked, as I attempted to follow her finger.

"Right. There."

I had no clue which flower Chole pointed at. I only knew my instincts screamed, *'Cry and hug her!'* But my stone-cold heart said,

*'Don't be a wimp!'* So, I gave a simple response with little to no feeling attached, "*Umm*...I see it. It's cute. Thanks."

Chloe ran into the yard and picked the only puffy white dandelion in the bunch. She gleefully ran back and practically shoved it into my mouth.

"What are you doing?" I pushed the puff ball out of my face, only to have it thrusted back in front of my chapped lips.

"Close your eyes, Bug, make a wish and then blow."

I hated closing my eyes and wishing for anything. Especially if birthday candles were involved.

I shoved the puffy flower out of my face again. "My wish is for you to make a wish, Chloe."

"Are you sure?"

"Absolutely. Make your wish for me. I insist."

"Okay. Here goes."

Chloe puckered up her pink lips, closed her eyes and then blew until the fluffy white ball had disappeared and what remained was a naked green stem.

"Know what I wished for?"

"You're not supposed to tell a wish dummy, or it won't come true."

"I wished you would smile more, Bug."

"You just wasted your wish."

"No, I didn't. I have faith one day you'll smile more."

"Never going to happen. Should have wished for something else. Maybe a new tape for your *Walkman*."

I had not believed in wishes for a long time. And smiles were for dreamers. The hard truth: I felt as disgusting on the outside as I did on the inside about myself. Far from beautiful. Repulsive felt more befitting. I wanted so much to hop over that fence and pull every one of those dandelions out of the ground so no more wishes could be made by anyone. Ever.

But I remained stoic, fixated on a sea of yellow topped weeds. I knew what happened to me in the past was not my fault. However, my mind could not and would not allow me to see myself other than repulsive, disgusting and revolting. Three words metaphorically tattooed on my forehead with invisible ink since the age of seven that only creepy men read.

My life was a persistent turnstile of whoring and drugging.

Whoring to earn for drugs.

Drugging to forget about the whoring.

I felt sick.

Unclean.

Ruined.

I was conflicted. I hated what I had in common with the dandelions, but I also secretly longed to be a dandelion, just so I could be doused in poison. My existence on this planet could then be all but forgotten. I would finally be free, freer then any of Chloe's feathers.

Chloe's sentimental babble wave had bummed me out. I needed to leave the area.

"Come on petal head. Let's go to the Beans & Jellies Café. Get a drink or something."

Chloe bent over and whispered to a clump of flowers basking in the sunlight, planted next to the sidewalk in front of the dilapidated house, *"Bye baby dandelions."*

I grabbed Chloe by the wrist. "Enough of the flower shit. Come on."

"Okay. Okay."

I snapped back, "Those weren't even baby dandelions. They were Biden daisies."

I turned into my mother in that moment. I did not mean to be so sharp-tongued at Chloe's sensitive nature.

So cold.

So hard.

So cruel.

Unlike my mother, I took no pleasure from cruelty towards, Chloe. I felt remorse but refused to show it. I was stubborn. I was weak.

Chloe turned back towards the flowers. "Sorry I called you the wrong name! Bye, daisies!"

I yanked her arm once more, "Let's go!"

"I'm going. I'm going," she replied with a fresh picked dandelion in her hand.

# Petal head (part 2)

Chloe habitually picked wildflowers by the roadside and handed them to random strangers.

"Why, Chloe? Why? Why do you pick flowers for people you don't know? Better yet, why don't you charge them for the flowers?"

She flashed a playful grin. "Because it's beautiful to give to others, Bug."

"That so."

She nodded her head up and down. "Flowers make people smile. I think everyone should smile. Don't you?"

"Not really."

"Here." She handed me a single flower. "Smile."

I grimaced at her gesture and said, "Picking weeds and giving them to strangers isn't beautiful. It's pointless."

"It's not pointless."

"It is."

"I think it shows love and care, Bug. *Sheesh.*"

Deep down, I secretly found Chloe's flower idea endearing. I was jealous of her ability to feel so open and free, despite the horrendous treatment she had endured during her young life.

I could never be like Chloe, even with a sprinkle of envy. I was far too jaded and damaged by others to pick flowers for myself. The world and everyone in it sucked in my opinion.

I often noticed the twisted-up faces people made whenever Chloe approached them with clumps of wilted wildflowers. They acted as if she shoved a sour lemon into their pretentious piehole. Most people avoided any encounters with the homeless on purpose. Even if the encounter included a clump of crappy, wilted flowers, from a hippy chick with a sweet innocent smile.

You know the look I mean. The classic: "*Oh, shit. Quick! Stare down at your phone or something else so the dirty, smelly homeless freak will pass you by and you can then pretend to not feel guilty for being such an ignorant asshole.*"

I wondered, '*Since when had humanity become so damn heartless?*' Then I answered my own question. '*Since I became old enough to see it.*'

I muttered, "Rich bitch," underneath my breath as a twenty-something year old girl pulled out her phone the moment Chloe and I passed her by on the sidewalk.

Chloe attempted to hand her a flower. "Here's a flower I picked specially for you."

The girl instantly recoiled and yelled, "Fuck off trash!"

I sneered at her overreaction and the words of disgust she hurled towards my street sister. She snapped a picture of us to post and mock us online.

"Don't take our picture, you stuck-up bitch!" I shouted in anger. "I'm gonna shove that phone straight up your tight ass!"

She tartly replied, "Why don't you take a shower and get a job loser!" She turned around and walked away.

"Bitch!" I yelled back. Chloe stood by my side, shocked by the interaction which had taken place.

I wondered, '*What if our roles had been reversed? What if life offered me better choices? What if momma chose me over her octopus' boyfriends and whiskey, instead? I could just as easily have been that girl and her me. I'll bet she has no idea how fortunate the cards she got dealt were blessed versus the ones dealt to me, cursed. She didn't struggle with addiction, live on the streets or in smelly shelters where you slept with one eye open to protect your shit and yourself from perverts. She could earn her money the right way. Not on her knees or on her back.*'

Chloe hugged the flower. "It's okay little one. We'll find you a good home."

"*Bet she has no idea how lucky she is,*" I whispered.

"Who's lucky, Bug?"

"No one. Screw her. I'll take your flower."

Chloe smiled, "Really?"

"Yes. Really. And look," I then smiled.

Chloe spun in a circle with her hands towards the sky, "I knew you smiled, Bug. I knew it!"

I playfully shoved her shoulder. "Stop."

It was pointless to compare myself to the snobbish girl. We were in two different worlds with no dramatic change forecasted on the horizon. I decided to erase the argument from my brain.

"Gone!"

"What?" Chloe asked.

"Nothing," I replied. I then gazed downward, and there in the middle of the sidewalk was a lone dandelion flower.

"Look, Chloe, it's a free growing dandelion, just like you."

She turned and gave me a hug. "I love you, Bug!"

"Right back at you, kid," I muttered. Showing my emotions was difficult. "Now get off me. I haven't showered today."

Chloe made a yucky face. "Ewww!"

"I know. I know."

"You might stink on the outside Bug, but the love oozing from within smells sweet."

I rolled my eyes. "Oozing? Really? You're such a weirdo, petal head."

"You love me. I know it."

I never uttered the word *love* to anyone because I never understood what it meant. Therefore, how could I speak or express the word with actions to anyone? I had never been loved by anyone my entire life. At least not in the proper way. Chloe was the only person who loved me in the right way.

I bent down and picked the yellow dandelion flower and tucked it behind Chloe's right ear. "Beautiful," I said, while I moved one of the blue jay feathers from her homemade headband out of the way.

The flower brought back an entertaining memory.

Chloe and I were panhandling by an exit ramp near I75 and Bruce B. Downs Boulevard. Chloe handed a man in a red Porsche a clump of daisies mixed with dandelions she had picked beside the exit ramp. In typical Chloe fashion, she innocently failed to notice the flowers were covered in fire ants.

The driver suddenly yelled out in pain, "You idiot!" before he exited his car and ran around it like he had ants in his pants. Which as it turned out, he did.

In a fit of understandable anger, he chucked the flowers back at Chloe and cursed out, "You dumb bitch!" before he jumped back into his car as the traffic light turned green.

I was left speechless and watched as Chloe nonchalantly brushed bits of flowers and confused ants off her dress.

She smiled at the red car as it sped away and yelled, "Have a groovy day!"

*"Unbelievable,"* I whispered.

"What?"

"You."

"What about me," she asked, confused.

"I would have punched that guy in the dick for throwing ants at me and cussing me out. How can you be so damn nice to people who treat you like shit, Chloe? I don't get it."

"Simple. Compassion."

"Compassion?"

"It was my fault."

"That he acted like a dick to you? I don't think so."

"No. Not that part. I should have checked the flowers before I handed them to him."

"Wait...What?????" My brain was ready to explode.

"And..."

I cut her off. I fumed, "You want me to find him and beat his ass for you?"

She put her hands on my arms to calm me down. "He's a lost soul, Bug. Let him go in peace."

The light bulb of Chloe's logic finally clicked in my brain. "Oh, I get it now. The compassion is for you, not him."

"The compassion is for both of us." She picked a fresh clump of flowers. No ants this time.

"You're too forgiving, Chloe."

"I know. But it's better to love than to..."

"Not loved at all?" I cut in.

"Something like that, yeah. Love feeds peace. Anger robs it."

I shook my head side to side, "Yeah. Yeah."

Chloe approached a white car as it stopped at the intersection. "Some flowers for you."

The woman inside the car took the flowers and smiled.

Chloe turned to me and smiled. She mouthed in silence, "See?"

I just shook my head, bewildered by her resilience. I mouthed back, "No, I don't."

# Cooked Cabbage

**I** met with Tiny and scored *dirt* tapped with a dash of ecstasy. Today was a day of celebration. Chloe's birthday.

"Happy Birthday, kid," I turned to Chloe and said as I paid Tiny.

"It's your birthday, Flowerchild?" He asked.

Chloe handed Tiny a flower. "It is."

"Well, I ain't gonna ask how old you are. I don't need to know that shit."

"She's old enough," I interjected and took the small baggie from his hand.

"Ah-right then," Tiny replied.

"Come on, petal head. Let's party." I waved the baggie before her eyes.

"Groovy."

Chloe and I headed to our secret spot to get high and celebrate her birthday. We also wanted to forget everything and anything about our crappy lives. Our secret spot was an abandoned, rusted out maroon *Ford Taurus* with four flat tires, in a weeded lot surrounded by boarded up, dilapidated buildings. Hidden in plain sight.

Chloe and I fixed up the inside of the wrecked car with fluffy throw pillows, blankets and small plastic plants found when we dumpster dove behind a *Kmart*. I was always blown away by what stores deemed trash.

Chloe always sat in the passenger seat.

Me, I sat on the driver side.

I pulled the small baggie of *dirt* tainted with ecstasy from my back jean shorts pocket. From there, the routine of preparing to shoot up commenced.

Pour heroin powder into a spoon hidden in the glovebox.

Add water from a bottle.

Cook it using a cigarette lighter stolen from a trick.

Once cooked, draw the brown liquid into two needles.

One for me.

One for Chloe.

Tie a shoelace around the upper arm.

Shoelaces were kept from view underneath the front driver seat.

Tap.

Tap.

Tap.

Success.

Veins cooperated for both of us.

Injection.

Lift off!

Injection.

Lift off!

Our journey to freedom from life's pain instantly ensued.

*Dirt* flowed through my veins like fresh, sweet, tapped syrup bled forth from a maple tree concealed deep in a Vermont forest.

Smooth.

Slow.

Syrupy.

*Dirt* hugged my innards like the loving arms of a parent. A feeling I never experienced from either of my parents. My mind soon, but only briefly, transformed into memories of my mom.

I quietly whispered, *'I love you mommy.'*

I laid my head back on the car's headrest and welcomed *dirt's* endless cascades of warmth with every fiber of my being. The silence was oh, so, golden until Chloe cheapened its value with her words.

"Man! I would have given anything to have celebrated my birthday in the seventies at Haight-Ashbury, Bug. This is the best birthday present, ever, Bug." She then clutched her heart.

I shot Chloe a side-eye and half-mumbled. "I'm pretty sure Haight-Ashbury was in the sixties, Chloe."

"Sixties. Seventies. Who cares?" She closed her eyes, hugged herself and rocked side to side. "It's all love and it's my birthday today. It's all so beautiful, Bug."

"Love is bullshit," I sourly sneered.

"But I feel it."

"What you feel is the love of Tiny's special birthday blend, petal head. Now hush. You're wrecking my high."

"But it's real, Bug." She then reached over and hugged me tightly. "Can't you feel it?"

"I can't feel anything. But I smell something ripe. You need to put some soap and a razorblade to those hairy armpits, hippie girl. Now shoo! You stink!"

She retracted back to her own seat and said, "You felt the love when I hugged you. I know you did. You can't fool me, Bug."

"Whatever you say. Happy Birthday, kid."

"Thanks, Bug."

Chloe closed her eyes. I, too, closed my eyes and allowed my mind to drift back to the syrupy sweetness of the maple trees and the *dirt* coursing throughout my veins.

'*A sweet day to be alive and celebrate… indeed.*'

# Pricks, Pennies & Pests

**I** continued my ride in the pickup truck towards North Nebraska Avenue with the blue-collared John. I was headed to meet Chloe, who was probably out front of our main hangout, The Beans & Jellies Café. I was late.

The Beans & Jellies Café was a standard mom and pop coffee house. It had vintage metal farm signs on the walls, mismatched antique tables and chairs. a distressed brown leather couch and a countertop lined with torn red Naugahyde stools. The place resembled a chic shithole. But it served the best damn jelly doughnuts and strongest coffee in the Tampa Bay area.

The owners went by 'Mom and Pop'. They always took care of the working girls. Mom thought of us all as her daughters. Their policy: you never paid for anything if you did not have money. You paid what you could when you could.

"None of my girls go hungry," Mom said, before always handing over a sugary donut and a mug of hot coffee.

Chloe was dressed in an orange sundress, vanilla Go-Go boots, and her outrageous homemade feathered headband. Torn yellow foam-covered headphones from her ancient Walkman hung loosely around her neck and blared inaudible music.

While she waited for me to show up, Clohe hustled folks for money while on their way to the bus stop located in front of the Café.

"Sir?" Chloe asked in her soft, wispy voice, before shoving a grimy used paper coffee cup towards a businessman about to pass her by.

The man sneered at Chloe and dropped one penny into the cup. "Happy now?"

Chloe peered into the cup. She then shouted at the businessman's back, "Peace and love!"

She resumed panhandling.

"Mam? Got anything you can spare?"

Just as the woman dropped two quarters into the cup, Chloe spotted the blue-collared John's pickup truck and screamed out at the top of her lungs, "BUG!"

"CHLOE!" I hollered back. I turned to the blue-collared John. "Hey, man! Stop the truck!"

The jerk braked so hard I nearly smashed my face on the dashboard. Payback I assumed for rejecting his advances during the ride.

I exited the truck, and a wave of relief instantly washed over me. The blue-collared John angrily peeled away from the curb. The once fresh crisp morning air became impaled with the smell of burned rubber.

"Asshole!"

A thirty-something lady walked by Chloe and me with a toddler in tow. Chloe multitasked. She half-hugged me and simultaneously shoved the filthy cup towards the woman's face.

The woman rummaged through her purse.

*Plop! Plop!*

Fifty cents went into the cup.

"Thanks, Mam!" Chloe then turned to me and whispered in shock, *"Fifty cents, Bug. Out of sight."*

I noticed since the last time I saw her; Chloe had added two more blue jay tail feathers to her headband. I grabbed hold of one of them.

"New?"

Chloe nodded her head. "Found them on the ground over on East Hanna under a tree." She gently moved my hand off the feathers. "Cool, right? I just love the colors."

"Cat attack, is my guess."

She pushed my shoulder and whined, "Stop it, Bug. The bird is okay. He just didn't need these feathers anymore. He grew newer, stronger ones. He is flying," she pointed towards the sky, "Somewhere in the sky."

"He's flying alright, inside some happy cat's belly." I reached forward and rubbed her stomach.

"Shut up," she cried and shoved my hand away.

"Okay. You're right. The little birdy is fine."

Chloe vacillated between a smile and a pout. I sensed she doubted by sincerity regarding the bird's well-being. I also suspected she thought I might be correct about the bird's true fate.

"Where have you been, Bug? It's been days," she grumbled. I knew she needed a fix.

I replied with an indifferent tone to my voice, "Here and there.".

Chloe did not need to know about where I had been, nor the things I had done to earn the money to help support our dependent drug habit.

Chloe nodded her head in the direction of the truck which had just left. "Groovy time?"

I turned towards my left and saw the blue-collar John disappear around the corner at the traffic light down the road aways. I adjusted my shorts in the front. The uncomfortable squirming done during the ride caused them to creep up. Everything below the belt felt numb.

"Better?" she asked with a quizzical look.

"Better."

To someone driving by, it looked as if I had caught a horrific case of college crabs.

I bumped Chloe's hip with mine. "Buy me a coffee and I'll give you *all* the filthy details about him." I nodded in the blue-collar John's direction.

Chloe paused and then shot a suspicious look at me. "Wait a minute."

I stuck out my bottom lip, "What?" I innocently asked.

"You've got money for coffee. You just tricked. You have been doing it for days, right? Or were you locked up?"

I grabbed the filthy cup from Chloe's hand. "I wasn't locked up, petal head. I never get locked up."

"So, why can't you buy your own coffee, then?"

"Because I hardly made shit the last few days. And what I did make…" I trailed off and grinned. "Well, you know…"

Chloe's bottom lip jutted out and her arms crossed. She snapped, "Bug! You promised you wouldn't score without me."

I shrugged my shoulders, "Shit happens."

"That's not fair. I've been going without…"

I cut her off. "Life isn't fair, kid. Thought you knew that by now."

"What about that guy?"

"What guy?" I asked. I played dumb. I knew who she meant.

"The truck guy."

"What about him?"

 Did he stiff you or something?"

"Oh, he stiffed me and something." I almost gagged as my mind re-lived the moment.

"Do you have money for Tiny?"

I raised my eyebrows. "I can hardly afford a cup of coffee."

Chloe grew pissed. I broke a promise we made. Neither of us scored *dirt* without sharing it. I had never kept my end of the bargain. If Chloe knew how many times I got high without her, I would have no family.

I jiggled the cup. Several coins clanked as they ran into one another inside the small space.

"Sounds like enough change for a cup of beans and a jelly doughnut." I gave her my best pity face. "Come on. We can share."

Chloe stared at me in disbelief. She clearly struggled to find a morsel of the peace and love jumbo she thrived on so much.

I got close to her face. "Come on, Chloe. Chloooo-weee! Bug needs her caffeine fix until she can get a..." My index fingers made air quotation marks, "...*real fix for both of us.*"

Chloe snatched the cup from my grasp. I felt the little bug legs as they began to scamper about my skin in various places. My countdown clock now officially ticked towards dope sickness soon. I needed to hit the streets and earn or else.

I fidgeted with the semi-fresh track marks on my arms. I then glanced down at the track marks hidden between my toes. My new spot. The veins in my arms were cooked.

I noticed I needed a new pair of shoes. My worn-down flipflops were eroded even though they managed to make my red painted toenails look nice; like a posh penthouse pet thrust in the middle of Skid Row.

Chloe muttered, "I can't talk to you yet."

She put her worn out headphones on for two *Led Zeppelin* songs. I had never seen her so mad over me getting high without her.

I never understood Chloe's rarity to get pissed off over anything. Angry Chloe was as rare as a sighting of the Loch Ness Monster or Big Foot. Even despite her mom's many boyfriends having done her wrong like momma's boyfriends had done me. Chloe's soul should have been destroyed, same as mine and others who lived on the streets. The worst thing the abuse caused was her addiction to drugs. Chloe remained kind, otherwise. A giant mystery, indeed.

I heard the faint sound of Robert Plant belting out, *"When the levee breaks, I'll have no place to stay"* from Chloe's Walkman, when she had finally removed the headphones from her ears.

"How long's it been for you?" she asked. "Don't lie to me. I'll know if you're lying." She stared into my eyes.

I gave my hair a good rustle and looked away. "Too long"

I lied. I was coming down. Chloe knew it, too.

"Liar."

I begged her again, "Please, Chloe? I need caffeine and sugar. Lots of sugar. Just something to get me over until I can get back out there for both of us."

She caved, "Fine," I knew I would win her over with promises of *dirt* in her not-so-distant future.

"You're the best, Petal head!"

"You want to know something, Bug?"

"What," I asked, as I took a hold of the cup.

"You're really living up to your name, today."

"How's that?" I asked.

Chloe playfully pushed me towards The Beans & Jellies Café door. "Bugging me for this. Bugging me for that. A real pest."

I turned around and coyly replied, "And you love me for it", before I planted a kiss on her dirt-smudged cheek.

"Think Pop's got any strawberry jellies today?" she asked.

# Another Day, Another...

**B**eing homeless and addicted to heroin was the closest thing to hell on earth in every sense of the word. There was nothing enticing about one second of it. Unless: puking, crapping your pants, losing teeth, sleeping with strangers for money just to score, having a tent to call home *(if you were lucky)*, rare personal hygiene opportunities, dealing with frustrated paramedics trying to save your overdosed ass, but struggling because you have blown out all your veins. And the worst part, never knowing if you would earn enough money in time for your next fix before dope sickness took over.

Being a homeless drug addict was never on my bingo card in life. Hell, either one would not have made it onto my *'bucket list'*.

But things happened or did not happen.

Directions changed.

Roads became bumpier or closed off.

Doors were slammed and sometimes nailed shut.

One was left with but a handful of choices to survive; quit while you were ahead, blend into your pathetic surroundings like a chameleon on a dead plant or fight like an angry alley cat to escape the bag of shit life tossed you into before it twisted that sucker tight and chucked you off the nearest bridge to drown in a nasty river of doom.

I chose the chameleon route.

I lacked survival skills in the beginning. I found it easier to blend in than to stand out. I gave up on life, but not entirely. I did, however, give up any belief in myself. I was weak. But not enough to quit just yet. Though I would be lying if I said the thought never crossed my mind.

Bad thoughts arose in my mind often like that one song on the radio you could never stand hearing. The song you would crawl across the floor bleeding out just to shut the radio off and never hear it again. We all have that one song.

Somehow, someway, no matter how gross life got, *dirt* was always there for me like a warm blanket, an old friend. It wrapped its arms around me and showered me with love. No questions. No judgements.

I felt warm.

I felt loved.

I felt content.

*Dirt* devoured every negative thought that swirled around inside my head. It embraced my soul. It pieced my broken heart back together with invisible duct tape.

The hurt…gone.

The shame…gone.

The anger…. gone.

The disappointment…gone.

The confusion…gone.

The loneliness…gone.

I eventually learned those were cliched lies I had told myself every time I shot up. Want to know the truly sad part about it all? I actually believed those lies every time I felt the warmth of *dirt's* touch ooze its way from the top of my head all the way down to my half-polished, raggedly looking toenails.

Addiction and homelessness coaxed me into doing things I never imagined I would ever have done for survival. The power of the drug, the power of starvation was overwhelming. I found myself doing or being done to by Johns, vile, unspeakable things. Things worse than what momma's boyfriends had done to me in the back bedroom of our trailer when I was a child. Things I will never utter, not even on my death bed.

As for my dreams of a better life? The dream of becoming something good in the world? *Fuck it.*

Once the streets, once *dirt* consumed me, nightmares became my dreams.

# Lather, Rinse, Repeat...

**EARLY MORNING:**

I woke up under an overpass.

My filthy body sprawled out.

I smelled like a decayed buffet.

And I looked even worse.

The circle of buzzards did not desire a taste of me.

Why would a John?

I was extremely hungover.

I needed a shower and a fix.

No. Wait. A fix and then a shower.

Typical junkie.

*Dirt* came before anything and everyone.

Always.

It was the first thought I had upon opening my eyes.

And the last thought I had when my eyes closed.

I failed to earn enough to score last night.

I mean, I had earned enough.

But I owed my dealer.

Tiny refused to front me anymore until I paid off my debt.

I had to compromise my craving for drugs with booze.

My head hurt badly.

My stomach yearned to lurch.

But it was too empty.

I had nothing on the inside to throw up.

Except my feelings.

My bladder was upset, too.

The moment I sat up, my bladder felt ready to burst.

I pee-pee danced my way to a gas station.

The bathroom was on the outside.

I needed a key.

A clerk rudely threw the key at me.

Bitch barely missed my eyeball.

I jiggled the lock to the bathroom door.

*'Finally!'*

The bathroom was dimly lit.

I could not say the same for the mirror.

It was bright and screamed, 'Clowny the Whore' back at me.

I felt like as if I were inside a funhouse at the County Fair.

Only this house, this bathroom was not so fun.

I stared hopelessly back at my pitiful reflection.

"Christ, Bug! You look like shit warmed over."

I looked as bad as I felt.

The porcelain sink had seen better days.

I used it to freshen up.

The pink soap oozed from the dispenser.

It reeked like an old lady's perfume.

I related to the small sink.

Its rusted pipes and chipped top.

Used.

Abused.

Unappreciated.

Despite the numerous services it provided for so many.

Hard brown paper towels chaffed my privates as I dried off.

I checked my bag.

No toothpaste.

No gum.

No money to buy them either.

"Dammit!"

I rinsed my mouth out with what remained of a now flat soda.

I purchased it last night to chase the cheap booze down with.

I fluffed up my greasy, blonde hair with my fingers.

I threw a scowl at my tired reflection.

"Time to go to work, skank-bait."

I turned off the light and opened the door.

The sun immediately delivered a bitch-slap to my pupils.

"Ooh!"

I covered my eyes with both hands like a Vampire.

My head pounded even harder.

I left the key stuck in the door lock and walked out.

"Screw that rude cashier. Let her come fetch the key herself."

Within minutes, I was approached by a trick.

We snuck into a nearby alleyway.

I provided him service with a *gag* - no smile.

I needed to earn more cash to buy *dirt* for Chloe and me.

Plus, a tube of toothpaste for just me.

Dope sickness started to set in hard.

I needed to band-aide the crappy way I felt - ASAP.

I mooched a cup of coffee with extra sugar.

Sugar is, was and will always be a dopers best friend.

A car honked for my attention.

It was a hefty geek who waved me over.

He wore a grease-stained Atari T-shirt circa 1980's.

"Probably still lives with his parents. Brilliant."

The day just kept getting better. *(sarcasm)*

But a hustle was a hustle.

Cash was cash.

*"Suck it up, Bug!"* I muttered.

I nearly retched climbing into the four-door white car.

The backseat was packed to the ceiling with garbage.

Old magazines, dirty clothes, and fast-food wrappers.

The view from the back window was blocked.

His nasty car made me feel momentarily clean.

One whiff of the inside of the car told me he was a hoarder.

He needed a shower worse than me.

*"You've got this, Bug,"* I whispered.

I repeated those words in my head until it was over.

Victory.

The geek was literally a *'one minuteman'*.

For once I felt the Universe was on my side.

A few more bucks had been earned.

Almost there.

I hid the money inside Chloe's Go-Go Boots.

I had *"borrowed them"* after one of my flipflops gave out.

I planned to steal a new pair next time I went to the store.

Chloe would be pissed I borrowed her boots without asking.

However, all would be forgiven once I gave her some *dirt*.

The geek dropped me off back in front of the Café.

It was not long before another horn honked for me.

East Hollywood Street, here I come.

Or he comes sooner rather than later, hopefully.

# LaRue

LaRue was barely eighteen and pregnant by a one-time John who refused to wear a condom when he had raped her. His violent actions were revenge after she rejected his offer for a date. She considered getting rid of it but changed her mind the moment she felt a slight flutter burst forth from a tiny butterfly growing inside her belly.

"I'm going to keep it, Bug," she would tell me, her brown eyes filled with signs of exhaustion. The closer LaRue got to her due date the harder it had become for her to work as many hours as possible on the streets. Extreme summer heat, lack of available food, no comfortable place to sleep, let alone sit and a strong addiction to *dirt* never often hindered LaRue. Despite the many odds against her, somehow, LaRue always managed to soldier ahead and get the job done.

I thought, *'It must be motherly instinct. Where a mother automatically protects her child at all costs, including sacrificing her own life.'* I mean, the sentiment from LaRue was there even while using drugs during her pregnancy. Addiction could have cared less about her baby. Heartless bastard.

Momma lacked motherly instinct. I worried sometimes that I might, too, because of genetics. I pondered this as I pressed my hand against LaRue's large ebony stomach. I tried to feel the baby kick. I secretly longed to feel maternal, just not pregnant. I could barely take care of myself, Chloe or a feral cat I fed scraps to. I named him, 'Unlucky'. After me.

I used to dream where momma cared about me. I mean, truly cared. Not because of an obligation. More like genuine, from the heart. A wished all my life before she died for one maternal instinct to shine through. Just one. One where she protected me from the wolves instead of throwing me right into their den. Never happened. Thanks to her lack of love and care, I believed dreams do not come true.

"This baby is going to help me get clean and stay clean, too. It's going to give me a purpose, Bug. You'll see."

"I know it will, LaRue," is what my lips spoke. But my head thought, *'No it's not. Dirt's got you too tight by the tail, tiger. It ain't letting you or any of us go. You've never stopped using dirt since you peed positive on a pregnancy test stick at some seedy gas station.'*

I suddenly looked up at LaRue, excited. "Hey! I felt it kick." I had expected the same excited reaction from her to my experience. Instead, I found her gaze fixed across the street at our dealer, Tiny. I gently patted LaRue's arm.

"I know. I know."

She rested her head upon my shoulder.

LaRue was thrown out of the house at sixteen for getting pregnant by her high school boyfriend. Before her ex-boyfriend arrived on the scene and convinced her sex was the same thing as love and basically ruined her life, LaRue had a bright future in journalism. She was on the right track with good grades and a part-time job at a local newspaper.

Now, the only tracks LaRue traveled on were composed of *dirt,* destination unknown and various unpleasant stops along the way. All it would take to derail her was one bad batch of *dirt.* Everyone on the streets knew the risk of taking drugs. But those same folks also believed *dirt* fixed the hurt. So, it was worth the risk.

*'Lies!'*

LaRue had lost her first baby two months into the pregnancy. Her boyfriend dumped her after the unfortunate tragedy struck. She was devastated and unable to function until someone on the streets introduced her to *dirt.* While her ex-boyfriend caught footballs on a college scholarship, LaRue caught STD's, missed their lost baby, and struggled daily to function. *Dirt* became the only thing which cradled the loss and pain LaRue felt on the inside.

LaRue's stomach and feet were so swollen. I helplessly watched as she waddled over to the passenger side of a car which had pulled up looking for a date. LaRue's royal blue mini dress clung to every nook and cranny on her body.

I waved in her direction and mouthed, *"be careful,"* as the car pulled away from the broken curb.

LaRue waved back and mouthed, *"I will."*

Every day LaRue promised herself she would get clean and be there for her baby. Yet, every day she remained *dirty* until the tragic end of her life arrived...exactly three months after the birth of her son, Trey.

"Sorry, Tiger."

# Paula

The corner of my eye caught Paula; a twenty-five *(who resembled more of a thirty-five-year-old)* 5'2" spitfire, with brown hair styled in two low-hung ponytails. She crossed the street to the other side without a care of on-coming traffic.

I screamed, "Lookout, Paula!" just as a maroon four-door car slammed on its brakes.

The driver laid down hard on the horn and yelled, "WATCH IT, WHORE!!"

"SCREW YOU!!" Paula retaliated and continued her strut as if nothing had happened.

Typical Paula. She never looked back. Literally or physically. She cared less about the guy who almost hit her with his car. The shocked bystanders stood with adrenaline pulsating through their veins. No one. Paula lived in her own freaky world. Paula lived by one rule; *Keep on moving. Never look back. Ever.* She practiced what she preached, too.

Paula tipped her head back and shouted out towards the sky as loud as possible, *"Boogie fever! Boogie down!"*

I shook my head and thought, *'High as fuck.'*

Paula donned a pair of red tracksuit pants with double-white stripes that ran vertically down the sides and a semi-dirty white tank top. A headband with two giant Styrofoam balls covered in red glitter and attached to long springs, bounced about on the top of her head.

*"Probably boosted that stupid thing from a Dollar Store,"* I mumbled.

Paula hollered from across the street, "Hey, Bug!"

"Hey, Paula!" I shot back.

"I got the boogie fever, Bug!"

Paula then danced to fit her wild personality.

*No shit. (eyeroll)*

"I noticed," I replied.

Paula was known on the streets to be hopped up on speed almost 24/7. She had no choice. Without uppers, Paula fell very low into the dumps. Paula's mood could plumet far enough where she has been talked off the ledges of several buildings in the Tampa Bay area by her street family and sometimes the police. Paula hated when cops got involved because it meant she would be put on a 51/50 hold. With her street family, she was guaranteed more speed to remedy the dire situation.

"Next stop – crazy town!" she routinely shouted out before the squad car door slammed shut and her voice was silenced for the next seventy-two hours.

Any time spent with Paula rivaled a circus loaded with insane clowns. One could never predict which way the pendulum of insanity would swing until they were under the metaphoric tent with Paula... *(aka: hanging out with her)*.

Paula's speed-fueled ventures literally had her talk, walk, and eat at a mile a minute. To try and edge a word into a conversation with her was simply impossible. And half the time, not worth the effort. Paula never heard your voice over the sound of her own, or perhaps the voices that chatted inside her head. If Paula's blood were ever to be tested it would be made of sugar, caffeine, speed, and one giant pinch of bullshit.

What rolled across Paula's tongue and poured out of her mouth was mainly nonsense. No one knew Paula's true story. Then again, no one really knew anyone's truth on the streets. People usually shared their version of the truth. Paula was no different. Except her stories typically exceeded the exaggeration bar.

Paula habitually lied. One time she claimed to come from a royal bloodline. Another, she was an orphan. And still another time, she was once a popular singer in a rock band who willingly gave up fame and fortune for life on the streets.

*'I think she and Chloe might be related.'*

No one understood why Paula turned lying into such an artform. Maybe the lies made her feel important and not so insignificant to the world. Insignificance was a feeling most homeless addicts were well acquainted with.

If Paula got caught in a lie, she claimed not to care what that person thought. Yet, more lies to cover a lie. She cared but would continue to spin lies faster than Rumpelstiltskin spun gold, until whoever the person she spoke with caved and let Paula's truth prevail. Even if it was still a lie.

"Who are they anyway? And why should I care what they think of me. Fuck 'em!" Paula said.

People on the streets drifted in and around Nebraska Avenue and its many side streets. Many for drug overdoses, some returned home, others were rescued from their pimps or traffickers by cops, street families broke up, some opted out of life, and others were in jail or rotting in prison in a 6' x 6' cell. And still many arrived fresh off the bus hoping for a better life in the Sunshine State. The influx never stopped. It merely rotated like a pig on a spit to avoid the burn.

The harsh reality? People on the streets were treading water in their individual cesspools of agony and torment. They had to decide to fight or drown. To fake as if all was right in their world, when it was not or face reality. Many were so preoccupied with keeping their head above water, they failed to notice those drowning right beside them. All of us were locked up in an indefinite self-preservation mode cycle.

Paula screamed out my name again from across the street, "Check it out, Bug!" She tilted her head forward and made those red-glittery head bopper things dance on top of her head.

"Gotta boogie on now, girl."

I called back, "Boogie on then, girl! Catch you another time."
I waved her on.

"Thank God she split! I don't have the energy for that girl today."

Paula eased down the sidewalk like one of those speed walking exercise soccer moms inside the *University Shopping Mall* until she transformed into a red speck far off in the distance.

I was relieved once Paula had disappeared entirely from my view.

*'Boogie down!'*

# Back to My Day

**I** am once again alone on the streets.

Purple tank top.

Cut-off jean shorts.

Chloe's vanilla-colored boots.

On the prowl for money.

A cute Wallstreet knockoff looking guy wanted a quickie.

The money pot was growing.

If this pace kept up, the pot would soon be traded for *dirt*.

**NOON:**

"Shit!"

The sun disappeared.

Out came the gray clouds.

It suddenly poured down rain.

I got soaked.

Florida and their damn spontaneous rain showers.

"Gee, thanks."

How I wished for a bar of soap.

It was a free shower from Mother Nature.

Might as well take advantage of the gift, right?

The rain should have made me cleaner.

But I felt far from clean.

No amount of rain could wash off the filth that covered me.

Inside or out.

Harder rain pelted downward.

Regardless, I continued to hustle until I no longer could.

No choice.

I needed *dirt* soon or else.

Cars continued to woosh on by.

The rain a worse turn off than my hygiene habits.

"Shit!"

Not one taker willing to risk it.

The rain cascaded even harder.

Business had officially halted.

"Damnit! I can't catch a break!"

Johns did not want rain-soaked whores in their car.

*'Selfish jerks!'*


**EARLY AFTERNOON:**

I huddled underneath a faded-white eve behind a store.

My dope sickness, stronger.

I needed candy to curb the craving.

I reached into Chloe's left boot.

A bag of shoplifted gummy worms successfully retrieved.

I ate the entire bag.

The entire bag.

My first meal of the day.

The strong jolt of sugar helped.

But not enough.

I still felt dope sick.

My toes hurt.

Chloe's boots were a size too small for my big feet.

I sat down on the semi-wet pavement.

I hugged my scabbed knees tightly.

I struggled to stay dry underneath the tiny white eve.

I felt like a smelly swamp turtle smushed inside its shell.

I needed a shower, badly.

I mean, badly.

The wind kicked up.

I was cold.

I was soaked.

And the tiny eve failed to protect me from additional
wetness.

I was not surprised by it.

Life never offered me protection.

Protection was a foreign experience to me.

My dad never protected me.

Momma never protected me.

Momma's boyfriend's sure as hell never protected me.

They always took advantage of me.

God never…

You know what?

Never mind.

God never loved me.

I never loved myself.

I hated myself.

Oh, how I despised dope sickness.

The days just sucked overall.

I wanted to quit.

Everything.

Right then.

Right there.

*Dirt.*

Hustling.

Life.

All of it.

Just one wrong batch of dope.

Just a little bit more in the needle than usual.

Bam!

Over.

But I lacked the courage and strength to follow through.

And even if I pulled the plug, I still had nowhere to go.

A potter's field maybe.

If they would have me.

But only if someone cared enough to acknowledge me.

The truth?

No one cared about me.

I was a drugged-out whore.

A life loser.

Maybe my street sister, Chloe, cared about me.

But who knew how long she would stick around.

We were both homeless junkies.

If I died, Heaven would say, "No thanks."

Hell would say, "Piss off."

I suppose I literally had nowhere to go.

On earth.

Or in the unknown.

Confusion washed over me in powerful waves.

Finally, the rain began to lighten to a drizzle.

I stared at the wet pavement.

My heart felt heavy.

I knew I could not abandon the streets.

I intently gazed at the track marks on my skin.

The marks soon merged into blurred lines.

It was then I had an epiphany.

*"My life's been just one pathetic, giant blur."*

The only thing I saw clearly...

I could not bring myself to ever abandon *dirt*.

I was too addicted.

Years of abuse and homelessness had convinced me of such.

Told me *dirt* had my back.

The streets were there for me when no one else ever was.

How could I go on without either of them?

The answer?

I couldn't.

I started to cry.

I thought about my dad.

My heart existed vacant.

Nevertheless, anger moved in.

I shouted, "Rot in hell, Asshole!"

I then thought about momma.

*I mumbled to myself, "Drunk bitch! I was there for you! I cleaned up your piss and shit! Your vomit! I held your hand as you took your last breath. All you ever cared about were your boyfriends. Loaded and laid was the motto you lived by until the very end. You never cared about what happened to me. Never! I hate you! Fuck your precious Jack, too!"*

Her octopus tentacle-handed testicle-driven boyfriends' came to mind.

Different sizes.

Varied shapes.

Some clean.

Some unkempt.

All putrid in appearance, regardless.

Their grubby hands.

Their contrast sized penises.

Both encompassed my childhood like horny villagers with tiki torches and pitchforks.

Each parked at the helm of my innocence.

All fueled by my fear.

Every one of them driven to action by the devil himself.

I thought of the endless parade of Johns trapesing in and out of my body parts like a 24-hour convenience store.

*'Always convenient for them. Forever inconvenient for me.'*

I grabbed handfuls of my shaggy bleached hair.

I shook my head side to side.

I screamed, "*Aaaaaaaaaaaaaaaaaaaaaaaa! Sick bastards!*"

A spark of fire erupted down inside.

The glow evolved into a flashover within seconds.

My insides burned.

My soul was torched.

My heart black as coal.

All that was within me now charred.

Rage consumed me further.

I stood up.

Then I repeatedly punched the white cinder block wall behind me.

"Fuck you! Fuck you! Fuck every one of you!" I yelled.

The mental, emotional, and physical pain released.

It was all too real.

Too overwhelming to contain.

The rage eventually brewed down to a simmer.

While the physical pain from hitting the wall set in.

I stared down my bloodied hand.

My knuckles tender to the touch.

I winced and scolded myself.

"Why'd you go and do that to yourself, Bug? Dammit!"

I needed some ibuprofen and bandages.

This meant less money for *dirt*.

And extra time on the streets to earn that money back.

*"Shit!"*

I fell against the same wall I punched the crap out of.

To my surprise, the wall did not punch me back.

It did not reject me.

It did not shove me off of it.

It did not try to fondle me.

Unlike people, the wall was not cold, cruel, or uncaring.

No.

The wall simply caught me as I fell.

It cradled me like a loving parent.

It gently guided my broken soul to the ground.

I was surprised by its kindness.

By its unyielding care.

It appeared to ask nothing of me.

It was just there.

For me.

Alone.

How I longed to be held with such unyielding care my whole life.

I curled up into a ball and cried.

I cried until I puked up the gummy worms and stale soda.

My sugar rush to stave off the cravings for *dirt* – vanished.

I was dope sick more than ever.

My head hurt badly.

My stomach officially emptied.

My heart, destroyed.


## LATE AFTERNOON:

I remained up against that wall until the rain stopped.

I thought, *'Time to pull your shit together, girl!'*

I dried what tears remained.

I wiped the puke crumbs from the corners of my mouth.

I dipped my bloodied knuckles in a puddle of dirty water.

I then entered a gas station store where I stole a packet of ibuprofen, band aides and some gum.

I was getting too dope sick to spend what money I had earned thus far.

Time to hit the streets, again.

Business immediately picked back up where it had left off.

I winced with each trick for the remainder of the day.

I was too sober.

I was too dope sick.

I felt all of it.

And needed to feel none of it.

What I needed was a fix… soon.

The ibuprofen failed to stop my hand pain.

Just one more trick and I earned enough to visit Tiny.

I finally landed one.

A regular.

A fast one.

Bonus.

The dope sickness had grown stronger, and I was weaker.

It felt like tiny little bugs were crawling underneath my skin.

Ten minutes later, I met up with my dealer, Tiny.

Waves of relief were washing over my body while holding
that small bag of powdered paradise in my hand.

Knowing all the emotional and physical pain I carried with
me, like ghosts trapped inside a haunted vessel, would soon
vanish back into their secret crevices.

At least for a while, anyway.

I had not seen Chloe, so I decided to use it all for myself.

*'Next time, Sis. I promise. I even took good care of your boots. See? No
puke or bloodstains on them.'*

I found a grassy noll out of the public view and sat down.

Lighter.

Check.

Spoon.

Check.

Water bottle.

Check.

Shoestring.

Check.

I cooked it and shot up.

I then lay back on the soft grass and watched the sky

morph from reddish orange to eventually black.

The sun had finally set on yet, another horrid day.

I had survived it all.

All thanks to *dirt* and that kind white cinder block wall.

Beautiful wall.

Loving wall.

My wall.

The moon would soon arise.

So, too, would I.

Eventually...I got really wasted.

I closed my eyes and placed my arms horizontally in the grass as if I were an airplane prepared for takeoff. The *dirt* had delicately merged together with my pain and blood which coursed within my weak veins, like a rampant mudslide. All of my bad memories instantaneously vanished into a sea of murkiness.

How I wished that feeling would last forever.

I knew it would not.

But I still wished for it anyway.

# Seeing Stars, Baby

**I** stood out in front of a combination gas station and convenience store. My small boobs were on low-key display courtesy of a yellow tube top I borrowed from big-chested Paula. I had to pull the top up every few seconds or risk being arrested for indecent exposure. I paired it with white shorts cut so high; you could have seen my panties…if I wore any.

The shorts used to be ripped up jeans I found at a clothing donation box in a parking lot. Someone failed to shove them all the way inside the container. Based on their condition and style, they sure had themselves one hell of a time in the 80's.

I borrowed a pair of scissors from Pop at the Beans & Jellies Café and trimmed them up. The only trouble was, I failed to follow the old rule; measure twice, cut once. So, the shorts came out shorter than I had intended. *Oops!* It turned out my mistake mattered not. It was better for business. Johns loved shorty shorts. The shorter, the better.

Once again, I found myself in need of cash to score *dirt*. No surprise.

Typical cycle of a junkie's life…

Earn the money.

Buy the dope.

Get high.

Earn the money.

Buy the dope.

Get high.

This *'hamster stuck on the wheel going nowhere pattern'* had to occur, no matter whether it was rain or shine to avoid the joys of dope sickness. Real fun stuff, too.

Runny nose.

Tingling vibrations when peeing.

Cold sweats.

Nausea.

Vomiting.

Body aches.

Diarrhea.

Depression.

Anxiety.

The sensation of bugs crawling all over your skin.

Feeling like your bones were injected with battery acid.

There were other reasons, too.

For me personally, *dirt* equaled avoidance.

Avoidance of emotional pain.

Avoidance of mental pain.

Avoidance of physical pain.

Avoidance was standard addict behavior 101. And I was an A+ honor roll student in the class. I believed if I kept it up, I would soon be crowned valedictorian of the streets.

Each avoidance appeared like a deep root attached to an olive tree who only bore forth rotten fruit. In my mind, it was easier to bury sullied pits inside the *dirt* for continued life, than to throw them in the trash and heal from the pain.

*'If healing from my past was even a remote possibility,'* I often thought.

I had no clue if I could or would ever heal.

I had no clue if I even wanted to heal.

Avoidance had become so easy.

Too easy, in fact.

It never mattered how disgusted I felt being touched by Johns, if I had poor hygiene, if I were dope sick or if I was in the midst of a mental health breakdown. I had to earn money for my habit or deal with my demons and horrendous withdrawals simultaneously.

I must therefore earn or experience the burn.

My options were none.

Nighttime was usually the best time to earn money. Although early morning was good, too. Both times had many horny men on their way home from a hard day's work or on their way to a hard day's work.

Countless men starved for affection and appreciation before getting neutered by grumpy bosses, wifey tailored honey-do-lists, daddy duties and more. I assumed their fruit trees which bore forth stiff bananas and wrinkled berries were just as rotten as that olive tree of mine.

I blocked out any guilt that attempted to creep in like a thief bent on awakening my conscience. Me, have compassion for their significant others or family; screw that. What I had been through. The hell I had endured which resulted in a life on the streets. Unloved. Plus, my need for a fix outweighed any morals, character, values, or integrity.

What I wanted is what mattered the most.

*'To hell with their perfect white picket fence lives!'*

The tables were turned in my favor.

My control.

I was on top of the world.

If it were upside down, that is.

Being upside down meant I was actually at the bottom of the ocean. Lower than a pile of whale shit.

Top of the world.

Hardly.

But I lied to myself that I was anyway.

I readjusted Paula's overstretched yellow tube top before my eyes got mesmerized by a blinking yellow traffic light perched across the street.

*Light.*

*Dark.*

*Light.*

*Dark.*

*Light.*

*Dark.*

The flashing light reminded me of a city firefly.

I remained fixated on that lone yellow traffic light and longed for the days when momma and I used to lay on our backs in the field at night and watch the fireflies twinkling.

Such simple times.

Happy times.

But those times died long before momma ever did.

Blinking lights, no matter what the source, bred soul aching memories bathed in sorrow, agony, anger, unforgiveness and regret. But they also conjured up longing, love and feelings that made me miss her sorry drunk ass. The result of both situations had evolved into a combination of euphoric anguish only a roll in *dirt* could understand, like a pig to a puddle of cool mud when it got too hot to shoulder any longer.

I thought, *The prodigal daughter has yet to come out of the hog pen and return home at this point in her life. More slop please. Just keep it coming. Nothing but crumbs and decayed scraps from the table will be acceptable and welcomed.'*

In my distorted mind, *dirt* developed into straggly arms that hugged me tight while I cried over what could have...no, what my life should have been.

It was a gentle hand that caressed my face and wiped away salty tears. *Dirt* whispered into my ear during dire moments, *"It's going to be alright. Let me in. Trust me."*

Part of me suspected *dirt* was a liar and deceiver like the many men I had encountered before becoming a whore and after. It really was no different than anyone who ventured into my life. Yet, it had such a strong hold on me. An ability to make me see what I wanted to see. To hear what I wanted to hear. To believe what I wanted to believe. To my deceptive heart and mind, *dirt* represented how my momma should have been towards me, but rarely ever was. It was also the many words my momma should have spoken to me but never uttered.

I was far from okay since the day my purity was stolen from me. The men from my past robbed me of my innocence like a callous purse snatcher on the streets. Just took it right from my firm grasp without permission.

My knees were spread apart like a golden clasp. Their wild, unruly, fondling hands rifled their way through my many pockets and folds, over and over in search of pleasure. I would be thrown to the side like trash, only to be snatched up again by another. I was unzipped and opened up, night after night. Rifled through until I was too sore to take being touched anymore. My fabric worn and torn almost beyond repair. But that never stopped them from opening me up in the hopes of more treasure. Despite that, all that remained of me was a handful of purse dirt.

Terrified.

Sick to my stomach.

I constantly fought back.

Always.

I kicked.

I screamed.

I begged.

I even vomited on some of them.

Other times I just laid there, stiller than pond water and begged for it to just be over. None of the past mattered now. It was done. The purse, my innocence had been thrown in a dumpster long ago. Nothing I could do about it.

I was aware that *dirt* fibbed to me on the regular. Plot twist. I too, lied to *dirt*. I pretended each fix cured everything wrong in my life. It did not. The truth: *dirt* was just a short-term distraction. A mere avoidance to my unpleasant past, my disgusting present and disappointing future.

I remained enthralled by the blinking yellow light like a cat drawn to a red laser beam, when a deep, chain-smoking tinged voice broke my stare.

"Hey, baby girl. Do you like to party?" the man asked before taking a deep drag off a cigarette. "Name's, Pete."

I sized Pete up straight away.

*'Around forty-five. Confirmed bachelor. Committed alcoholic.'*

The noticeable, deep crow's feet perched next to each eye gave his true history. Too much smoking and drinking had clearly taken their toll on Pete's outside. I shuddered to think of his insides. I was certain his liver would survive without issue stuffed inside a mason jar. No need for any alcohol-based preservative.

*"Just like Momma's,"* I whispered. *"His and hers pickled white-trash pâté. A perfect match."*

I saw Pete at the Beans & Jellies Café. We never actually spoke. He worked in construction. Sometimes his crew stopped in for coffee on their way to work. Pop's coffee had a reputation for curing vile hangovers. And Pete undoubtedly loved his nightly beer.

A very unshaven Pete stood before me in a pair of tight blue jeans and a white T shirt. He had a six pack of beer nestled tightly under his left arm. By the look of his bloodshot green eyes, Pete was already two hours into his own party.

"Can I have one?" I asked, as I nodded at the six-pack.

"Well, that all depends, darlin'," he replied.

I played dumb and twirled my hair. "Depends on what?"

Pete eyed me up and down like a porterhouse steak. I shivered at his stare, not sizzled.

"What you gonna give old Pete in return?" He then licked his lips. "Do you like to party?"

I instinctively revolted at the thought of sleeping with him. But, I had a habit that needed to be fed. So, I forced my typical 'hooker smile', adjusted my top and asked, "What did you have in mind, Pete?"

Pete dug a wad of money from his front jean pocket and waved it before my hungry eyes. He raised his left eyebrow.

"How does partying with Pete under the stars sound to you?"

"Okay. Sure." I looked around. "You got a truck or something?"

"What's your name, darlin'?" Pete then leaned in and sniffed my dirty neck. He gave it a quick lick. "Hmm…salty. Too bad old Pete doesn't have some Tequila for body shots." He winked.

I wanted to vomit. I gently eased him off my neck to nail down the negotiations.

"Ease up. No freebies. And my name doesn't matter."

"Well, it does to, Pete. Come on, darlin'. Pete's your friend , right?" He once again waved that thick wad of cash before my desperate, drug starved eyes.

I caved. "They call me, Bug."

"Bug, huh? What, like one of those black widow spiders or something?" He then poked my right ribcage with his index finger in a teasing manner. "Or are you a furry little caterpillar, instead? Hmm?" He reached out to grab my crotch.

I successfully stepped backwards, and he missed.

*Like I haven't heard that stupid joke a hundred times.'*

"Fuzzy everywhere, I'll bet." He licked his lips again.

"It's just, Bug. No meaning behind it. Okay?" I snapped back.

Pete leaned in and whispered into my ear, *"Do you like seeing stars, Bug?"*

"Who doesn't?"

Pete grabbed a beer from the six pack and offered it to me. I reached for it. But just before I could grab it, he pulled it out of range.

"*Eh. Eh. Eh.* Not so fast. Hold on just one second my fuzzy little caterpillar."

I immediately thought, '*Stop calling me that asshole!*'

He eyed me up and down. "The way I see it, ol' Pete's offered you a beer and the stars. Romance." He took a chug of beer.

*'Dirt's the goal, Bug. Just swallow your vomit, flirt with this loser and get the cash.'*

I took a deep swallow and cooed out to him, "Bug will give Pete the stars and anything else he wants. How about we start with Pete handing Bug a beer."

"Well, ah' right then."

I swear, I never chugged a beer down so fast in my life.

Pete and I made our way behind the convenience store. He did not want to use his truck. Said the wife might smell me. We drank for a bit and set the empty beer bottles on top of an A/C unit behind the store. Pete left at one point to buy another six-pack. We wound up chugging a twelve-pack between us.

119

Once the beer disappeared, it was not long before Pete worked up the nerve and mashed me up against the outside back wall of the store. He kissed and licked my neck aggressively.

'*Gross! Just gross. Just stop already. Let's get this over with.*'

Pete attempted to kiss me on the mouth numerous times. Each time, I turned my head away and protested, "No mouth kissing."

"Alright. Alright. Take it easy baby." He resumed kissing on my neck. "Ol' Pete's kisses feel good, don't they?"

"Yeah, sure. Whatever."

Apparently, my sarcasm mixed with my obvious desire to not screw Pete did not bode well with his ego. The next thing I knew, Pete slammed me incredibly hard against the building's blue cinderblock wall. I knew Pete was going to beat my ass. I was in real trouble. I could have screamed for help, but no one pays any mind to a whore in danger. All I could do was try and stroke his bruised ego and hope for the best.

"They feel good, don't they? Say it, whore!"

"What, they?" I asked, a slight tremble to my voice. I feared saying to wrong thing.

"Pete's kisses." He slammed me again and demanded, "Say it!"

I nodded my head up and down and almost in a whisper replied, "Yes. Yes. They feel good. Pete's kisses feel good."

Pete pulled back from me and stared dead into my eyes. I watched his green eyes instantly morph into jet black. His face grew contorted. He was no longer the surly, redneck I had initially engaged with.

*'I'm so fucked! Help!'*

"Liar! Say it again and you better mean it or else," he hissed, as I got slammed up against the wall again. He unbuttoned my shorts with such force, they almost tore. He kissed me on the mouth and let go. "I want to hear you say it!"

"Pete's kisses feel good. They feel good. Take it easy, baby."

But it was too late. Pete's anger over my rejection erupted. There was no amount of water to extinguish the fire I inadvertently started with my smart-mouthed attitude. I knew in that moment I was in deep shit.

Pete grabbed me hard by the throat and choked me. All the while his other hand ventured south, down inside my shorts. My metaphoric purse clasp flipped apart so callously. His hands were rough. He hurt me on purpose with each touch, jab and penetration.

"You are going to love the way this makes you feel darlin'. Ol' Pete's going to have you seeing stars. Right?"

I said nothing. I could not respond with his other hand around my throat.

He slammed me up against the wall, "Answer me, whore!"

I barely managed to utter, *"Rrrrrrright."*

I attempted to pry Pete's tight hands from around my throat. I could barely breathe. I felt faint. He was too strong for me. Nothing Pete did felt good, around my neck or inside my shorts.

I knew death was certain if I did not act fast. I had to get his hand off my neck. I brought my right knee upwards and kicked Pete square in his balls. He released a cry worse than that of a mother at her child's funeral.

"I don't do that Ted Bundy, psycho shit," I yelled out and pushed him off me. "Asshole!" He stumbled backwards and clutched his aching balls.

Pete continued to rub his crotch and winced in horrible pain with each fractioned move. I delivered a solid kick. I felt proud. But my pride did not last for long. Once the impact of my attack on his family jewels subsided, Pete lunged at my throat with vengeance.

"You ungrateful bitch! You said you wanted to see the stars. Well, ol' Pete's gonna make damn sure you see those stars now whore!"

He tightened his grip around my throat even more. Both hands this time.

I panicked and between gasps of air stammered out, "Stop it! Stop it. You're hurting me. Let go of me!"

Pete forced a kiss upon my mouth. I then kicked him in the shin, and he released his grasp. I managed to push him backwards once again, only harder. And because Pete was so drunk, he lost his balance and fell to the ground.

I stood over him and yelled, "We're done here. Keep your money. Sick asshole!"

I turned to leave. Pete reached out, grabbed me by my right calf and yanked me to the ground beside him. He then rolled on top of me and landed several hard slaps across my face.

He bellowed out, "Where do you think you're going, you worthless whore! I ain't done with you! You gotta see the stars ol' Pete's made specially for you."

I kicked and flailed my arms wildly. I tried to strike him anywhere I could. He was too powerful. I lost what little control I had in the situation.

Pete grabbed me by my hair with one hand and proceeded to beat me to a bloody pulp with the other in the form of a fist and alternated open hand. Punch. Punch. Slap. Slap. Punch. Punch. When he grew tired of the slaps and punches, he stood to his feet and kicked me repeatedly in the ribs.

As Pete's slaps, punches and kicks reduced my body to a pile of bruises bathed in blood, all I could say to myself inside my head was…

*The streets are mean. They don't care anything about you. They punish you for things you never done to anyone in your life. Robbed. Raped. Beat up. Infected. You're invisible to the world. A nobody to everybody. Until somebody needs a warm body to rub against. Then you're anybody they pay you to be. Being somebody for a moment is better than being nobody for a lifetime, I suppose.'*

Pete mercifully grew tired of beating on me. I think he feared if he kept going, he would catch a murder charge.

"Ain't no whore worth going to jail over."

He released his grip on my shoulders and allowed my battered body to fall to the ground. I landed on my left side. I felt worse than flattened roadkill. I clutched my abdomen.

I thought Pete was done until he suddenly stood, straddled over top of me. I grew terrified. I was defenseless and badly beaten. He used his right foot to forcibly roll me onto my back. He wanted to ensure I saw his nasty face one final time. And to confirm I was still breathing.

He quickly rifled through the pockets of my bloodied, torn shorts and retrieved his money. He then hit my nose hard with the wad of cash. "Taking this back. Bitch!"

Pete remained towered over me. He was dominant and clearly in control. He relished in overpowering a prostitute. "I got something else for you, whore!"

I feared the end had come for me. I felt devastated I would be unable to tell Chloe, "Goodbye," or have one last moment alone with *dirt*. I closed my eyes and awaited my demise. Then, I felt something cold and hard land on me. Pete had retrieved a penny from his pocket and tossed it onto my exposed, beaten chest.

"You ain't even worth that much," he said, then spit beside my head and walked away.

Pete left me bloodied, bruised, and abandoned behind the convenience store. Just me, along with chirping crickets, the sounds of traffic, twelve empty beer bottles and a shiny penny.

I remained motionless on my back for what felt like an eternity. My eyes barely focused due to the swelling that had started to set in. I stared at the stars. They were far more beautiful than the ones Pete had shown me as he knocked me around. I started to cry. In the stars I noticed the letter J.

*'Momma always warned me about those who fake making the letter J.'*

I coughed.

I hurt.

I tried to move.

I hurt even worse.

I knew I had to muster the strength to sit up and move or I could die if Pete came back for round number two.

I sat on the pavement, held my aching head, and thought…

*The worst is when the streets go lifeless. You get nothing. That's when sickness sets in. It's the worst fucking feeling in the world. The puking. The chills. The pain. The itching. It's like thousands of tiny bug legs are scurrying underneath your skin. The bugs won't stop terrorizing you until they feel the sensation of dirt coursing through your veins to quiet them once more.'*

My tracked-up arms itched terribly. I tried to stand up but fell down a few times from dizziness. Pete had worked me over well.

*'Bwah-astard!'* I mumbled through swollen lips.

Pete was not the first to beat my ass. And he certainly would not be the last. Unfortunately.

I eventually managed to stumble away from the convenience store parking lot and to a hospital for treatment. Thankfully, Pete never returned.

I told the nurses I fell. They knew I was full of shit but could do nothing about it. I refused to press charges or give up any information. I was treated and released the same night with a handful of aspirin and another notch added to my nightmare belt. Though Pete may not have gotten off with me that night, he certainly got off from being arrested that night because of me.

*'How do you like those stars, ol' Pete?'*

# Alleys Aren't Only for Cats

*Light.*

*Dark.*

*Light.*

*Dark.*

*Light.*

*Dark.*

**I** noticed a blinking streetlight whose bulb had seen better days because it had begun to short-out.

I eased my way down a dark alleyway to meet up with my dealer, Tiny. I was in desperate need of a fix. And Tiny held the cure for all which ailed me. I had to score *dirt* for Chloe, too.

Tiny was anything but tiny. He stood almost six-foot-five and was covered in tattoos. There were too many to count. I tried on several occasions with no luck. Tiny appeared burly but was a softy to those who knew him.

"Whatchu need tonight, cock," he paused, "roach."

I jumped at the unexpected sound of his deep voice. "You scared the crap out of me, Tiny. Damn. Don't do me like that." I then tried to catch my breath.

"Thought my good looks startled you, baby," he teased. Tiny notoriously flirted with all the whores on Nebraska Avenue.

"Cockroach, huh?" I replied with a quizzical stare.

He laughed. "Yeah, cockroach."

"Why's that?" I countered with my hand on my hip.

"Cuz you be creepin' and crawlin' in the dark like you're on the hunt for somethin'." He proceeded to mimic someone creeping and crawling.

I rummaged through my tattered purse which I had found in a dumpster. I was in search of the money I had earned earlier in the day.

"Shit! Where is it?"

"You lookin' to get dirty tonight, huh?" Tiny asked.

"Hang-on a minute." I grew nervous. *"Ah! Found it!"* For a moment I panicked and feared the money had fallen through some unknown hole inside the purse.

"Tiny's got whatchu need if you've got what Tiny needs." He then waved a small baggie before my eyes which contained my sweet delight. *Dirt.*

I handed the money over to Tiny. He began to count the dollar bills when a strange look suddenly washed over his face. "This ain't enough."

"I know. Business is slow tonight." I forcibly cuddled up to him. "Wanna take the difference out in trade?" I really hated the idea of banging Tiny. It would not be our first time doing so. But I was so desperate to get rid of the dope sickness setting in. Customers screw their dealers all the time. Having sex for drugs was no biggie. I did that for a living. I just found screwing any man for any reason repulsive in general.

Tiny pushed me off. "Nah. You know I ain't down with that nasty shit with you girls no more."

"Since when?" I asked.

"Since I figured what I get doesn't even out."

"Come on, Tiny. Please. I'm begging you. I really need it." I stuck out my bottom lip and tried to play cute like a toddler.

Tiny shook his head side to side, "*Tsk*. Man." He was clearly frustrated on a potential loss of sale, money or not.

The dope sickness grew stronger. I asked, "What can I get from you for what I gave you? It's all I got. Honest. I'm not holding out. And you know I'm good for it. We're friends, right?"

"Friends ain't got nothin' to do with it. It's business. No money. No business. You sure you don't got nothing else on you?" he asked in a tone of skepticism. Tiny was well aware that junkies lied and tried to pull fast ones.

I pondered.

"Well?" He waved the baggie of *dirt* before my eyes. "Talk to me."

I hesitated, before I reached down into my purse and grabbed ahold of something I was hesitant to part with. But desperate times called for desperate measures. And I was pushed almost past the point of basic desperation.

Tiny waved the baggie with his distinct logo pasted on it, a Sloth, before my eyes again. "Sure, you got nothing else? I know you want it, girl. Come on. Whatchu you holding out on? Show Tiny. I know you got somethin'."

I reluctantly handed over a prescription bottle of uppers.

"I swiped this off a customer. I was saving it for Paula. I owe her some money."

Tiny carefully inspected the contents of the bottle before he jammed it firmly into his front jacket pocket. He handed me the baggie of dope.

"Thanks, Tiny!"

"Bounce before I change my mind." He playfully smacked my bottom.

I silently crept my way back out of the alley and onto the street like a feral cat who had just eaten the canary without a single feather of evidence left behind.

# Spinning Wheels, Going Nowhere

*Light.*

*Dark.*

*Light.*

*Dark.*

*Light.*

*Dark.*

I sat in the driver's seat of Chloe's and my secret hideaway. I was entranced by the orange flame of fire that shot forth from a lime green lighter I repeatedly flicked on and off.

"Hurry up, Petal head," I snapped. My patience was depleted.

The harsh tone of my voice caused Chloe to hesitate with further movement. To breathe. To even pour forth the powder

I purchased from Tiny onto an old metal spoon that was balanced upon her knee.

My last high had worn off and I needed a fix, like yesterday. The spoon we used to cook the dope had seen better days. But it got the job done to satisfaction. So, why trade up and steal a shiny new one from the Beans & Jellies Café', right?

Chloe wore a look of suspicion.

"What's wrong?" I asked. I assumed Chloe's paranoia resided from the sized baggie I had purchased from Tiny. It was smaller than usual. But all I could afford. The morning had been less than satisfactory for available Johns.

"You sure this is as good as what we usually get, Bug?"

*'I was right. Classic case of baggie paranoia…self-destorya!'*

I snatched the small baggie from her hand and snapped back, "I got it from Tiny." I then flipped the baggie over. "See, there's the same decal, right on the bag. It's good. Trust me. Tiny's never done me wrong." I dipped the tip of pinky inside the baggie and sampled the product for her reassurance. "It's good. Prep it." I then tossed the baggie back over where it landed on Chloe's bony lap.

"But it's so little. Are you sure it's enough for both of us? I need to feel out of sight right now, Bug. I really, really do. It's been a bummer of a day."

"It'll be enough. Trust me. Pour."

"This John, well, he…" she started to say.

"Pour, Chloe and you'll forget about that asshole."

She reluctantly shut her mouth and poured the powder onto the spoon.

I was far from being in the mood for chatter. Especially words or phrases centered around nameless, faceless, smelly, uncouth, Johns. Normally I helped Chloe navigate through rough patches. But I felt super selfish at that moment. Entitled. My fix mattered more. It always did. Ask any junkie if I am lying. Fix over friendship. Always.

Besides, no one was immune to rough days. Whether on the streets, in a posh apartment or even inside a gated mansion. If your lungs breathed life, rough days were guaranteed.

I felt terrible having dismissed Chloe's need to vent. But *dirt* took priority. My day had not exactly been a bed of soft roses either. It was a day peppered with countless, viny thorns. Not a single delicate second in the day. I was beyond eager to stave off the withdrawals, along with any unsavory memories from my entire life.

Chloe shifted her left knee. The one which held the spoon and powder upon it. My nerves went on immediate alert. One wrong twitch and the spoon would tip over and there went our small, but powerful dope.

"Careful, Petal head. Or you're going to spill it."

"I won't. I won't."

"Seriously. Be careful, Chloe. I mean it."

"I am, Bug. I am."

The spoon wiggled slightly side to side.

"Careful…" I reiterated, only louder.

I wanted to snatch the spoon off her animated knee. But I refrained from doing so. I knew Chloe was hurting and I did not want her to feel even more 'less than' then she already did.

I grew moody. Chloe knew it, too. She flipped her internal switch from dreary and antsy, back into her standard happy hippie mode. A tactic she used often to avoid arguments.

"You really need to relax more, Bug. Stress is not good for the soul. Breeds negative vibes. Breathe in fresh air and release your negative energy out and up towards the sky on an exhale."

I felt a bit tart at her suggestion. "So, if I get to breathe out all of this," I used air quotes, "negative energy" …

"Right. Right."

"Okay, let's say I do it. Where does the negative energy go?"

Chloe just stared at me in wonder.

I snapped my fingers in front of her zoned-out gaze. "Hello?"

She popped back. "Huh? What?"

"I asked you where the negative crap I breathe out goes. What happens to it?"

Chloe nodded her head up and down a few times. "Right. Right. The wind. It becomes part of the wind."

"So, it doesn't become someone else's negative energy, then? I mean, I did release it so technically it's free to find another, right?" I was totally screwing with her at this point.

"It becomes part of the wind. It's free to just be."

I shook my head. Bewildered by Chloe's illogical reasoning.

"Watch what I do." Chloe then demonstrated. She took one deep inhale, a deep exhale, followed by a blank, continual stare at the stained roof of the car.

I felt the needle on my annoyance meter climb. "My anxiety…"

"Stress," she corrected.

I shot her a look of death. "Whatever."

"Breathe in," Chloe said.

I quickly inhaled, then exhaled.

"Better, right?" she asked.

"Look, kid, my stress, negative whatever you want to call it, will be released once you stop shaking your leg with the spoon on it. You're making me very nervous."

"Just breathe, Bug. It's fine." She smiled big.

"Focus, Chloe. Just focus on what you're doing. Okay?"

"I'm trying, Bug," she whined. "I think I've got the jitters."

"Just breathe," I replied sarcastically.

"I'm coming down. I'm sorry," she pleaded with those puppy dog eyes of hers.

"I am coming down too, so you can't lose what we've got. I don't have the energy right now to earn cash to buy more. Tiny's shit costs."

"I'm sorry, Bug. I'm really trying to hold on."

"I always buy from Tiny. No one else. You do the same. Got it?"

Chloe despised being bossed around by anyone. It's one of the key reasons she ran away from home. Between her mom constantly in her face and her mom's boyfriends always creeping into her bedroom at night, she could not take it anymore. So, she split. She hoped for greener pastures. It was not long before she realized the green grass in the so-called 'greener pastures' was loaded with piles of steaming manure. Step after step Chloe found herself covered in metaphorical crap.

Chloe disengaged from her hippie mode and straight to a smart-mouthed teenager who thought she knew it all. Annoyed by my advice, she sourly replied, "*Yeah. Yeah.* Tiny's stuff. I know. You never stop hounding me about it. Over and over. You sound like my bitch of a mom."

I reached over and grabbed her firmly by the left arm. I was pissed over her ungrateful attitude and insulted by her calling me a parent. Being called a big sister, I could manage. But being a parent no thanks.

I had been careful in my grab to not cause the spoon, now full of sweet, sweet, *dirt,* to spill onto the floorboard by her shocked reaction. She had instinctively grabbed the spoon handle with her free hand.

"I mean it, Chloe. I'm not screwing around. There's a lot of bad junk on the streets right now. Almost everything is laced with Fentanyl. You buy from Tiny, only. Always. Understand?"

Chloe jerked her arm from my grasp and sneered back, "I heard you the first ten-thousand times you've told me since I've known you. I'm not dumb. Geez. *Tiny. Tiny. Tiny.* You sound like my mom. Always bitching. You're starting to ruin my positive vibe, Bug." Hearing her say, 'positive vibe' indicated hippie Chloe had begun to beat back bad attitude Chloe.

"Okay. Okay." I released the hold I had upon her arm and quietly retreated to my seat. "Just trying to keep you safe, kid."

"I know. And I love you for it, Bug. I really do." She then blew an air kiss in my direction.

I playfully ducked. "Missed me."

Those sad eyes of hers glanced my way as she whispered, *"Always do when you disappear from me for days."*

I successfully fought back tears. "I know, kid." I resumed flicking the lighter off and on. "But I gotta do stuff sometimes without you around, ya know, so I can keep getting you the good stuff."

She replied in a somber tone, "Yeah, I know."

I stuck a syringe into a bottle of water hidden underneath the driver's seat, added the water onto the spoon and mixed it in with the powdered *dirt.*

Chloe remained jerky. Both physically and verbally. The spoon somehow miraculously stayed on top of her left knee. Meanwhile, I continued to fight the overwhelming feelings of nervousness that our dope was going to spill into the floorboard.

"Stop moving, Chloe."

"I'm trying. Honest. But I'm crashing, Bug. Bad."

I grabbed hold of her leg and firmly held it in place. "Well try harder. The sooner you hold still, the faster it'll be ready."

"Okay. Okay."

I let go of her leg, added more water, and continued mixing. Stirring *dirt* into water with a needle was no easy feat. It required diligence and a shit load of patience.

"I've told you already. I can't go score more dope right now."

"Well, I can't either," Chloe shot back.

I continued to mix the water and powder together.

I had grown suspicious of her quick excuse not to pitch in for *dirt* should we need to score more.

"Why can't you earn? You've only had two Johns today."

Chloe opened and closed her mouth several times. "I think I got lockjaw from the last guy."

"He a regular?"

"Maybe."

"What name does he go by?"

"I call him Mr. Took Too Damn Long."

I carefully removed the spoon off Chloe's knee and held it up into the air before sliding the lime green lighter underneath it. I turned towards her and winked. "Yeah, I think I know that guy."

Chloe let out a snorted laugh.

"We call him 'Forever Freddy'. Tall. Slim. Black hair. Beady eyes. Drives a white classic *Cadillac*. Right?"

She nodded her head up and down fast. "Yup. Yup. That's the one."

I smirked. "Forever Freddy. Pays good. But he makes sure you earn every dime."

She rubbed her jaw again. "Yeah, no kidding."

Chloe stared at the spoon like a yearning child at Christmas time over a present.

If only I truly understood that feeling. I was lucky if I got a 'Merry Christmas' from momma. Never mind a present. I used to see and envy the happy kids I saw with their families I watched at the mall as they took pictures on Santa's lap and got to tell him what they wanted for Christmas.

In our trailer, it was Christmas year-round. Momma's perverted boyfriends always pulled me onto their laps. The only difference: they told me what they wanted, not the other way around.

"Blech."

"What's wrong, Bug?" Chloe asked.

I had accidentally reacted to my bad memories in her presence.

"Just a bad burger or something."

"Oh, okay." Chloe resumed her mediation breathing routine she always did before shooting up.

I recalled how each Christmas eve, I left Santa Claus a list of what I wanted. My requests were never demanding. I always asked him for love, time with momma, for momma to quit drinking, and to stop bringing nasty men around me.

We rarely had fresh milk in our trailer, so I left Santa, a glass of water and that old can of peas. The same can of peas that had been there since we moved in. I figured maybe Santa could share it with his reindeer. But Santa never brought me shit. Maybe if I had left milk and cookies...maybe.

"Whatever."

"What did you say, Bug?"

"Nothing, petal head. Keep exhaling your bad ju-ju out."

"Oh, okay."

I resumed cooking the mix.

One year I drew a little Christmas tree on my bedroom wall with a broken crayon. I put my newspaper dolls next to it. The only gifts I recycled and gave to myself year after year until I outgrew them and Santa Claus. Santa had been a constant no-show. Wonder if he knew my daddy? He was a no-show in my life, too.

Chloe and I sat in those worn-out car seats for what felt like an eternity. Our eyes heavily fixated on the spoon and flame as they worked together in harmony for our pain-relieving benefit.

Chole rubbed both of her cheeks, "Oh, my jaw hurts. I think I got lockjaw."

"You know you can't get lockjaw from doing that thing with 'Forever Freddy'. I've told you a hundred times, if they can't deliver in five minutes, you're done. Forever Freddy could put you out of business for hours while you heal up. That's a lot of lost earnings. Why do you think we all try and avoid him every time his car is spotted? Huh?"

"But…"

"Listen, kid. I've also told you a hundred times, lockjaw comes from Clostridium tetani. Not doing that." I pointed at her jaw. "But you can get other things from doing that, just so you know."

Chloe recoiled. "Ack! Gross, Bug! I don't like to think about it."

"Well, you need to think about it because it's true. Lots of ooey, gooey yucky stuff. Germs. Bacteria. Fungus. People are flat nasty with washing themselves. Putting their privates in all sorts of dirty places."

Chloe attempted to cover her ears. "I'm gonna puke. Stop it, Bug."

"I'm just sayin'."

I was astounded by Chloe's naivete after being on the streets for a bit. One could lightly toss a stone out the window of a passing car on Nebraska Avenue and hit plenty of working girls who got side-lined due to an STD.

Some girls ignored medical advice and overall consideration. They were junkies. Or, they had a pushy pimp who forced them work regardless and continue to spread the "love" until they were too rank or sore to earn further.

While other girls on the streets easily viewed catching STDs as a game of 'tit for tat', *"I caught it from a John, so I'm gonna give it back to a John. Fucking pigs!"*

Chloe stared at me wide-eyed like I was an all-knowing Guru. "You're so wise, Bug."

"About what?"

"Lots of things."

"Yeah. Sure. Okay." I refocused my attention back onto the spoon and flame. Chloe decided to add a small braid on the left side of her face.

I do not understand how or why Chloe found me wise. I was far from it. I did not know much at all. Sure, I picked up a few things along the way; some basic knowledge, an STD or two and a good street dumpster recipe. But my life tended to resemble that of a bird. I winged it.

I watched Chloe as she gently swayed her head side to side up against the seat rest. Lost in a maze of fantasy.

I thought, *'Too much exhale and not enough inhale… of oxygen."* She tenderly said, "I wish I could be you sometimes, Bug."

I abruptly replied, "No, you don't, kid. Trust me."

Before Chloe could respond, I looked down at the spoon and knew the *dirt* had been cooked enough to bake us both into a short-term oblivion.

"It's done."

Chloe let out a huge sigh of relief. *"Ohhhhh."*

I drew up the freshly prepared liquid into separate needles

I handed a needle to Chloe, "One for you."

She nodded her head like a grateful hippie and said, "Peace and love, my street sister."

"One for me." I gave the needle a flick of the fingers to release any trapped air bubbles.

I had begun preparations to shoot myself up when Chloe stopped me. "Wait. You can't do it yet, Bug."

I was momentarily confused and hoped she was not going to whine again about any uncertainty of the drug. "Why?" I asked.

"You forgot to do me first. Remember?"

"Yes, I remember. I didn't forget." I had actually forgotten. I was in such a rush to get numbed. I forgot about Chloe's phobia.

"You know I hate needles." Chloe then gave me her best irresistible 'pretty please' pout.

Yet another Chloe mystery for the books. How could a junkie who shot up drugs not be able to stick the needle into their own damn vein?

Chloe was my street sister. I had her back. She desperately needed to be set free from her emotional pain. Pain, she thought she kept well hidden by cloaking it with consistent happiness with her hippie jive routine. But I knew better.

Chloe assured me she had dealt with her past. But I knew Chloe was a liar. She was just like the rest of us junkies. I understood why she lied. Abuse hurts. Remembering it. Talking about it. What better way to hide a revolting past than to enter the current world of denial. A place where happiness thrives and lies are just lies you convince yourself are the truth about your newfound street life.

Pain such as Chloe's never fled with the snap of the fingers. Nor could it be ignored, no matter how hard one tried to pretend it did not exist. Life altering pain will remain silent until a weak moment. It is then the pain pounces upon the person's brain, soul and heart until they fall onto their knees and beg for a guillotine to shut the pain up for all eternity.

Freedom for those who run from pain comes in the form of our favorite type of guillotine. Drugs. Only out of ignorance, whether deliberate or innocent, drugs were just a pathetic mirage. There was no freedom with using drugs to silence pain. Our *'so-called-freedom'* came at a high price.

The cost of getting physically hurt while earning.

The cost of getting drugs that might kill you.

The cost of being killed for your drugs or money.

The total cost of what drugs took on your body, inside and outside.

Freedom?

Hardly.

We were each locked in our own prison. To be paroled meant one had to be brave enough to face their inner demons. Get clean. Leave the streets. Or remain stuck in the confines of this prison of hell until an eventual overdose.

But the fear of an overdose was forever trumped by *dirt's'* ability to squash the pains of the past. The basic mindset was,

*'Well, it might happen to you. But it will never happen to me. I can handle it. So, it's worth the risk to march towards the guillotine and silence the pain if only for a little while. Off with her head!'*

"I forgot. Sorry."

Chloe smiled and handed her needle over.

"Look away, Petal head. I got you."

I tied a shoestring around her left arm and then shot Chloe up. She immediately fell under the enticing embrace of *dirt* and melted into the passenger car seat.

"Definitely out of sight stuff, Bug."

I untied the black shoestring from Chloe's arm and tried to fix myself next. The veins in both of my arms were not cooperating. Typical hassle for a true junkie. Blown veins. I was forced to be creative.

"Between the toes it goes."

And so that sweet, brown-sugar delight went inside my veins, smooth as butter. At first, anyway. It was not long before the unbearable temporary pain of the location I had chosen for the injection set in.

*"Ouuuuuuuuuuuuch!"*

My left foot recovered, as I too melted into the car seat beside Chloe.

At first, the trek was serene.

But soon, the monsters from my past crawled out from the walls.

Snarled teeth.

Bad breath.

Groping hands were felt running all over my body.

*"Momma's men,"* I mumbled. *"Get away from me. Don't touch me!"* My hands pushed at their ghostly hands.

I was in the throes of a bad ride.

*Shit!*

No one could help me escape the road I walked upon. I had to save myself. Only question…did I want to be saved?

My mind played horrific, taunt-fueled tricks, as the *dirt* surged throughout my body.

First, I saw men.

Lots of men.

From my past.

From the present.

From the past again.

Back to my present.

Then, my past on the streets.

Men were everywhere.

I was surrounded.

Submerged by them.

I felt their hands.

I felt their hot, smelly liquor-scented breath on my neck.

I shuddered.

Suddenly I saw an insect who dug like a maniac in earthly brown dirt. Its small legs worked overtime as it dug and dug. The hole grew deeper and deeper. The pile of dirt it kicked up mounted higher and higher. The bug bore deeper and deeper into the ground.

I begged, *'Let me join you. Please!'*

My mind jumped back and forth between both scenarios.

The men.

The insect.

The men.

The insect.

Over and over.

My soul thrashed about in torment. Pure hell.

My mind thought, *'Dirt, what is wrong with you? You are always my fortress. You deaden my damaged soul. You purge those painful memories from my past. You erase the sensations of filthy hands groping at my ripe, tender breasts. You dull the feeling of rough fingers prying apart my delicate flower, petal by petal. You blur the sight of countless smug, selfish faces who have climbed on top of me. You have hushed my inner screams upon penetration. You deafened my ears to the echoes of fast panting climatic breaths. And you numbed my nostrils of the putrefying scent of hormonally charged pheromones. All my life I have loathed men. And, yet all my life men have lusted after me. A mere glance from a man prevailed my desire to dig deeper into the comfort you always offered. But not on this journey. What changed between you and I, dirt? Why the betrayal?'*

My mind snapped back and concentrated upon the insect who dug. I watched as the insect bore deeper into the ground until it got swallowed up by the actual dirt of the earth and took the many men from my past and present along with it..

An epiphany arose from within.

The collapse had not occurred due to the depth of the hole dug by the insect. But rather the instability of the hole itself. I saw this vision as a foreshadowing of the inevitable downfall of my own life. The bug in the scenario was me. The stark revelation of my grim future caused my high to wind down.

I had dug myself into a dark hole where I was buried alive. Despite suffocating under the weight of each spec of soil, I still managed to breathe. How?

# The Prodigal Daughter Flees

**I** felt as if I died on the inside with each injection. *Dirt* was never going to release me from its firm grasp. Not without a one hell of a fight.

I knew it.

I despised it.

But it was the bold truth.

I was to blame for the mess my life had become. So, I thought. Momma's men never forced me take drugs. The only needle they stuck into parts of my body were the needle in their pants. No syringe dared to touch my veins until I decided when.

The disgusting, unspeakable things their pants needle did to me as a child, sent me down a treacherous road that was hard on my soles and my soul.

When *dirt* introduced itself, suddenly the rough pathway I walked all those years suddenly felt smoother. It lent a softer touch and caressed the bottoms of my feet. It offered comfort to my spirit. I foolishly embraced its false security and assurance. I believed if I remained on the trail with it, *dirt* and I united, no more troubles would befall my life's journey. And if it should, *dirt* would whisk the strife away from my soul.

*Dirt* could be an entitled bastard when forced to let someone go. I feared ending up like LaRue. A girl who succumbed to *dirt's* sadistic trickery in a seedy alley. I also feared becoming strangled to actual death because of *dirt's* firm grasp on me. I did not want to be found alone in a random back alley, dumped in a ditch by a scared John. Or worse, unrecognizable because no one noticed I had been missing for weeks.

I failed to reason out my fears and courage to continue my dance with *dirt* simultaneously. I dealt with abandonment issues for a long time. I suppose *dirt* feared abandonment, too. Maybe that was how I managed to succeed.

I acted tough as nails on the outside. But inside I was full of painful rusted holes. I prayed for death to put me out of my misery before I was ever forced to breakup with *dirt*. Death for a junkie over a breakup was always the easy way out. No responsibility. No accountability. No withdrawal suffering.

But I was deeply enslaved to *dirt*. It had me tight by the tail. The same as it once had LaRue. Its grip was strong, tight and unrelenting. I tried to breathe but could never quite inhale enough oxygen. I felt braindead.

Every day progressed into a tug-of-war. Part of me desperately wanted to dump *dirt* and never look back. Yet, another part of me could not resist *dirt's* persuasive charms whenever internal trouble brewed and bubbled over. I instantly fell prey to it every single time.

How could I resist?

How could I be so weak?

Pathetic?

Helpless?

Needy?

Easy.

*Dirt* always helped me to forget.

Everything.

Anything.

Sometimes nothing.

To me, and others like me, *dirt* was a great catch.

A good boyfriend.

Lover.

BFF.

Parent.

Boss.

Doctor.

Shrink.

Anything you wanted or needed *dirt* to be.

It just was.

It always would be.

My aqua blue painted eyelids fluttered as they struggled to open and remain as such. I needed to get my bearings. I had absolutely no clue where I was. How I got there. Or, how long I had been there. Unfortunately, I still knew who I was.

*'A worthless piece of shit! Whore! Junkie! Loser! Nobody!'*

The persistent closure of my eyelids took the lead as I struggled in vain to keep them open. In between hard blinks, my eyeballs glimpsed the sun. Its rays glared through rustled leaves from the big oak tree which towered over me. The tree looked down at me like a disappointed parent.

*'Stop staring at me, jerk! It's rude!'* I mumbled to the tree.

The sun rays stung my eyeballs again. Its beams felt like drops of acid with each forced peek-a-boo glance I took.

*Light.*

*Dark.*

*Light.*

*Dark.*

*Light.*

*Dark.*

I shifted my glance to the right and saw a marque sign which read, *Holy Redeemer Church* in big, bold black letters. I was somewhere near Hanna Avenue. My drugged-up ass apparently passed out in the flowerbed of a church.

*'Well Hallelujah, Bug!'*

I lay flat on my back, on top of a bed of gorgeous yellow Coreopsis and pink Petunias. I resembled a disheveled weed.

Messy haired. Smeared make-up. Stinky armpits. I absolutely reeked of cigarettes and stale greasy fries. Yet, another night of tricking, binging and *'I can't remember what the hell else I did or didn't do'* tucked underneath my *'I'll regretfully remember it one day belt'*.

"*Bet you're proud of me now, huh, God?*" I whispered, before I gave a thumbs up towards the sky.

The tree appeared to stare down at me again. Only this time, the look it offered was one of pity.

"Stop staring at me you pile of dehydrated toothpicks," I snapped out, before I turned my back on the tree and curled up into the fetal position. I needed more sleep.

I noticed the white building before with its giant cross mounted on the roof which glowed at night. The church caught my eye many times as I strutted up and down Nebraska Avenue during a John-fueled, drug-seeking prowl. I often tried to shield my eye away from the building due to the overwhelming shame it brought to my doorstep. I felt awful about myself and everything I had done.

"*Like looking in a shattered mirror,*" I mumbled.

For years I purposefully avoided going anywhere near the church, or any church. Many times, I received invitations from non-judgmental church folk to come and join. But I declined. I feared churches. It was the whole brimstone and fire thing.

Plus, the years I had been told what an abomination and mistake I had been since birth. Momma made certain to sear that thought deep into my brain before she died. My relationship, or non-existent relationship with churches and God was void.

*'Dirt, you clever bastard. You are the one who brought me to this church didn't you. Why? Are you trying to dump me? Do you not want to be there for me anymore? Have you stopped loving me?'*

I assumed God was persistently disappointed and pissed at me. I swore there were times I felt His anger and other times I felt His love. If only for a fleeting second. But it was not enough to convince me that love was stronger than disappointment and anger.

One casual glance at my whorish, junkie, raped, molested, momma wished I had never been born, lifestyle was all the proof I needed to justify any wrath he chose to thrust upon me. I deserved it, too. I was the one to blame for a pathway to hell, after all.

My countless mistakes in life had begun with being breast fed as a baby instead of by bottle. Momma's milk was a White Russian served at the local titty tavern. She once said, "You only kept my pickled milk down. You puked up formula." Further proof I was destined for a shit-stained life.

"Where were you God when I really needed you?"

No sooner had those words tripped over my chapped, dried lips, when the dark brown door to the *Holy Redeemer Church* opened. A young priest stepped out onto the smooth white concrete steps. I froze like a snowman about to be melted by a blow dryer if I dared move.

I remained in the fetal position and squinted my eyelids tight. No light filtered in. Natural or Godly. I felt disgusted with myself. Unworthy to be in the presence of a priest. The presence of God. The presence of the church building. The feelings of condemnation were strong. I even felt unworthy to be in the presence of the flowers and the giant judgmental tree. I felt utterly worthless and flat gross.

I heard the priest's soft, gentle footsteps. They grew louder as he slowly approached. I was nervous on the inside but remained silent and very still on the outside. I slowed my breathing to a super shallow mode. I appeared dead.

The priest bent down.

I tensed up.

I feared what he might do.

The possibilities were endless given my life experiences.

Most men were not noble.

Clothed or otherwise.

I peeked ever so subtly out of my left eye.

I watched as the young priest looked me over.

I wanted to shudder at his glance but hesitated.

What did he want with me?

Mercy?

A mercy screw?

Did he pity me?

I peeked at him again.

His eyes dropped towards my chest.

I thought, *'I knew it! A pervert! Stop staring at my chest!'*

But then something changed.

He stared back up at my face and leaned closer.

I tensed up even more.

The priest was searching for signs of life.

He was not a pervert.

So I hoped.

The priest appeared genuinely concerned and uncertain if the girl lying in his church's flowerbed were dead or alive. I relaxed, when the priest suddenly reached forth, placed his hand upon my shoulder, and rolled me onto my back. He then shook me.

"Hello," he said, then shook me again.

At first, I was unsure of how to react. *'Do I come around? Do I punch him in the face and run away? Do I spit at him? What should I do?'*

My immediate instinct was to clock him hard in the face and go on a cussing rant about keeping his filthy hands off my body. But he was a priest. But he was also still a man underneath that pristine uniform. I found myself in an awkward situation.

I had never encountered a real priest before. At least not knowingly. But Johns do lie about themselves. For all I know, I could have slept with one or two. Who knows. Only God, I suppose.

He shook me again.

I remained still.

I honestly did not know how to respond to this man.

"Hello. Hello," he repeated and gave my shoulder another firm shake. "Hello. Can you hear me? Are you alright?"

I had grown nauseous from so much movement. I needed to do something before I puked or got arrested.

"Hey. Are you alright?" He asked me again, only a bit louder.

*'It's now or never. Get your fists ready, Bug, just in case.'*

I slowly *fake* opened my eyes. Closed them. Then opened them again. My head felt like a thousand ants tap danced all over it. It felt itchy and painful at the same time. My brain felt like it had been dipped in formaldehyde. My stomach wanted to empty. My bladder did, too.

I wondered, *'What's the priest going to do with me?'*

In my best *'out of it sounding voice'* I replied, "Huh? What?" I then half-rubbed my eyes and tried to focus before I sat up.

In a concerned tone the priest asked once more, "Are you alright?"

I said nothing. I just stared at him and then upwards at the tree that scowled back down at me for playing games with the kind priest.

I tried to sit up but fell back down. My body was not as awake as I had originally thought.

"Here, let me help."

Even though I did not want to be touched, I welcomed the priest's hand onto my left wrist as he helped pull me upwards.

"What happ...," I started to ask, when the priest reached forth and touched the same shoulder as before.

157

*'Big mistake!'*

This time, I reacted tartly and smacked his hand away.

"Get your Godda…" I stopped myself from finishing the crude reply.

He instantly retreated. "Sorry. I'm sorry."

"It's cool. Just don't touch me anymore. Okay? Unless you want to pay for something. Then…" I eyed him up and down with a coy smile.

The man was young, slightly older than I, but still young. But he was a priest. A dedicated man of the cloth. A man married to God. But a man is a man, nonetheless. I felt oddly compelled to be a bitch in his presence. To me, this priest's kindness was probably a mirage left over from last night's drug bender.

I allowed my loose shirt to purposefully slide off my shoulder and raised both eyebrows in a flirtatious manner. "Well? Do you wanna touch…"

"I…ummm…I…," he stammered. The priest blushed and cleared his throat. Clearly uncomfortable.

*'Mission accomplished. Not a pervert.'*

"It's okay." I pulled my shirt back up and jokingly added, "I didn't think so anyway. But it was worth a shot. I gotta go."

I gathered up my things. My filthy blue dumpster purse. A half-smoked pack of cigarettes. An extra concert shirt of some shitty boyband I kept on hand in case I puked or got puked on and needed to change in a pinch. And my infamous lime green lighter.

I lost my balance on the way to standing up and instinctively leaned half-way into a strong hedge until my composure was regained. I dropped the lime lighter during the fumble. I went to retrieve it, when the priest beat me to it. He picked it up and handed it back to me.

"Thanks." I then lit up a cigarette and took a deep drag. It was then I noticed the priest had kind eyes.

"You're welcome," he replied.

As I remained fixated on his ocean blue eyes, I almost felt like a normal person. A person who never whored, used drugs, was pure and ever messed with. A person with goals. Hopes. Dreams. But my dreams had long ago morphed into well documented nightmares

I thought, *'I wonder what his name might be. David? Mark? Perhaps, Luke? It's probably just Father. They're all called 'Father'. Lucky me. I have daddy issues. A perfect divine appointment if ever. Screw you dirt for bringing me here.'*

I took another deep drag and rustled the back part of my greasy, dirty-blonde hair with my left hand. It was then I embarrassingly noticed the fresh, visible track marks on my arm.

*'Crap! The priest probably saw them, too.'*

I pretended to scratch an itch on my back to hide my tracked-up arm. It was not a full-on lie. I did have an itch. *Dirt.* And the desire to scratch it needed to be satisfied. Soon.

I felt ashamed. Weak. Pathetic. No right to exist. Too unpure to have set foot upon church property. Who did I think I was? I had no right to be in the presence of a man who loved God. A man who knew God so intimately. A man who believed in His existence. The priest was a pure man. He was a clean man.

I felt like a wash rag taken from its clean packaging and used up until I was covered in dirty, putrefied liquids and various rotten particles picked up along the way. My fabric now worn so thin I was ready to disintegrate at any moment.

I took another drag off my cigarette. "Can I ask you a question?"

"Of course." His voice sounded compassionate. Unlike the gruff, graveled voices of the chain-smoking, hard-drinking Johns I was accustomed to hearing.

Their disgusting requests.

Their loud grunts.

Their fast-paced moans.

Their endless grumbles when it came time to pay.

My guilt-ridden eyes averted away. I struggled to gain the courage to ask my question. I blamed momma. She always made me feel stupid every time I opened my mouth and spoke. Her boyfriends on the other hand made me shy. But not in a cute, good way. More like the, *'if I speak, I will get hurt and messed with even more ways'*.

"It's just that...well...well..." I stammered.

"It is alright. Take your time, child."

*'Child? Child? Child? Oh, God. He sees me as a child.'*

Fire ignited in my eyes over being called a child. My soul seethed. I never wanted to be a child again. Ever! I would rather burn in hell.

I half-yelled, "I ain't no one's child."

"I'm sorry. It's just a term. I did not mean to upset you."

I glared at him.

"What shall I call you?"

"Nothing," I bitterly snapped back. "Child. Child. CHILD!" I started to work myself up again. The priest appeared frightened and unsure of what to do. "Are you fu…nevermind."

"I'm sorry. I won't say it again. Please forgive me."

I took a drag from my cigarette and calmed down. "Whatever."

"What is it you wish to know…" He began.

"Bug."

He nodded his head once. "Bug. What is it you wish to know, Bug?"

I paused. He said nothing. He dawned the patience of a saint. After a few more moments of *'Chloe type silent treatment'*, I replied, "What did I do wrong?"

"Wrong? What do you mean, what did you do wrong? Do you mean sleeping in the flowerbed?" He gestured his right arm towards the semi-smushed bed of flowers. "You did nothing wrong. It happens more than you think. This place…"

"What about this place is so damn special."

"Not special. Peaceful. Anyone is welcome."

"Anyone?" I asked with skepticism.

"Anyone. We're all God's children."

I grew angry again. "I'm not anyone's child." I readjusted my purse strap on my left shoulder. "Never mind. Forget it. I need to go."

I felt the urge to flee. I sensed the priest about to open my pandora's box. Though I knew what contents the box held, what I did not know was what my reaction might be to their reveal. Or, if I would be able to repack any of it back into the box.

"Wait. Please. Don't go," he begged.

I felt dumb in that moment. I sensed momma laughing her dead ass off at me for talking to a priest. I changed my mind. I no longer wanted to know the truth about what I had done wrong. If time had taught me one thing, it was ignorance is bliss.

Why did I need an answer in the first place. I had done wrong all my life. Momma said as much. Plus, I did drugs. I abused my body. I slept with countless men. Momma did not love me. My father walked out on me. I endured endless sexual abuse. The list of condemnations rolled onward and downward. Like a filthy snowball growing bigger by the minute.

I turned away to bolt. The priest grabbed ahold of my left hand. When I looked back, I was shocked. There stood a man who was not angry that I wanted to leave his presence. He was not upset that I had yelled at him. What remained was a man with kind eyes. I was unsure of what to do. I never met a man who only wanted to help me, not help himself to me. It was new.

"Please," he said.

I hesitated. "I really gotta….you know…I gotta…" I pointed in the opposite direction.

"Go?"

I gave a sheepish gaze. "Something like that. Yeah."

"I understand. But can you sit for just a moment.?" He pointed at the concrete stairs in front of the church entrance. "Please. I would like to try and answer your question."

I released a huge, very loud *sigh* bathed in annoyance, before I reluctantly followed this kind man over to the stairs. I sat beside him, as he continued to hold onto my hand.

I remained on the stairs, locked inside my own private room of silence.

"Do you trust me?"

I scoffed and jerked my hand out of his. "Trust you? I don't even know you. You're probably just some prick," I corrected myself. "Sorry…some guy who…well I don't know what you want from me."

"Not everyone is bad."

"Not everyone is good."

He tried to take hold of my hand again but failed.

I grew spiteful, "You think you can help me, huh?"

"I would like to at least try."

"Okay, 'Mr. *I want to help the wounded druggie whore*', answer me this; Why do men like to make the letter J for me since I was a little girl?"

His reaction was one of perplexion. "The letter J?"

I lit up a fresh cigarette. "That's what I said. The letter J."

"I'm afraid I don't understand."

I immediately stood up. "I knew it. Men. You're all liars. Phonies. Help me, my ass. You damn well what I'm talking about."

"Can you please tell me what you mean by the letter J. I'm afraid I'm a bit confused," he nervously replied. For whatever reason, maybe because he was a priest, I believed his confusion. He appeared sincere. I sat back down on the stairs beside him.

"Why have men always liked me in that, you know, way all my life?"

I pulled my hair behind my ears and hugged my knees up to my chest. I turned to my left and noticed the priest looked sad.

*'Why did this man care what other men did or had done to me since I was little? Did he really love all of mankind same as God?'*

The priest took both of my hands in his and proceeded to answer my question the best way he could. Unfortunately, my rebellious, angry attitude, along with anxiety of learning the truth that it might have been my fault all along, caused me to block out his answer consciously. Though my subconscious had other plans and secretly retained his words.

The priest rambled on for what seemed like an eternity.

My bladder was about to burst. My stomach was starving. And I still had a *dirt* itch which needed scratching.

I thought, *'Hurry up so I can go already.'*

I finally caught a break when a car horn honked, and I snapped out of whatever Led Zeppelin song I forced to play inside my head the entire time the priest spoke. It was then I heard him say, "God loves you so much, child."

The moment I heard the word child again, tears started to well up in the corners of my eyes. The bad memories of my childhood flooded forth. I panicked and jerked my hands from the priest's.

"Don't call me child! I hate that fucking word!"

I then ran away as fast and as hard as I could. I ran from the young priest, the church, God. All of it.

# Pull Me Under

*Light.*

*Dark.*

*Light.*

*Dark.*

*Light.*

*Dark.*

The sun's rays burst forth across the surface of the rolling Hillsborough River. Its reflection nearly blinded anyone who glanced its way. The sun acted as a shepherd. The beams, its staff, protected its flock from grazing too close to the river's edge.

Many dangers lurked beneath the murky surface of that riley waterway. Alligators. Undercurrents. Big fish. Small fish. Crabs. Various items of trash. Snakes. Vegetation. Contaminants. And the occasional Bull Shark. Whether on land or in a boat, I realized nowhere was truly safe in the Tampa Bay area.

It had been a week or so since I encountered the young priest. He was the only man I ever crossed who wanted nothing from me. He wanted to give, not take and help guide me towards a path towards redemption.

*'Whatever that meant.'*

Since our fateful meeting, I tried my best to sack his words deep inside my mental *file thirteen* to be silenced forever. While I appreciated his kindness, I had little to no faith for any possibility of changing my life.

I felt the young priest had wasted his precious breath on me. My life was destined to end sooner rather than later. I saw no point in changing my trajectory. I was a whore. That was not going to change. I was also a junkie. Not going to change that, either.

It's not that a part of me did not long for change. I was just not ready to let go of *dirt. Dirt* was not ready to release me either. I found a sick, twisted comfort in that revelation. Or deception, as I am certain the young priest would have emphasized regarding my lost soul.

I had traveled alone around the Tampa Bay area since a spontaneous decision I made the last time Chloe and I got high together. The same day I met the young priest.

I woke up the following morning and simply wandered off. I never spoke to Chloe about it. As I stared out over the river, I recalled how angelic and sweet she looked the last time I saw her. Like a sleeping bunny, as I, the seedy serpent, slithered away coated in the diamond patterned skin of a coward.

I felt restless, discontented and agitated. Over a week was the longest I had been away from my street sister, ever. The only other time I abandoned Chloe was when she was arrested for panhandling. I could not afford bail. And because *dirt* came first, Chloe remained in jail over a long holiday weekend until her court hearing.

Chloe was lucky. The judge, being a prior hippie himself, took an immediate shine to her. Who did not love Chloe? Sure, she could grind on your nerves with all that *peace and love* jive. But at the end of the day, her heart was pure gold. The judge saw it, too. Her feathered headband. Her love for *Led Zeppelin*. Her love for one another outlook. He dismissed her case on the spot.

Later, we celebrated at the Beans & Jellies Café. Pop hooked us up with the best chocolate covered chocolate donuts in town. And all of the coffee we could drink.

I worried about Chloe. I hated being away from her. I was concerned about her innocently wandering the harsh streets of Tampa Bay alone. I was not by her side to protect her from shady Johns. Chloe's kindness and naivete had gotten her in serious, dangerous trouble more than once. I hated not being there to protect her, as always. I hoped she was safe. I was a selfish jerk for taking off without a word. But I had to be alone. I needed space to sort shit out.

As I meandered around Tampa Bay, I struggled to comprehend what fueled such a disconnected attitude inside of me. A need to rumble aimlessly about the concrete jungle alone. Though I was naturally disconnected from others by choice, this time the desire felt even more intense. Grinding. Unrelenting. It felt like a hundred chickens pecking at a little black blemish on my soul. I had to figure things out. Soon.

*'I have to get back to, Chloe.'*

I worked despite my mysterious restlessness. Quick tricks, only. I loathed being touched even more now than before. But I had to feed the withdrawals. As the sun rose the next day, my entire body sank. I felt very unwell. *Dirt's* subtle reminder who was truly in control.

*'Definitely not you, skank bait!'* I thought. I then fumbled through my purse to find the only thing to fix that which ailed me.

I snuck behind a bush and shot that sweet, brown colored, sugary delight, between my toes. The amount was not nearly enough to get bombed into an oblivion. Which I needed. But I could not afford to pay. It was the price one waged when not turning enough tricks. Tiny refused to front anyone.

"Dammit, Bug! Every. Damn. Time," I harshly bitched out loud at myself. "Idiot!"

I bled between my toes. I normally could have cared less. But I borrowed Chloe's boots without asking. I left a pair of raggedy sneakers behind in their place. She was going to be pissed. And even more pissed if I returned her boots in the condition befitting of a crime scene on the inside.

I hobbled my way down to the Hillsborough River's edge to wash my bare feet off in the cool, crisp water. I was concerned an alligator might smell the blood and tear my foot off. However, I feared Chloe's wrath more. So, I took the risk.

The sun felt strong, and its rays glared hard as I approached the shoreline. I hoped I did not step in anything nasty on my way down; used needle, used condom, dog shit, etc.

The blades of soft grass were tall and comforted my sore toes. The city had not tended to any landscaping on this side of town for a while. I believed it to be a deliberate attempt by City Officials to hide the true ugliness of Nebraska Avenue and its surrounding areas.

I reached the edge. "Finally!"

I dropped Chloe's precious vanilla Go-Go boots off to the side. The small lapping waves washed up on shore and sounded soothing. I was struck by the reflection of myself as it bounced on top of the river's surface. I shook my head side-to-side and fought back tears.

*"Who the fuck are you anymore, Bug? Do you even know?"* I muttered.

I despised the disgusting, unrecognizable reflection that stared back at me. I reached for a small rock close-by and threw it hard at the mirrored image.

I shouted, "Whore!"

The rock was not strong enough to curb the fit of self-hate I experienced. I spit at my reflection, too. By now, blood had pooled beneath my toes. Larger, cold waves caused by the thrown rock washed up and placed gentle kisses on the tips of my filthy toes.

"*Burr!*"

The face of the priest flashed before my eyes as I squatted down to wash off my feet.

I thought, *'No one ever noticed my broken, battered spirit hidden behind my two crystal blue irises.'*

I momentarily paused. *'But he saw me. The real me. The me I so longed to be, but never could.'*

I washed my feet harder.

*'His kind words. His soft stare. My soul was naked before him. The most naked I had ever been. My naked soul felt unashamed. Every spot, blemish and wrinkle of life exposed without judgement. None of my own self-disgust repelled him. It did not turn his gaze away. Nor did it cause his private parts to stir with wicked desire. He was not like the others. For a moment I swore I had seen God's love for me in his eyes.'*

The more I thought about the priest and our conversation about God and His love for me, the harder I tried to scrub the spiritual and physical filth away from my flesh.

I grumbled, *"The letter J."*

I scrubbed even harder. My violent scrubbing motion caused the silt on the bottom of the river to stir about. I noticed curious fish swim close by. My feelings of revulsion became almost too much to bear. I wondered how those fish tolerated being near such a putrid existence.

I hissed out, "Jezebel is what you are. You, retched whore! It's who you've always been. Momma was right."

A TV preacher who I saw on a TV in a room after a trick with a John popped into my head. I could still hear him as he spoke about a woman in the Bible named Jezebel. A whore who enticed men to sin. This preacher said, "All whores shall burn in hell come judgement day," before he slammed his fist down hard onto a podium. I immediately turned off the TV and hid in the bathroom shower until the John left.

Momma somehow managed to put the fear of God in me, despite not being a true, God-fearing woman herself. Another one of life's great mysteries, I suppose. I did not realize this to be the case until my feet were put towards the fiery furnace. My face shoved into the hellish belly of truth. My soul, prepared to burn to a crisp.

Just the thought of that TV preacher caused me to scrub my skin even harder. I tried in vain to wash the memory away.

"Fuck him! I ain't no Jezebel! They are! All those filthy, rotten, disgusting men!"

I thought, *I never forgot the way the TV preacher described hell. He talked about it before launching into the Jezebel speech. I also recalled the way momma described it, too. The thought of burning in hell scared the crap out of me. But the thought of not being able to squirm on my belly in dirt like the worm I had become was even more frightening. I knew down inside my soul teetered at the brink of brimstone and fire from the sins that were committed all due to the letter 'J'.'*

I shuddered.

The water was cold.

My thoughts, colder.

When I looked down at my foot, it was redder than a vine ripened tomato. My skin felt raw and tender to the touch.

"Oww!" My mind wandered away from the external pain and back to the internal agony.

*The priest said God loved me no matter what bad things I had done. That those inappropriate touches by others weren't my fault. Nor was the path I currently walked upon to try and forget about it all, either. He said I could be someone new. My painful past all but forgotten. I desperately wanted to believe him. I truly did. But I lacked the ability or perhaps the guts to try and find a way to make it so.'*

I stood up and looked out at the water.

*'But the constant reminder of the vile things I had done. The things I still do. The thing I just did which led me down to the river to wash myself clean...'*

I reached down, picked up another rock and threw it out into the river.

*'The vile things done to me. I felt gross. Ashamed. I wanted to scream every time I was touched. But my lips would never part. My voice always grew mute. My tongue twisted up. My throat tightened. Fear emerged from a dark place. It grew, and grew, until there was no longer any room left for my lungs to draw a meager breath. So, I turn and run.'*

"I'm still running. I probably always will."

I stared down at my distorted, rippled reflection in the river, again and whispered with a tear formed in my eye, *"Maybe."*

# Lost

*Light...*

"Let's move it along. Come on. Scoot, scoot," a police officer said, as he shined his bright flashlight directly into my pea-sized pupils.

I snapped back, "Okay. Okay. Get that fucking thing out of my eyes. I can't see shit."

"Aren't we the cheery one." He then turned his attention at other people who were passed out in the alley and yelled, "Party's over folks. Let's go."

The passageway soon filled with sounds of cussing, coughing and one unlucky person retching.

"What time is it?" I asked.

"Time to get moving."

"No kidding. What actual time is it?" I inquired as I gathered up my things.

He shot a look of disgust in my direction. "For you, I'm sure it's five o'clock somewhere."

I stared at him, bewildered by such a belligerent attitude. Most seasoned police officers knew us by name and/or by collar. He must have been a transfer from another department. "I don't drink."

"It's four o'clock. Happy."

"No. You woke me up."

"Let's *gooooo* people!" He shone the light on several homeless people's faces as he continued clearing the alleyway. He turned back to me, "Come on. Move it, princess. Stop stalling."

"I'm going. I'm going."

He nudged the foot of a passed out old man. "Come on, Sir. Or it's a comfy night at *Chateau Le Jail* for you." The homeless elder, we fondly called Jerry, waved the cop's threat off and drunkenly stumbled out into the night.

"It's moving day folks. Time to pack your shit and get."

All the drugged up, drunken degenerates, including myself, scattered from the once serene alleyway like wasted cockroaches.

"Thank *yooooooou!*" the officer taunted. He added insult to injury with a sarcastic waving of his right hand. "Nite-nite! Sleep tight. Or it's into the slammer for my delight."

"Asshole," I replied.

"Have a good night, princess."

I stuck my tongue out at him despite wanting to give him the middle finger.

It had been around two weeks since I abandoned Chloe in the car. Despite my time away, I failed to resolve whatever bothered me. That upset me even more. Something still brewed within my craw, and I had no clue how to lower the heat. I decided it was time to give up and return to Chloe.

Chloe was going to be so happy to see me and her prized boots again. How she managed to wear them and not get blisters on her feet was yet another 'Chloe Mystery'. Since my time away, I developed a new appreciation for the raggedy sneakers I had left behind.

The following morning, the first place I checked for Chloe was at the Beans & Jellies Café. I knew she panhandled in front of the building most mornings.

No sign of her. Though odd, it was not out of the ordinary. Panhandling sucked in the area sometimes, so she relocated.

I spotted Paula strutting down Nebraska Avenue. I shouted, "Hey, Paula!"

"Hey, Bug!"

"Have you seen, Chloe?"

Paula shot back, "Haven't seen her! Gotta boogie! I'll let her know you're looking for her!"

"Thanks!"

"You got it! Boogie-fever! Boogie-down!"

My next thought, jail.

"I hope that petal head didn't get herself arrested. I only have enough money to score *dirt*."

I asked Pop if I could borrow the café phone and the white pages.

"Sure," he replied.

"Sorry. There's no Chloe Littlefield here," the jail clerk on the other end of the line said.

*"Well, shit,"* I muttered underneath my breath. "Thanks." I then hung up the phone.

Next, I called the local hospitals. I struck out there, too. No patient named Chloe Littlefield had been admitted.

"Thanks, Pops." I handed the white pages back to him.

"Did you find her?"

"Nope."

Sensing my concern, he reached out and patted my hand in a gesture of reassurance, "You will. Don't you worry yourself." He put a plate before me. "Have a jelly donut. It's on the house." He then gave me a wink and a smile.

I half-heartedly whispered, "Thanks Pops."

I was the most difficult one to find, not Chloe. She could always be found. I stared at the yellow telephone and waited for it to ring with an answer.

"Where are you, kid?" I asked of the still phone. No response. I released a sigh, grabbed the donut and exited the café.

I needed to meet Tiny and score, so I took a break from hunting down Chloe. Between the stress of her absence, to the last time I got high, my withdrawals were on the rise.

Tiny handed me a small plastic baggie with his signature design on it. I took it and shoved it into my back pocket.

I looked side to side, then back at Tiny. "Hey, have you seen, Chloe, Tiny?"

"You mean, Flowerchild?"

"Yeah. Her." My heart picked up the pace. I hoped for a "yes" to my desperate question.

"Haven't seen her in like a week or something, cockroach."

I thought, *Dammit, Chloe! An entire week? How are you getting by without being sick. I hope you're not lying somewhere by yourself too ill to get help. I must find you quickly.'*

I dug some cash out of my front jean shorts pocket and paid Tiny. I did not have time for further conversation. I had to split.

"If you see her, will you let her know I'm looking for her?"

"You got it."

"Catch ya later, Tiny."

"Scram, cockroach!"

"It's, Bug!" I shouted back.

"Yeah, I know. I know."

Another girl soon walked up to Tiny to score.

I heard him ask, "Whatchu need, baby?"

The only place I failed to search for Chloe at was the abandoned car we fixed up. My stomach flipped at the idea of seeing my smiling hippie street sister at the car anxiously waiting for me. She would have a flowery weed in her hand and Led Zeppelin IV blasting from the worn-out headphones of her Walkman that hung around her neck.

I rounded the corner and made my way towards the car. I left Chloe there two weeks ago.

"Maybe she never left after I did," I said to myself.

The thought vanished as I immediately noticed no signs of movement in the passenger seat underneath a lump of clothes. I looked up and saw seven buzzards circling in the blue sky above. My legs felt weak, but I forced them to move forward.

"A poncho," I said, as I picked up one of the garments and inspected it. I rifled through the rest of the pile. "Shirts. Dresses. Shorts. Where did you get all this crap, kid?"

I looked around the front half of the car. All appeared intact. Nothing inside appeared to be missing. I carefully peeked into the back seat of the car in case she was in a ball sleeping. No Chloe. Just two messed up bohemian blankets.

I shook my head side to side, "What is going on?"

I plopped into the driver's seat, flipped the visor down, then up and glanced around the inside of the car again. I stared at the *polaroid* picture of Chloe and I, taken in front of the café, placed next to the speedometer.

"Come on kid. Give me something, here."

My eyes aimlessly searched around the inside of the automobile for a clue as to where Chloe might be. Nothing stood out. Then, I remembered Chloe kept a diary. I reached over to the passenger's side of the car and stuck my hand underneath the seat.

"I better not get bit by a spider, petal head. You know how I hate those eight-legged bastards!"

My hand fumbled about and touched various hippie trinkets Chloe kept hidden underneath the seat. Bird feathers, bottle caps, rings and other assorted stuff either found or stolen. Basically, an entire collection of junk she viewed as treasure.

"I know you're here. She never takes you out of the car. Where are you?"

My hand eventually felt something familiar shoved almost into the backseat. "Ah-ha! Gotacha!" I slowly removed Chloe's diary from under the seat. The loose trinkets on top of it, spilled across the floorboard.

"*Oops!*"

Chloe's diary was a black and white Mead Notebook she wrote random thoughts in. She was extremely sensitive about its contents. I would never have violated her privacy, but I felt this was an emergency. No one had seen her in days. No one had heard from her in days. She was not arrested. She was not hospitalized.

"Shit! I forgot to check the morgue." I suddenly felt sick at the thought of her being dead.

I snorted a dab of *dirt*. Though not my usual method of getting high, it was not my first time doing it that way. I needed a boost of courage to read what Chloe wrote. I did not care what most thought of me. But I did care what she thought. Only I never let her know I did.

"Here we go, kid."

My mind instantly tripped into another dimension as I thumbed my way through the wrinkled, liquid stained pages. There were no dates or times to mark events Chloe journaled. Entries were scattered throughout the book. Her mind was unfocused. The more pages I read, the more various layers of Chloe emerged.

# Chloe's Far-Out Feelings

I met a groovy girl today underneath the bridge. Her name's Bug. I don't think that's her real name. But maybe it is. I will ask her. She saved my life today. I could have drowned in the river when I slipped on the ground and almost fell in. No one ever saved my life before. I mean, except for the doctor when I was born. My mom said when I was born, I had low oxygen or something because the cord was wrapped around my neck. I had to stay in the hospital for a while until I felt groovy again. This chick Bug I met is so cool. She's the first person I've met on the streets that hasn't tried to rob me, rape me or beat me up. I'm so happy I met her. I think we're going to be best friends. Maybe she can be the sister I always wanted to have but never got. The end.

My eyes welled up with tears. "Glad I met you that day, too, petal head."

I've been thinking about my mom a lot. I called her last night, and she said I could come home. She misses me. I miss her, too. She said we could work on the house rules together and that she dumped that creep who used to come into my room at night to mess around with me. He thought I was foxy or something. Gross! I want to go home soooooo bad. I mean, I love the friends I've made while being on the streets. I would miss them soooooo much! Especially Bug. Maybe my mom would let me bring Bug home with me. Then we could be sisters forever! She could sleep in the spare room. It's across the hall from my room. Then, when my mom goes to bed, I could sneak into Bug's room where we'd talk and laugh all night and pig-out on ice cream! Gosh, I miss my mom so much. I miss my soft pink bed and my stuffed animals. But I like having no one telling me what to do all the time. Well, except for Bug. But she's my big sister. She's supposed to boss me around. I'm kind of glad she does. I feel loved. Bug is so groovy. The end.

"Why didn't you tell me about being homesick, Chloe? Geez?" I shook my head, dumbfounded by her true feelings sealed in silence. "You miss your stuffed animals, huh? Sometimes I forget you really are still just a kid. What the hell are you doing on the streets? Seriously?"

The more entries I read, the more I realized I did not really know Chloe as well as I thought. Her entire hippie, peace and love routine was a show she put on to everyone. Including me. The reality? She was just a scared, homesick child.

"I feel so stupid. How could I not have seen it?"

Through reading Chloe's diary, I discovered her honest feelings. Shame they had been for the diary's eyes only all this time. I should not have been so surprised. Most people on the streets are never truthful about who they are, how they feel or how they end up on the streets. We all pretend, like professional unpaid actors.

Every.

Single.

One.

Of.

Us.

I read Chloe's second to last entry and hoped for a hint where she might be found.

"Okay. Let's see what you have been up to since I've been gone, petal head."

I don't have enough money to buy stuff from Tiny. He wants too much. Bug's always riding me about going to Tiny only. Tiny! Tiny! Timy! I'm so sick of being hassled about where I score. My mom always hassled me about how I spent my allowance. Maybe I should leave, Bug and go back home. At least I wouldn't have to hear the name, Tiny anymore. I'm so sick of being treated like a child. She can go off and do whatever she wants, whenever. But if I do it? Noooooooo! That's it! From now on I'm going to do what I want. The end.

"Did you go home, Chloe? If you did, why didn't you leave a note or tell someone? Did you leave me out here alone?"

I had become mad at the idea of being abandoned by the only family I had left in this world. I threw the diary across the car. I felt hurt. Discarded.

"Fucking bitch! Who needs you anyway!"

But why was I so angry at Chloe? I had done the exact same thing to her two weeks ago. Left without saying one word. In fact, I had been leaving Chloe for days at a time since we first met.

I took another bump of *dirt* and reached over to pick the diary back up. The faint sounds of emergency sirens wailed in the background. Nighttime had approached. It started to sprinkle rain. I turned the page and landed on what seemed to be a section which contained some of Chloe's final entries.

Woke up today and Bug's gone. She does that sometimes. Disappears on me. I hate it. I feel lonely without her. I'm mad at her. She took my boots without asking. I'll try and make some money today passing out flowers. I saw a yard full of dandelions in front of a house

185

that's been condemned. Hopefully no one has mowed them before I can get there. I haven't been making much money lately and I don't want to trick. But I need drugs, so I might have too. The end.

Bug still isn't back. It's been five days now. How could she leave me for so long? I miss her. I feel so sick. I hope I make enough today begging and handing out flowers at 1275. Things around the café have been dead. Haven't been able to make shit. I need stuff badly. I feel so sick. The end.

Finally, a clue.

My heart leapt for joy. A sense of calm washed over me. Although that particular diary entry was written almost two weeks ago, Chloe decided to remain in that area.

Tomorrow morning, I planned to hitch a ride to the Busch Boulevard exit ramp and look for Chloe. If I had no luck, I would hitch my way over to the Hillsborough Avenue exit ramp, next.

"Hopefully I find you at Busch, petal head."

I resumed reading her diary in search of another clue.

I remember the day Bug and I bought my vanilla boots at the Salvation Army Store. I didn't have enough money, so Bug loaned me some. She knew how much I loved those outta-sight boots. She always knows just what to say or do to keep me high in the clouds. But I wish she hadn't taken them without asking. Her feet are waaaaaaaay bigger than mine. Probably gonna stretch them out wearing them this long. When is she coming back? It's been so long. I need her help.

"So, what are you saying, Chloe? I have clown feet compared to your dainty ballerina toes?" I rolled my eyes. I could just hear her whining about how the boots felt too big now for her tiny feet. I recalled countless times she wanted to go barefoot like a true hippie. But after I explained to her the dangers of stepping on dirty needles, she promised to wear shoes and only go barefoot in our car.

"Deal?"

"Deal."

We then pinky-finger swore on the promise to seal it forever.

Oh, I see Lyla. Be back soon diary. The end.

"Who the hell is Lyla?" I asked.

I'm back. Sorry it's been a few days, diary. I was busy with Lyla doing stuff. She's groovy, too. Just like Bug. But she doesn't boss me around and stuff. Maybe because we're the same age.

"What stuff and you and this chick doing, kid? I'm going to have to track this Lyla down and find out what her story is."

Anyway, back to my boot story. Later, Bug and I went to the park and got stoned. It was far out! We did not feel like working. It was such a beautiful day. The sun was shining. I made Bug laugh with my goofy faces. It's not easy to get her to laugh, but I keep telling her how stress is no good for her soul. She needs to ride shit out. Go with the groove.

"What groove took you away from me, huh?"

A group of people were at a nearby pavilion at the park. They were having a party. All I remember is they played some groovy tunes on their radio. I closed my eyes and felt every bit of the rhythm...

I palmed my forehead. "Ugh! Seriously, Chloe? That's such a hippie thing to say, *"Felt every bit of the rhythm."*

The rain started coming down harder.

I heard more emergency sirens wail, only louder.

"Must be a fire somewhere." I resumed reading.

I danced and danced and danced until my feet made me feel like I was floating over the grass. I was flying, like a robin. I did not want to stop, even after the rain started to fall. Bug was mad and wanted to leave. But I grabbed her by the hand and soon we were both dancing and laughing.

The emergency sirens grew louder.

I tried to do a Rockette kick and landed flat on my back. I started laughing as I lay in a puddle of muddy, rainwater. The laughter stopped and Bug

...

I heard a lot of commotion close by. So, I left the diary, leapt out of the car and ran to see what was happening. As I rounded the corner, I saw paramedics running towards a body lying in the middle of a side street in a muddy puddle of rainwater.

*"Bug? Bug?"* Chloe barely whispered out into the open air, between fading breathes. *"I feel cold, Bug. I'm scared. Why is it getting so…"*

# Smack in the Heart

*"…**d**ark?"*

My eyes had become fixed on the flashing emergency vehicle lights.

*Light.*

*Dark.*

*Light.*

*Dark.*

*Light.*

I watched in horror, along with other spectators, as a lone paramedic performed CPR, while the other paramedic squeezed a blue bag over the person's face. They tried in vain to resuscitate the still person.

The flashing lights drew me in like a moth to an old familiar flame. I unknowingly stepped closer towards the person lying in the street. I was in a trance. My ears detected a  gruff sounding police officer's voice, who stood behind me. He forced everyone to step behind the newly placed yellow tape. I ignored his command and continued inching closer to the body.

I was halfway there when a hand grabbed a hold of my arm and yanked me backwards. I turned around and noticed it to be the same cop who had shooed me out of the alleyway the night before.

"Come on, princess. Behind the tape with the other looky-loos. Let's go."

Another police car pulled up. It's headlights glazed across the person in the street. My knees immediately buckled. I violently jerked my arm from the officer's grasp. "Let go of me!" I ran towards the paramedics and shouted, "No! No! No!"

The cop yelled, "Get back here." I continued to run.

"No! No! No! Please, no!" I resumed shouting until I reached…Chloe. It was then I released a wailing scream only a parent releases upon discovering their child on the brink of death or death itself. *"Ahhhhhhhhh!"*

The cop caught up to me and tried to arrest me.

"It's resisting for you, princess."

"Stop! Let me go! That's my sister they're working on."

A paramedic overhead me. "Your sister? Do you know her?"

The cop released one of my arms.

I was out of breath from my fight with the cop and the shock of seeing Chloe lifeless in the street. "I do. I do. Please! Please! Help her!" I then broke completely free from the cop, dropped to my knees beside Chloe. "Don't do this to me, Chloe. Please. You can't leave me. Not like this. Please, Chloe. Not like this."

I tried to hug her, but the cop pulled me back.

"They can't help her if you're in the way."

I sobbed uncontrollably. "Chlllllooooooooeeeee! Plleeeasse!"

"What did she take?" a paramedic asked.

I wiped my face and shook my head side to side, "I…I don't know."

I stared down at a motionless Chloe. "What did you do, Chloe? What did you do?" I tried to lunge for her again. And again, I was restrained.

"Stop it or I'm going to put you in the back of my car."

"Fuck you!" I snapped back. "Get your hands off me." I then jerked my arms free from his grasp once more. My uncontrollable sobbing returned.

The paramedics spoke with one another, but I failed to hear what they said. One of the them turned to me and in a stern tone said, "Look. We can't help your friend if we don't know what she took. So, what is it? Smack? Molly? Blues? What?"

I was about to violate Chloe's privacy for a second time today. "Sh..sh…she usually does smack. Sometimes a little weed."

I reached out to hold Chloe's right hand. It was balled up into a fist. The paramedic noticed and pushed my hand away. He carefully undid Chloe's tight fist and discovered a hidden baggie shoved up against her palm. I immediately noticed the logo was not Tiny's. I did not know whose it was or what drugs had been inside of it.

I lunged at Chloe again. I was angry. I got my hands onto her shoulders, shook her and screamed, "What did you take, Chloe? What the fuck did you take? Why? Why? Why didn't you listen to me? Dammit, Chloe! Dammit!"

"That's it," the angered cop snapped out as he snatched me off Chloe and dragged me towards his car. I kicked and screamed violently the entire time.

I looked back and watched the paramedics push Narcan into Chloes arm. She did not respond to it, nor any other attempts of lifesaving.

I thought, *Folks always say you know how you can tell when a junkie is lying? The answer…their lips are moving. It's always the truth…forever wrapped in a convincing lie.'*

We reached the car. I begged the cop to let me return to Chloe.

"Please. She needs me."

"What she needs are paramedics, not another junkie who might give her more drugs."

"Screw you!" I wiggled about. "Get your hands off of me."

He opened the back door, "Get in the car."

"No!"

I turned around and saw the paramedics shock Chloe with the paddles several times but to no avail.

I thought, *'An addict is a lot like the boy in the fairytale, The Boy Who Cried Wolf. Nobody believed the wolf was real because the boy had lied so much about it being real. Much like an addict who says they want to get clean, even though they keep on using drugs in secret. No one believed the boy in the story about the wolf. No one believes in an addict's words, either. No...one...believes...'*

The one paramedic looked towards the police officer and shook his head side to side. I released a guttural cry. "Chloe! Noooooooo!" Chloe was dead.

The cop released me, and I fell to the ground in my own muddy puddle of rainwater. I stared hopelessly and hypnotically at Chloe's body as it rested in the same muddy cold rainwater. She was soon picked up, placed on a gurney and covered with a white sheet. I would never see her smile or hear her kooky words ever again. She was gone. Forever.

I watched a lone feather from her headband fall to the ground and float upon the water in the street. The only evidence of where her soul had departed from the harsh streets of the planet.

The cop decided not to press charges on me. He felt the loss of my street sister was punishment enough. I walked over and retrieved the lone feather Chloe had dropped before the ambulance took her away. I held that feather close to my heart. As I walked past a bar, an all too familiar song blasted from the speakers. Tears rolled down my face as I walked off into the dark, unforgiving night.

*"Fly Robin. Fly. Up, up to the sky."*

# Down

**I** sat half slumped over, supported by a graffitied concrete Jersey Barrier. An old gray shawl was wrapped around my body for warmth. I was stoned out of my mind on *dirt* and repeatedly blinded by headlights as cars bounced up and down on the rough, pot-holed asphalt towards their intended destination.

*Light.*

*Dark.*

*Light.*

*Dark.*

*Light.*

I needed to work, but the last thing I desired was smelly, demanding Johns. I had to numb myself further to get through it. So, I shot more *dirt* between my toes. The veins in my arms and hands were still not healed.

"*Dammit!* That hurts!" I complained, despite the welcomed surge of pain at the injection site. I deserved to be hurt. I failed Chloe.

The sun rose and set fourteen days since Chloe died. I remained in complete denial over it. I never returned to our car after that night. In my mind, if I did not go back, Chloe was alive. Hard as I tried, though my heart knew the truth. It relentlessly ached.

The only true friend, the only real family I ever had on this shithole planet abandoned me. Nothing remained for me to give a crap about anymore… except *dirt*. How I prayed it would not leave me, too.

"Please, don't leave me. I need you. You're all I've got," I rattled off to a baggie coated in the powered remains of *dirt* I had used earlier.

I felt certain Chloe's diary still rested on the passenger seat, exactly where I had left it in the car that fateful rainy night.

I sighed and said, "I watched you arrive to me in the rain. I watched you leave me in the rain. Fuck you rain!"

I momentarily closed my eyes. When I opened them and turned to my right, Chloe was beside me, up against the Jersey Barrier and held onto my left hand.

I stared in disbelief. Half-dazed I asked, "Chloe?" I squinted harder. "Is that really you?"

"It's me, Bug," I heard her reply. The headphones around her neck blared Led Zeppelin's song, 'Stairway to Heaven'.

*In a tree by the brook, there's a songbird who sings*
*Sometimes all of our thoughts are misgiven*

"But I saw you die that night on the street, in the cold rain."

She shivered. "The rain sure was so cold that night, huh."

"You're here."

"I am."

"How?"

She reached over and touched my heart with her hand but said nothing.

"Where have you been, Chloe? I have missed you so much. I looked for you on Hillsborough Avenue, Busch Boulevard, Fowler Avenue. All up and down Nebraska Avenue. I couldn't …" I stammered, "I couldn't…I couldn't find you. But you're here. You came back to me. You really didn't leave me." My eyes welled up with tears.

"You always worry too much, Bug." She caressed my tear-stained cheek. I stared back at her like a helpless, lost puppy.

"Why, Chloe?"

"Why what?"

"Why did you do it?"

"Do what?" she tipped her head side to side in curiosity.

"Why didn't' you score from Tiny? Was it because of that bitch you met, Lily? Did you trust her more than me, your street sister?"

"Lyla."

"Lyla?" I scoffed. "Well, if I ever find Lyla…I swear," I snapped out with gritted teeth.

"Like the song says by *The Youngbloods*, Bug, *we have to love one another right now.*"

I rolled my eyes. "That's such a hippie thing to say, petal head." I then laughed through thick, dripping snot and falling tears. I wiped my nose on the shawl. "I've missed you so much, petal head."

"I know. I'm sorry. You know…"

"Know what?" I asked.

"I've missed you, too."

"I'm sorry I left you that morning. I'm sorry I always went off and left you alone Chloe. I'm such a piece of shit. Why didn't I just stay. You'd still be here and not off with" I changed my tone to sarcastic anger, "Lyyyyy….la. The first part of her name says it all. Lie!"

"It's okay, Bug."

I shook my head side to side and through more snot and tears protested, "No it's not. It's not okay. You're not here anymore, Chloe and it's all my fault." I sobbed uncontrollably. "I miss you so much, Chloe. I don't know how to go on without you. It hurts so much. I hate that you got in."

"Got in where?"

I punched my chest. "Here! In my heart. I worked so hard to keep people out because they hurt me. I trusted you. You hurt me, Chloe. You hurt me when you left. I miss you so much."

"I miss you, too, Bug. Bugging me for this. Bugging me for that. A real pest."

"You're the pest not me, petal head," I teased back. The tears resumed. "Oh, Chloe!"

"*Shh.* Bug. It's okay." She pushed my hair behind my ears. "Here, take this."

I looked downward as Chloe placed an object into my hand. My eyesight was too blurred. "Wha..what is it?"

"Close your eyes, Bug. Listen to the lyrics." The music coming from her headphones had grown louder. "Rest."

I did as Chloe asked. Lyrics from 'Stairway to Heaven' filled the air.

*And it's whispered that soon if we all call the tune*
*Then the piper will lead us to reason*
*And a new day will dawn for those who stand long*
*And the forests will echo with laughter*

The last thing she spoke before I drifted off into unconsciousness, "I'm with you. I'll forever be with you. I love you, Bug. Peace."

My eyelids opened an hour later and found Chloe no longer by my side. I looked down and noticed a lone feather from her headband rested in the palm of my hand. The same feather I picked up from the street the night she died. The one I barely released from my grasp ever since.

I looked around. "Chloe, come back. Chloe. Chloe! Don't go! I miss you! I need you! Please! Don't leave me!" I begged and panicked through more tears.

Chloe was never there. Her entire visit had been a drug-fueled mirage. The harsh reality of her absence once again became too much to endure.

"Fuck you, heart! It's not true! It's not true. IT'S NOT TRUE!" I shouted.

I cried nonstop and hugged myself as tightly as I possibly could. I shot up again to numb the pain even further. The fresh rush from the *dirt* quickly embraced me. I soon felt less alone as I slid, willingly, into *dirt's* open arms once more for comfort.

I remained slumped up against the cement barrier stoned out of my mind. I continually nodded off, only this time, no vision of Chloe. Instead, I flashed back over the past days of my life since she died.

I passed out at various locations around Nebraska Avenue. Sometimes I woke up with my clothes on. Sometimes naked. Almost every time, absolutely no memory of what happened. I blacked out. I no longer cared what happened to me. I earned enough to buy *dirt* to remain numb and keep Chloe at bay.

I wandered the streets aimlessly in her vanilla Go-Go boots, lost in my own world. The boots were the only tangible thing I had left of her. I felt her presence with every step I took. Each one hurt worse than my cramped-up toes.

"I don't care if you hurt. Keep moving, feet."

I tricked whoever crossed my path for whatever they wanted to pay. Five dollars. Ten dollars. Twenty-five dollars. It did not matter. "Just pay me and fuck off!" were the only words I said to a John, minus, "Yes, I'm available. What do you want? How much you got to pay for it?"

I tried to panhandle, but it never worked out for me unlike Chloe. Maybe because she offered flowers in return for the money. I could never bring myself to pick, nor even look at flowers. It hurt too much.

I rubbed my sore toes where I had shot up. If the area was infected, so what.

I spoke to my foot, "I hope you're diseased. Then you can rot off, along with the rest of my limbs until my soul is finally free and I no longer ache and can be with Chloe again."

I knew I needed to relocate soon. I was certain Officer Dickwad would cruise by the area eventually and threaten to arrest me.

"What do you know about loss? Huh, Officer Dickwad? You don't know shit. That's how much you know. You only know how to arrest people and kick them out of alleyways when they're trying to sleep. No sympathy. No compassion. No idea what the word family means. Like when you kept me from being with Chloe. She was my sister. She died alone, without me holding her hand. And it's all your fault, asshole!" I shouted out at his imaginary image which appeared before my stoned, glazed-over eyeballs. *Dirt* took over and I nodded off again.

Hours later, the sound of a loud horn honk stirred me awake. My eyes were blinded once more with bright headlights.

"Turn your damn brights off, jerk!" I shouted at a green SUV. The driver drove past and never noticed me.

I looked at my left wrist as if I was wearing a watch. "How long have I been out?" I shrugged my shoulders. "Fuck it. Who cares. Time means nothing anymore."

I attempted to stand on my feet but fell. After a few more tries, I held my balance. "Let's *mooooove* it, Princess," I said to myself with sarcasm and then stumbled out onto the street. "Officer Dickwad and the calvary are probably on their way."

Another loud car horn sounded off as I nearly tripped into oncoming traffic. I flipped the bird to the irritated driver in the classic purple dune-buggy and shouted, "Loser!"

I staggered back up onto the sidewalk and glanced around. I was so wasted. I needed to gather my bearings. I was disoriented, but the area felt oddly familiar.

I looked in both directions and asked myself, "Which way should we go, Bug, left or right?" My body lost its balance and leaned towards the right. "Right, it is then. Let's *gooooo*, Princess."

I tripped, stumbled and tumbled about on the uneven sidewalk. The chunky heels of Chloe's boots continued to snag on the bits of broken cement.

A forty-something guy in a blue muscle car approached me. "Hey baby, how much?" he asked.

"Fuck off, loser!" I snapped back.

"Oh, come on baby. Don't' be like that. How much for a good time?"

"Leave me alone, asshole!" I picked up a piece of loose concrete and threw it towards his car. I was so wasted I had no idea if the person was even real or just another figment of my warped imagination.

"Bitch!" He yelled, followed by the sound of screeched tires as he peeled off from the curb.

"Guess you were real. Whatever. I don't give a shit." I laughed and resumed my wasted walk down the sidewalk. "You got the boogie-fever, Princess!"

I was almost past a building, when my eyes were drawn towards a light that flickered from underneath a door. Before I rationalized what I had seen, my feet changed direction, and I found myself headed up a short flight of stairs.

*"What is happening?"* I whispered.

# Dirty

*Light.*

*Dark.*

*Light.*

*Dark.*

*Light.*

The glow from several candle wicks, danced bright orange and yellow flames before my hazed eyes. Their ferocious interpretive dance appeared to say, *"Come in."* I did.

"What is this place?" I asked, as I peered around.

The door clicked loudly behind me. I jumped. "What the…"

I turned around and as my eyes focused, I noticed crosses, stained glass windows, rows of dark wooden pews and a large altar with an oak podium at the front.

"I think this is that church with the kind priest." I shouted, "Hello? Are you here kind priest?"

No one responded.

I shrugged my shoulders, *"Oh, well."*

The air conditioner kicked over. A breeze from the ceiling vent titillated the brightly colored flames of the candles, as they vied for my attention. I looked to my left and saw a side-altar in front of the candles.

In my dazed condition, I spoke to the candles. "Why did you playful little cuties want a whore like me to come in here? Do you want me to get set on fire so I can burn? Do you think I deserve to burn in hell for all the bad things I've done. You know, I belong in the darkness, not the light, right?"

The candles flickered brighter.

"Oh, I think I get it. You think I should be in the light and not the dark, right? Interesting."

I ran my hand across the top of the flames.

"I feel you. So warm, not boiling hot like momma used to tell me the fire of hell felt like. She's probably burning there now." I then mumbled, *"The bitch."*

The candles flickered stronger.

"Sorry."

I observed a statue of Jesus. It rested on a pedestal behind the candle stand. The stand held several dozen candles nestled inside small red jars. In front of the stand was a prayer kneeler.

Most of the candles had been lit by people. Some still remained dark. I related to both types. I understood the lit candles because of the fire. To me, fire represented the anger I felt burning within and also the light I longed to be bathed in. I valued the unlit candles because of their darkness. They had no light and were unchosen, much like me. I thought it to be a much-deserved punishment for all that I had done in my pathetic life thus far.

When I stared upwards at the statue of Jesus, my legs gave out. I unintentionally yelled, "Jesus!" and reached backward with my right arm and grabbed the back of a pew for support.

I was too high on *dirt*. I had not eaten, nor slept in days. Plus, the emotional rollercoaster ride I had endured since the death of Chloe. It finally caught up to me. I was exhausted.

"Wait a minute", I said, as I regained my composure and stumbled back towards the statue of Jesus and the rows of flickering candles.

"Jesus starts with the letter "J". God! I can't escape that fuc…I mean, dang letter even in a church."

I felt defeated.

"Why? Why? Why?" I shouted out.

The air conditioner responded with a loud click as it shut off until the next cycle.

"Figures."

I tipped my head slightly to the right, and then to the left at the Jesus statue. I had never been inside a church before in my life. I was clueless about how to behave or what to say. I looked upwards at the ceiling and honestly awaited a lightning bolt to strike me dead.

"The nerve of me to be in such a sacred place. I know."

Momma used to say to me, "You are so disgusting to God. If you dared to set foot inside His house, He would strike your sorry ass dead with a bolt of lightning before you even blinked those same eyes you love to bat at my men so much."

"I hope lightning bolts are striking you non-stop wherever you are now, momma! Liar! I came through the doors of this church and not one bolt of lightning hit me."

I remained fixated on the ceiling and waited a little longer for the deadly strike to happen. After two minutes, nothing. It was confirmed. I hissed, "Should've known you were full of crap like always, momma."

My gaze dropped downward. It briefly halted on Jesus' eyes, before it continued down to His feet. Lightning bolts or not, I still felt ashamed to be inside a church.

"I don't belong here. Liar or not, momma's right. I am disgusting."

A red piece of paper taped to the wall caught the corner of my eye. I said, "What the hell is that?" I squinted my eyes hard and tried to read it. I mumbled the words out loud to help better understand them in my wasted condition.

"One. Identify a candle that has not been lit. Two. Select an unlit match from the box of matches sitting near the candles. Three. Using the flame from a lit candle, light the match. Four. Light the unlit candle of your choice. Five. Make a donation for the candle."

I released a sigh. "I can do that."

I chose an unlit candle on the bottom shelf, took a match from the box, put it over a lit candle and the match sparked.

"Holy sh…!" I quickly recalled I was in a church and whispered, *"Sorry."*

I lit the candle, shook the match and put it on a white ceramic plate with the other used matches. I wanted to jump onto the plate so badly and join them. I felt as burned out and used as them.

I re-read the last line on the red paper again. "Make a donation for the candle."

"A donation?" I asked, confused. "What kind of donation do they want? Money? Because if it's that, I don't have any."

I rummaged through my pockets. I had nothing but a powder coated, used bag of *dirt* and Chloe's lone feather.

"Not giving you those."

I shoved the baggie and feather deeper into their respective pockets. I was unsure of what to do. I feared my candle would be extinguished and my cries unheard if I offered nothing.

I threw a nervous glance around the church and searched the floor for loose change. I found nothing.

I said in a note of sarcasm to the statue, "This is different. I'm usually the one who asks for," I used air-quotes, "'donations' before any kneeling."

I felt as if the statue looked down upon me with pity.

"Don't look at me like that. You know it's the truth."

The statute remained silent.

"Look, all I got to donate for the candle is myself. I know I'm not worth shit." I whispered, "*Sorry. I'm trying not to cuss. Force of habit. I mean with the ass…I mean jerks I deal with. Well, you know. I'll try and do better.*"

I released a loud sigh and resumed my original speech. "I know I'm not worth anything. I know I don't deserve to be inside a church. I know I don't deserve to be talking to you. I don't even know if you can hear me. Or, if you want to hear me." I almost started to cry. "I don't know anything anymore. I just hope I'm enough for a candle and…" I then whispered, "*…some of your time.*"

I knelt on the prayer kneeler with a wobble. I was still very high. My eyes stared at Jesus' feet. I clasped my hands together.

I looked up at Jesus, winked and said, "Saw people do this with their hands in a movie once on our television back when I lived in the trailer with momma. By the way, I like your toes."

I felt confused and nervous. I had no idea what to say. In my head, I swore I had heard Chloe talk to me in that moment. She said, "Close your eyes and let your heart speak, Bug."

And so, I did.

I opened my mouth and stammered out, "I-I never prayed before. I – I don't know how to start. I don't even know why I'm here."

I opened my eyes and looked up at Jesus again. Perhaps for his approval, but probably more for his help. I suddenly found myself mesmerized and confused at the same time.

"You know something? You have kind eyes like that priest. He looked at me just like you are. Like I never done nothing bad my whole life. But I know you know that isn't true. I've done lots of bad stuff. Really bad stuff."

I lowered my head as humiliation washed over me, along with various tainted, sour memories.

"I had lots of bad stuff done to me."

I shook my head side to side as I recalled the countless number of men who took advantage of me. Their images seared deep inside my brain. I rustled the back of my filthy blonde hair with my left hand like a dog with an itch. I attempted to toss the bad memories off me like unwanted fleas.

I was so embarrassed about my life. I then worried because Jesus had seen me with all those men since I was five years old up until now.

Momma always said, "God sees everything you do. So, you can't lie to Him and tell Him you ain't no filthy jezebel because you are! He's seen you and the nasty things you've done!"

"I hate you, momma!" I yelled out before anger, fear and abandonment took over.

"I changed my mind. I don't want to talk about the dirty

stuff done to me. Or the dirty stuff I have done to myself. I might vomit."

I thought of Chloe.

"I miss Chloe so much. You would've liked her. She loved everyone. I guess. I don't know. The things she wrote in her diary were so different than who she was on the streets. But I know she loved me. I know it. I suppose she was the only one who ever really did. Well, except for momma in the beginning of my life before her boyfriend's got a hold of me."

I wiped a tear from my eye.

"Jesus? Why is Chloe gone and I'm still here? I don't understand."

I sucked loose snot back up into my nose. "I feel like I really fuc...I mean, screwed up with Chloe. I shouldn't have  left her alone for so long. I blame myself for what happened. It's all my fault she's dead. I murdered her. I'm going to burn in hell even more now, huh?"

I shook my head side to side, as I fought my inner demons. In an agitated voice I argued out loud with myself. "No! No! No! Bug. Chloe told you it was okay. It was not your fault what happened to her. You tried to warn her. Tiny only. Tiiiinnnnyyyy ooonnnnllllyyyy! Chloe didn't listen. It's her fault she's dead, not yours. It was her fault not yours. It was her fault not yours. No, it was mine. All mine. All mine. All mine."

I stared up into the Jesus statue's eyes and sought reassurance from Him that it was not my fault Chloe had died. He only offered more pity.

My head dropped down, and I sobbed uncontrollably and blubbered, "I'm so sorry Chloe. I'm so sorry. I'm so sorry. I'm so sorry," I heaved. "I don't know what to do without her. Tell me. Please." I begged.

The Jesus statue remained silent and stoic.

"Thanks for nothing."

I became overwhelmed with emotion and passed out.

# Devoted

*Light.*

*Dark.*

*Light.*

*Dark.*

*Light.*

**A** buzzing sound and ceiling lights that flickered awakened me. At first I had thought it to be the priest. Perhaps he saw me and turned the light switch off and on to wake me up. It soon was apparent the lights that flickered above my head were due to a bulb about to die. The kind priest was not there.

I wiped the drool off the side of my face, regained my bearings and started to chat with the Jesus statue again.

"I don't understand why all those men did such disgusting things to me when I was little. Always wanting to make the letter

'J' with me once the alcohol had put momma to sleep. Why did they do it? Why did they hurt me?"

I grew angry.

"I gave up my dream of being a nurse to care for that evil bitch until the day she croaked."

I wagged my index finger at the statue. "Did you know not once did she ever say sorry for what her men had done to me. Not once. Even though I changed her shitty diapers, cleaned up her vomit and put up with her endless hurtful, hateful words."

I slammed my hand down hard on the top of the prayer kneeler.

"Not once did she ever say it wasn't my fault. She always blamed me, instead."

I slammed my hand down hard on the top of the prayer kneeler again for emphasis.

"Not once did she ever believe me when I told her the truth."

I slammed my hand down again.

"Not!"

Another slam.

"Even!"

Again, with a slam.

"Once!"

My anger meshed into sadness again.

"Maybe it really was my fault. Maybe I stole momma's boyfriends like she said. Maybe I deliberately got hooked on *dirt* to forget. Maybe I wanted to become a whore on the streets and not a nurse in a hospital. Maybe I wanted Chloe to die, so I could die now, too. I have nothing to live for anymore. I'm such a piece of shit, aren't I?"

I looked up at Jesus' eyes.

"You don't have to answer that question. I already know I am."

My anger flared back up.

"I hate myself! I hate them! Every one of those fucking men! I can't close my eyes anymore without seeing them mount me one after the other."

I grabbed chunks of my own hair in an attempt to physically yank the disturbed memories out of my head. The rustling of my hair, the shaking of my head had not been enough to complete the job. Those memories held on to my hair strands with all their might and refused to release me. It was a tug-of-war from hell.

"Let…me…go!"

"No!"

"Let….me…gooooo!"

"Nooooo!"

"LET! ME! GO!" I then threw clumps of hair to the floor and felt a momentary glimpse of victory. "Take that you motherfu…perverts!"

Silence fell over the church and inside my mind simultaneously. But the silence did not last for long. The horrible memories soon returned with vengeance.

I looked up at His eyes with my own eyes, they pleaded for help.

"Why won't they leave? No matter what I do to make it all stop. The visions. The voices. The pain. None of it goes away."

I hugged myself.

"I constantly feel their soft hands, their calloused hands, their rough hands, touching me in every wrong place. Whispering nasty things into my small, delicate ears. Begging me to call them 'Daddy'. They're not my daddy. I don't even know who my real daddy is. I'm not sure momma did either. She just assumed it may have been this one guy. If the truth were known, I think momma was the actual whore in our demented family."

I shivered at the thought of the countless repulsive hands and vile, nasty words.

"I feel so vile. Like a legion of demons have squatted inside every crevasse of my body. My soul feels trapped inside a temple riddled with mass destruction. I don't understand why all those men did such disgusting things to me. Why would they want to do those disgusting things to anyone, ever? What did I do to make them want me? Why won't someone tell me the truth?"

I gritted my teeth and hissed, "I can't stand the way I feel about myself anymore. I want it over with. All of it!"

I wiped fallen tears away. "How do I silence the anger and the hatred? How do I erase all of it from my head? Tell me, please?"

I looked up at the statue as the tears continued to pour down my rosy cheeks.

"I'm *sooooo* tired of running from my past, Jesus. I don't have the strength to outrun it anymore. I'm sick of crawling in the *dirt*. It doesn't work anymore. *Dirt's* not there for me like it used to be. My soul is suffocated by so much hate and anger built up inside of me. I need to let go and be free, like petal head. But I'm scared. I'm all alone now. No Chloe. And now, no *dirt*. I have no one. Nothing."

I sniffled.

"I don't know who I am anymore without *dirt*. I don't know who I want to be. I don't know how to start over with so much bad stuff in my life. Please, help me."

I then released a loud sigh. I said nothing for a few moments. I was unequivocally drained by my giant emotional purge. I had finally opened the door to set the pain and hatred free from my heart and without realizing it, allowed Jesus in. I wiped my face free from what tears lingered and placed my hands into my pockets for a tissue. I did not have one.

"Is it okay if I rest here with you for a while? I'm exhausted."

I did not wait for His response. I leaned forward and hugged Jesus at the ankles. As I turned my head to the left to rest my right cheek upon the top of his feet, the right palm of my hand opened up, and the baggie of dirt dropped to the floor behind Him. In my left hand, Chloe's feather remained.

I whispered, "Thank you, Jesus," and closed my eyes.

# My Coda

"Victims of dirt are more than society's throwaways. They are someone's daughter, mother, grandmother, aunt, uncle, cousin, son, father, and friend. If you happen upon a firefly soaring over a dewy meadow, look for me....in the light."

If you would like to be healed from past hurts, be able to have forgiveness, be able to make a change in your life and be able to have an honest relationship with God, please see *The Salvation Prayer* below to help open the door to your broken heart so God can begin healing you. This is not about religion. This is about healing and having a relationship with God.

The Holy Bible says:

Jesus said to them: *"I am the way, the truth, and the life. No one can come to the Father except through me."* (John 14:6)

*"For whosoever calls upon the name of the Lord shall be saved."* (Romans 10:13)

If you would like to receive the gift that God has for you today, pray this with your heart and lips out loud:

*"Dear Lord Jesus, come into my heart. Forgive me of my sin. Wash me and cleanse me. Set me free. Thank You that you died for me. I believe that You are risen from the dead and that You are coming back again for me. Fill me with the Holy Spirit. Give me a passion for the lost, a hunger for the things of God and a holy boldness to preach the gospel of Jesus Christ. I am saved; I am born again; I am forgiven, and I am on my way to heaven because I have Jesus in my heart."*

All your sins are forgiven. God loves you and has a great plan for your life.

## You are going to be okay, kid!

# Bullied: Dying to Fit In

book 2

*Bullied: Dying to Fit In* was nominated and received the
**Advocacy/Social Justice Award** for the **2019**
**In the Margins Book Award**
**School Library Journal**

This is every bullied person's story.
Will you listen?

Metamorphosis is to evolve from one creature, like a caterpillar, into another, a butterfly.

 Bullied.

 Healing.

 Free.

Being bullied can make you feel like a bug that can get squashed at any moment. But, once you realize by transforming yourself and becoming who you really are, you can develop into the butterfly that takes wing and is set free from the pain.

# Bullied

## Dying to Fit In

Normandy D. Piccolo

**NBI**
**Normandy's Bright Ideas**

# contents

*Bullied Dying to Fit In* is for the bullied and the bully. It reveals the raw feelings and emotions a person might experience because of bullying. It also shows a strong correlation between bullying and mental health issues, like depression.

Did you know a bullied person's feelings and emotions can overwhelm them to the point of considering suicide to stop the pain?

Stories about kids committing suicide because of bullying make daily headlines around the globe and yet, the number of deaths because of bullying continue to rise and the ages are getting younger. Why? Because the emotional/mental fallout from being bullied has not been recognized, nor understood well enough.

Too much effort is spent on promoting T shirts, bracelets and witty little sayings against bullying. While those things help bring awareness to the issue of bullying and certain mental health issues amplified or formed due to bullying, they do not offer solutions.

Keeping things surface and *"not going there"* because the topic of depression, self-harm and suicide is too unpleasant, is getting us nowhere. We need to deal with this unpleasant topic head-on and acknowledge the gritty, raw side of bullying and intensified mental health issues either amplified or formed because of it.

*Bullied Dying to Fit In* talks to you. Not at you. It helps one to understand the reality of what can happen if bullying goes too far, before transitioning into positive reinforcement, guidance and wisdom.

After reading this book, a person being bullied will hopefully understand why they are being bullied, how to stop being a victim of bullying and develop a realistic, but, still positive outlook on their life.

**warning:** The desire to quit life is expressed in parts of the book because that is the truth. Committing suicide is strongly discouraged as a solution to fixing bullying and/or mental health issues. If you or anyone you know are struggling with any of those issues, please seek help at a support or crisis center in your area or online through local and national organizations.

**SUICIDE IS NEVER THE ANSWER.**

sadness

bad days 95%
good days 5%

## how should i end it and if i did would you care?

How should I end it and if I did, would you care?
I could cut my veins open and let blood ooze everywhere.

How should I end it and if I did, would you run?
I could wrap my lips around the barrel and pull the trigger of a gun.

How should I end it and if I did, would you feel a sharp pang?
I could noose a belt around my neck, jump off a chair and hang.

How should I end it and if I did, would you let out a shrill?
I could get a glass of water and down a bottle of sleeping pills.
Why should I end it? It's because of your hate.
You say hurtful things, you spit on my lunch plate.

You say you're just kidding, but that's not the truth.
Want to know how I know?
I'll tear open my chest and show you the proof.

My heart is riddled with pain, hurt and misery.
Why should I end it?
It's because you won't let me be.

Maybe I'll fight back...maybe, we'll see.
But, if I should end it just know this one thing.
I ended it because of you, you cruel, heartless, mean thing.

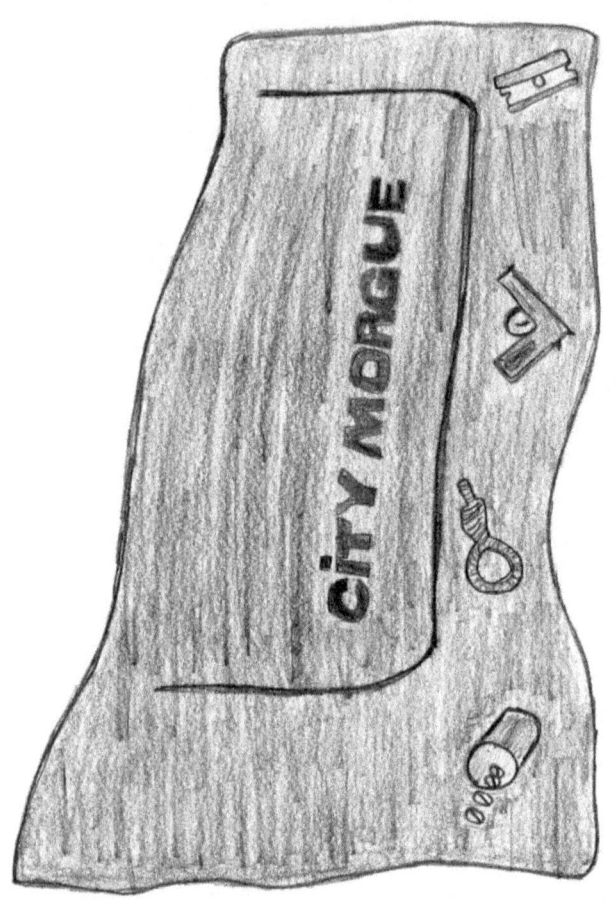

Dying to fit in
Dying to be someone's friend
Died because the bullying never came to an end.

## OBITUARY NOTICE

✝

The Kid Whose Name Nobody Knew, 14, died January 20, from a self-inflicted injury due to relentless bullying.

The Kid was talented, intelligent, caring, giving, thoughtful, and a hard worker. But, due to the ignorant cruelty of fellow classmates, only the Kid's family knew of those things.

The Kid was born surrounded by love and died alone, feeling rejected, depressed, hurt and confused. The Kid will be best remembered as the one who got pelted in the school halls with water bottles, gossiped about on social media, punched, kicked, spat upon and excluded from social events.

The Kid lived what's deemed the "best years", as the "worst years". The Kid never understood why nobody would be a friend. The Kid tried to be a friend to everyone.

The Kid is survived by two grieving parents who will spend the rest of their days brokenhearted, trying to understand why their child chose suicide as the answer to being bullied.

In lieu of flowers please contribute to the Kid's memory by not being a bully.

# beware of the closet

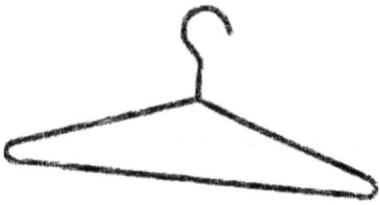

Beware of the closet
It is where hurtful secrets hide
Beware of the closet
Venture inside and you might die

Beware of the closet
A roped serpent dangles above from a wire shelf
Beware of the closet
Peace may not thrive while hanging yourself

Beware of the closet
Rumors and lies are meant to deceive
Beware of the closet
Stop! Don't hand your life over to a lying thief

But, I want to go into the closet
Make a noose, let the pain end
I want to go into the closet
For I am nobody's friend

I want to go into the closet
I hate the way I feel
So, what if I hang myself?
It's not that big of a deal

I want to go into the closet
Silence the repetitious voices inside my head
I want to go into the closet
Kids at school say they wish I were dead

I want to go into the closet
Nobody wants me around anyway
I want to go into the closet
I want the world to stay away

The closet represents darkness
It's where truth, half-truths and skeletons reside
But, if I choose to stay out of the closet
Then, I won't, I don't have to die

One step in
Another step back out
I pull on my hair
I scream, and I shout

F**k you!
I hate you!

You fail me again and again
Why do I have to make this choice?
Why did you push me to the end?

No! No! No!
I scream then slam the closet door shut
I drop down to the floor
And tell the pain, *"Shut up!"*

I then let out a wailing cry
God, please show me how to survive
Life, come on, stop failing me
Please, help me, I need to revive

I mean, why should I give up?
Why should I let them beat me?
If I go into the closet and hang myself
I'll be labeled a sell-out, a wimp or a wussy

Church once taught me that suicide's a sin
So, if I quit and go into the closet

I lose
They win

No! No! No!
I won't give up that quick
I won't let them get the better of me
I'm no longer absorbing their sh**

I am staying out of the closet
At least, now, for me
I am not going to exhale
No! Instead, I am going to breathe!

I never knew a text
That became a private sext
Would be sent out to everyone
by a bitter, spiteful Ex

Hester Prynne always felt hexed
A giant red letter placed upon her chest
But, that was not my case
I did not lust after another or give chase

So, why is an A now on my chest?
What? Because I sent my then boyfriend a sext?
Seriously? That makes me a slut?
I feel like I've been punched in the gut

I wish I could take it back
I wish I could take it back
I only wish

If I had known my bitter Ex
Would show the world the private sext
I never would have sent it
And now, it's too late to relent it

But, I do know this one thing
I will never, ever send another sext
I will not dare trust, nor flex

For if you should ask me for a sext
My reply to you will simply be, NEXT!

Punch me
Slap me
Say mean things about me
Guess what? I feel
How can you not believe my pain isn't real?

I am broken.

Meet my friend
Who goes by the name of unbelievable pain
It resides deep inside my heart
And courses through my veins
Thanks to your unbelievable pain
Life is no longer fun
Then, more vicious verbal vomit spews forth
And everything comes undone
That is when it ventures outside
By rolling down my cheeks
Encased inside many salty tears
The only way it speaks.

I am not a slut
You said that you cared
I believed that you liked me
Not because of a frat boy dare

I let you take pictures
You promised not to share
But, you betrayed me you liar
And now, the pictures are everywhere

You made me popular
But, not in the right way
Girls want to kick my ass
Boys look to get laid

I hate you! I hate you! I hate you!
How could you do me wrong?
I would never have hurt you
I had loved you for so long

The pain that you caused me
Can never be erased
Nor can the pictures,
Now the world knows my face.

Pump me
Hump me
Then treat me like trash
Popular I've become
Voted the school's favorite piece of ass

With boys in the dark
I'm pretty, I'm the bell
However, by myself
I'm ashamed, I'm in hell
If, I don't do what they ask
I won't be desired, I won't be wanted

Little did I know in the end
I'd be rejected and brutally taunted

A thousand douches, a million showers
Won't ever make me feel clean
I've gone from being popular
To a, *"She'll do it with anyone"* sleaze queen

Comments written on social media walls
Vulgar words shouted in the halls
*"For a good time, call"*
Scribbled inside a bathroom stall

I don't care
Say what you will
Your words can't hurt me
Remember, I'm so popular, I'm chill

But, that's the problem
The reality is, I do
I can try to front until I graduate
But, down inside it's the painful truth

Sleeping around to be popular
Is not all it's cracked up to be
I wish I could go back on it all
Erase it or undue everything

But, I felt insecure
And wanted to fit in
Like the other girls
I was lonely, in need of a friend

I'll never understand
Why it's okay that some girls can
While other girls who do the same
Get slut-shamed, again and again.

A release from the pain
The razor blade exposes my sins
Penetrating, slicing, it rips apart my skin

I don't want to die
I just want some peace
With each cut I make
I begin to feel some relief.

My emotional wounds run deeper than the cuts on my flesh.

This cut is for wanting to belong and not.
This cut is for life not getting better even when I try.
This cut is for getting beat up when I speak up.

This cut is for the rumors spread about me.
This cut is for the shame I now feel about myself.
This cut is for the sorrow I'm drowning in.

This cut is for the rejection.
This cut is for feeling isolated.

This cut is for making me hate myself.
This cut is for feeling so helpless, weak and pathetic.
This cut is to awaken the numbness.

This cut is to feel something. I feel nothing anymore.
This cut is for being a loser. A nothing. A nobody.
This cut is for being empty inside.

This cut is for being bullied.
I'm running out of places to cut.
Please bring it to an end.
I don't think I can take much more!

I once was a seedling
planted into the ground
I grew big, I was strong
until they cut me down

I was pressed and pressured
and watered down
Before being placed in a factory where
others like me abound

Scissors and razor blades
They brought me relief
Tormented inside
I found a release

I'm but a paper doll
Fragile and weak
Rough around the edges
Too pathetic to speak

A paper cut I can give you
Compared to what you gave me
The pain of rejecting myself
Pain so strong, I can hardly breathe.

Playing 'Rock - Paper – Scissors' with a bully.
Rock I throw at you.
Scissors I cut with to relieve the pain you've caused.
Paper I write my final goodbyes'.

The cuts continue to appear
Though I keep hoping to disappear

From my body, the blood runs down
But, I hear not a single sound

Just the faint whimpers of my soul as it cries
Why? Why? Why? Oh, why?

Drip, by drip, by drip
On their radar of destruction,
I am nothing to them but a blip.

My family thinks I'm strong
A bully sees me as weak
A smile for Mom and Dad
Secret slaps across my cheek

I wish I could tell my parents
So, they might help it stop
But, if I open my mouth and speak
The bully finds out, I'll get popped

So, I front for Mom and Dad
Weep silent tears into my sleeve
Reaping kicks, hits and punches
In private, I continuously grieve.

Overwhelmed
Under-loved
Beaten badly
Constantly shoved
Bruises hurt
Tears trickle down
Confusion sets in
So much hurt I could drown.

I feel sad.
I feel depressed.
I feel anxious.
I feel sick.
I feel unwanted.
I feel left out.
I feel lonely.
I feel so tired.
I feel like giving up.
I feel I can't take another day.
I feel lots of other things, too.
But, I don't feel loved or that I'll be missed.

Wish I could say
But bad feelings won't go away
I want so much to stray
But, something keeps making me stay

I really want to live
I have so much to give
But, no one seems to want me
Everyone in school endlessly taunts me

I cup my hands over my ears
Sing loudly so I can't hear
But, the hateful words manage to seep in
I fight back the tears, but the crying begins

Alone under the stairs
No one seems to care
I hold my knees close to my chest
I feel as if I'm failing life's test

Dork, Jerk, Geek, Loser, Ass
The bell just rang, now I'm late for class

I don't want to come out for fear of being hit
Why am I always picked on?
Why does the world think I'm shit?

See me with a bullet in my head?
See me with the noose wrapped around my neck?
See me swallow an entire bottle of pills?
See me slash my wrists until the blood spills?

Watch me get lowered into the ground
The dirt covers me over
You say no words, make no sound

You won't shed one tear
No water for my flowers to grow
Only emit cheers of joy and say,
*"Another dork dead. That's how it goes."*

I will be, but a memory is what I've been told
My locker will be emptied, my clothes will be sold

No one will miss me, or so they type
Sure, my death will be news, until the next hype

Stupid, dumb, ugly, fat, loser, lame
You should die they said, imagine the fame

Newspapers, Television, Facebook, Twitter
Problem is, my parents said they didn't raise no quitter

Miss me, don't miss me, I suppose that's your choice
Will your heart even break?
Will your eyes become moist?

Do it
Don't do it
Not sure which one will win
Die before it's time
Heard that's a big sin

Stupid, dumb, ugly, fat, loser, lame
How I wish I could start over
How I hate this hurtful game.

Would you miss me if I went away?
Would you pause for a moment?
Beg me not to die, not to decay?

Is there someone, anyone, willing to say,
*"Please, stay."*

Nothing but silence.
Apparently, not today.

I never wanted to cry because I was bullied.
I never wanted to cry for being called hurtful names.
I never wanted to cry for being beat up for no reason.
I never wanted to cry for rumors spread about me.
I never wanted to cry because of those things.
But, I cry now all the time.

Sometimes I just need a hug and to be told, *"Everything is going to be all right"*, even if it might never be.

So young.
So beautiful.
So tragic.
Now gone.
Will you even miss me?

I need love. Not hate.

No Slut Am I
I will always deny
The vicious rumors you
continually spread
To silence your voice
I shall have to be dead
To get your hateful words
Flushed out of my head.

No one cares.

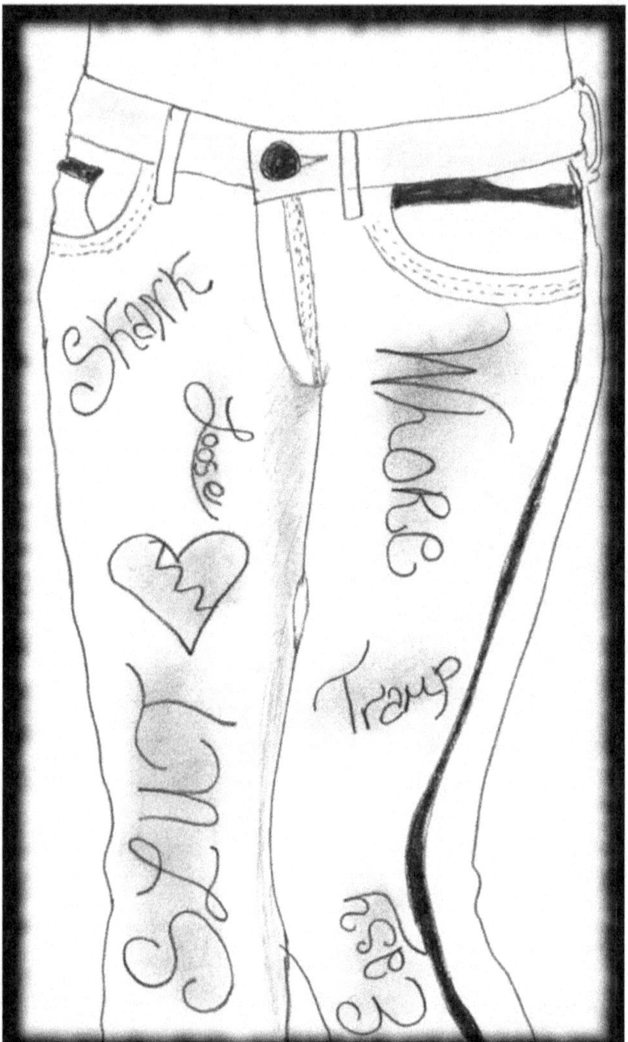

Nobody cares.
They stare.
Or, they glare.
Speak a kind word to me?
Pah! They would never dare.

I am a light.
I want to shine.
But I can't.
They won't let me.

Why don't I fit in?
Why won't they let me fit in?
I don't understand.

Sorry I'm not perfect like you.

So, I'm short
So, I'm a little fat
So, my hair's curly
Instead of being flat
I like myself.

So, I love to smile
So, I sometimes cry
So, I don't give up
So, I give it another try.
I like myself.

Then I met you.

Now, my feelings hurt
Now, you make me sad
Now, I smile no more
Now, I always feel sad
I hate myself.

I hate that I am short
I hate that I am fat
I hate my curly hair
I wish it would go flat
I hate myself.

I no longer smile
All I do is cry
No matter what I say or do
My life is full of sighs
I really hate myself.

What did I do wrong?
Why do I even give a damn?
I am so tired of trying to prove myself to you
Why can't you just accept me the way that I am?

While I loathe you, just know, I hate myself even more.

If you prick me
I bleed just the same
You call me a slut
But, that is not my name

If you hit me
I shed tears
But, do you?
The pain that I feel
I hope someday you feel, too

Please, please ignore me
Disappear and go away
Never bother me again
That's all I must say.

Shut up! Shut up! Just go away!
Social media sites are where you go to say
Hurtful, hateful, cruel remarks you proudly speak
Singling me out because you assume I am weak

But, you are the one who is weak
For you type crap, but never speak
I dare you to say those words to my face
To come and invade my personal space

You can't, I suppose.
I'm not surprised, it figures.
You're just a coward behind the keyboard
Typing lies with a click and a snicker

You are pathetic!

I left something for you at your front door last night.
My shoes.

I wonder if you will dare to wear them.
To step into the hell, you have created for me.

I wish you would put my shoes on your feet.
I wish you would feel the pain you have caused me.

I want you to feel each step taken as if it were going to be your
last. Because, that is how I feel every single day.

Dammit!

I just want you to feel what I feel.
If you did, maybe you would stop bullying me. But, I doubt it.

You can keep my shoes as a reminder. To never forget what you
did, even though you will probably forget about me.

# will you?

Will you punch me when no one is around?

Will you always call me hurtful names?

Will you line up chairs at the head of the room and mock my funeral when I come into class?

Will you write nasty limericks about me on the bathroom wall and proudly sign your name?

Will you shove me?

Will you throw water bottles at me and get everyone else to do the same as I am walking down the halls at school?

Will you get someone to pretend to like me, so I will share my innermost thoughts, then use what you learned about me against me?

Will you nominate me for Class President and get my hopes up to win, only to have the whole school laugh at me?

Will you post endless lies about me on the internet?

Will you harass me to the point where I don't want to leave my house anymore?

Will you invite me to a party and then, when I show up, pretend you never invited me?

Will you do those things?
Will you?

Your answer is YES, you will. Because you have already done those things to me.

Since you are so willing I would like to know...

Will you help me drape the belt up in the closet?

Will you form a strong noose to break my neck?

Will you kick the chair out from underneath me?

Will you hold my feet, so they don't wildly kick about while I'm asphyxiating to death?

Will you even try and stop me from ending my life?

Your answer is NO, you will not. Because you willfully drove me to this decision.

Will you wait around while my organs shut down?
That is, assuming my neck doesn't snap right away.

Will you still wait anyway, as I linger for a while, breathing very, very shallow breaths. This could take a while. Hope you brought something to read.

Will you watch my face twist and contort?

Will you take pictures and post them?

Will you then brag and say, *"Look What I Made Happen."* You must be so proud of yourself.

Will you cut me down or leave me hanging alone in the closet?

Will you leave the closet light on or leave me swinging ever so slightly, back and forth in the dark?
I can't help but wonder.

Will you clean me up after I have crapped and pissed my pants?
You know that happens during asphyxiation, right?

Will you clean up the mess I made?

Will you redress me?

When my parents ask you, *"Why did this happen?"*

Will you tell them the truth?

Will you tell my parents about all the mean things you said and did to me?

Will you tell my parents how sorry you are for doing and saying mean, hateful things to me?

Will you even mean it?

I doubt it.

Will you help my parents plan my funeral?

Will you help my parents pick out a coffin?

Will you help my parents pick out an outfit for me to be buried in?

Will you place a flower, or an apology note on my coffin?

Will you say something nice about me at my funeral?

Will your words be full of regret for the way you treated me while I was alive, or will you spew more hate?

Will you even comprehend the money my parents had saved for my college fund is now paying for my funeral?

Will you even care that instead of a graduate certificate, I get a death certificate now, instead?

Will you help my parents pack up my room and donate some of my stuff while storing the rest?

Will you keep in touch with my parents? See how they are doing as time marches onward?

If your answer is, *"No"*, then leave me the hell alone!

Rumors. Lies. Punches. Slaps.
I am as numb on the inside as I am on the outside.

Watch what you post
Watch what you say
The rumors you type won't ever go away

You can try to delete them, but they spread very fast
Be careful speaking untruths about someone's past

The pain you cause will never go away
So, think before you act
It's all I must say.

Could have been something.
Should have been something.
Might have been something.
Schoolmates think I am nothing.
Because of your lies.
Now, I think I am nothing, too.

I am damaged by your cruel words.
I am ravaged by your hateful friends.
I am savaged by your punches and kicks.
I am bloody.
I am wounded.
I am done.

I am plastic wrap, invisible until you spy me.
Then, I become wax paper.
Torn apart easily with your words not watered down.
You think yourself to be tinfoil.
Tough and durable.
But, what do I know
I am only plastic wrap.
Invisible.

I am so tired
I cannot sleep

Eyes open
Eyes closed

Matters not I still weep

I try to be like the other sheep
But I am cast aside and called weak

How I long to drift off,
drift off,
drift off,
And sleep

I am so tired
So tired of being called pathetic
Of being called weak

Inner strength why won't you arrive?

Until you do, I shall sit alone in my closet and weep.

I hope, one day the word BULLY disappears from the dictionary!

Monday, I got beat up.
Tuesday, more rumors were spread about me.
Wednesday, I got beat up again.

Thursday, even more rumors were spread.
Friday, I went completely numb.
Saturday, I cried in bed all day.
Sunday, I wanted to be dead.
Monday, the cycle repeats.

I am so tired of failing at life.

I am lonely.
I am heartbroken.
I hate going to school.
I love my teachers.
I hate my bully.
I want to stay home.
I never want to leave my room.
I just want to be left alone.
Why can't the world just leave me alone?

I once was a nobody
Until you made me somebody
A person who's hated by everybody

At school, I get treated like an antibody
I live inside a torn and bruised up body

Because my life you chose to disembody

I am constantly tormented soul and body
I wish I could have never been somebody
Other than that, whom I used to be, nobody.

My existence feels like one meant for you to destroy.
How I wish I did not exist right now.
How I despise your evil ploys!

A punch to my stomach.
A punch to my head.
Why prolong the misery?
I know you wish me dead.

Mean words hurt.
Cruel words cause death.
Overwhelmed by hateful blurts.
I want to take my last breath.

I stare into the bathroom mirror.
I admire zero things about myself.
I write hateful words over my reflection.
Letter by letter they effortlessly appear.
Each word, reaffirming my feelings about myself.
I spit at my reflection and scream out loud,

*"Ugly! Loser! Pathetic! Nobody! Worthless! Disgusting!"*

I then punch my reflection.
My hand does bleed.
My hand surely hurts.
But, if you compared that pain to that of my shattered heart —
no contest. My heart hurts more.
I hate the one who I see looking back at me, more than the one
who has now made me see myself this way.

I care what you think of me
I wish I knew why
Continually seeking your approval
Again, and again I try.

Why do I even bother?
What makes you so great?
You are nasty, cold and cruel.
So bitter and full of hate.

I am not okay. I may never be.

Die stupid loser.
Why are you even here?
Nobody wants to date you.
Nobody wants to be your friend.
You may as well close your eyes.
You may as well be dead.

I thought you should know, not that you care. But, what cruel things you said will hurt me forever.

You do not know me. So, shut up!

I really want to say goodbye.
I really don't want to give it another try.
Listen close.
Hear my final sigh.

Screw you once for writing mean crap on my locker.
Screw me once for not erasing it.

Screw you twice for spreading rumors about me.
Screw me twice for not telling everyone you are a liar.

Screw you three times for beating me up.
Screw me three times for taking your abuse.

Screw you four times for creating fake social media accounts in my name.

Screw me four times for not getting those accounts shut down.

Screw you five times for getting others to bully me.
Screw me five times for not reporting you.

Screw you six times for being a bully.
Screw me six times for being a victim.

SCREW YOU X infinity!!!!

Congratulations. You broke me.

A frown cannot be turned upside down, if one keeps getting beaten down.

When you call me a mean name, I feel worthless.
When you punch me in the face, I feel worthless.

When you steal my stuff, I feel worthless.

When you spread lies about me, I feel worthless.

When you bring up past mistakes I made, I feel worthless.

I wish you could understand how worthless your words and actions make me feel.

I try and feel worthy.
But you steal my joy away.
And I feel worthless, again.

I wish I was strong enough to resist your hate.
To realize you are the one who is worthless.
But I can't.
I'm too beat down.

It's raining, it's storming
Why's my life so boring?

Because…

I had some friends
But, that's come to an end
Thanks to a selfish bully.

My name is not slut.
My name is not skank.
My name is not whore.
My name is not tramp.
My name is not loser.
My name is not fat pig.
My name is not idiot.
My name is not stupid.
Do you even know my name?

My pages,
please stop stalking.
Your rumors,
please stop talking.

Smiles can be faked, you know.

Hours.
Minutes.
Seconds.
Mornings.
Afternoons.
Nights.
Days.
Weeks.
Months.
Years.
Time is no longer a friend of mine.

I don't know you.
You think you know me.
Do me a favor, huh?
Leave me be.

I am not as strong as I pretend to be.

Dejected...Subjected...Objected...and

Injection Of Your Painful Neglection

EMO REJECTED R LON FR FREAK WEIRDO STRANGE

Unprotected From Your Subjected Physical Objections

Quit The Conject and Eject From My Life!

If I change the shape or color of my eyes, will you see me differently?

If I shave my nose down, will you stop calling me names?
If I get my ears pinned back, will your mean words finally get blocked out?

If I grow my hair out, cut it short, change the color, straighten it, curl it, will your criticism cease?

If I pump my lips up or thin my lips down, will you stop running your lips about mine?

Nip, Tuck, Cut, Suck
My looks have now changed
And, yet, your hate remains.

My head hurts because you hit it with your fist.

My arm hurts because you twisted it behind my back.

My stomach hurts because you punched it with your other fist.

My back hurts because you kicked it with your foot.

My cheek stings because you slapped it with your hand.
My heart hurts because you spoke horrible words.


Aspirin, ibuprofen, acetaminophen, an ice pack won't stop the pain.

An apology from you would have stopped the pain.

Leaving me alone in the first place could have prevented the pain.

I fake a smile for Mom.
I fake a smile for Dad.
I fake a smile for my little sib.
I fake a smile for my Grandma.
I fake a smile for my teachers.
I fake a smile for my counselor.
I fake a smile for my friend(s).
And when I look at my reflection,
I fake a smile to myself.

You hear laughter
I shed tears
You see beauty
I feel fear.

Please remember only the good things about me.
I was good at solving problems except for my own.
Please don't remember the bullying done to me.
Please remember to miss me.
Please never forget me.
Please.

## REPLACEMENT PARTS

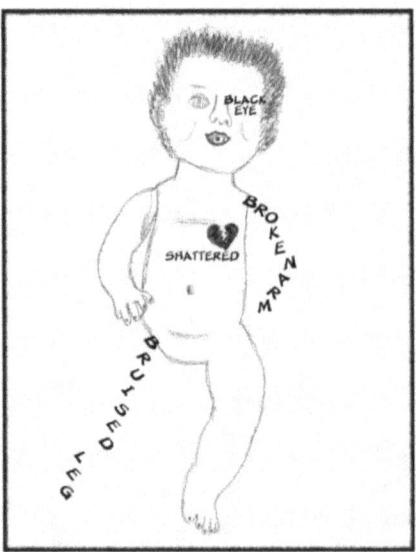

## BECAUSE OF A BULLY

Seeking new parts to replace ones damaged by a bully. I need a new eye. My left one got punched and is now black and blue. I need a new arm. My left arm got broken when it was twisted behind my back. I need a new leg. My right leg is very bruised from repeated kicks. Finally, I need a new heart. Mine has been shattered into tiny pieces.

Star Light
Star Bright
The Pain They've
Caused Me
My Tears
Aren't Slight

I Wish I May
I Wish I Might
Not Have
My Heart
Broken 2Nite

Emotionally wounded
Emotionally cocooned
My soul has turned charcoal black
Pain-filled tears stain my face blue
Life has little meaning
I wish your hateful words had little meaning, too.

I'm done!

I'm going into my closet
But not for what you suppose
I don't care what I wear
This isn't about clothes.

I stand alone in the closet
Thinking over what next to do
Debating if I want it over
And wonder if you ever, even knew?

You think I am a waste of life, huh?
You suggest I should kill myself, already?
What if I did as you asked?

You'd probably say I was being petty

Why do you want me gone?
What did I ever do to you?
Why do you attack me online?
Why do you insist on not telling everyone the truth?

I don't know who you are
You won't tell me your name
Yet, you claim that you know me,
Call me an emo, loser and lame

You're not very original
Though you think you are
Hiding behind your computer
Causing emotional scars

Gutless, coward!

I've got an idea
Why don't you take my place?
You can walk down the halls
Get shoved and spit in the face

Let me type vicious lies, spread a rumor or two
Hey, keyboard commentator
Come and step into my shoes.

Whatever! Jerk!

I want to be somebody else.
I no longer want to be me.
I'd gladly be anybody.
Anybody, other than me.

I trusted you with a secret
You blabbed it to the whole school
Now everyone knows about it
You broke the pinky swear rule
I hate you!
Why did you pretend to be my friend?

If I could talk about it, part of me knows I would feel better. Just
wish I knew how to start.

I don't know who I am anymore.

A bully's recipe for Pound Cake:

2 Punches to the stomach
2 Slaps across the face
2 Kicks to the shins, one each
1 shout of *"Dork!"*
1 shout of *"Loser!"*
1 shout of *"Slut!"*
5 Others to yell the same

Mix it all together.
I lost my appetite for life.

I wish I could tell my parents what's wrong. But, I can't. They wouldn't understand.

Depressed.
Tears.
Cast aside.
Incomplete.
Thrown out like trash.
Miserable.
Bruised.
Blue.
Bloody.
Frowning.
More tears.
Sad.
Lonely.
Done.

How are you doing?
Fine.

Are you lying?
Yes.

Why?
I don't know.

What's going on?
Nothing.

What's wrong?
Nothing.

Will you talk to me?
No.

Why not?
Why should I?

Because, I care.
No, you don't.
No one does.

A damn liar is what you are
Weekends were supposed to be fun
But, your hateful words took things too far

You called me a slut, a whore and a skank
My low self-esteem I now have you to thank

What you spoke was far from the truth
You knew nothing about me, so, where was your proof?

Being the new kid in town is never an easy road
You made sure the journey was bumpy for me
Ah, the vicious seeds you and your friends sowed

Running, running, running, your little lying mouths
The lies that spilled forth sent my entire reputation south

All I sought was acceptance, approval and love
But, you and your immature friends made certain each weekend
was full of spite and shoves

A damn liar is all you will ever be
I did not have clear eyes before,
Oh, but now, how I do see

No more tears will I shed
No more wishing I was dead
No more wishing death for you
No more forgiving will I do

So, call me what you want
Think what you will
Now and forever
Your hateful lies mean nil.

I wish you would like me.
I wish you took the time to get to know me.
I wish I could tell you how much you have hurt me.
But, my mouth stays shut.
I say nothing.
Why bother.
It's obvious you don't care.
You just want to hurt me.
Why, I have no clue.
Wish I could understand what I possibly did to you?
For now, though, I think I'm just about through.

Everyone has a story to tell
Most are a journey straight into hell
Mine is no different
I'm willing to bet
It's the same as yours
Full of endless regrets.

I feel worthless
I feel blue
I feel like crap
How about you?

Oh, wait, that's right
How dumb of me to forget
You're so perfect and cool
Not like me, a social reject.

Please turn my upside-down heart right side up.
*"How do I do this?"*, you ask.
Start giving me love.
Not repeated hate.

I am tired of being the exception to your social acceptance rule!

*"Get out!"*
*"Piss off!"*
*"No one wants you!"*
*"Pathetic reject!"*
Those nasty tunes of yours are blasted into my eardrums daily.

I wish the batteries that run your mouth would die.
I wish I could smash your verbal speakers.
I wish I could change your playlist.
I wish I could find the switch that turns you off.
I wish I could hear only silence.
While I continue wishing,
You, little bully, continue performing.

The world never sees the real me.
When facing my direction, it appears to be blinded by endless
hate and disappointment.

A black eye and a broken nose
A twist to the arm
It's how my day goes

Bruises, slaps and kicks
My head punched so badly
I now feel awfully sick

Overwhelmed by grief
A razorblade cut penetrates my skin
Blood seeps out
So, begins my relief.

Perfect little bitch
Do as I say
Not as I do
You have no clue
How much I despise you, too
You're mean
You're nasty
You don't care what you do
How I wish you could be weak like me
How I wish I could be strong like you.

I was dead on arrival
The first day of school

A loud-mouthed bully
Found out I wasn't cool

I'm like, *"But you don't even know me"*
And the bully's like, *"I don't even care"*
I got shoved into some lockers
My new shirt received a tear

Kids pointed, laughed and stared
Feeling completely humiliated,
I ran home to hide in my lair.

Hur-ray! Hur-ray! Step right up!
Guaranteed this isn't a hoax.
What is so fascinating to see, you ask?
Me - God's perfect little joke.

Welcome to the show.
It's certainly one you don't want to miss.
Watch as I get kicked, punched and shoved.
Looking away will be hard to resist.

Enter the big Ol' bully
Who doles me a hearty black eye.
Watch it turn purple, ebony and blue,
as I hold it like a wimp and cry.

*"Here comes the bearded lady"*, they shout,
as I walk from class to class.
Sometimes I am tripped in the halls
and I fall flat on my ass.

Other days, I'm thrust onto
a troller-coaster ride from hell.

Both hands raised high up in the air,
as I open my mouth and yell.

Living life under the big school tent,
I'm labeled a circus freak.
I don't exist to entertain and amaze you
But, I just thought I should finally speak.

Dear Bully,

I have a question I need to ask.
I promise it won't be a daunting task.
How did you know I was a loser before I did?

You're gonna miss me when I am gone. Right?

I give
You take
I love
You hate
I fail

You try
You laugh
I cry

Lost and not found
My self-esteem and confidence have disappeared
Maybe they're hiding underground
Constantly jeered at and ruthlessly smeared

I don't know where they are
Not sure if they ever existed
I do know I am scarred
I do know being bullied is twisted.

They're only words.
No, they're not!
They're verbal daggers
My soul you rip and shred

I am nothing.
A shell now.
An oxygen sucking loser.

Words don't hurt, huh?
You're right.
They destroy!

Your false projections
And ridiculous trajections
Have caused senseless rejections
Feelings of unnecessary subjections
I should have added some objections
Perhaps pushed for your ejection
Someone should have placed an interjection
Before my cries grew into introjections
I reside in complete dejection
Feelings of worthlessness are now repeated injections.

Someday, I will stand up to you.
Someday, I will not allow you to disrespect me anymore.
I wish someday was now.

I am a lonely girl.
I am a lonely boy.
Feeling like one of God's rejected, unwanted toys.

I don't feel loved.
I don't know what that is.
I only know hate.
I only know put downs.
I wish I knew what it felt like to hear someone say, *"I love you"*
instead of *"I hate you"* or *"I don't want you around"*.


I am so full of pain.
Why don't people like me?
What did I do?
Why won't anyone be my friend?
Why????

I'm nice and yet, I don't get treated nice.
What did I ever do?
What????
I'm so confused.

I feel so lost.

Why can't they see the real me?

I am,
a mistake,
a disgrace,
a screw-up,
a loser.
Who are you?
Bet I know.
Thankful you are not to me.

Making me weak
Such a clever technique
Never any shame
When calling me hurtful names

Picking on my size
Never caring to realize
How worthless you made me feel
The punches you threw, all too real.

My life feels like a blur
My pain is all too real
My head and heart concur
I wish no longer to feel.

# death by hanging

Death by hanging has become a common solution to ending pain because of bullying. Many online sources claim, death by hanging is fast and painless. They are lying. The odds of breaking your neck right away are highly unlikely. That only happens in TV and movies.

Death by hanging is extremely agonizing and unpleasant. You will suffer. Here are some possibilities of what could happen to you during a hanging:

You might see flashes of light. This is no '*cool rave' effect*, as some websites describe. You are dying. Do you get it? DYING!

You might hear ringing in your ears.

You will lose consciousness, but it might not happen right away.

You will feel your organs shutting down. Organ failure hurts - a lot.

Your arms and legs will flail wildly about. This is an involuntary action. You cannot stop it or control it.

Your face will contort worse than Katie's, from the movie *"The Ring"*. By the time it is over, you may not even look like you.

Due to the violent shakes and convulsions your body experiences while being deprived of oxygen, the ligature you used to hang yourself might break. If this happens, you will drop to the ground like a rock.

You may or may not be dead at this point. You might still be alive, paralyzed or in a vegetative state. The outcome varies based upon how long your brain has gone without oxygen.

Eventually, your last breath will escape from your body.

You will pee and/or crap yourself before it is all over.

If you are a male, you might get an erection.

Your heart might beat for an additional 20 minutes. When it finally stops, you are officially dead.

You have endured a horrible physically painful experience to relieve emotional pain brought about by a bully.

Would you seriously consider ending your life because of a bully? Would you really allow someone to have that much power and control over your life?

No words, actions, behavior, or thoughts by another towards you, are ever worth ending your life over. Your life is not worth their power-trip.

Seriously, suicide IS NOT the answer to whatever problems or issues you have going on in your life. Circumstances are always subject to change. Instead of being a memory, choose to stick around and make memories.

Life is a precious gift.

Death is final.

You have a lot to give and the only way to do that is to live. So, live!

# what is negative?

rumors

gossip

teasing

insults

threats

name calling

mean words

harassment

sadness...

facts

# there are 3 types of bullying

✓ meᵑTal

✓ physical

✓ emoTional

Most assume physical bullying to be the worst of the three. Wrong. Though bruises may heal, broken hearts do not always do the same.

The pain borne from cruel, hateful words by far outweighs a fist punch. Words can cause destruction, emotional damage and sometimes provoke devastating life decisions, especially when coupled with social isolation. This often happens during bullying because words that have been weaved into lies and rumors.

The taunting phrase, *'Sticks and Stones may break my bones, but words will never hurt me'* has been proven to be nothing short of a cute saying wrapped up in a big lie. Words do indeed hurt.

'Folk Phrases of Four Counties' by G.F. Northall published the infamous *'Sticks and Stones'* taunt in 1894. Other versions include:

*'Sticks and stones may break my bones, but words will never break me.'*
~ The Christian Recorder (1862).

*'Sticks and stones may break my bones, but names will never harm me.'*
~ Tappy's Chicks: and Other Links Between Nature and Human Nature by Mrs. George Cupples (1872).

*'Sticks and stones may break our bones, but words will break our hearts.'*
~ All I Really Need to Know I Learned in Kindergarten by
Robert Fulghum (1989).

*'Sticks and stones may break my bones, but names will never down you.'*
~ The Quiet One by The Who (1981).

*'Life and death are in the power of the tongue'* (Proverbs 18:21).
Therefore, speak life (positive words) over someone, including
yourself. Because to speak negatively over someone or yourself,
serves only to generate pain, sorrow and the destruction of the
spirit which lives inside each of us.

If you have been speaking ugly to someone or even to yourself,
ask yourself these questions:

"Why am I deliberately choosing to speak death, when I can
choose to speak life?"

"Why am I speaking bad about someone, when I can be
speaking good about someone, including myself?"

"Why am I sowing rotten seeds that will leave my field with no
crop, when I can sow healthy seeds that will have my field
overflowing with many crops?" *(In other words, why am I robbing
someone of joy, including myself, when I can be spreading joy?)*

# did you know?

### one:
Each year more than 160,000 students are absent from school due to bullying. Others are being removed from the system to get homeschooled.

### two:
Bullying will always exist.

### three:
How bullying situations are handled is changing. Stiffer laws and consequences for unacceptable bullying type behavior are currently being put into place to address this growing issue.

### four:
Many people believe that *"A child's brain is not fully developed until they reach maturity so therefore, they know not what they do."* Wrong. Kids are taught the difference between right and wrong early in life. Bullying someone is wrong.

### five:
When you think about it, bullying such as; spreading false rumors about someone is considered to be slander. Slander is a crime.

### six:
Newspapers from various states are reporting cases where bullies are being charged for their actions. The Department of Justice (DOJ) has invested close to $2 million dollars for *'youth courts'* where middle school and high school kids act as judge, jury, prosecutor and defense in cases of bullying. They have the discretion to administer the appropriate punishment for the charge.

## seven:

Today's bullying is very different than the bullying of yesteryear. Back in the day, when bullying became an issue, a kid was removed from one school and put into another and life was good again. Such is not the case anymore. This applies to homeschooling, too. The reason? Social media. The only way a child receives a break from the persistent badgering from their peers outside of school is to deliberately disengage from social media.

## eight:

Bullying is capable of *"jumping over the pond"*. Thanks to the internet, bullying continues no matter where you are residing on the planet. There are several documented cases of bullied kids who moved to a new country to start over, only to have their past bullying issues discovered and spread all over their new school via social media.

## nine:

Bullying *(especially cyber-bullying)* and intensified mental health issues either amplified or formed because of it can lead to suicide, especially for kids in their tweens and teens. The youngest case to date is that of a five-year-old.

## ten:

Suicide is the wrong solution to end the pain you feel from being bullied. There is nothing worth ending your life over. Nothing! Your life matters. You matter.

## eleven:

Did you know committing suicide due to bullying and intensified mental health issues either amplified or formed because of it, causes the following:

Devastated, heartbroken parents, who will struggle for the rest of their lives to try and understand why their child made such a harsh choice.

Siblings who will carry guilt for feeling they were not a better sister or brother.

Friends, who will think *'would have, could have, should have and if only'*.

Everyone left behind will wonder how they missed the tell-tale signs and experience what is known as, *"misplaced blame"*.

facts…

scoop

# social-bullying: would you miss me?

Would you miss me if I went away?
Would you pause for a moment?
Beg me not to die, not to decay?
Is there someone, anyone, willing to say,
*"Please, stay."*
Nothing but silence.
Apparently, not today.

Why are people more appreciated and adored in death rather than in life?

T-Shirts plastered with photographs of a loved one gone too soon.
Faces stained with tears.
The sharing of memories.
Precious, heartfelt words rolling off tongues.
Confusion.
Anger.
Endless questions.

Amazing how we tend to take people for granted, isn't it? Especially a bully who intentionally generates anti-social behavior to their victim from themselves and others. They never dreamed their relentless ridiculing and isolation tactics could result in something as tragic as their target committing suicide.

Bullying is not just punching, rumor spreading or calling someone mean names.

Sometimes, people are bullied with silence. They are purposefully ignored or deliberately excluded from events that include their peers. They endure vicious rumors spread about them and are sometimes humiliated in public for amusement by their bully.

Other times, they are briefly acknowledged as either a cruel trick or when someone needs to use them for something. Otherwise, they are made to feel useless and unwanted by anyone for anything.

Social rejection is one of the harshest forms of punishment one human being can do to another. The emotional wounds run deep and take years to heal, if ever.

Victims of social bullying are often labeled *"worthless"* until they are gone. Only then do these sweet souls become encapsulated in acceptance, love and held in high regard.

Odd how they were hated, ignored and mistreated while breathing. Yet, suddenly they are loved, cherished, and memorialized after death.

Why? True guilt for those who caused the person to make such a harsh decision due to bullying. And, survivors guilt by those who maybe abandoned the victim due to peer pressure or felt they should have expressed their care for the person more than they did.

Victims of social Bullying often suffer in silence. They keep their pain well hidden. Some are so good at hiding it, even Sherlock Holmes, Inspector Gadget and Dick Tracy combined would have no clue what was going on.

Unfortunately, it seems only after a bullying victim is gone do the puzzle pieces fall into place. The subtle hints they may have dropped all along like bread crumbs on a trail, now light up brighter than an atom bomb. But, by then, it is too late.

Instead of someone reaching out and asking, *"Hey, would you like to hang out sometime?"* a lonely soul hangs alone in their room. Their body swaying silently side to side.

The question, *"Why didn't anybody like me?"* echoing inside their head until that last breath escapes their body. Alone in life. Alone in death. But, it does not have to end up this way.

**never cause harm to yourself because of social bullying.**

Haters are always going to hate someone or something for some reason. They have a problem. And, that problem is not you. Nor, does it have anything to do with you. The sooner you can get this – the sooner you can move past it and get on with your life.

Stop wasting your precious time caring, worrying or trying to prove yourself to be worthy of someone's time and attention who basically treats you like crap. You owe them nothing.

Believe it or not, the world is full of good people. You just happen to have had the misfortune of crossing paths with a jerk and some of his/her friends. If anything, be thankful you're not them. That's one way to look at it.

Stand strong and love and accept yourself, even if right now you feel like nobody else feels the same way about you. Do it for you.

Believe it or not there are people in your life who love you and want you around. They just need to speak up and let you know. Try taking the focus off the bully. You might then realize people are letting you know they care in their own unique way.

If you see someone being socially bullied, try and step outside of your comfort zone. Talk to the person. Stop caring what others around you might think if you do. Be a friend. Say, *"Hi"* or *"We're having an event, like to come?"* Compliment them on their wardrobe or if they are creative say, *"I really loved the short story you wrote and read in class today."* You never know how much your kind gesture might mean to them. It literally could be a matter of life or death.

Being bullied sucks. Stop caring what the bully thinks of you. Start working on developing some self-confidence.

**to the bully:** If you are socially bullying someone, stop it. No one likes a jerk. You might think they do. But, they don't. Keep in mind, you reap what you sow. You could just as easily find yourself being bullied, instead of being the bully. Don't be quick to scoff. It could happen. Instead of tearing someone down, your time might be better spent working on your own issues.

*Being a bully is a lame lifestyle choice.*
*Stop being a jerk.*
*Start being a friend.*

# no angel am i

No angel am I
Heard sleeping around is a sin
Not ready to go to heaven
Won't dare let you boys win

My reputation got branded
Slut, whore, easy, bitch
The boys did call me by my name
Until I scratched their horny itch

How dare you boys spread rumors
How dare you boys scoff
My intentions weren't only
To get your worthless rocks off

I sought acceptance
I wanted love
I needed affection
Help from above

But, your hate fueled strife
Made me as popular as Hester Prynne
Slut shame comes with a price you know
Now, everyone knows where I've been

I got used, I got damaged
Lied to and mislead
A human mattress the boys called me
*"She'll sleep with anyone"*, they said

The viral cyber campaign launched
Left destruction that can't be erased
No matter which State I move to
The world forever knows my face

Inbox offers from strangers

They keep pouring in
Lay on your back or kneel
Delete and into the trash bin

I'm not a Heavenly Angel
Not literally anyway
Because someone reached out
Someone begged me to stay

No matter what I've done
I'll always be better than you
The angels have given me wings of flight
I now rise above the hateful things you do

I'm free from the shame
My future is looking bright
My life has again become mine
I'm still here, now bathed in sunlight.

SEEK     WANT     NEED
ACCEPTANCE * LOVE * AFFECTION

## slut shaming

Per *Webster's Dictionary*, Slut Shaming is: the action or fact of stigmatizing a woman for engaging in behavior judged to be promiscuous or sexually provocative.

Slut Shaming has gained attention because of stories about teenagers harming themselves or committing suicide because of it, are being written in local newspapers and picked up by the national media.

People slut shamed by a bully are called, *'whore, slut, skank, tramp, bitch, ho, tease, loose, easy and nympho'*. A person being slut shamed has rumors spread about them. They also endure the exposure of any nude or semi-nude pictures or video of themselves being shared via text and/or cyberspace without their permission.

No one should ever be made to feel bad about themselves because of the number of sexual partners they have had, the nude or semi-nude pictures they sexted to someone or risqué video they may have willingly taken themselves or video unknowingly taken of them by someone else.

Is it wise to take nude or semi-nude pictures of yourself and then send them to your current love interest because they asked you to do so or because you felt like doing it? No. It is not a wise thing to do. It is also not wise to make risqué videos of yourself either.

Did you know most states consider nude and semi-nude material of someone under the age of eighteen to be child pornography? This applies to print as well as video.

Did you also know, if you are caught having possession of nude or semi-nude material (photos/video) of someone under the age of eighteen, you could be prosecuted and have your name put on a sexual predator list?

Did you know sending nude or semi-nude material (photos/video) of yourself to someone, whether requested or not, will not make them love you or serve to maintain their interest in you if they are pulling away?
Do you seriously want to risk having nude or semi-nude material (photos/video) of you floating around in cyberspace?

Taking such a drastic, demeaning approach will only gain you the wrong type of attention. Do it, and you flush your self-respect right down the toilet. Is having that person's attention worth giving up your self-respect?

Keep in mind, most relationships sour. I know that is hard to imagine being young and in love. But feelings do change. People fall out of love, just as quickly and easily as they fell in love.

When a relationship ends, sometimes one or both parties can be vengeful and cruel. Therefore, it is not a smart idea to record or snap nude or semi-nude material (photos/video) of you and/or your partner performing any type of sexual behavior. Because it can and most likely will be used against you.

The phrase, *"It will be for our eyes only"* is a LIE! Do not fall for it. Naughty stuff always has a way of finding a slut shaming audience. Keep that in mind if your partner says, *"Let's make a sex tape or send me some nude photos of you."*

Think before you act.
Think about the outcome.
Think about your ability to handle the consequences.
Think about your future.

We all do reckless stuff when we are young. No one is exempt from that rite of passage. However, regardless of the number of people someone sleeps with or the fact they may have sexted pictures or recorded risqué videos, no one should be singled out and humiliated for it. Especially to the point of choosing to end their life.

Let's not forget, it takes two to tango. So, if one person in the same scenario is going to be humiliated and slut shamed, perhaps the other participant(s) should step on up and claim their shame tag(s), too. If not, then they need to rethink their actions and behavior before being so quick to label someone a 'Hester Prynne'.

Unfortunately, because of social media, your wild past might linger. But, fear not. You have the power to overcome it, even if you cannot erase it. You can choose to move onward with your held high and not skulk.

Know this. It is easier than you think to be taken advantage of. The use of alcohol or drugs, smooth talkers who can be very persuasive, and your own burning desire to be popular and socially accepted, can all play a role in making not so wise choices. These are reasons, not excuses. And certainly not something you should feel ashamed of or be condemned for having done. Part of life is learning. We learn mostly from mistakes.

Remember, we all do things we regret. Add youth, inexperience, raging hormones and misguidance to the mix and you have a recipe for poor choices. Life is about improving, growing and developing ourselves into the person we want to be. The person we are destined to be.

What can drive a person to participate in promiscuous behavior boils down to three simple things; they seek acceptance, they want love and they need affection. Just so happens, they go about it the wrong way.

Did you know what is deemed 'slut shaming behavior' is not always about the act of sex itself? It is also about trying to fill a void from within. Something inside of the person acting out is broken.

The healing process of promiscuous behavior begins by first, figuring out the issue. The true root cause of why you are choosing to behave this way. Second, the issue, once figured out, needs to be addressed and sorted. As you heal, your self-respect will return, and you will start feeling good about yourself again. Despite what you may have done in the past.

My heart breaks each time I read another story about someone who chose to harm themselves or end their life because of slut shaming.

Being slut shamed hurts.
You think your life is over.
You think your life is ruined.
You think you will never be happy again.
You feel powerless because the pictures and/or video are out there in cyberspace and you cannot take any of it back.
You hate that everyone has seen the photos and/or video.

You feel embarrassed.
You feel humiliated.
You feel tired.
You hate yourself.
You hate everyone.
You are sick of being put down and made to feel bad about
yourself.
You want it to stop.
You feel dirty.

**question:** *"How can I make it stop and go away?"*

**answer:** Develop an *"I don't give a crap"* attitude. I realize this is
an easier said than done scenario. But, try. You have nothing to
lose. And, quite honestly, it cannot get any worse than it is right
now.

You have the power within you to rise above any mistake(s)
made.
You have the power to conquer a bully.
You have the power to make changes for YOU.

Did you know if a bully fails to get a reaction out of you they
eventually grow bored and move on? It might take some time,
but they will move on. Just do your best to hang in there until
they do. Do not give up. Do not let them win.

Keep your focus on what you can do about the situation at hand.
Not what you cannot do about it. That is where the frustration
lies. Feelings of powerlessness. Again, you are not powerless.
You have just been made to feel that way. So, why continue
allowing a bully to have that control over you?

**please note:** If you feel you have been sexually violated in any
way, seek legal action immediately. Talk to your parents, a school
counselor and the police.

If you simply made a bad judgement call, let it go. You cannot
take it back. You cannot erase it. It does no good to churn your

guts up about it. It is done. You can choose to change in your reaction or keep repeating the same depressing cycle. Again, your choice.

The bully wants you upset. Wants you hurt. Stop letting the bully have his/her way. Why give them that power over your life?

We have established the battle between you and your bully is over your damaged reputation. Control is what a bully wants. Now, is your time to take the control back.

When a bully slut shames you, you feel defeated. You have every right to feel this way because your reputation is being sullied. I am not saying you do not. But, if you hold your head high and display an *"I don't give a crap"* attitude, the bully is going to be left feeling confused. Your emotions are no longer being controlled by their cruel behavior. You are no longer reacting. You have taken the control back. You have the power.

No matter what life may throw at you, and believe me, it will throw some curve balls, always try and do your best to remain confident when handling the situation.

Be strong.
Be true to yourself.
Believe in yourself.
Love yourself no matter what.
We all wear battle scars in one form or another.
Nobody is perfect. NOBODY. Mistakes happen, and that is okay. It is how we learn, grow and move on.

# rejected

*"Emo!"*
*"Freak!"*
*"Weirdo!"*
*"Reject!"*
*"Nobody likes you!"*
*"Nobody wants you!"*
*"You don't belong!"*
*"Why are you still here?"*

The all too familiar phrases repeatedly shouted out by a bully and his cohorts, while hurling empty soda cans and catapulting spit balls at a kid dressed in all black.

The kid, a sensitive, kind soul, quickly finds solace, hiding in the darkness behind a set of stairs, before the bullies can witness a steady stream of painful tears, certain to wash away the black eye make-up, placed heavily underneath his blue eyes. The kid sits down, pulls out his private journal and scribbles:

> *While I despise your cruel objections*
> *And wish to initiate identical subjections*
> *For you to feel your own hate-fueled injections*
> *My thoughts now dwell on various life ejections*

> *Live. Die. Live. Die. Live. Die. Live. Die. Live. Die.*

> *Your relentless cruelty*
> *has made this choice an obsession.*
> *Which one I'll choose matters not*
> *because according to you*
> *My existence is that of a faceless reflection.*

To survive in life, human beings require three basic things. Food, shelter and love. Without food, we starve. Without shelter we perish in the weather. Without love we feel rejected and alone. According to the *Bible*, *"It is not good that Man should be alone"* *(Genesis 2:18)*. It is almost impossible not to know what the unbearable pain of rejection and isolation from our peers feels like, if that statement were not true.

The emotion of loneliness we, as human beings, feel from time to time, lends merit to its verification. Though we may choose to be alone sometimes for assorted reasons, in the end, there is a significant difference between choosing to be alone and forced into loneliness.

Human beings are social creatures by nature. But, to get love, we must first learn how to give love. First to ourselves. Then, to others.

Let's look at the word reject from which the word rejection stems. According to *Webster's Dictionary*, the word 'reject' means; to refuse to accept, consider, submit to, take for some purpose, or use.

Rejection is one of the worst behaviors one human being can exhibit towards another. In college, Sociology 101, teaches the importance of belonging and being accepted within our species. Every human being craves it. No matter what their race, sex, sexual orientation, economic or social standing is.

Connecting with other human beings helps generate feelings of inclusion and belonging in the world. Again, it goes back to how human beings are wired. To not be alone.

People tend to believe if they do not fit in with a certain group or fail to meet a level of what society deems *"socially acceptable"*, there must be something wrong with them. Examples being; they are not popular in school, are not earning enough money, are not married, they do not have kids, etc.

It is a downright tragedy how many good people are made to feel bad about themselves over societal expectations they may or may not have any control over.

When a person of any age faces social rejection, the fall-out can be very detrimental. Some never fully recover from this type of deliberate social isolation. They carry the painful scars for the rest of their lives.

Some are unable to cope with social rejection and end their suffering via suicide. Sad. Nothing or anyone or their opinion of you for that matter, is ever worth ending your life over.

People deemed *'social rejects'* by society, tend to become fixated upon what they feel is wrong with them to land them in that category. They do this to try and justify the rejection and/or make changes for the sole purpose of gaining social acceptance. If you are being treated like a *'social reject'*, ask yourself these questions:

*"Are there any changes necessary to make?"*

*"Am I basing the changes I want to make on a person's opinion about me?"*

*"Or, am I choosing to make changes based on my own self opinion without being influenced?"*

*'Social rejects'* pick apart their hair *(the color, the style, the length or the texture)*, their make-up *(too heavy, too dark)*, their clothes, their body shape, their weight, their height, their eye color, their nose formation, how their lips look *(too skinny, too plump)*. Even the sound of their own voice can become an issue. Some go so far as to despise their birth name, and have it changed.

The list of *"things I hate about myself"* can run into infinity if not reigned in. It is very heartbreaking to watch someone tear themselves apart simply because they were made to feel socially unacceptable. A bully. Amazing how one person can come into another person's life like a wrecking ball and leave so much destruction.

*"Okay. So, you spouted off all this advice. But, how do I become socially acceptable?" you ask.*

For starters, stop criticizing yourself. Are you perfect? No. Do you deserve to be treated like a social outcast because of any imperfections? Never.

Tune out anything negative anyone says about you. Accepting their negative opinion of you is wrong thinking on your part. Whether you realize it or not, up until now you have been agreeing with their negative opinion of you enough to tear yourself down and question everything about yourself. Stop. You don't deserve it.

We all have faults. We all mess up. But, that is no reason to be singled out and treated like a social misfit just because one person gets the ball rolling based on their own judgmental opinion. Continue absorbing the negative garbage being said about you and it will destroy you.

Burn this into your thoughts so that it never leaves: *"There is no one else on the planet like you. You are not a perfect person, but you are not a mistake either."*

Instead of allowing another to tear you down, lift yourself up by embracing who you truly are. Love yourself. Accept yourself. Your opinion of yourself is what matters. Not a bully's. Or anyone else's.

If there is something about yourself you are not pleased with, change it. But, do it for yourself. Not because you are trying to gain social acceptance.

Those worthy of your time and love will love you back, faults and all. Those who choose to love you only without faults are shallow, narrow-minded people who are not worthy of your time, friendship or love. Forget them. Move on.

Listen, before you can expect anyone to love or accept you, you must first learn to love and accept yourself. Cliché, yes. But it is the truth.

# shut the f-up!

Shut the F-Up
I don't care what you say
Shut the F-Up
Leave me alone, just go away

You pretend to be my friend
You pretend to care
Shut the F-Up
Erase that shocked stare

Shut the F-Up
I'm onto your lies
I know exactly who you turned into
your little bully spies

Shut the F-up
You'll not hurt me any longer
Shut the F-up
That's right, I'm getting stronger

Shut the F-Up
For it's my turn to speak
I said Shut the F-Up
You're the one who is pathetic
The one who is weak

Shut the F-Up
I'm not heartless like you
Shut the F-Up
I've spoken my peace
We're officially through

Shut the F-Up
I refuse to end my life
Shut the F-Up
I'm unconsumed with strife

Shut the F-up
I'm a winner and life chooser
Shut the F-Up
You sorry, little, bully loser.

# i had no idea

*Dear Mom,*
*Dear Dad,*
*I need to tell you*
*I'm feeling sad*

*You need to listen*
*For I need to speak*
*Things suck at school*
*My outlook on life has turned bleak*

*I'm being bullied, picked on, and teased*
*No matter what I try, my enemies are never pleased*
*I need your help for the bullying to end*
*I tried to handle it, but, by myself, I can no longer defend*

*The hatred, the lies, the rumors, the pain*
*At school or at home, it all feels the same*
*I need your strength, guidance, support and love*
*No judgements, anger, disappointments or shoves*

*Please be my parents*
*Don't be my friends*
*Help me, please, help me*
*Bring this bullying to an end*

*I love you.*

Time and again the phrase, *"I had no idea"* is uttered by the parents of children who committed suicide because of being bullied or because their child was dealing with a mental health issue that became amplified or formed due to bullying.

They had no idea their child was being bullied. They had no idea their child was struggling with mental health issues. They had no idea their child was in so much pain. They had no idea their child was contemplating committing suicide. Sadly, they had no idea.

Because our society has become so busy and quite frankly, self-absorbed, it is easy to overlook those silent cries for help uttered by hurting children. If they ever even cry out for help at all. It is not uncommon for many to suffer in silence.

The world has evolved into a society of *"Go! Go! Go!"* We go to work. We go to school. We go to practice. We go to social events. We keep going until we think we cannot. And then, we go again. We have too or else we get left-behind. There is no rest for the weary. Nor, time for the hurting. This is what we have been led to believe. Guess what? It is all a lie. A lie that is costing us, mentally, physically and emotionally.

We no longer stop and smell the roses. Let alone water them. Our lives have tilted so far out of balance, along with our priorities.

Gone are the days of sit down meals and open discussions at the family table. Life now revolves around social media. There is no more talking. Only staring down at our individual phones, fully engaged in utter rubbish. Plenty of parents are just as guilty as their kids when it comes to this type of behavior.

This desensitizing behavior needs to stop. Now. Parents, put your phone down. Have your kid(s) put their phone down. Talk to one another. Really, talk. Openly. Frankly. Honestly. No judgements.

Listening to your kid smack their lips on fast food while rambling on about an after-school activity while sitting in the backseat as you drive them to the next event, does not qualify as an in-depth conversation with your child.

*"I'm too busy"* is no excuse. You made time to create your child. Now make time to be there for your child. No exceptions. It is important as a parent that you and your child look each other in the eye and have undivided attention. No distractions. Find out what is going on in your child's life. And, if you are the child – talk to your parents. Or a trusted adult at least. Stop holding in your feelings. You do not have to spend your life in pain.

Kids can be very good at hiding emotional pain. You might fire back with, *"I know my kid!"* Are you sure about that?

When was the last time you sat down with your child and had a real heart-to-heart conversation about things besides homework or the last sports game they played?

I can remember as a kid growing up, my family would sit down at the dinner table and talk about our day. My parents always took the time to talk to us kids no matter what was going on in their lives.

I can remember approaching my Dad in his workshop many times over the years and he would always stop what he was doing, pull out a stool and say, *"Have a seat, kid. Tell me what's going on."*

Because we had a bond, which both of my parents took the time to nurture, as kids, we felt comfortable enough to talk to our parents about anything and everything.

My parents were never nosy. They were in tune with their kids. They always knew when something was wrong. Even if they had to sometimes drag it out of us.

Because our parents had laid out that foundation of communication and trust when we were young, it helped us reach out to them when we were being bullied and when I especially felt overwhelmed and suicidal because of bullying.

A lot of parents make the mistake of trying to become their child's friend rather than being an actual parent. I am not saying that you cannot or should not be friends with your child. I think you should, once your child becomes an adult. But right now, they need guidance, love and protection. From you. The parent. Not their friend acting as if they are their parent when necessary.

I know it is natural for teens to rebel against their parent, but I also know teens can and will come to their parent, if they know their parent will be there with a hand stretched forth to help lift them up when they are down.

As a parent, please keep in mind that bullying can make a child feel very helpless, isolated, alone and like no one cares or understands what they are feeling or going through.

Often, a child will keep the bullying they are enduring to themselves out of fear of appearing weak, fear of retaliation from the kid who is bullying them, fear of rejection by their peers, fear their parent or another adult may judge them or punish them for being weak.

Please take the time to talk to your kid. Take the time and make the time to really get to know your kid.

Be a parent, not a friend. Your child needs you.

## signs a child is being bullied

Unexplainable injuries
Lost or destroyed clothing/ books/electronics/jewelry
Feeling sick or faking illness
Changes in habits
Skipping meals or binge eating
Frequent nightmares
Difficulty sleeping
Not wanting to go to school
Declining grades
A loss of interest in schoolwork
Avoiding social activities
A sudden loss of friends
Decreased self-esteem or feelings of helplessness
Self-destructive behavior like running away from home,
harming themselves or talking about suicide

## signs a child is bullying others

Getting into physical or verbal fights
Have friends who bully others
Shows signs of increasingly aggressive behavior
Frequent visits to detention or the principal's office
New belongings or money that can't be explained
Blames others for their problems
Refuses to accept responsibility for their actions
Are competitive
Excessive worrying about reputation/popularity.

# flip the bully script

Here is some information to help change a bullying situation around.

*Put negative feelings aside and stop making them the center of your life.*

You have every right to feel those negative emotions based on how terrible you have been treated, but the key, which is always over-looked is: YOU ARE IN CONTROL. Despite how it all looks, you are in control of your life and how you feel and react to situations.

The more you focus on the negative, the bigger and more out of balance feelings and thoughts can become.

*You are a strong person.*

Go look at yourself in the mirror. Really look. There is no one else on the planet like you. You are very special.
You are unique. God has a good plan and purpose for you in life. Say, *"I'm Okay"* - every day, several times a day, if necessary until it sinks into your heart and you believe it. The more you believe in something, the truer it becomes. How do you think the bully wore you down? Because you believed what they spouted off about you.

Replace the negative names with positive ones such as; smart, beautiful, handsome and a winner. Try and see yourself in a positive light instead of dogging yourself all the time. Eventually, others will begin seeing you in a positive light, too. It takes time, so be patient.

*Take a time-out.*

Stay off the internet for one week or even a month. Shut down your social media accounts. Once you remove the bully's ability to strike out at you online, you have taken the power back.

Let them type what they want. If that is how they choose to waste their time, let them do it. You do not have to waste your time reading their garbage. It's a choice.

*Texting.*

Ignore text messages from anyone other than your family or people you know are your friends. Delete any text message that comes in a bully. Do not read it. Delete it. The purpose of a text from a bully is to hurt you. So, do not give the bully the power.

If you are building a case against a bully, do not delete the messages. But, do not read them either. Give your phone to your Mom or Dad so they can read the messages from the bully and save them for law enforcement. It is okay to let your parents protect you.

*You will never please everyone.*

It is impossible. So, stop trying.

*Get a "So what" attitude.*

So, what, if there are pictures of you out there. You can't take them back. Learn from it. Do not do it again. Move on.

And please stop being hard on yourself if you sexted someone who then shared your private photos. You are not the first person to make this mistake. Unfortunately, you won't be the last one, either. Everything is going to be okay. It will take time for things to simmer down. But they will.

*Do not give up on yourself.*

Believe you can survive being bullied and you will.

If you act like you don't care on the surface, *(even though inside you do care)*, the bully is robbed of the thrill they are seeking by causing you pain. Once a bully realizes they cannot get a reaction out of you, the game is over for them. You win. They lose and move on.

*Ignore the rumors spread about you.*

Never allow anyone to make you feel pressured into proving or defending who you are. Let them say what they want about you. So, what. You never have to prove anything to anyone about yourself to win approval.

*Ignore the bully while at school.*

This might not be possible all the time. But, try your best. Nothing upsets a bully more than to have their power taken away. You accomplish this task by simply ignoring anything they say to you.

*What if a bully is beating on you?*

If you have a bully who hits you, make sure you are never alone. You should also tell your teacher and your parents if you are being physically attacked. No one deserves to be hit.

Telling someone you are being bullied does not make you a tattletale. You were not put on this earth to be someone's punching bag. That is called ABUSE. Abuse of any kind is never okay. Tell an adult if you are being abused by anyone, please.

*Talk to a trusted adult about being bullied.*

Talking to an adult about being bullied is wise because believe it or not, they may have been bullied too and have good advice to share.

Again, you are not a tattletale. You are seeking a reasonable solution to a problem. There is no shame in getting help for a problem. And being bullied is a problem.

*Tell an adult if you are feeling suicidal or having bad thoughts about yourself.*

This applies whether you are being bullied or not. There is nothing wrong with getting help. There is nothing wrong with seeking out advice. It does not make you weak. It makes you brave.

Please do not keep those bad feelings to yourself. The longer you hold bad feelings in, the worse they become.
So, talk to a responsible adult about them NOW!

*Take the focus off yourself.*

You think your life is bad? I can guarantee you, someone out there has it worse than you and would give anything to be in your shoes. For real. Everyone thinks their issues are MAJOR. To most, they are. And some may very well be. But, if you were to take a room full of people and stack their issues up against yours, you might be surprised at how different your situation looks to you now. Maybe you might realize that it is not as bleak and hopeless as you thought. Stay focused on the positive things. Let go of the negative. You are in control of your life, your destiny.

*In the end.*

Everyone makes mistakes. Mistakes are learning experiences on what not to do again. They are not a means to continually punish ourselves, nor allow anyone else to punish us for them, either.

Things happen in life, whether good or bad. They do not define who you are as a person. Please remember it was/is one moment in your life. Not your entire life.

You have a long life to live. Don't quit now. Give yourself a chance. I think you're worth it. You should, too.

## put the right foot forward

*Right foot. Not Left*
*I've made my choice*
*Hateful words matter not*
*Now hear my strong voice.*

We have choices every morning we wake up. For example, we can choose to get out of bed in a good mood or a bad mood. The circumstances matter not. It is how we choose to handle the things in our life, no matter how pleasant or unpleasant they might be.

The same decision making can also be applied when hearing rumors spoken about yourself or other people. You can choose to believe the rumors or not.

You can also choose to believe positive things about yourself such as: amazing, creative, happy, beautiful, strong, and loving.

346

Or, you can choose to focus on the negative things from a bully, such as: loser, dumb, ugly, dork and slut.

You always have the power to choose which path you want to walk. You never have to tolerate negativity in your life unless YOU decide to do so. It is your choice.

One way to look at is like this. Just because the mailman brings you a package, does not mean you have to accept what is inside the box.

Make the decision today that from now on you are going to believe only good things about yourself and no longer focus on negative energy from a bully.

What you think of yourself is so important. More than you may realize. You need to stop caring what a bully thinks about you. You do not need their approval to be acceptable in this world. You are acceptable. Here. Now. Just as you are. You have value, a purpose, a plan. Never allow anyone tell you otherwise. If they should, know they are lying.

Here are some questions to consider that might help skew any negative perspective you may have of yourself due to someone's unfortunate opinion of you.

*"Who put a bully in charge of deciding you were not socially acceptable?"* The answer will surprise you.

You did.

*"But how?"* You ask.

The moment you chose to believe their negativity about yourself. Fear not though. The good news is you can turn it around.

*"How?"*

By choosing to focus on the positive things in your life. Even if it is only one minor thing. It still counts. And, by blocking the bully; mentally and emotionally.

*"How do I accomplish this?"*

You just decide to do it and follow through. It might not be easy at first. Mind of matter never is. But, with practice and dedication, it will become a new and improved way of thinking which will serve to benefit you in the long run.

You can defeat your bully and neigh Sayers. Maybe you never realized it until now or maybe you felt like you were not strong enough. But you now know you have strength, power and control over your life.

A bully cannot have power over you unless you allow it. They only want the power because they are nothing more than insecure people trying to appear powerful. Once you recognize this, their power is stripped away.

You must decide - right here -right now:

*" Do I want to take the control and power back in my life?"*

Every day is full of choices. Which foot do you want to choose to lead with, starting now?

I have no doubt you will make the RIGHT choice.

# quick chat for girls

Maintain self-respect in all areas of your life. Never allow anyone to pressure you into doing anything you feel uncomfortable doing. Especially in the hopes of gaining their approval. For example: doing drugs, drinking, having sex or sexting.

If you have been having sex, simply in the hopes of winning someone over - STOP. You will not win. That is not the way. If someone truly cares about you and really loves you, they will treat you with respect, acknowledge any boundaries you set in place, and never pressure you into going against your morals and values.

If someone cannot treat you with the respect you rightly deserve, you do not need them in your life. Promptly show them the door. And never look back.

In the end, sleeping around to gain popularity, social approval or what you believe to be love, will you get nothing but a bad reputation and a broken heart. Ask yourself if it is worth the sacrifices you must make.

You will not be popular in the way you think.
You will gain a negative reputation.
You will most likely get slut-shamed.
You will not feel good about yourself on the inside.
You will not win over *"Prince Charming"* or his friends.
Sometimes sacrifices are worth making. This, however, is not one of those times.

Do not do it.

And, if you have been doing it, stop. Right now.
It is never too late to make a change.

As a female, but more importantly a human being, you never deserve to be used, mislead or *'Slut-Shamed'* no matter what you have done.

The right person will come into your life and treat you like a queen, a lady, when the time is right. It is better to hold out, then to hold on to something that is no good for you. The right person will not treat you like a booty call. If a person treats you this way, dump them. They are no good for you.

Did you know loose behavior is likely the result of misplaced feelings, not because someone is *'easy'*?

Believe it or not, you might be seeking acceptance, wanting love, needing affection or trying to fill an empty void inside of yourself. Or you might be reacting to some type of trauma you are either consciously aware of happened to you or something that was done to you that you cannot recall. You just know something is not quite right down inside. Recognizing there might be an issue is the first step towards getting it sorted and making changes in your life for the better. Do not lose hope. There is always hope in every situation.

Never compromise your morals or values for anyone. Sacrificing your self-worth is not worth it. Value yourself and the right guy will value you in return. Be a virtuous woman. You are a precious jewel worthy of special treatment. Never settle for anything but the best treatment.

*"When will I know it is the right person?"*

*"You'll just know."*

Watch for the frogs on the journey to meeting your Prince.

# quick chat for guys

Being a tough guy has its time and place. Acting like a bully is not one of them. Be considerate of other people's feelings. Treat people with respect, the way you would want to be treated. Why choose to do wrong when you can choose to do right?

When it comes to the ladies, remember they are someone's sister, daughter and mother, should you become tempted to 'slut-shame' or disrespect them in anyway.

One day you might have a daughter. Would you want your daughter to be disrespected and mistreated by someone? The answer is, *"No!"*

Never be afraid to open-up to someone if something is eating away at you. Share what is going on inside. Unburden yourself from that weight. There is no need to carry it around.

In society, men are taught to hide their feelings. This is wrong teaching. It is okay for a man to feel and express his emotions. It is okay for a man to cry. Crying can be healing. This does not make the man weak or any less of a man for that matter.

If you are ever feeling confused about things in your life or how to handle a situation, please do not be afraid to open-up and talk to a trusted adult about it. Let it out. Do not hold it in.

Avoid being concerned with how others might see you. A real man stands proud and own who he is. He does not care what others think. A real man deals with situations. A real man does not run like a coward. A real man never cares others might think about him. A real man has self- respect and shows respect to others.

You have one life to live. Live it the way you see fit. But, keep in mind to also live it in a way that does not deliberately cause harm or pain to others.

# quick chat for both

Ignore the haters.
Plan your future. *(Yes, you have one.)*
Stay focused on school.
Ignore the negativity.
Do not be led by confusion.
Nor distracted by scattered thoughts and emotions.
Keep your attention centered on your goals.
What goals?
Graduating. Then college. Then a career. Etc....

Yes, school might be a drag because of bullying and other teen/life issues. There are also break-ups and failed grades. No shame in either. It is a part of learning and developing into the person we want to be.

Try developing a better attitude. You have a future to plan for. Whether you realize it or not, school is only a temporary stop. It is not the whole journey. Even though it might feel like it right now.

Where do you see yourself a year from now?
Where would you like to be a year from now?
How are you going to make it happen?

Where do you see yourself five years from now?
Where would you like to be five years from now?
How are you going to make it happen?

Where would you like to go to college?
What grades do you need to make to get accepted into the college of your dreams?

How do you plan to make your dreams come true?

Don't feel overwhelmed. Planning for a future is exciting. It gives purpose. Something to look forward to working towards, whether you get there or not. Or, something better comes into our lives along the way. It does not matter if you fail. What matters the most – you try.

If time permits and you can manage to keep up your grades, consider getting a part-time job doing something you enjoy. You can use the money earned to buy a car or put it towards college expenses. Having a job and saving money for something is a great self-esteem booster. It feels good to earn things in life. Not have them handed to you.

Despite the negative parts of being a teenager in high school that feel like your whole life, try and get some enjoyment out of those youthful years. They can be some of the best times of your life if you so choose. They only happen once. So, make the most of them.

Do not worry about racking up random hook-ups, getting married or having a baby right now. Save those moments for when you are more mature and settled. This is your time. It is okay to be a little selfish and focus on yourself during this time.

Keep your eye on your goals. Get something positive going for yourself first before you share it with someone else. Do not be afraid to pursue that career you want or eventually buy/rent a place of your own *(when you are old enough to legally move out)*. Go for it.

Take this valuable time to get to know yourself during these *'growing years'*. Stop worrying about trying to be something you are never going to be no matter how hard you try. Perfect. Being perfect is an unrealistic goal. To avoid this trap set by your bully, you must learn to accept yourself, flaws and all. And realize, everyone has flaws. EVERYONE.

Love yourself. And, always be yourself no matter what.

Never change who you are to please someone else. Stand by your boundaries. Never settle for anything less.

You are special. You are you. There is no one else like you on the planet. Hold your head up high and be proud of who you are. Of who you are evolving to be.

Make your mark in the world. But, check any ego issues at the door. Being proud does not mean acting like a diva or a jerk.

There is an old Latin quote which goes, *"Illegitimi non carborundum"* which means, *"Don't let the bastards grind you down."*

*You can make it.*
*You will make it.*
*You are making it.*
*I am proud of you.*
*You should be proud of you, too.*

# which secrets to keep
# which secrets to share

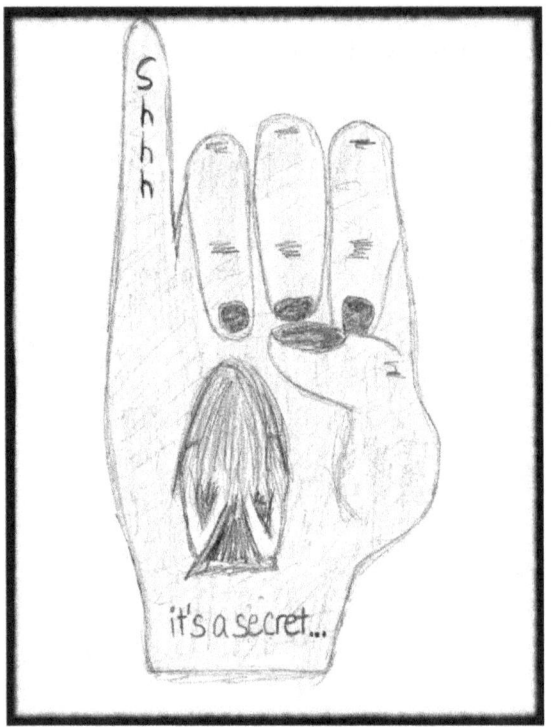

Friends tell each other secrets all the time.
Who their crush is.
What they think of their parents.
What they dream about.
A pinky-swear. A tick-a-lock. And the secret remains between them forever.

But sometimes a friend might tell a secret that should be shared with a trusted adult and not be kept a secret.
Why? Because certain secrets can literally be a matter of life or death.

**these are secrets to share with a trusted adult:**
*if someone is talking about killing themselves.

*if someone is talking about cutting themselves.
*if someone is talking about feeling depressed.
*if someone is talking about crying all the time.
*if someone is talking about quitting/giving up on stuff.
*if someone is talking about hurting others.

The right thing to do if you know of someone who is talking about hurting themselves is to tell a trusted adult about it. You are not a snitch if you tell. You are a lifesaver. You are brave. You are a hero. You are a friend.

Do not worry if you lose your friendship with the person whose secret you shared. Even if it might seem like the end of the world to you at the time. Better to lose the friendship for a while and save their life than to sit back and do nothing. Hopefully with time and treatment, they will see what a loyal, caring friend you truly are.

A person who goes the extra mile for another is a rare find. A treasure. You are very blessed if you have a friend like that in your life. Someone who 'has your back'.
Words may hurt. But, they can also save a life. Do not be afraid to speak up. Be a friend. Tell if you know.

## words do hurt

We have all heard the saying, *"Sticks and Stones may break my bones, but words will never hurt me"*.

I suppose that depends on who is saying the words, what words are being said and why they are being said. Some will argue the classic saying holds true. Others will strongly disagree and state, *"Words most definitely hurt and can cause lifelong damage to a person."*

From birth, until death, people will be speaking into our lives. Some will speak positive. Some will speak negative. And some, will fall under the category of constructive criticism. Those people have intentions of helping one to become the best they can be, especially when that person fails to see potential within themselves.

It is only natural we revel in joy with positive words. Positive means acceptance and approval. But, when the words spoken to us are negative, rejection and hurt feelings surface.

We either consciously or unconsciously, seek acceptance and approval from family members, friends, co-workers, a crush and even a stranger we pass along the way.

Society has falsely taught us to automatically accept and value other peoples' opinions of us over our own personal feelings about ourselves. No questioning why. No exceptions to how. It is wrong thinking and very destructive to our self-esteem.

What other people think of us matters so much it can affect our mood and how we think and feel about ourselves 24/7. What an unnecessary stress and burden to carry.

When a person's opinion of you comes to a point where you turn on yourself, that is a red flag. A warning to stop and reevaluate that person and their purpose in your life. It is also a time for you to reevaluate your own thinking and to discover why you are allowing one person to have so much control over your life to the point where you are becoming your own worst enemy.

*"How do I change the way I have been thinking about myself?"* you ask. Sociology classes teach us that people need people. The *Holy Bible* even states it in *Genesis 2:18, "It is not good for man to be alone."* Before we were born, we were loaded with expectations: to walk, to talk, to go to school, have friends, to graduate, go to college, have a career, get married, have a family, retire, become a grandparent and finally live out our golden years playing checkers and doing prune juice shots at a nursing home until our time comes to sprout wings and hold a harp.

Should we fail to participate in those areas of false expectations, we are doomed to feel like a failure and an outcast. Again, this is wrong thinking and very destructive to our self-esteem.

Because of the ingrained need for approval and acceptance from others, it can be incredibly damaging to be bullied and socially isolated. Receiving this type of harsh treatment goes against everything we were taught.

Animals, insects, and humans survive within a *"pecking order".* Someone is the leader. Someone is always fighting to take their place. This natural order of things does not mean bullying is an acceptable behavior in which to achieve said coveted position. There is a clear difference between being a strong leader and being a bully.

A leader should be respected, not feared. A leader should never bully.

A bully is not respected and is feared. A bully is not a true leader. A bully does not lead. They control another by breaking them down through mental, emotional and physical duress. Bullying is about humiliation and submission. Not leadership.

If you are following a bully, now might be an appropriate time to reevaluate why you are doing so and to stop.

If you have been allowing another person's opinion of you to override your own opinion of yourself, now might be an appropriate time to stop and reevaluate why you are allowing it to happen.

You've made me cry
Only you know why
Seems no matter how hard I try
My words keep getting twisted into lies
You might be slick, even a little sly

But, I have a secret.

So, take a breath, let out your annoying sigh
You will not defeat me, make me quit life and die

To your cruelty, torment, negativity I say,
"goodbye."

To my joy, happiness and positive outlook I now say,
"hi!"

Weirdo. Freak. Emo. Strange. Odd. Geek. Misfit. Samples of hurtful insults often hurled by a bully. But, what if you looked at those words in a new way? Instead of horrible, how about *"Unique"* or, even better, *"YOU-nique"*, instead?

If no one has told you before, I am going to now. Being *YOU-nique* is chic. Being yourself is good. Not bad as a bully may have been portraying it to be.

Tim Burton's film, *Frankenweenie,* features a character named *"Weird Girl"*, along with her clairvoyant pussy cat, *Mr. Whiskers.*

*Frankenweenie's* Wiki page describes *Weird Girl as,* "Someone who does not fit in well with other kids. She delivers ominous pronouncements in a monotone voice. Her cat, *Mr. Whiskers,* is a constant companion. *Weird Girl* and *Mr. Whiskers* both have an unnerving, unblinking stare. *Weird Girl* loves to share *Mr. Whisker's* dreams to those whom he dreamt about."

*Weird Girl* is never bothered by the social bullying she receives from the other kids. *Weird Girl* embraces who she is, from her large staring eyes, to her monotone voice, to her psychic abilities to read *'signs Mr. Whisker's leaves in the litter box'.*

*Weird Girl* is unique. Her style of clothes. Her hair. Her voice. Her personality. Everything about her is kooky and quirky, but unique and adorable at the same time.

*Weird Girl* does not hide who she is. She could care less what others think of her. She displays her unique personality traits proudly. She never allows anyone to make her feel ashamed of who she is just because they may take issue with it. She is clever enough to recognize that is their problem. Not hers.

Being unique does not have to be a curse. It can be a blessing. It can also be fun, too. The choice on how you manage your uniqueness is yours alone no matter what unique qualities you adorn:

Your physical appearance (eyes, nose, mouth, hair, height or weight).
Your clothes.
Your voice or manner of speech.
Your personality.

Your quirks.
Your taste in TV/Movies/Music.
Whatever.

Never give someone the power to make you feel bad about your uniqueness. Embrace it. Do not hide it, feel ashamed or put yourself down about it, either.

If someone doesn't appreciate your *YOU-niqueness*, that is their problem. Let them keep it. They are most likely jealous and wish they had the guts to stand proud and be who they are, wear what they want, say how they feel, etc...

Thought stated already, it bears repeating. There is no one else like you. You are special and here for a great purpose. You are not here to be abused physically, emotionally or mentally by someone who does not understand or appreciate you and your uniqueness.

*Weird Girl's* quotes from the movie *'Frankenweenie'* read, *"Mr. Whisker's had a dream about you last night. If Mr. Whiskers dreams about you, it means something big is going to happen."* That something big could be you deciding to love yourself, to accept yourself, to be proud of yourself, to embrace who you are.

Be yourself no matter what anyone else says. Being YOU-nique is chic.

question...

"Who put a bully in charge of deciding being yourself wasn't good enough?"

reply...

You did once you caved into their pressure and hid your uniqueness. Do not feel bad about yourself for doing so.

solution...

Brush off their hate. Brush off any self-hate you are feeling.
Love and accept yourself just as you are.
Change for no one.

# bullied kids getting homeschooled are earning an "e" for emotional pain

Natural parental instincts are to protect your child. Especially when it comes to the issue of bullying. No one wants to see their child in pain, whether it be physical, mental or emotional. Witnessing your child being hurt is one of the worst feelings for a parent to experience.

So, what is a parent to do if their child is getting severely bullied at school?

Parents - talk to your child and find out what is going on. Kids can be secretive and may not be forthcoming with their situation. It is not uncommon for victims of bullying to hide their pain due to feelings of shame, helplessness, depression and frustration.

Be the parent, not the buddy to your child right now. You must open the lines of communication and dialogue with your child. A child in pain needs unconditional love, security, strength, wisdom, guidance, reassurance and a solid foundation that only you, their parent, can provide. They need you now more than ever.

Kids – do not be afraid to talk to your parents or a trusted adult about your feelings, no matter what they may be. For every problem, there is a solution. You do not have to keep feeling bad. Nor do you have to silence your pain by ending your life. That is not the answer. Do that and you lose. They win. Talk to someone. You will feel better.

Parents - visit your child's school and find out what they *(teachers, principal, counselor, superintendent)* know about the bullying happening to your child. Cooler heads prevail. So, as much as you may want to lash out because your baby is being hurt, reign it in. Again, for every problem, there is a solution.

If you discover the school is unaware your child is being bullied, make them aware of it. Provide calm, reasonable conversation and any proof; text messages, emails, etc.... Find out what the school plans to do about the bullying and make sure they follow through. You will probably need to be proactive in this situation with periodic talks with your child, meetings with the Principal and/or teachers to ensure the bullying issue is getting resolved.

Getting proactive with the school system may or may not solve the problem. It is not uncommon for many parents in your situation to be left feeling frustrated with the entire situation and get left with no other option but to homeschool.

Many parents are opting to homeschool their children due to the school system's failure to prevent their child from being bullied. Homeschooling is being viewed as the best solution to this ever-growing problem. In some cases, it has proved to help resolve bullying issues when the school failed to do so.

However, no system is perfect. Homeschooling can raise additional problems for a bullied child: social-isolation, an inability to develop coping mechanisms to handle challenging issues and not dealing with the existing emotional fall-out from being bullied.

One critical area often overlooked before homeschooling even begins is existing emotional damage done to the child by the bully. No amount of homeschooling will ease those hurt feelings. Be aware, removing your child from a bullying situation does not remove the pain caused by the bully. Professional help may be needed.

Protection and privacy have a fine line between them that must be crossed sometimes, for the right reason. Bullying is one such reason. Parents have the right to monitor their child's computer and phone activity. Kids need to be told why it is happening and assured it is not an invasion of privacy, but for their protection.

Being a parent today is no easy task. Neither is being a kid. Talk to your child. Hug them often. Tell them you love them, and you are there for them no matter what. Keep in touch with what is happening in their life whether you choose home schooling as the solution to your child's bullying issue or not. A bullied child needs support and assurance to help them overcome the damage done to them because of the bullying. Be there for them.

# don't let them break you!

The thought of High School reminds one of the John Hughes flick, *'Pretty in Pink'*, and the creatively dressed character Andie, played by actress, Molly Ringwald.

Andie was a girl from the poor side of town who got bullied by the rich kids at her school because she was different. She was a talented designer and a caring person who never judged anyone for anything. She accepted people as they were. Rich. Poor. Ugly. Pretty. It did not matter. She never judged. Her heart was pure. She was real and could not be bought or impressed by money.

The rich kids knew down inside Andie was a better person than they would ever hope to be. They had plenty in materialistic items, unlike Andie. But, also unlike Andie, they lacked character and integrity. Two things money cannot buy. They resented and bullied Andie for this reason.

A classic line Andie quoted from the movie, when her Dad asked her why she was still going the prom despite having been dumped by her date *(who happened to be a rich guy)*. Her simple reply was; *"I just want them to know that they didn't break me."*

Social media, daily interactions at school or after-school events have made bullying almost impossible to avoid nowadays.

Victims are being broken to the point where they are turning the malice vented by the bullies, at themselves. It is called self-hatred. Self-hatred seeks to destroy. The good news is, you have the power within you to prevent it from happening.

A new school year brings about the perfect time for changes. Rise above the nonsense of put-downs and gossip. Those things are driven by jealousy and serve only to keep you distracted from what is important in life. Your future.

You have an amazing future waiting for you. Do not allow bullying to destroy all you have worked so hard for: good grades, getting into the college of your dreams, etc.... Stay focused on what is important. Your life. Your future. Your goals.

Always strive to be the best you that you can possibly be. But, do it for you. No one else. You do not ever have to prove anything to anyone. Even though it might come across as being narcissistic, it is not. This is not about a big ego, acting like a diva or thinking you are better than anyone else.

*Do you want to know the secret to avoid someone destroying your self-esteem?*

For, every tear down someone gives you, give yourself two build-ups. Stop taking crap. Stop accepting what a bully says about you as gospel. For example: if your bully says, "You are stupid." You automatically reject what they said before it has a chance to take root and say to yourself, "No. I am smart. I am somebody."

Unfortunately, people say and do horrible things to one another all the time. The important thing to remember is how you respond to what is said or done. I say, *"Be strong and rise above it!"*

The only way someone can break you is if you give them the power to do it. So, don't.

# being bullied made me become a bully. Why?

The question, *"How did being bullied turn me into a bully?"* has been asked time and again by those who have been bullied.

Anger, insecurity, jealousy, hatred for others, hatred for self are just a few of the many reasons why someone chooses to become a bully. Then there are those who start life full of love and compassion for others. But, because of bullying, the love and compassion sours and they end up becoming a bully, too.

No matter how bullying starts, in the end it always boils down to one objective. Control. Bullying is nothing more than the need to control another to help the bully feel better about themselves. It really is that simple.

A bullied person, who then becomes a bully, not only carries the pain caused by their bully, but also the guilt of bullying others. Why? Because no matter how much the love and compassion for others seems a distant memory, down inside, being a bully goes against their nature: to love and have compassion for others.

The fact that a bullied person evolves into a bully is not their fault. They are what is called, '*A Victim of Circumstance*'.

Being a VOC is not a viable excuse to bully. In fact, there is no viable excuse for bullying another. Period. However, if a VOC had not been bullied, they most likely would have never developed into a bully themselves.

Unfortunately, hurtful circumstances can cause a VOC to make bad choices when it comes to the treatment of others. But, if a VOC feels guilt over bullying another, clearly, they still have a heart and a conscience. They are just overloaded with pain and acting out because they do not know what else to do. They are overwhelmed and confused by too many emotions.

It is perfectly understandable if VOC wakes up one day and feels guilty for their past behavior towards others. They turned into the very type of person they spent years fighting so hard against.

*"What can one do to ease the guilt and shame that comes with being a VOC bully?"*

Recognize the past is the past. As much as we all wish we could go back and undue stuff, it's impossible. Let it go. It's over. Done with. Gone. Move on. You cannot change it. So, stop exhausting yourself physically, emotionally and mentally

Forgive those who have bullied you. Forgiveness is often the hardest thing in the world to do, but also, the most rewarding for your own self-preservation. Forgiveness is a very important, necessary step. By forgiving the one or ones who did you wrong, you will begin to heal from the pain. You may never forget what was done, but through forgiveness, it won't sting like it used too.

Walking in forgiveness, rather than in bitterness, anger and hatred is best. Negative emotions do nothing more than cause destruction in health and other areas of your life. Is a bully worth doing that to you? Stop giving your bully the control.

If you became a VOC, forgive yourself for the bullying that you did. You were a victim. Both in bullying and of circumstance. It was not your fault what happened. Yes, you may have done horrible things, but the time has come to let it go, forgive and move on.

Do not be afraid or shy to talk to someone about your feelings: a parent, a teacher, a doctor, a school counselor, a pastor or a trusted adult in your life. Keeping bad or sad feelings bottled up inside is not healthy for your mental or physical well-being. So, talk to someone. Let those feelings out before they smother you.

Forgive the bully, forgive yourself and then, move on.

# 8 miles of bullying

One day, I channel surfed upon the movie, *"8 Mile"* starring *Eminem, Kim Basinger, Mekhi Phifer* and the late *Brittany Murphy*.

I had not seen *"8 Mile"* since its release back in 2002. My timing could not have been better. *Eminem's* character, *B-Rabbit* and his rival, *Papa Doc*, were about to battle for the title of best rapper in Detroit.

Forget for a moment these two Actor/Rappers are playing characters. Forget that the rap was pre-written, based on scripted events in the movie.

What made this scene in *"8 Mile"* stand out was the fact that *Eminem/B-Rabbit*, took the power away from *Papa Doc* – a bully.

In the movie, the MC flipped a coin and *Papa Doc* had the option to go first or pass. He passed.

See, *Papa Doc* thought he was slick by letting *B-Rabbit* take the mic first. *Papa Doc's* cocky, bully attitude allowed him to falsely believe he was going to win simply by ragging on *B-Rabbit* using typical bully put-downs.

Watch the movie *'8 Mile'* for *Eminem/B-Rabbit's* rap off scene mentioned. You can see for yourself how *B-Rabbit* begins with telling the crowd the negative things he knows *Papa Doc* is going to say about him. But then there is a twist. *B-Rabbit* goes on to share things about *Papa Doc*. He then tosses the microphone over to *Papa Doc*, who is left speechless. Why? Because *B-Rabbit* took the power back.

The character *B-Rabbit* owned the good, the bad, and the ugly about himself. He acknowledged all the things in which *Papa Doc* found fault. That is how he took the power back. Once *Papa Doc's* power was stripped away, he had nothing. He could no longer hurt *B-Rabbit*.

What makes a bully appear strong and more superior is their ability to deflect their own issues. That is how they become the bully and not the bullied. But, underneath the tough exterior they front, is nothing. They are a weak, pathetic and lost person with issues that will most likely require professional help to fix.

Despite being a *jerk*, a bully should never be made to feel shame or be ridiculed for their issues. Do that, and you are not better than them. Look, we all have issues – some just happen to be better at handling them and not taking them out on others.

Even though a bully may know WHAT they are doing to you, they do not know WHY they are doing it to you.
They may not even know WHY they feel hate for you.

It is not entirely impossible to believe down inside, they may like you and respect you. But, either they don't see it because they are so consumed with jealousy and envy. Whatever a bully's problem with you might be, remember they have the problem. Not you.

 Do not allow yourself to feel like you must pick up their mantle of hate, self-loathing and despair in return. And never turn on yourself by believing the vile vomit spewed forth about you by your bully. That is their false opinion of you. That should never be how you think about yourself.

If you find yourself believing their lies, you need to adjust your unproductive thinking.

You are wonderfully and skillfully made. There is no one else out there in the world like you. You never need to change anything about yourself to please a bully or someone else, for that matter. You make changes for you. You oversee you. No one else.

The next time a bully strikes out at you, remember they are hurting inside. They are only trying to hurt you to help them feel better about themselves. It is their twisted way of dealing with pain. It does not make it right. This type of cruel behavior is completely unacceptable. But, understanding why they do it will hopefully help you not take what they have to say to heart.

When you forgive the unforgiveable, you're free.

# hurt feelings

If you are feeling hurt because of something mean someone said, what can you do about it?

**one:**
You can try and talk to the person who hurt you.

**warning:** If the person who hurt you is a bully, ideas *'two'* or *'three'* might be better options for you to take.

Bullies do not care if they hurt you. That is the reason why they bully you. To hurt you because they are hurting and need to deflect their pain to not feel it themselves.

**two:**
Pretend the person who hurt you is looking back at you in the mirror. Tell your feelings to your reflection. By doing this exercise, it does not mean you are talking to yourself. Your reflection is standing in proxy for the person who hurt you because you are unable to talk to them directly. You can do this same exercise and talk to yourself.

*"Why should I talk to myself? I did not hurt my own feelings."*

Maybe you have and never realized it. Maybe you called yourself hurtful names or you did something harmful to yourself physically that you now feel bad about. Sometimes we are cruel to ourselves out of frustration because someone has been hurtful to us. We unconsciously or sometimes consciously turn on ourselves. It is okay to apologize to yourself. It is healing.

**three:**
Write your feelings down on a piece of paper and then tear it up afterwards.

**four:**

Tell your feelings to a stuffed animal. Sounds silly, but getting those hurtful feelings out is relieving.

Do not allow yourself to stew over it. Stewing only makes the issue feel worse. It solves nothing.

The sooner you talk about your feelings – no matter what they are - the better you will begin to feel.

# know who you are as a person. That's what matters!

Andy Biersack from the band, *"The Black Veil Brides"* once said, *"As long as you know who you are as a person, nothing else in the world matters."*

What you think of yourself is more important than what others think of you.

Unfortunately, there will always be someone who does not like you no matter what you do, say, wear, eat, where you live, work or who you choose to love. You can run yourself into the ground from exhaustion seeking an unattainable acceptance.

Ask yourself, *"Why do I need this person's approval of me?"*

*"Who gave this person whose approval you seek charge of what is and is not acceptable?"*

The answer might surprise you. But, you are the one who did.

You may ask, *"How did I do that?"*

Simple. Once you began devaluing yourself based on someone's refusal to give you their approval. No one should ever have that much power over you and your life.

Just because someone cannot see how wonderful you are does not mean you must stop seeing yourself as being wonderful. You are wonderful.

You have the option of choosing to accept their point of view about you or not. Rejection works both ways. You can just as easily reject their negativity about you, as they have rejected you. It honestly is your choice how you choose to see yourself.

The time has come to begin making positive changes in your life. If, that is what you choose. Again, almost everything in life boils down to choices.

Keep in mind, nothing happens overnight. That type of *'false reality'* exists only in television and movies. Real life issues take work. But, start somewhere.

Work on seeing yourself in a positive light, not the darkness you have been standing in because of a bully.

*Light or dark.*
*Free or held captive.*
*The choice is yours.*

# fighting a bully battle

The first rule of any battle is - know your enemy.

Although you may never learn the reason why a bully chose you. Just know they are the one with the problem. Not you.

*"But, why are they picking on me?"* you ask.

The answer may never be known. It doesn't mean there is something wrong with you. There is something wrong within them and they are taking it out on you for some reason only they know why.

A bully lacks the ability to feel compassion or care for another. Their empathy button is broken. They do not care if you cry or kill yourself because of things they did to you. They do not express remorse or regret. They seek pleasure from destroying you. Maintain your power by not showing them they are getting to you – if they are.

"Did you know bullying is just a pathetic ploy a bully uses to keep from dealing with their own issues and pain?"

Until a bully can resolve what is wrong within themselves it is unrealistic to assume they will feel any remorse for their actions towards you. They will continue to gain pleasure from your pain.

The good news is **you can defeat a bully**. And it is easier than you think.

**first**, get some confidence in yourself.

**second**, no one is perfect.

Everyone has faults and shortcomings. But, those faults and shortcomings should never be used as ammunition to fight a bully. Pointing out what is wrong with someone makes you a bully, too. Don't do it.

**third**, stop being so hard on yourself for mistakes or things you may have done that you wish you hadn't.

Those things are over, done with and gone. You cannot go back and undo them. If they were recorded, again, you cannot undo it. The only choice you have is to learn not to do it again. One bad moment, one poor decision in life, does not define who you are. Nor, should it make you feel bad about yourself.

**fourth**, control is a bully's secret weapon.

Without control, there is no one to put down, belittle or beat-up to help make them feel better about themselves.

Did you get that?

**they pick on you to feel better about themselves!**

Life is full of battles and obstacles. Anyone who says life is perfect is full of crap. We all go through stuff. Some go through more than others. Those who do, will be stronger in the end if they keep moving forward.

Learn to overcome bullying now and you are well on your way to becoming a Five Star General in the bully battles of life.

Bullying does not end when you graduate high school. But, do not let that scare you. Learn how to defeat bullies now and you will succeed at doing so in your adult life. The only difference is, by then, you will be a much stronger and wiser person. Strong enough to endure the crap. And wise enough to know how to stop it before it destroys you.

Do not be surprised if you end up helping others learn how to fight and win the bully battle, too. The sharing of knowledge is one of the most precious gifts you can give to another person who is being bullied.

Life is more than whispers in the halls, rumors, the passing around of sexted pictures and videos, bumps, bruises, etc. Please do not give up. Please. Your life has meaning and purpose.

Many schools have put bullying programs in place that offer various suggestions on how to handle bullying. Make sure to check your school for those programs.

# how to beat a bully at their own game

*"How do I defeat a bully?"*

Take control of your life. You do not have to announce it. The result will show when you no longer react to what the bully says or does to you. Not reacting is the worst thing you can do to a bully. To them, it means they have failed and you have successfully stripped their power over you.

*Would you like to be my buddy?*

Find one person you can befriend in your neighborhood, at school or at church. But, use caution. Keep your guard up. Do not share any secrets about yourself unless that person has truly earned your trust. Protect yourself.

If you have a friend or two who have earned your trust, try and hang out together, especially if you are getting physically attacked by a bully. Being in a small group should help prevent those attacks from happening. There is strength in numbers.

*Did you know bully spies exist?*

A bully spy is usually tight with a bully. If someone who never paid you any attention, that you know is friends with the bully, suddenly pretends to be enemies with the bully and now wants to be your friend, beware.

Watch what you say and do around a potential bully spy.

Keep them on a *"need to know"* basis. Many have fallen victim to this trick. Do not beat yourself up if you get tricked. They are called spies because they are good at blending in and faking people out. Anyone can become a victim to this trick, especially someone who has been bullied.

*How do I avoid a bully?*

When a bully comes towards you, walk in the opposite direction. This does not make you a coward. YOU are the one choosing to walk away. The bully is not making you. You are taking control away from the bully.

*Do I get mad or even with a bully?*

Neither.

Even if you happen to beat up the bully, do not believe for one minute you won. The bully will try something else to even the score. Many have been fooled into believing after a fist fight, where they kicked the crap out of their bully, that they and the bully could become friends.

In almost every one of those cases, the bully got even.
How? The cruelest way possible. They pretended to be their victim's friend, and, like a venomous snake, struck when their target was at their weakest and most vulnerable state. Beware what you share.

*What about giving a bully a taste of their own medicine?*

Physical violence and name calling only amps up the tension already brewing between a bully and their victim. Avoid doing it, if possible.
Very rarely does a bully see what a jerk they are. A victim tends to hope down inside a bully will see the error of their ways and stop. But, the truth is although a bully may recognize their own issues, they either do not care or are afraid to make positive changes.

There are some cases where a bully expressed remorse after their victim died. Some bullies joined up with the parents of the victim to help put a stop to bullying.

*"What if I just kill myself? That will show them"*

That way of thinking is a complete load of crap. You do not show anyone anything by ending your life because someone decided to treat you horribly. Your death will prove one thing to a bully. The had complete control over you. NEVER give a bully that kind of power over your life!

All your death will succeed in accomplishing is putting your family and friends in an immeasurable amount of unnecessary pain. Before long, classmates will forget about you, graduate and move on with their lives. Meanwhile you will be getting eaten by worms or resting on your parent's mantle in a jar. The bully graduates with a diploma and you get an obituary notice in the paper.

**your existence above ground, not your demise underground, is the best revenge to level against your bully. it means you are a survivor – because you are.**

*So, how do I get the bullying to stop?*

**ignore the bully.** Ignoring a bully is the ultimate up yours. Ignore the bully and you take their power away. It is one of the best moves you can ever make for your own self-preservation. Don't smirk, smile or look pissed off while doing it. Do those things, and the bully knows they can still get to you. Go on with your life as if the bully no longer exists.

If the bully steps into your path, politely ask them to *"Please step out of my way."* If they refuse, do not try and push past them. That is what they want you to do. Instead, turn and walk away. You are not being a chicken. You are taking control of the situation and handling it like a mature person.

**tell a trusted adult you are being bullied.** It is not uncool to do so.

Nine times out of ten these are people who may have been through it, too, and can provide useful advice on how to handle the situation. Telling an adult, you are being bullied does not make you a snitch, tattle tale or any other childish name.

Telling an adult about a bully, especially a bully who is inflicting physical harm to you or causing you to want to inflict physical harm upon yourself makes you smart! So, do not be afraid to tell.

**leave your stuff at home.** Whatever the bully wants to take from you, like your IPOD for example, do have it on you. If you do not have your IPOD on you, then the bully cannot take it from you. Does it suck to not be able to have your cool gadgets with you like everyone else around you? Yes. But it is a temporary situation. The bully will eventually understand you have chosen to no longer take their crap and move on.

**stop giving the bully ammunition to use against you**. Watch what you post online or text on your phone. Keep your private life, private. Try and stay off the Internet as much as possible. *"If you don't have something positive to say, keep your mouth shut and your fingers to yourself."*

**take a social media vacation.** This will help reduce the stress in your life because you will not be subjected to any negative stuff being said about you. Stop reading the negative things written about you on social media. Shut down your social pages if necessary. Use the block option, too. Avoid sites where you know people are writing mean stuff about you. It is pointless to upset yourself over what trolls write. You will exhaust yourself trying to defend yourself against people who take pleasure in your pain.

So, what if they say stuff about you? So, what! You know the truth and that is all that matters. You do not have to prove anything to anyone. You do not owe them any explanation about your life and your choices.

Believe it or not, years from now all the negative stuff being said about you won't mean a thing to those saying it. Hard to imagine, but it is the truth. Trolls have very short memories. They move from target to target. A year from now, they will be attacking someone else and you will be off their radar.

Are you beginning to understand now how small-minded bullies are?

# a time-sucking vampire bully

Do you realize how much of your valuable time is wasted caring about a bully's opinion of you?

Do you realize the bully is literally draining the life out of you like a time-sucking vampire?

Holy Water. A Cross. A Wooden Stake. Sunlight. None of those will help rid you of a TSV Bully. Well, perhaps a bit of garlic breath might keep a bully away for a bit. But, when the garlic disappears, and the bully reappears, then what?

*"How do I get rid of a TSV Bully?"*

Stop allowing the bully to rob you of your precious time.
Your life matters. Your time matters. And it should not be wasted on a minion who thinks so little of you.

Unlike most Hollywood Vampires, there is nothing mysterious, sexy or cool about a TSV Bully. In fact, they are the reason why many wonderful people end up lying inside of a coffin – having committed suicide.

A victim of a TSV Bully has a right to live their life in peace without being judged for who they are: *gay, straight, bi-sexual, tall, short, skinny, fat, ugly, pretty, smart, dumb, etc...*
Only, the TSV Bully makes sure they don't know it.

Consider a TSV Bully to be a master of illusion. Much like an actual vampire, they cannot see their own reflection. So, instead, they deflect what they know to be the truth about themselves onto others.

*"How much time and energy do you spend focused on the way a bully makes you feel about yourself?"*

Is it from the moment you wake up until at night when you put your head down on your pillow to sleep? And, even then, the pain you feel because of their behavior is managing to turn pleasant dreams into nightmares.

You probably go through a dozen wardrobe changes, hairstyles, make-up applications, and such, before heading off to school.

*"Do you realize you are doing those things for a bully and not yourself?"*

A TSV Bully will never be won over, so stop spinning your wheels and trying to be perfect for their approval. Perfection is not only overrated, it is impossible to achieve, especially with a TSV Bully.

Take a moment and ask yourself, *"Why do I care what a TSV Bully thinks of me?"*

Hasn't this TSV Bully stolen enough from you already?

There is no pleasing a selfish, immature, misguided person with issues that can only be resolved once they realize that:

1. They have a problem.
2. They want to fix the problem.
3. They are sincere in wanting to change their mean ways.

A bully will continue being a bully until they fix what is broken from within. There is nothing you, nor anyone else, can say or do that will change their behavior.

A bully has the power of choice, same as you. They can choose to change their life and get help, or they can choose to remain in pain and continue tormenting others to help them alleviate it.

If a bully chooses the later, it does not mean you must remain in misery. Their choice does not have to be your choice, too. You can choose to act and take your life back.

question:

*"Who can be a Time-Sucking Vampire Bully?"*

answer:

*Any person who willfully, maliciously and deliberately chooses to steal time away from another person's life by methods of distraction such as; calling them mean names, spreading rumors and/or inflicting physical harm.*

Ask yourself, *"Who allowed a TSV Bully control over my life?"*

This question has a two-part answer.

**first,** you are to blame.

*"How am I to blame? I'm the victim."*

A TSV Bully got a hook into you, once you allowed what they said and/or did to you, to steal the joy from your life and focus

all your attention, time and feelings on them. Please understand, this is not your fault. Believe it or not, this is the way most people respond when attacked. It's normal, until you gain better knowledge on your enemy.

You need to realize that you are the one who oversees your life. You are the one who determines what you will/will not accept in your life.

*"Are you going to continue allowing a TSV Bully control to have control over your life?"*

Look at your experience with a TSV Bully as a wake-up call. Recognize the areas in your life that need work and put your focus on it. By doing so, you will begin developing into a

389

stronger person who is better able to handle issues and not lose their power, again.

No matter what a TSV Bully has said or made you believe about yourself, start accepting yourself, faults and all. Stop feeling bad about yourself just because someone does not like something about you. That is their misfortune, not yours. Never feel like you must change who you are to please someone else.

Everyone is a work in progress with varying issues, even your bully. Scary thought, right? You are not alone. If it means talking to your parents, talk to them. If it means getting professional help, get it. Stop allowing the joy to be robbed from your life, whether it is because of a bully or what they may have stirred up that already existed down inside of you.

You deserve happiness. Question is, do you choose it?

**second**, a TSV Bully has what you might call '*A God Complex*'. They are a legend in their own mind. They are incapable of seeing the arrogant, pompous, cruel, narcissistic human being they have evolved into because of their own pain.

Yes, you read that last part right. They are hurting, too.
The difference between you and a TSV Bully is, they choose to cause hurt to others to deal with their pain instead of getting help and learning better coping skills.

A TSV Bully is not the boss of you. So, stop taking orders from them. The time has come for you to take a stand for your life. You oversee you - no one else.

Do remember one thing. Your parents have a say over your life until you are 18 years old. Do not forget that. Always respect your parents, even when you disagree with them about something. You may not always listen to what they have to say, (*which is normal*), but respect them always.

Life truly is too short to waste away on a TSV Bully and their negativity. A TSV Bully will not even matter once you graduate and move forward with your life. So, why allow them to matter now?

If you are reading this in the morning, today is a new day.

If you are reading this mid-day or at night, tomorrow is a new day.

Be free. Live your life. You only get one. Make the most of it.

# was a bully the only one who hurt me?

It never feels good to hear someone say to your face;

*"You are stupid."*

*"You are ugly."*

*"You are a loser."*

*"You are nothing."*

Ask yourself, *"Are the salty tears rolling down my cheeks because of what the bully said to me or, did those hurtful words trigger a hidden pain I never realized existed?"*

If the hurtful words triggered a hidden pain, you may be wondering, *"How did the bully know something was going on inside of me before I did?"*

A bully does not need to know the root of your pain. They sense a weakness in you, and then zero in on it like a heat seeking missile.

In the wild kingdom, it is common for animals to attack a weaker, sicker member of the pack or deliberately isolate them from the group.

True, a bully is not an animal, despite their behavior dictating otherwise. But, like an animal in the wild, they sense weakness and then attack and socially isolate their prey.

Ask yourself the following questions:

*"What is the true root of your pain?"*

*"Did your parents got divorced?"*

*"Do you lack a close relationship with your Mom/Dad/Sibling(s)?"*

*"Did you lose someone who you were once close to?"*

*"Did you lose someone you admired?"*

*"Did you lose someone who helped you feel good about yourself? If so, do you feel lost without them?"*

*"Do you not feel good looking enough?"*

*"Do not think you are smart enough?"*

*"Are there any family secrets you may have blocked out or are afraid to tell someone about?"*

*"Do you feel that something might be your fault when it might not be your fault at all?"*

Close your eyes and search down in your soul for the honest answer. Only you know what key will open your Pandora's Box. Think.

Do not get frustrated or upset if the answer does not come to you right away. It will, when the time is right. Once you learn the issue, seek help to resolve it, heal from it and then put it behind you.

*"How do I do this?"*

Talk to your parents, a professional counselor or a trusted adult who can help you take the next step towards healing.

Do not be afraid to put a light on whatever the issue may be and deal with it. Stop letting it torment you and cause you pain and distress. You do not deserve or need to carry it.

No matter your age or how long the issue has been going on, it is never too late to seek help. Why spend your life full of pain when you don't have to? Deal with it and heal from it.

So, are you ready?

The time has come to step boldly towards a new, brighter and happier future.

Stop letting a bully feed on your existing pain like a life-taking, blood-sucking leech. You have the ability and the power to starve them. How? By no longer reacting or responding to their attacks.

Aren't you sick and tired of hurting all the time?

It takes a very brave person to face their demons, no matter what they might be. And you are brave. Whether you realize it now or not.

Being able to sort out your issues is a courageous step towards healing and recovery. Nobody else can get inside of your head and heart and fix things. Only you have the power to make it happen.

Through hard-work and dedication on your part, you will reach a place where you can live a more balanced, productive life and be free from past pains.

Living the perfect life is unrealistic. No one lives a perfect life. No one. If you expect to live a perfect life, you will gain nothing but endless struggles and disappointments.

So, expect to live a life full of ups and downs. By recognizing this realistic fact, you will lead a more balanced life with a solid foundation.

Though you may not forget, you will eventually get to a place where you can forgive. And once you forgive, you are free. You are healed.

# franken-bully

If you are a bully, please consider a change in your cruel behavior. Being spiteful and nasty to others is not what your life is supposed to be about. Behaving like a jerk does not make you a better or stronger person. Nor, does it make you a leader worthy of respect or recognition. Acting vile towards someone only reveals you have serious issues in your life that need to be dealt with on a professional level. Know that anyone who teases you for that has now become a bully, too.

There is no shame in wanting, needing and getting help for your issues. It takes a courageous person to acknowledge they have a problem and then take steps towards healing.

*"Why go through life being pissed off, hurt and acting mean to people just to help ease your own pain?"*

*"Why behave this way when you can heal from the pain and live a happier life?"*

*"Are you ready to make an appointment with Dr. Franken-Bully and stop being a bully?"*

**new brain:**
think before you speak.
think before you act.
think before you react.
think.

**new eyes:**
to see things differently.
to notice others besides yourself.
to view others in a positive way instead of being so judgmental and critical.

to view yourself in a positive way instead of being so judgmental and critical.

**new mouth:**
say something nice to someone.
say something nice about someone.
say something nice about yourself.
learn to keep your mouth shut if you cannot say anything nice.

**new heart:**
feel compassion towards others.
feel empathy towards others.
feel love towards others.
feel love towards yourself.

**new hands/arms:**
to shake another's hand with.
to write an apology to those whom you have hurt.
to wave "Hello" instead of giving someone the middle finger or punching them.
to give hugs to others.
to give hugs to yourself.
to accept hugs from others.

**new legs and feet:**
to walk away from a situation before starting anything you will regret.
to walk up to someone whom you have been bullying and say, "I'm sorry."

# so, what do you think?

Up until now, you have believed everything a bully said is wrong with you. You've cried, gotten mad, felt frustrated and more. Are you ready to throw their negative opinion of you in the garbage and develop a positive opinion of yourself, for yourself, instead?

*"How do I get positive opinions of myself?"*

You can start with talking to the important people in your life: Family members, friends, teachers, counselors and your pastor.

Their input might help inspire you to see the positive things in yourself you have been overlooking because of being overly focused on the negative things. Sometimes a little constructive criticism helps open our eyes to that which we are unable to see.

Here are some examples of questions to help get you started:

Listen, it never hurts to ask. You will not know the answer until you do. You can do this. You need to do this to start seeing yourself in a new, more positive light. You need to get control of your life.

*What do you think of me?*

*What do you like about me?*

*What don't you like about me?*

*What is your favorite thing about me?*

*What do you see in me as weaknesses?*

*What do you see in me as strengths?*

*If you could improve one thing about me, what would it be?*

*If you could change one thing about me, what would it be?*

*If you could leave something about me the same, what would it be?*

Constructive criticism should never be viewed as a terrible thing. If what is being said to you is constructive, take it under advisement. If it is destructive, throw it in the trash.

Constructive criticism can sometimes come across harsh. Try not to get defensive or dismissive. Keep an open-mind. Take the time to think over what was said. The constructive words may not be what you want to hear, but they might be what you need to hear to become a better, stronger person.

# coffin-quences

*Dear Bully,*

*Why are you choosing to act mean towards others?*

*Does it make you feel better about yourself when you put another person down?*

*Do you feel like an important person while acting like a bully?*

*Do you feel special? Needed? Accepted by others when behaving like a bully?*

*Do you lack the ability to have control your own life so, you must control other people's lives?*

*Do you even recognize how your cruel actions towards another cause devastating consequences, some that last a lifetime?*

*Do you even realize how your vile and vicious actions towards another might cause them to end their life?*

*Do you even care?*

While **legally** bullying someone to death does not make you a murderer - **technically** it does.

True, people are responsible for the choices they make. And if a person chooses to end their life, that is their choice.

But, what if your cruel behavior towards the person, forced the person to make a choice they might not have otherwise made without your cruel influence? Can you see the possibility of that happening? All behaviors, right or wrong, have consequences. If you bullied someone and they ended their life, **YOU made them CHOOSE** that harsh solution to their pain based on your selfish, relentless, cruelty, just to relieve your own pain.

*"Who put you in charge of deciding who has the right to be left alone and who has the right to be bullied, sometimes to the point of committing suicide because of it?"*

To those who bully others, take this under advisement and consideration for which is intended:

*'Just because you choose to behave in a vindictive, cruel manner does not make it acceptable behavior: socially, morally, or ethically.'*

You have no right to mistreat another person for your own personal amusement. You are making a choice to behave this way.

You have no right to mistreat another person to help relieve your own pain. Get professional help. Grow-up. You are making a choice to behave this way.

You have no right to tear someone down in the hopes of building yourself up. You are making a choice to behave this way.

It is never too late to correct unacceptable behavior. Are you ready to stop being a bully? If your answer is "No!", you had better hit your knees and start praying for mercy, because you are going to need it for the rest of your sad, hate-fueled, miserable, empty life. Do you honestly want to live your life feeling that way?

Ask yourself these questions and really take some time to think about your answer:

*"What has got you so upset down inside that you feel the need to strike out at people?"*

*"What do you really get out of behaving like a bully towards others?"*

*"Does acting like a bully make you feel good about yourself?"*

*"Do you feel bad about yourself when you bully someone?"*

*"Do you feel like you are accomplishing something when acting like a bully?"*

*"Did someone teach you how to be a bully? If so, who? Why?"*

*"Do you have any self-respect?"*

*"Why are you so full of hate and anger towards the person whom you bully?"*

*"Do they remind you of the person you wish to be, but can't?"*

*"Are you jealous of them?"*

*"Do you envy something they have?"*

*"Why are you behaving like a bully?"*

Have you ever heard the saying, *"You catch more flies with honey than with vinegar?"*

Being nasty to others gets you nowhere in life. You might feel big, tough and mighty, pushing your weaker peers around, but, you are acting like a small-minded fool.

If you do not get to the root of what is really eating at your soul you will wind up leading a very shallow, empty, meaningless, cold, hard life. No joy. No peace. No true happiness. Nothing.

On the surface, you may appear to have everything. But, deep down inside where you really live, you will be empty.

Now, ask yourself the same questions asked of those whom you have bullied:

*"What is the root of your pain? Your anger? Your self-loathing?"*

*"Did your parents got divorced?"*

*"Do you lack a close relationship with your Mom/Dad/Sibling(s)?"*

*"Did you lose someone who you were once close to?"*

*"Did you lose someone you admired?"*

*"Did you lose someone who helped you feel good about yourself? If so, do you feel lost without them?"*

*"Do you not feel good looking enough?"*

*"Do not think you are smart enough?"*

*"Are there any family secrets you may have blocked out or are afraid to tell someone about?"*

*"Do you feel that something might be your fault when it might not be your fault at all?"*

Close your eyes and search down in your soul for the honest answer. Only you know what key will open your Pandora's Box. Think.

Do not get frustrated or upset if the answer does not come to you right away. It will, when the time is right. Once you learn the issue, seek help to resolve it, heal from it and then put it behind you.

Right now, you are viewed as the enemy.

But much like those whom you have picked on and put down, you too can change your situation around. You can choose to stop being the bad guy. The bully.

You can choose to live a life of happiness instead of anger. If you do decide to shed your evil ways, it will not make you a punk, a wussy or a sell-out. You will be a mature person who is trying to make changes for the better.

Through hard-work and an honest effort, you can become a person who will earn the right kind of respect, instead of demanding what you thought was respect from others, but was, fear.

Being mean to others is not respectful. It is disrespectful.

If you grew up in a household where you were taught to handle issues by being physically/mentally/ emotionally cruel to others, it does not mean you must continue the cycle of abuse. That is what you have endured. Abuse.

If you continue to willfully behave like a bully, you will eventually be held accountable for your actions. It might not be today. It might not be tomorrow. But, it will happen.

It is inexcusable, unacceptable behavior to hound somebody day after day until they cannot take it anymore and are forced to do something drastic to stop it – like committing suicide.

*"How would you feel if the shoe were on the other foot?"*
Take a moment and step into your victim's shoes.

*"How would you feel receiving harassing phone calls, to be beaten up daily, to have people throw water bottles and trash at you, to have rumors posted about you on social media?"*

It is so pointless to be at odds with someone you hardly know over nothing, or perhaps something that will not even matter a year or two from now.  Grow-up. Choose a better path. Stop making people hurt so you do not have to hurt. It is cruel, childish and selfish.

If you choose to screw your life up, fine. That is your choice. But, you do not have the right to screw someone else's life up in the process.

The time has come to work towards making positive changes and becoming a better person, not only for you, but for those around you, too.

You need to let that better person, the one who has been living inside of you since birth, the one who has been smothered by the angry, hurtful person you have had on display, free.

Are you ready to make a change?

# signs i'm being bullied

I cannot sleep well.
I have bruises and cuts that I hide.
I cry for no reason.
I make up excuses like I am sick, so I don't have to go to school.
I do not want to eat.
I feel sad.
I am moody.
I get called mean names.
Nobody wants to by my friend.
I want to go to sleep and never wake up.

**if you are feeling suicidal or having bad thoughts of any kind, please do the following right away:**

**\*Tell your parents**
**\*Call a Suicide Prevention Hotline**
**\*Call 911**
**\*Talk to your teacher, your counselor, your principal**
**\*Talk to your pastor**
**\*Contact a Bully Prevention Organization**
**\*Talk to a responsible adult**

There is nothing to feel embarrassed or ashamed about when asking for help.

**UNDER NO CIRCUMSTANCES SHOULD YOU END YOUR LIFE.** Ending your life is not like a video game. You cannot hit the *"start over"* button if you change your mind and decide to live after you are already dead. Get it? Got it? Good.

# how to heal from being bullied

**first.**
Turn it over to God.

Before you get all self-righteous, let me point out something. This is not a religious matter. This is more:

*"Hey, I'm tired of carrying the burden. Here, God, you take it for a while. I need a break."*

Giving your problems over to God is a way of letting go. It begins the healing process and helps ease the burden off you. You have been carrying undeserving and unnecessary garbage long enough. Wouldn't you agree? So, hand it over.

**second.**
Forgive the person(s) who did you wrong. This does not require you to say it to their face(s). In fact, you can think it in your head, feel it in your heart, write it down on paper for your eyes only and then tear it up or tell it to your stuffed animals.

Ask yourself, *"Do I want to give a bully power over me to the point where I spend the rest of my life bitter and angry because of what they did to me?"* If you want to be free from it, your answer should be *"No!"*

Carrying bitterness and anger is not worth the long-term damage it will do to you physically, mentally and emotionally. A bully is not worth it. It has even been proven that sickness can develop from unresolved anger. Forgive them and move on.

**third.**
Forgive yourself. You are not to blame for being bullied. The bullying you received or have been receiving was probably done through no fault of your own. But, it has left you feeling bad about yourself, mad, confused, depressed and who knows what else.

The important thing to note is you have eyes now to see what went wrong. So, forgive yourself for being lost for a while.

The healing process can now begin.

**scoop…**

hope

bad days 50%
good days 50%

# a splash in the rain

instead of wishing the rain away
this time i think i'll go out and play
as grown-ups, under the covers we huddle
As kids, we jump and splash in the puddles
gene kelly adored, *"singing in the rain"*
an umbrella, a heel kick, a twirl of the cane
earthworms squiggle up from beneath the ground
i stretch forth my arms and spin around
such fun to let your tongue catch the drops
until the sun appears, and the rain finally stops
hence, from now on, if it should rain
instead of complaining of it being a pain
i'm going to head outside through the door
to jump and splash in puddles forevermore.

Who is your best friend?
Who is your worst enemy?
Who gives you love?
Who gives you hate?
Who encourages you?
Who discourages you?
Who believes in you?
Who doubts you?
Who has a gallon of fear?
Who has a pint of faith?
You.

Real courage is bravery
that builds with each challenge.
No one can scare it or chase it away.
Real courage roars when pushed
and purrs when nudged.
Real courage conquers uncertainity
and replaces doubt.
Real courage rids the mind of fear
and replaces it with faith.
Real courage arrives when least expected
and vanishes just as quickly.
Real courage flouishes with each
bold step taken in life.

Self-worth cannot be purchased.
It is not found on a store shelf.
Self-worth is a value that fluctuates in life.
Self-worth prospers with positive words.
Self-worth becomes poor with negative words.
Self-worth conquers weaknesses
and replaces insecurities.
Self-worth replaces misery with contentment.
Self-worth is easy to possess, but just as easy to lose.
Self-worth, although free, can also bear a heavy price when choosing to value yourself.
Self-worth remains if you let it.

Confidence is strength residing from within.
No one can defeat or take it away,
 unless you permit it.
Confidence speaks with force and yet,
 listens with a tender ear.
Confidence overcomes fear.
Confidence crushes barriers
and opens roads and doors.
Confidence demands respect, but not arrogance.
Confidence aides your future with each step taken.

The circumstance is always subject to change.

You don't have to fit in.
It's good to stand out.

Be yourself! If someone does not like you for who you are that is their problem, not yours. Aren't you exhausted from being a people pleaser hoping to win someone's approval?

Each snowflake is unique just like you. There is no one else on earth who can be you, except YOU. Be yourself.

# Curiosity
# killed the cat!
# Ur NOT a cat!

Deactivate Ur Social Networking Accounts!
Don't Peek!
Don't Go Back!
Block The Drama!
Delete Negative Stuff From Ur Life
And U Defeat The Bully!
Disconnect Social Media —
Reconnect w/Life!

# One step at a time defeats a bully

*"Which step are you standing on in the bully battle you have been fighting?"*

The 'I can't' step or the 'I can' step?

*"Are you ready to stop allowing a bully to have control over your life and dictate how you should feel about yourself?"*

If so, you just took the first step. *"Congratulations!"*

No one recalls what we were like at birth. We don't remember how all we could do was lay wherever Mom or Dad put us. We soon learned to roll over and, eventually crawl. And, after some trial and error, we mastered walking one wobbly step at a time.

The point is, you may stumble. You may even wobble and fall over. But, the key is to get back up, dust yourself off and try again.

If you want to succeed in life, you need to keep on climbing the steps and never let anyone or anything stand in your way.

Success is not measured by popularity, money in the bank or a job title. Success is trying – even if you fail. At least, you tried. And that is more than most people do.

Speak outward and you will be heard.
Continue speaking inward and you won't.

Sometimes we really need to talk to someone.
Sometimes we really should talk to someone.

But how do you talk to someone?
What do you say?
How do you start?

Are you afraid what you want to say might come out wrong?

Are you worried that if you talk to someone they will even hear what you are saying or truly get how you feel?

The only way you'll ever know is to speak. Talk to a trusted adult: a Parent, an Aunt or Uncle, your School Counselor, a Police Officer, a Fireman, or a Teacher.

Nothing in your life will change until you speak up and let someone know you are hurting.

H8ters are gonna h8te
Playas are gonna play
Bullies are gonna bully
I'm gonna stay.

Shut the F-Up
I don't care what you have to say
Shut the F-Up
Leave me alone, just go away

You pretend to be my friend
You pretend to care
Shut the F-Up
And get rid of that shocked stare

Shut the F-Up
I'm so onto your tricks and lies
I know exactly who you turned into your little bully spy

Shut the F-up
You'll cause me to hurt no longer
Shut the F-up
Yup, that's right, I'm getting stronger

Shut the F-Up
For it's my turn to speak
I said Shut the F-Up
You're the one who is pathetic
The one who's weak

Shut the F-Up
I'll never be heartless like you
Shut the F-Up
I've spoken my peace
You can leave...we're through

Shut the F-Up
I refuse to end my life
I refuse to let you win
I refuse to be consumed with strife

Shut the F-up
I'm a winner

A life chooser
Shut the F-Up
You sorry, little Bully loser.

Cutting causes pain
Cut downs gnaw at my brain
I wish your slander out of my head
Before I wind up lost and dead.

Call me what you want
My guts I refuse to spill
You cannot break my spirit
Or rob me of my will.

Go look in a mirror and say all that bad sh** you say about me
to yourself. I realize now you are really talking about yourself.

Don't kill yourself.
Will yourself to live.

The bully can get to know my back side, as I walk away from their hateful crap.

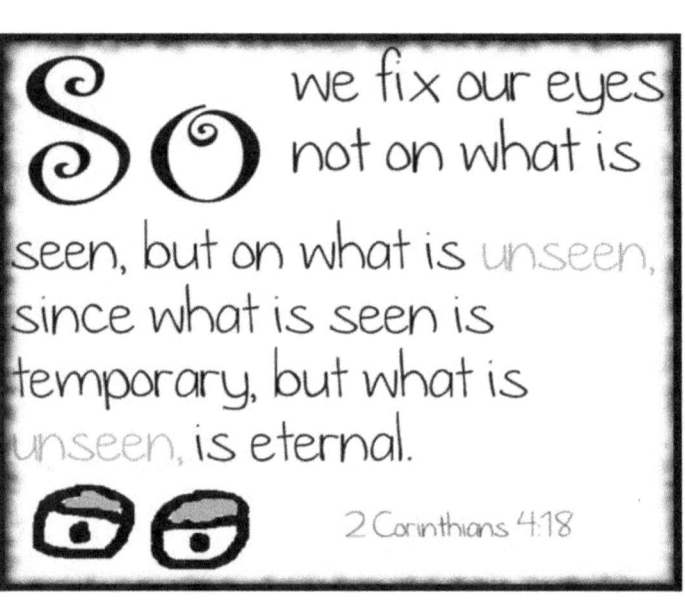

So we fix our eyes not on what is seen, but on what is unseen, since what is seen is temporary, but what is unseen, is eternal.

2 Corinthians 4:18

Isn't it ironic
Being a bully made you iconic
Having people live in fear
Afraid of their reputation being smeared

Wish everyone had eyes to see
The pleasure you take in causing their misery
Shallow and weak is what you are
With a heart coated in painful, hidden scars

I long for the day bullies get taken down
I long for the day they are run out of town
Then their bullied victims will finally be free
To be who they are and live a life full of glee.

Did you know salmon swim upstream, enduring and overcoming countless obstacles along the way?

Weak salmon cannot take the ups and downs of the journey and quit. Strong salmon overcome the odds and thrive.

Contrary to what a bully might think, you are not a weak salmon. You are a strong salmon, capable of metaphorically swimming against rushing currents, leaping over large rocks and escaping the fierce clutches of your enemies.

Life will toss obstacles into your path to make things difficult. Like a bully, for example: who will call you mean names, spread rumors about you or physically assault you.

No matter what is tossed into your path, remember, you are a strong salmon. Strong salmon do not quit! Strong salmon continue swimming forward, leaving obstacles, hidden in a flurry of bubbles stirred up by their tail fin.

To quote *Dory* from the movie, *Finding Nemo*, "*Just Keep Swimming*" no matter what obstacles are put into your path.

End the pain. Start talking.

"*Hi!*" friend
"*Bye!*" friend
Did you know I'm bringing my life to an end?

Of course, you don't
You never had the time
Always mistaken me for a pathetic mime

I pass you daily in the hall
I listen carefully
But my name you never called

I needed a good friend
Not a "*Hi*" and "*Bye*" friend
Someone to be an actual friend

I'm tired of being picked on
Being alone and treated like crap
So tired, am I, of the daily fighting
My zest for life is zapped

Every night before I go to sleep
I pray to the Lord my soul to keep
And if He should be able to work it in
I hope you and I will become real friends.

**i will not** put myself down.

**i will** use my mind and not my hands if an unpleasant situation happens.

**i will not** sext.

**i will** appreciate the body I was given.

**i will** work hard for what I want.

**i will** accomplish all my goals.

**i will not** compliment myself too much, nor put myself down.

**i will** have patience when I am in a hurry.

**i will not** argue with my parents.

**i will** be faithful in my choices.

**i will not** envy others for the things they have.

**i will** trust myself.

**i will not** be cruel to someone who has been cruel to me.

**i will** lose my heart to someone.

**i will** remember that I don't have it that bad, but only when I think that I do.

**i will** love myself even if I don't feel like it.

**i will** dig deep inside for strength when I feel that I am weak.

**i will** respect my parents/guardian/foster.

**i will** learn right from wrong.

**i will** use manners when eating with a poor man and practice the same manners with a rich man.

**i will not** be greedy.

**i will not** destroy my body. I will respect it and expect others to do the same.

**i will** deactivate my social media accounts for a month and see if helps me feel better.

**i will** stick up for someone who is being bullied.

**i will not** bully anyone for any reason.

I have rights.
I have the right not to be hit.
I have the right not to be called mean names.
I have the right not to be judged.
I have the right to defend myself.
I have the right to be left alone.
I have the right to exist.

Here is a little secret: "*Bullies are unhappy with themselves. It is the reason why they hurt you.*"

You hate my face
I hate yours more
Do me a favor
And hit the door!

I'm sick of your ranting
Your teasing and lies
I'm especially sick
Of your internet spies

Crawl back under the rock
From whence you came
If the truth were known
You're the one who is lame

But, you keep on bullying me
While in the past that used to work
You no longer have power over me
You are a pathetic lost jerk.

Block. Delete. And, you defeat cyberbullying.

A bad moment in life does not define who you are.

Never say something to someone you would not want said to you.

Love is always stronger than hate.

If opossums could speak, they would understand how it feels to have lies spread about you.

People tell lies about opossums all the time. Most are borne out of ignorance, much like a bully does to their victim.

Opossums are judged by their appearance, what they eat, for playing dead *(a defense mechanism against predators)* and for hanging upside down *(a myth)*.

The truth about opossums: they *"play dead"* or go into a catatonic state to avoid danger, they hiss and show their teeth to scare you away, they only bite if you try to pick them up, they carry fewer diseases than cats and dogs, they are very clean, despite stinking sometimes if they rummaged through trash looking for food, they are immune to most snake venom, they have opposable thumbs on their rear feet and, their fur feels kind of like a stuffed animal.

Despite those confirmed facts, it is difficult convincing people to see them any other way besides, dirty, nasty and diseased – per the misinformed lies or rumors.
But, circumstances are subject to change for the opossum, and you, too.

Thanks to Dr. Claire Komives with the *San José State University*, things for opossums are about to change. Dr. Komives is currently working on developing an opossum-based snake bite antidote that could one day save a human from a venomous snake bite. Amazing, right?

Just like there is wonder in an opossum yet to be realized, there is wonder yet to be realized in you, too.

Although you may never convince a bully or anyone who believes the lies the bully spread otherwise, you know the truth. And, believe it or not, that is what matters.

Sometimes ignorance cannot be overcome. But, that is okay. Those who are worthy of your time will not listen to the lies. Those who do? Forget them. They are not worth anymore of your valuable time.

Vicious rumors and lies never stopped an opossum from living its life. Why let the lies and rumors stop you?

It's *im-possum-able* to please everyone. Stop exhausting yourself trying.

You say you're not mean
I don't know what you mean
Because your actions towards me
Don't justify the means
Why are you so mean?
Do you know what I mean?
I don't think you have the brains to get what I mean
But, I get what you mean
I do understand what you mean
The fact is, you are plain mean.

The bully waits patiently to cast their hex
Reading everything you post on-line or in a text

The bully comes disguised as a friend, but is a foe
Never trust someone you do not really know

Beware of what you post on-line or in a text
It lives forever passing from one bully to the next.

Bullies hate themselves more than they hate those whom they pick on.

Better to be unpopular than be a bully. It is not worth treating others poorly to feel better about yourself.

Bullies have issues.
I can see that now.
I may not be perfect.
But, I am finally free.
I know now who you really are.
Yet, you still don't know me.

If you cannot accept the way you look, then why should you expect others to do the same? Accept yourself.

Sometimes a good cry helps release the pain.

It is okay to love yourself.

You do not deserve to be bullied.

Your future is waiting. But, you must be here to live it.

It is not the garbage a bully says or writes about you. It is how you receive it. Garbage comes in. Garbage goes out.

Everyone is beautifully flawed.

Accept what you can change.
Let go of what you cannot change.

You have the power to choose.

A bully sees flaws because they are flawed.
You see character because you are real.

You do not need someone to make you happy. Be happy with
yourself, first.

An internet bully is just a lost soul trapped inside the body of a heartless troll.

Be yourself.

When a bully talks you walk away.

Shove me?
I will not shove you back.

Steal my laptop?
I will use pen and paper.

Take my iPod?
I will whistle instead.

Write nasty things on my locker?
I will paint it.

Try and start a fight?
I will ignore you.

I'm sick of your demented games.
You, bullying me, has become really lame.

I will stand up.
I will speak out.
I will help a kid who is being bullied.
If I don't, then I am saying *"It is okay to bully"*.
And it is not okay to bully.

Lips may flap, words may fly.
I know the truth and can hold my head high.
It does not matter what I have done or said.
Facing my bully, I now no longer dread.

If you do not want it spoken about you, do not speak it about
someone else.

Though I may be in pain, I refuse to die in vain. Bullying is not
worth ending my life over.

I am not nothing.
I am something.
I am not nobody.
I am somebody.

God does not make mistakes.

Live in peace. Do not rest in peace.

Respect yourself.

It is okay to feel mad sometimes.
It is okay to feel sad sometimes.
It is not okay to feel mad and sad all the time.

90% of what you feel is all about your mental attitude. Keep it positive.

Every day is a choice.

Speak pleasant things over yourself or *"Shh!"*

The bullied do not always become the bully.

Learn from it.
Move on.
Don't repeat it.

Being bullied is not your fault.

You have strength to survive. Draw on it. You got this!

I have no friends.
I have no money.
All I have is rumors, bruises, heartbreak and pain.

I do have one thing.

I have God.
He's on my side.
He'll never betray me.
He'll never lie to me.
He'll never use me.
He'll never smack me.
He'll never steal from me.
He'll see me through this time in my life.
He'll always stand beside me and be my friend no matter what others say or do to me.

My life might not mean much to you.
But, it means something to me.
I refuse to allow a bully take that away from me.

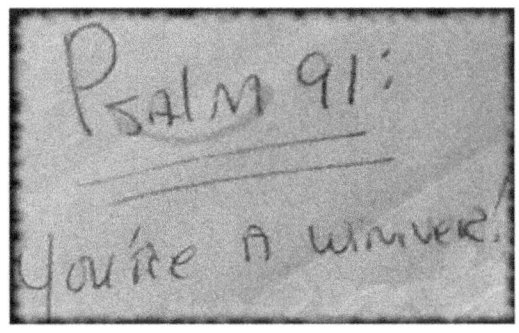

## PSALM 91
### © Amplified Bible/Lockman Foundation

[1] He who dwells in the secret place of the Most High shall remain stable and fixed under the shadow of the Almighty [Whose power no foe can withstand].

[2] I will say of the Lord, He is my Refuge and my Fortress, my God; on Him I lean and rely, and in Him I [confidently] trust!

[3] For [then] He will deliver you from the snare of the fowler and from the deadly pestilence.

[4] [Then] He will cover you with His pinions, and under His wings shall you trust and find refuge; His truth and His faithfulness are a shield and a buckler.

[5] You shall not be afraid of the terror of the night, nor of the arrow (the evil plots and slanders of the wicked) that flies by day,

[6] Nor of the pestilence that stalks in darkness, nor of the destruction and sudden death that surprise and lay waste at noonday.

[7] A thousand may fall at your side, and ten thousand at your right hand, but it shall not come near you.

[8] Only a spectator shall you be [yourself inaccessible in the secret place of the Most High] as you witness the reward of the wicked.

⁹ Because you have made the Lord your refuge, and the Most High your dwelling place,

¹⁰ There shall no evil befall you, nor any plague or calamity come near your tent.

¹¹ For He will give His angels [especial] charge over you to accompany and defend and preserve you in all your ways [of obedience and service].

¹² They shall bear you up on their hands, lest you dash your foot against a stone.

¹³ You shall tread upon the lion and adder; the young lion and the serpent shall you trample underfoot.

¹⁴ Because he has set his love upon Me, therefore will I deliver him; I will set him on high, because he knows and understands My name [has a personal knowledge of My mercy, love, and kindness—trusts and relies on Me, knowing I will never forsake him, no, never].

¹⁵ He shall call upon Me, and I will answer him; I will be with him in trouble, I will deliver him and honor him.

¹⁶ With long life will I satisfy him and show him My salvation.

Before you were born, God had already created you to be someone very special. You have a great purpose, worth and value in this life. Do not listen to the haters. Trust what God said. He's been here longer.

Please, stay.

You have a voice. Use it. Speak up.

Was once introverted because of a bully.
Now I'm extroverted because of courage.

Why does a bully, bully?
Because they are hurting.
Because they are insecure.
Because they need to feel better about themselves.
Because they want attention.
Because they seek approval.
Because they think they are cool.

You can handle life.

Delete accounts.
Unfriend foes.
Liberate yourself.

Be a Prince
Don't react and be mean
People will adore you
The bully now bows to the new King.

447

You are what a bully says you are, but only if you believe them. So, don't.

If you want to have a good attitude about yourself, you can. If you want to feel sorry for yourself you can do that, too. It is always your choice.

The day a bully no longer controls you, is the day you are free.

Think before you react.

I will still be standing when you fall. And you will fall. All bullies do.

Bullies enjoy calling their victims hurtful words. But, what do the words a bullied victim gets called really mean?

Let's look at some words bullies say:

**slut:**
A person who is sexually promiscuous or has loose sexual morals.

**ugly:**
Unpleasant or repulsive in appearance.

**useless:**
A person who has no ability or skill in a specific area or activity.

**loser:**
A person who is unable to succeed or is incompetent.

Notice how nowhere in any of the definitions above does a name appear. Your name. Once you understand the words a bully says about you, they lose their meaning and power. Why? Because they are untrue and therefore do not matter. Especially coming from the mouth of someone with issues of their own.

**words do not define who you are as a person.**

Words only have life if you choose to believe them. If you choose to ignore them, they die on the tips of your ears and never to take root in your heart.

Killing yourself doesn't show *"them"*.
Surviving does.

Shut down all social media accounts during a bully attack. If a bully cannot reach you, they cannot hurt you.

Royal bully sitting upon thine throne
Telling the school to ignore me, to leave me alone
Barking orders and acting like you have got class
But, remove the crown and staff you hold
What's left? Nothing but a royal pain in my ass.

My head is held high
My foot is out the door
I am choosing to step into a new life
One where I will not tolerate being bullied anymore.

Feeling wounded
Drowning in dread
A million random thoughts
Circle inside my head

You are better off dead
Is what they speak
Maybe they're right
I am pathetic, I am weak

Am I as bad as they have made me out to be?
Wait! No! I am not!
It is they, who are pathetic
It is they, who are weak

It is easy to deflect
What you'll never be
A caring, loving person
You'll never be like me.

Uncover.
Discover.
Recover.
Live.

What would you do
If I suddenly walked up to you
And ordered you to take that back
Bet you'd launch into a panic attack

Well, what are you waiting for?
Take it back, right this minute
I am not kidding with you
I am serious, I mean it

I dare you to treat me nice
I dare you to be my friend
*Aww,* what's the matter, bully
You don't know how to pretend?

Relax
I will show you how it is done

You smile for the world
In private you come undone

Punching, screaming, hating
So many feelings, it's overwhelming
Your nose will start to run
Tear stained eyes grow red from the swelling

What's that you say?
You don't have time for this sh**
I should go and do what with myself
Look out! Right hook! Here comes the hit

I finally did what was long overdue
Thought hitting someone is not the right thing to do
But I needed to take control of life back
Not to be vengeful, but to prevent more bully attacks.

Deliberately being cruel to others to feel better about yourself
is seriously messed up thinking.

*How does someone defeat hurtful feelings and thoughts?*
With strength from within. It cannot come from anyone else.

The person being bullied needs to realize for themselves they are
not the one with the problem and tune out anything the bully
says or does.

The person being bullied must make the decision they will no
longer rule their mood, feelings, emotions or choices based on
what a bully says or does.

The person being bullied needs to know they are not alone when it comes to being bullied. There are many others out there who have been bullied, too.

The person being bullied needs to understand they are not the one who is weak, pathetic, dumb, or a loser. The bully is merely deflecting their own hurt feelings.

The person being bullied needs to know they do not deserve to be mistreated or abused by anyone for any reason. Stand tall. Square your shoulders and take back what is rightfully yours: your dignity, your self-esteem, your self-worth and your life.

## may, you
may you find happiness
may you find love
may your heart never grow weary
may you no longer get shoved
may you find courage when times are tough
may you never lose strength
may you never give up
may you stay the course
may you never lose sight
may you admit when you are wrong
may you rejoice when you are right
may you come to realize you have so much to give
may you know here and now the time has come to live.

**breaking news for bullies:** freedom of speech does not include the right to mouth-off hate-fueled speech and be a deliberate jerk to someone just because you have issues of your own and need someone to take them out on.

## what is positive?
hope

amazing

capable

wise

confident

strong

love

talented

over-comer

happy

optimistic

reassure

praise

amazing

hope…

to be honest
#tbh

good days 80%
bad days 20%

# #tbh

The #tbh *(to be honest)*, section of the book is not about pep talking you into a better mood by seeing the silver lining of a dark cloud or cuddling kittens and puppies while standing underneath a rainbow.

The phrase, *"Everything is going to be perfect from now on"*, is a lie. It won't. Everyone's life has ups and downs. Things will get better, but they will never be perfect. Once again, perfection is an unrealistic, unattainable expectation.

Even though you may deal with more garbage than others, have faith in yourself that you can handle whatever life throws your way. Even if your faith is the size of a mustard seed. A small amount of faith still counts.

The truth you hopefully learned about your bullying situation from the prior pages of this book, should help you begin to make positive changes in your life and adjust your negative thought process.

Positive changes are what you need to focus your time and attention on. Starting now. You have wasted enough time being bullied.

Some of what you are about to read might sound familiar. But sometimes good points bear repeating. But, I promise you, there will be no judgements, criticisms, bashing or bullsh**ing. Only the truth.

Change is a good thing. People tend to buck change due to the discomfort or a fear of the unknown. Yes, change can suck sometimes, too. But, like it or not, life is about change. Nothing ever stays the same. So, either roll with it or get run over. Your choice.

What you have the power to change is how you look at things. The choice has always been yours. Maybe you did not realize it until just now.

You can choose to look at your life as hopeless and negative. You can choose to throw out that old way of thinking and start over. Or, you can do nothing.

No one can get inside of your head and turn your thinking process around. Only you have the power to make that happen. You have a choice to make.

Don't you think it is time to take control of your life?

**#tbh:**

Stop allowing negative people to speak negative words into your life. Stop believing negative things being spoken about you. If you easily believe the negative things, you can just as easily believe the positive things, too.

Get out a piece of paper and draw three columns.

**in the first column:**
Write down the negative things you think/feel about yourself.

**in the second column:**
Write down the negative things a bully(s) says about you.

**in the third column:**
Write down the positive things you think/feel about yourself.

Now look at it. Columns 1 and 2 are longer than column 3, right? But, guess what? The first 2 columns are garbage. Tear up Columns 1 and 2.

Take column 3 and put it up on your bedroom wall or inside your locker. Anytime you start believing the negative words from Columns 1 and 2, put your focus on Column 3.

You might be thinking, *"I don't think anything good about myself."* Everyone may have a million things they hate about themselves, but somewhere down inside hides one good thing they like about themselves. Take some time and really think about what you do like about yourself.

The truth: sometimes it is hard to override the negative and focus on the positive. But, it can be done with determination and choice.

**#tbh:**

Do you remember the section in the book about how much time you have wasted focusing on the bully and the effects of their negativity in your life?

Do not tear yourself down over it. Focus on the positive. Forget about the negative. Again, with determination and choice, bullying can be overcome.

**#tbh:**

Self-acceptance is important. It is more important than having acceptance or approval from others. If you cannot love and accept yourself, how do you expect anyone to do the same? So, love yourself, even if others never do.

**#tbh:**

Do not commit suicide because of bullying. Bullies are not worth it. You are worth something. Ignore what they say to you. Choose to live.

**#tbh:**

You are special.
You are important.
You are wonderful.
You are beautiful inside and out.
You are smart.
You are talented.
You are gifted.
You are unique.
You are important.
You just are.

# DREAM

**#tbh:**

You deal. You heal.

**#tbh:**

You take control of the pain from being bullied instead of the pain taking control of you.

**#tbh:**

Time is a great healer. Give yourself time and you will.

# FAITH

**#tbh:**

Today will be different than yesterday. Tomorrow might be even better. Yesterday is over. Let it go.

**#tbh:**

The sun always rises the next day bringing with it a chance to start over.

# HOPE

**#tbh:**

You are not a problem. You have a problem. A bully. And, problems can always be resolved.

**#tbh:**

Start seeing your future through the eyes of *'can do'* instead of the eyes of *'can't do'*.

**#tbh:**

Sometimes a chat with a trusted adult like your parents, a teacher, a pastor, a counselor or a bully prevention hotline can help if you are being bullied. There is nothing wrong with asking for help.

# LOVE

**#tbh:**

A bully is emotionally and mentally dysfunctional. They inflict pain upon others, hoping to feel better about themselves.

Did you know, a bully's own self-hate could rival the misery you feel about yourself? It's true.

Like you, a bully has choices. They can choose to change their behavior or remain in a life of misery. It is their choice and bears no reflection on you or anything you say or do. The problem is them. Not you.

Bullying someone is not cool. It only reveals how broken they are inside.

**#tbh:**

Sometimes a bully can indirectly bring something to your attention you have been carrying around inside, like a painful memory, but you never realized it before.

**#tbh:**

Are you ready to get to the root of your pain and heal?

**#tbh:**

Ending your life
Brings sweet relief

465

But leaves behind loved ones
Tormented and full of grief
The bully is the only one
Filled to the brim with joy
Mocking you even after death
Gloating over whom they destroyed.
Suicide is not the answer to your problem(s).


**#tbh:**

You are okay, Kid!


**#tbh:**

All of life is precious whether it is something as small as a beetle or someone as imperfectly made as you. *"Imperfectly"* because no one is perfect.

Striving to be perfect is a waste of time. It is an unachievable and unrealistic goal meant to steal the joy out of your life.


**#tbh:**

To heal from the pain caused by a bully or anyone who harmed you, you need to forgive them.

*"What? Why should I do that? They hurt me."*

Because forgiving someone who has hurt you is how you let go of the pain and heal. It does not mean you must be friends with them, tell them you forgive them or forget what they did to you.

Even after you have forgiven someone who did you wrong, it might not feel that way. This is a normal feeling. You need time for the initial hatred to fade.

*"Why should I forgive someone who did me so wrong?"*

You do it for your own self-preservation. You do it because it is the right thing to do. You do it because it is healthier, mentally and physically, to walk in love instead of bitterness and hate.

Forgiveness is something you must realize within yourself. Forgiveness must be something you are willing to do from the heart. Nobody can make you forgive someone. Only you have the power to make that choice.

You may not feel like forgiving someone who has been unbelievably cruel to you. But, you should consider giving it a try. Not for their sake. For yours.

Back in the old days, when someone committed a murder against another, the Romans would tie the corpse to the murderer. As the body rotted, the murderer became sick with disease and died a miserable death.

It is a proven fact that anger and the unwillingness to forgive will make you sick. Is a bully worth doing that to your health?

#### #tbh:

Any amount of gratitude, whether the size of a mustard seed or as large as a boulder, can give you a better attitude about life. It is not easy to hold the line and remain positive when things are going wrong. But, with determination and effort it can be managed. Things will go your way if you believe they can. It's the power of positive thinking. It works.

# ACCOMPLISHED

**#tbh:**

See yourself as worthy: worthy of having good friends, a joyful life, being treated with dignity and respect. If you do not see yourself as worthy or recognize your value, how do you expect others to? Believe you are worthy, and soon others will, too.

**#tbh:**

Have you been making personal sacrifices to please someone else while destroying your own life in the process? Are you making these sacrifices to seek someone's approval?

Ask yourself these two questions:

*"Why do I need their approval?"*
*"Why does their opinion of me matter so much?"*

You should never sacrifice who you are as a person to please someone else. Respect is earned, not bought. Respect yourself. Stand up for yourself and what you believe in, no matter what anyone else thinks. Just don't be a jerk about it.

**#tbh:**

Retrain your brain to *"I can"* not *"I can't"*.

# VALUABLE

**#tbh:**

Words always matter. Words can lift you up. Words can tear you down. Always choose them wisely.

**#tbh:**

If you are failing school because of being bullied, there are two things you need to do: stop focusing on the bully and get focused on yourself.

Bullying is ruining your future. It needs to stop right now. Try setting a goal for yourself to start bringing your grades back up before the school year ends. Make it a realistic goal. The object is to help you, not stress you out. For example: go up one grade or even half of a grade - like a C to a C+.

When negativity strikes, it is very important you remain focused on the positive things in your life.

It is pointless to destroy your future over someone who (believe it or not) will not even matter a year from now. Do not give a bully the power to wreck your future.

**#tbh:**

Staying true to yourself is the best thing in the world you can do.

# CAPABLE

**#tbh:**

You have the right to feel good about yourself, even if someone does not agree you should.

**#tbh:**

Everyone has the potential to be *something* and to be *somebody*.

Being somebody does not mean being famous. Being somebody can be as simple as: being a person who is kind to others or a person who sets goals and tries to accomplish things in life.

You are somebody with the power and ability to be anything and everything you want to be. Never quit, compromise or give up on yourself.

# AMAZING

**#tbh:**

Contrary to what you might think about yourself or what others may have told you, you are not weak. You are not a loser. You are not pathetic. You are not a slut. You are not a nerd, a dork or a geek. Why are you giving negativity a place in your life and ignoring the positive stuff? Did you know you can choose to put the bullying garbage out on the curb and stop tolerating it in your life?

# BOLD

**#tbh:**

Boundaries are meant to protect you. They help you maintain control of your life. Boundaries are not about becoming a diva or a snob. The purpose of setting boundaries is to not allow people to abuse you physically, mentally or emotionally. Setting boundaries will ensure you are to be treated with respect, dignity and courtesy or not at all. What boundaries are you prepared to set?

**#tbh:**

Respect yourself enough to never settle for anything less than what you would do to or for another.


**#tbh:**

Did you know you have a right to protect yourself?
Did you know you do not have to tolerate abuse?
Did you know you can speak up and ask for help?

Being mistreated by someone is unacceptable behavior on their part. You should never allow someone to have that kind of abusive power over you.


# DARING


**#tbh:**

Did you know everyone is going through stuff?

Granted, their issues may or may not be as serious as yours. But, to them, they are the most important thing in the world. You are not the only one in pain, feeling hurt, disappointment, sorrow, anger, confusion, sadness or depression.

Everyone, from your teacher, to your parents, to your friends, are all dealing with something - including your bully. Though it may appear everything is perfect in their life, do not be fooled. Some people are good at hiding their issues or handling them better than others.

You are not alone in having to *"deal with stuff"*. Everyone must deal with unpleasant issues at some point. Nobody rides for free in the ups and downs of life.

*"Okay. But, how does this help me when it comes to being bullied?"*

You need to understand that the bully has issues they are dealing with, too.

*"Yeah, but the stuff I am dealing with is because of the bully. What about that?"*

The difference between you and a bully is: they choose to act out their pain by behaving like a jerk. And you choose to react when they do.

*"How else am I supposed to act when someone hurts my feelings?"*

The natural reaction is pain. But, although you may feel it, you do not have to act on it and show a bully they got to you. Think about it.

A bully strikes out at someone to help ease the pain they are dealing with down inside. For them to stop feeling pain for even a second, they must take it out on someone. It is inexcusable, unacceptable, thoughtless, abusive behavior on their part.

But they are choosing to behave that way. You can choose not to react to it from now on. Just because someone dishes garbage to you does not mean you must accept it.


**#tbh:**

You have nothing to prove to anyone other than yourself.

**#tbh:**

If you want to feel whole and complete, first, love yourself.

**#tbh:**

Those who love you for you will be there. Those who want to use you, show them the door.

**#tbh:**

You can flee from a bully, but you cannot escape from yourself. Acknowledge your issues and pain. Then, heal from it and move on.

**#tbh:**

Looking up to or imitating someone who lacks patience, kindness, a tolerance for others, acts prideful, rude, nasty, violent, or spreads hurtful gossip, is physically abusive, lies, yells, cusses people out, is not a good example on how to behave and be respected by others.

**#tbh:**

Always be polite until there is a valid reason for you not to be. Treat others how you would like to be treated, even if they fail to return the same. You do it not to win their approval or because you expect something in return. You do it because it is the right way to behave.

**#tbh:**

Take the high road, when someone takes the low road with you. It is not always easy to walk in love when someone is so hateful towards you, but you will be a better person for having done so.

**#tbh:**

Love grows and flourishes. Hate withers and dies at the root. Better to love than hate.

**#tbh:**

There is a saying out there that goes something like this:
*"The dash between your date of birth and the date of your death is your life."*

Make your dash count.
Your life matters.
You matter.
Never forget that.

**#tbh:**

Always do your best. If it is not good enough for someone, they are not good enough for you.

**#tbh:**

Learning to love yourself, after years of self-hatred, takes time. Be patient with yourself.

**#tbh:**

If somebody loves and respects you, they will not force you to send naked pictures of yourself to them.

**note:** *Check your State Law. If sexted pictures you received are from someone under the age of eighteen, you are in possession of child pornography. You could face criminal charges, jail time and must register as a sex offender.*

No matter how much in love you might be or how great you think the person you are with is, you need to know that feelings change. The same person you thought would never hurt you, could destroy you. Protect yourself. If someone walks out of your life because you would not send them naked pictures of yourself, then they did not care about you from the beginning. They were only using you. You deserve better.

# THANKFUL

**#tbh:**

So, you have a problem with a bully. But, you are afraid to tell someone about it. You fear that if you talk to an adult, you will be made fun of or seen as being weak or uncool. Or, you are afraid your problem might be viewed as unimportant or silly when it feels like a matter of life or death to you.

You should not have to wake up every day feeling sad, depressed or angry over someone's thoughtless actions towards you. If that is how you are feeling, you need to talk to someone you trust about it. And, by someone, I mean preferably an adult. Yes, you can talk to your friends, but they might not know what to do or they could violate your trust and blab it around school.

Knowledge is power. You acknowledge that you have a problem and need help for that problem. This is a powerful step towards healing. Do you realize that? Find someone you feel comfortable enough talking to and share what is bugging you. Once you start talking about it, you will feel like a giant weight is lifted off you.

**#tbh:**

The phrase, *"It's hopeless"* is a lie. Life is full of challenges. Some you will win. Some you will lose. Nobody can be a success all the time. It's unrealistic. The key is to remain balanced when changes and challenges arise.

**#tbh:**

No situation is ever hopeless. You may feel like right now you have no control over your life, but that is not true. You DO have control. You have had control all along. You just did not realize it until now.

**#tbh:**

You have a good future ahead of you, even if it does not look like it right now.

# GENUINE

**#tbh:**

The mind is a powerful thing. It can make you see the good. It can also make you see the bad. It can influence you to do right. It can influence you to do wrong. It can make you believe lies and rumors a bully spread about you. It can also make you believe positive things people say about you. It is all in what you allow to come into your head and take root inside your heart. Although the mind is a powerful thing, you are still the one who is in control. You are the one who has the power to choose what you want to believe.

**#tbh:**

Stop comparing yourself to others. You are beautifully and wonderfully made. You are perfectly flawed, as you should be.

You are not perfect. You never will be. Neither will anyone else. Those unique qualities you get picked on for, are what make you special. There is no one else like you on the planet. Be proud of who you are and never allow anyone to make you feel bad about yourself.

**#tbh:**

Put your right hand on your left shoulder, your left hand on your right shoulder. Now give yourself a hug.

**#tbh:**

Please, aspire to love yourself. Not with arrogance or pride. Love yourself with appreciation, joy and kindness. Take the time to get to know who you are as an individual. I have said it before, but it bears repeating. For others to love and accept you, you must first love yourself. If you do not love yourself, how do you expect anyone else to love you? There are plenty of reasons to love yourself. Just look in the mirror.

# FAB

**#tbh:**

Never feel ashamed or bad about yourself if you fail. Part of trying anything is failing. It is okay to fail. You tried. And that counts for something. So, what if you fail? Big deal. People try and fail all the time. If you happen to fail at something, try again until you succeed. Failure is viewed as a bad thing only if you never tried in the first place.

**#tbh:**

Believe in yourself.

**#tbh:**

You do not have to play the hand you were dealt. The beauty of cards is you can always change them or reshuffle the deck.

# HAPPY

**#tbh:**

God does not make mistakes. You are not a mistake. You are not a disgrace. You are not a screw-up. You are not worthless. You are not naïve. You are not a loser. But, you are not perfect, either. No one is. You are going to be okay.

**#tbh:**

Do not grow weak and weary during trying times. Those who persevere stand strong like a tree against a mighty wind. Those who are weak snap like a twig in a light breeze. Things will get better. They have too. Do not give up. You are a strong mighty tree.

**#tbh:**

Nothing is ever hopeless or out of reach. Nothing is ever an overnight fix, either. If it were, we would all be going around twitching our noses like Samantha from the TV Show

*"Bewitched"*. But that is not real life. Real life is ups and downs. Everything takes work. That is the truth.

# MOTIVATED

**#tbh:**

You have nothing to be sorry for.

**#tbh:**

Do ever wish you were someone other than you?

Stop thinking this way.

The only person you need to be is yourself. There is nothing wrong with you. If you think there is, that is a choice you are choosing to make based on false ideas you have of yourself or what a bully has said to you. You can choose to accept yourself, just as easily as you can reject yourself.

You should know not everything is as it seems. People are good at hiding shameful secrets and pain. Stop putting yourself down and comparing yourself to others. You do not know what goes on behind closed doors in their life.

If you do not like something about yourself then change it. But, change it for you. Do not make any changes to yourself or your life because you are trying to please someone else. Being a people-pleaser is a waste of your time.

# VICTORIOUS

**#tbh:**

Establish a healthy relationship with yourself. It does not have to be perfect. No relationship ever is. All relationships take effort and commitment.

**#tbh:**

It is a good thing sometimes to spend some *"me time"* getting to know who you are. Get to know who you are as a spirit and a soul. Only you can know who you truly are down inside. Do not be afraid to get to know yourself. Stepping outside of our comfort zone and learning who we are is a good thing. It can be an exciting time to learn what you like and who you want to be in life.

**#tbh:**

Exit the pothole ridden road which you have been traveling down. It is time to hit the metaphoric *"open road"*, roll the windows down and enjoy a new journey.

**#tbh:**

You are not worthless.

**#tbh:**

If you take the high road you will not get a nose bleed. Sometimes the best way to handle someone who has done you wrong is to do nothing. If they cannot upset you, the thrill for them is gone. You win - they lose. Pretty neat trick, huh?

# STRONG

**#tbh:**

Stop living in the past. You cannot undue what has been done. It is finished. It is pointless to continue dipping back into the *"what was"* or *"what could have been"* or *"how it should be"*. Let it go. Live in the present. It is time to take a bold step towards a future that can be anything you choose it to be. You are in control of it.

**#tbh:**

There will never be another you. Appreciate your life. Take care of yourself. Love yourself.

# OPTIMISTIC

**#tbh:**

You have a mind. The bully does not matter.

**#tbh:**

Recognizing the root cause of an issue gets you 50% closer to resolving it and living a more peaceful life.

# SERENE

**#tbh:**

Beware of the metaphoric octopus tentacle that brings about past hurts and other negative stuff in your life.

There will always be a tentacle from the past trying to ensnare you and keep you from moving forward. The tentacle is meant to make you feel your situation is never going to change or getting better. It is a lie and a deception.

When a tentacle from the past tries to enter your mind or your life, say, *"Be gone!"* and then continue moving forward.

You have the choice not to be trapped in misery due to lies, deception and situations that have long been over. While you cannot undo what has already been done, you can choose to not let it hinder you anymore. Severe the tentacles from the past. Be free.

**#tbh:**

Ask yourself this one important question:
*"Who am I?"*

Not,
*"Who am I according to what others think of me?"*

Get a journal and write down everything about yourself from your likes to dislikes, favorite things, stuff you cannot stand, what you love about yourself, what you wish you could change about yourself and why, etc... Find out who you are for you, not who you are according to how others define you.

**#tbh:**

The beautiful thing about life is you get to start over again and again, no matter how many times you mess up. The same cannot be said about death. Death is final.

# INSIGHTFUL

**#tbh:**

Even if you are being treated like a social outcast, try and be a friend to someone who you think may be in the same boat. Taking your mind off your own troubles and giving time to another does wonders for your self-esteem. You never know what type of impact your gesture of kindness could have on someone in pain. It might literally be their last life line.

**#tbh:**

These five words can mean a lot to someone in pain: *"I am here. I care."*

**#tbh:**

The only person you must please when you look in the mirror is yourself.

**#tbh:**

The only two places the word *"Perfect"* exists is in a dictionary and the Bible. Stop exhausting yourself trying to be someone you cannot possibly ever be. Perfect.

**#tbh:**

Forgive those who have done you wrong. Forgive yourself for things you said or did or allowed to happen. Forgiveness is the key to releasing the hurt and healing.

# YOUTHFUL

**#tbh:**

Not being popular or not having alot of friends should never make you feel bad about yourself. This is no reflection on you as a person. Having a few friends, one friend or even no friends does not make you any less of a person than someone who does.

*"School Popularity"* is a brief time in your life, not your entire life. You should never look at not being popular
as *"the end of the world"*. So, what if you don't become prom queen, head cheerleader, school stud or the class president? It is okay if you want to strive for those titles, but if you do not achieve them, know you are still a terrific person.

**#tbh:**

What matters is quality, not quantity, in every area of your life.

# BLESSED

**#tbh:**

Sometimes life stinks. But, that's no reason to quit living it.

**#tbh:**

Things will work out.

# WISE

**#tbh:**

Laughter really is the best medicine when you are feeling down. Laughing releases feel good hormones called endorphins which make you happy. Try laughing. It might help make you feel better, even if only for a little while.

**#tbh:**

When you have done all you can do, stand tall.

# DETERMINED

**#tbh:**

Have courage, stay committed, remain consistent and you can achieve anything in life.

**#tbh:**

You are the head and not the tail! You are above and not beneath! Never forget it!

**#tbh:**

Even though things may appear bleak and you feel like you have wasted your time or missed out on things, know that you have not. Everything you think you have been robbed of will come into your life even better than you could have ever imagined. If you stay focused on getting your life in order, things will work out for your benefit.

# EXCEPTIONAL

**#tbh:**

You were born for a good purpose in life. Your Creator knew you even before you were born. And, even though right now, you might be feeling like your purpose is to be treated like garbage, please know that is simply not true.

You are loved. God loves you. People in your life love you even if they have a tough time saying it or showing you. You are not alone. You really aren't. There is nothing that will stop God from loving you and wanting only the best for your life. God is love. He loves you unconditionally. Love yourself, too. You are worthy of being loved. You deserve to be loved.

**#tbh:**

Imperfections are beautiful.

**#tbh:**

Be in the present. Let go of the past. Look forward to your future.

OVERCOMER

the end of the book.
the beginning of your new life.

# normandy d. piccolo

# q & a

# questions

# answers with

## *normandy d. piccolo*

**Q. How did you become involved with bullying?**
I was severely bullied from the age of five until my mid-twenties.

**Q. Were you ever suicidal because of being bullied?**
Yes. It did reach a point where I attempted suicide one time.

**Q. What stopped you from ending your life?**
I realized that if I ended my life, the bullies won. And, they were not worth my life. I decided I wanted to no longer be a victim. I wanted to overcome the pain and help bullied kids to not feel the horrific pain I had experienced for years.

**Q. Did you write 'Bullied Dying to Fit In' as a way to help you heal from being bullied? It is put together in an unusual format, not like most books about bullying.**
Yes and no. Yes, because it did help me heal as the words poured forth. But the main reason I chose to write *'Bullied Dying to Fit In'* and, in that particular format, was because the market is flooded with so many "my

bully story" books. I wanted the reader to know that "I get it". I understand how they feel because I have been there. But, at the same time, I also wanted to allow the reader *(a person who is being bullied)* to see it as "their story". I also wrote it this way for those who have never been bullied, to help them realize how painful it is to be bullied. And, I am hoping to help parents who have a child being bullied or lost a child who was bullied to understand the pain and maybe answer some of the 'whys' which are often asked after a tragedy.

**Q. What do you hope the book accomplishes for those who are being bullied?**
By the turn of the last page, I want bullied kids to see their future in a positive light and to heal from the pain and know that they are not alone. The book contains five sections; hurting, facts, scoop, healing and #tbh, which range from the pain of being bullied, to information, to the bold truth about bullying and how to gain strength to rise above it.

**Q. How do we end bullying?**
Unfortunately, there will always be bullying. Bullying exists even in the animal and insect world. As for humans, hopefully through better education programs at school, more communication at home with their parents, the teaching of basic manners, learning how to agree to disagree and develop better acceptance and tolerance of others. As a society we need to become more sensitized and less

desensitized. This happens by having more human contact vs electronic communication.

Taking these steps, a bullied victim will better understand how to stop being a victim and see their bully through new eyes. The same goes for the bully. Hopefully he or she will learn how to better communicate with others without using physical, mental or emotional abuse towards them.

**Q. What was one of the most surprising things you learned while writing 'Bullied Dying to Fit In'?**

I discovered I had a lot of pain that was tucked away down inside that I never dealt with.

**Q. And have you since dealt with the pain?**

I have. But, I would be lying if I told you everything in my life is perfect since dealing with and healing from the pain. Perfection is an unrealistic goal. And, if anyone tells you otherwise, they are mistaken.

**Q. If you had one piece of advice to give, what would it be?**

Life throws us challenges every day. It's how we choose to handle those challenges that makes us or breaks us. You have the power – you have had it all along. The power of choice. You can choose to allow a bully to ruin your life. Or, you can choose to take your life back. Your choice.

**Q. What do you think makes a good story?**

The truth.

**Q. What were your goals and intentions in this book?**

To help someone not feel the way I did about myself for the longest time because of bullying. Having people hate you hurts. And, I did hate myself right along with the bullies. When someone says hateful things about you over and over, it's hard not to believe them after a while.

**Q. How do you feel you achieved your goals and intentions in 'Bullied Dying to Fit In'?**

If I help only one person overcome bullying and heal, then mission accomplished.

**Q. What was the hardest part of writing this book?**

I would have to say the section entitled, "hurting" because I had to reach deep down inside and basically bear mine and every bullied person's soul. It was a very painful, and yet at the same time healing journey. Being bullied is very damaging to a person mentally, physically and emotionally. It goes deeper than I think most people realize.

**Q. What did you enjoy most about writing this book?**

I really enjoyed writing the section entitled, "#tbh" because it is truthful, honest and positive. The section talks to you, not at you. So, for those who have no one to talk to or get advice from, this section can be helpful.

# Why is Kristyn A. Kutter?

book 3

*Why is Kristyn A. Kutter?* won two awards and was placed in the TOP 10 List for Fiction/Non-Fiction and the Fiction Recommendation List.

**2021 In the Margins Book Award/ School Library Journal**

Instead of talking about her problems, Kristyn A. Kutter's rebellious spirit and self-hate has led to episodes of depression and self-mutilation when things go wrong. It did not help that her best friend committed suicide, leaving her to wonder if she will end up the same way. This book arms the reader with resources for crisis intervention through national centers and online support sites.

**\*Trigger Warning:** Includes strong language, non-graphic depictions of self-harm, drug and alcohol usage and sexual situations. Recommended for ages 16+\*.

# Why is
# Kristyn A. Kutter?

Normandy D. Piccolo

**Normandy's Bright Ideas**
**Florida**

Why is Kristyn A. Kutter?
Printed in the United States of America
Copyright ©2019, 2023 by Normandy's Bright Ideas
ISBN: 978-0-9979349-5-3

Pixabay.com Photos Credits:
Alexandr Ivanov
Gerd Altmann
Alexas Fotos

**www.normandydpiccolo.com**

# TRIGGER
# WARNING

*Why is Kristyn A. Kutter?* discusses serious and difficult issues regarding self-harm, depression, and suicide. If you or anyone you know are struggling with any of those issues, please seek help at a support or crisis center in your area or online through local and national organizations.

National Alliance on Mental Illness (NAMI)
800-950-6264(NAMI)
info@nami.org
Text "NAMI" to 741741

Suicide Prevention Lifeline
800-273-8255

Includes strong language, non-graphic depictions of self-harm, drug and alcohol usage and sexual situations. Recommended for ages 16+*.

## SELF-HARM IS NEVER THE ANSWER.
## SUICIDE IS NEVER THE ANSWER.

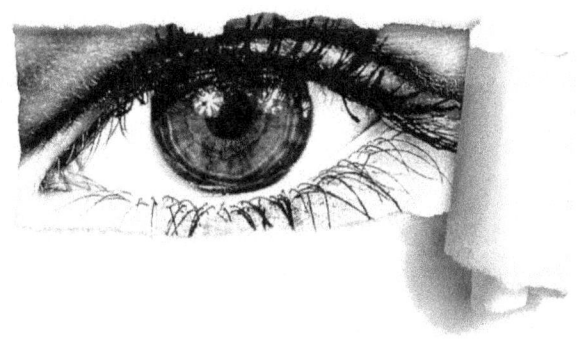

"This cut is for..."

Kristyn Amelia Kutter

Location, New York City.
Born of British American parents.

Beautiful, but awkward.
Fragile, yet able.
Lost, but still somehow existing.
Happiness - a long-forgotten sentiment.

Headstrong, yet submissive.
Crass, but delicate.
Consumed with vulnerability.
Persistently fearing emotional intimacy.

A peppered British and North American accented voice.
A wicked flirtatious laugh.
A smirk *always* displayed upon the face.
A daredevil who will try anything, except *Fugu*.

Secretive, yet sometimes forthright.
A truth seeker, but a liar, too.
Honest feelings often hidden behind sarcastic remarks.
Pain masked using drink, drugs and self-harm.

A master of illusion.
But, also a failure at acknowledging her own delusions.
Believing herself to be clever and in control.
Allowing one to see only what she is willing to reveal.
Nothing more.

Petite.
But, not too short.
Slender.
But, not overly thin.

She has porcelain skin, dark hair and smells of coconut.
Light pink lip gloss hides her naturally plump, pursed lips.
Both sapphire blue eyes coated with smudged black eyeliner.
Hints of light peach blush coat her strong cheek bones.

She always wears frayed hem, bootcut, ripped jeans.
A black long-sleeved burnout T-shirt with the collar cut off,
loosely hangs off her boney right shoulder.
Burnout fabric means to her, *'I exist, but not really'.*

Graffitied red sneakers hide her size 6 feet.
They're littered with vile words and band names in black ink.
She removes the right sneaker.
It drops to the floor.

The word *slag* scribbled on the left shoe catches her eye.
She angrily throws the sneaker across the room.
Her bare feet and painted dark blue toenails are now exposed.
The only hidden part of herself she is willing to reveal, so far.

Most think they know her.
They do not.
She does not even know herself.
*"Want to know me? Fuck off!"*

A faded-red antique wing armchair cradles her tiny frame.
She glances down at her cellphone and scowls.
Another rumor about her has landed on social media.
She mutters, *"Wankers!"* and slams the phone down.

She pulls both knees in towards her chest and hugs herself.
Vibes of nervousness begin to encroach.
The room feels cold, lifeless – a kismet vibe to her soul.
She shudders and lights a cigarette.

Her eyes scan the room.
Boring furniture and four drab painted walls.
There is a lone spider plant in need of watering.
A cricket trapped inside a floor vent can be heard chirping.

A digital audio voice recorder rests on a table before her.
A hand reaches forward and pushes the *record* button.

# chapter one

*A feminine, soft-spoken American accented voice begins speaking.*

Q. "Testing. Testing."

*Kristyn inhales a drag off her cigarette and replies in her mixed accent.*

A. "'S working."

Q. "How do you know?"

*With cigarette in hand, Kristyn points at the device.*

A. "The red button 's lit."

*The playback button is pushed, and the recorded 'testing' is heard.*

Q. "*Ah*, so, it is. Still getting used to this thing."

*The record button is pushed again.*

Q. "Let's begin, shall we?"

*Kristyn inhales a deep breath then, slowly exhales. She senses her sarcastic defense mechanism already kicking in before the first question is even asked. She takes one more drag off her barely smoked cigarette before dropping it into a soda can.*

Q.  "Who are you?"

*Kristyn shrugs her shoulders.*

Q.  "Is there something about yourself you wish to share?"

*Kristyn scoffs. She decides to test the boundaries and see what she can and cannot get away with.*

*'Let's see how you react to this one.'*

A.  "Here's a clue 'bout me."

Q.  "Okay."

A.  "I'm Miss Scarlett, chattin' up Colonel Mustard in the Conservatory, while smoking some spliff."

*She then smirks.*

A.  "Satisfied?"

Q.  "Interesting."

A.  "Which part?"

Q.  "I thought you were Kristyn sitting in a chair deliberately avoiding giving my question a serious answer."

*Kristyn arch's her eyebrows.*

*'Ah, a challenge. I think I might just fancy these sessions.'*

A.  "What if I am?"

Q. "We have a lot to cover. The sooner you answer my question…"

A. "The sooner I can get the hell out of here?"

Q. "Not exactly."

*Kristyn glances around the room before returning her gaze forward.*

A. "What do you want to know 'bout me?"

*She leans forward and lowers her voice.*

A. *"If I'm super wicked? A mega bitch? Prude with the girls?"*

*She then wiggles her bare shoulder in a teasing manner.*

A. *"Loose with the boys? What?"*

Q. "How about starting with your name and go from there."

*Kristyn sighs.*

*'Well, this just went from challenging to boring. Fine. We'll do it your way, or I might never get to leave.'*

A. "I'm Kristyn Amelia Kutter. Age seventeen and three-quarters. I drive a 1975 mauve VW Beatle. I make stupid decisions. But I am smart enough to be taking college courses while still in high school. I hate brussels sprouts. Oh, and I can't stand talking 'bout myself. Ever."

*She smirks.*

A.  "Are we sorted?"

Q.  "No."

A.  "Too bad. I'm leaving."

*Kristyn reaches for her brown fringe cross body purse and gets up from the chair.*

Q.  "Sit. Back. Down. Please."

*Kristyn hesitates. She wants to run away from the room, but even more from herself. Only she cannot seem to force her feet to take a step towards the door. So, she grudgingly plops back down into the chair.*

A.  "This is shit."

*She then slams her purse hard onto the table.*

Q.  "I detect insolence in your voice."

A.  "*Um*, because there is."

Q.  "Are you not ready to do this?"

*Kristyn looks at the door. She imagines herself leaping out of the chair and running away, leaving her purse, her shoes, her phone — everything behind. 'Oh, how I want to bail. Badly. But I can't. I mean, I can, but I can't. Grr. Why are issues so damn annoying? Or maybe it's just me. Maybe I'm the annoying one.'*

A.  "Let's get on with it."

*Her eyes lock on the door again.*

Q.  "Do you have somewhere else to be?"

A.  "Not really."

Q.  "Then why are you in such a rush to leave?"

A.  "Because any place else is better than being here."

Q.  "Why?"

A.  "Just 's."

Q.  "No one is making you stay."

*'Bollocks. You are. Okay. Okay. Maybe I am, too There. I owned it. Satisfied?'*

*Kristyn turns her gaze from the door to the window. She watches the wind playfully tease dangling leaves on a tree.*

Q.  "These sessions are to help you deal with your issues, Kristyn."

*She mutters.*

A.  *"Brilliant."*

Q.  "If you choose to be difficult about things, you are not only wasting my time, but yours, too."

*'My entire life is a waste of time. So, fucking off more time in sessions doesn't really matter, right?'*

*Her blue sapphire eyes fixate back on the door, again.*

Q. "Why do you avoid talking about yourself?"

*Kristyn shrugs her shoulders.*

A. "No point, really."

Q. "The truth, please."

*'It's one version.'*

A. "Fine. I don't like talking 'bout myself. I told you already. Apparently, you don't listen very well, do you?"

Q. "Why do you not like talking about yourself?"

A. "*Umm*...I'm not a narcissist."

Q. "Talking about yourself, especially when getting help, does not make you a narcissist."

A. "I disagree."

Q. "Do you want to know what I think?"

*'Not really. But I have a feeling you're going to tell me anyway despite my protesting.'*

A. "What?"

Q. "I do not believe..."

*She rolls her eyes.*

*'Here we go.'*

Q. "I do not believe concerns about narcissism or a dislike of talking about yourself are the reasons why you work at dodging the topic of 'you'."

*Kristyn crosses her arms and scowls.*

A. "Are you calling me a liar?"

Q. "More like an avoider."

*'I'm currently trying my best to avoid answering your annoying, meaningless questions. It's not working.'*

*Despite being annoyed, an ounce of her becomes a little curious.*

A. "What am I avoiding? I mean, according to you because personally, I don't give a shit."

*She then spitefully adds.*

A. "For the record."

Q. "I believe you are avoiding self-discovery."

*She cranes her neck back and scoffs.*

A. "Self-discovery?"

*She snickers.*

A. "That's your amazing answer?"

*She is now angry at herself for being curious enough to ask.*

*'You should have kept your mouth shut. Idiot.'*

Q.  "I think you are afraid to discover who Kristyn Amelia
    Kutter truly is. Could I be right?"

*Kristyn shrugs her shoulders.*

A.  "I don't know. And, I don't care to know, either."

*'You do know, and you do care. Stop lying.'*

Q.  "I think you care, or you wouldn't be here."

*Kristyn bites down hard on her bottom lip. She winces from the pain at
first, before a rush of calm washes over her.*

*Typical self-harming behavior: to seek physical pain to get immediate relief
from emotional distress.*

A.  "It doesn't matter who I am in this gutted existence you
    call life."

*'Psst. I already know who I am. A loser. If you were smart, you would
have figured it out already and saved us both a lot of time.'*

Q.  "Why do you think you do not matter?"
A.  "What makes me *not* think it? Can we talk 'bout something
    else? This whole *'getting to know Kristyn'* chat is getting
    tiresome."

*Kristyn runs her hand through her hair.*

Q.  "It is important for you to know who you are to heal."

*'Request denied. Why am I not surprised?'*

A.  "Why does it matter who I am? I don't care who you are."

Q.  "Because you matter."

A.  "Yeah, until this session ends. Then, I'll be a file 13."

*Kristyn points her index finger straight ahead.*

A.  "You know it."

*She then points back at herself.*

A.  "I know it."

Q.  "Is that how you see yourself? A file 13?"

A.  "Pretty much. Rubbish. Garbage and the like."

Q.  "Why do you think you feel this way about yourself?"

*Kristyn shrugs her shoulders.*

A.  "I don't know."

Q.  "Stop saying *'I don't know'*. Be honest. You do know."

A.  "You want me to be honest?"

Q.  "It would help."

*Just remember. You asked. I tried to spare you the agony of hearing my pathetic life's story.'*

A.   "*They* think I'm shit. I happen to agree."

*Kristyn then scrunches up her face like she bit into a lemon.*

*'Happy now?'*

Q.   "Who are *they?*"

*Kristyn begins picking at her fingernails.*

A.   "Everyone."

Q.   "Everyone?"

A.   "Yeah. *Everyone.* What part of *everyone* don't you understand?"

*'And here I am thinking I'm an idiot. Nice to know in some way I'm not alone.'*

Q.   "Can you be more specific?"

*Kristyn releases a sigh laced with annoyance while continuing to pick at her fingernails.*

A.   "Kids at school. Family. Strangers. You know, *everyone.*"

Q.   "I am confused."

*She stops picking at her fingernails and looks up, perplexed.*

A.   "Seriously?"

Q.   "Yes."

A.   "Maybe I should be asking the questions then and not you."

Q.   "Sorry?"

*An alert sounds off on Kristyn's cell phone. The hangnail she had been working on is shoved to the side, as she mutters under her breath, while typing at the same time.*

A.   *"How in the fuck would you and your wee willy know anything at all 'bout my shagging skills? Little liar!"*

Q.   "Please put your phone away."

*She adds repeated exclamation points after 'Little Liar!!!!!!!!!' before slamming the phone down.*

A.   "Sorted."

Q.   "You seem upset by whatever you just read on your phone."

A.   "Like I said. *Everyone* thinks I'm shit."

Q.   "Not everyone is bad, Kristyn."

*She launches into a rant.*

A.   "*They* are. *They're* soulless. *They* won't leave me alone. It's like *they* want me six feet under getting ravished by worms until there is nothing left but bones sucked dry of marrow. Then, *they* want to torture my bones until each one is reduced to powder, and it still won't be good enough."

Q. "Someone's negative opinion of you is just that. Their opinion. It does not mean it is true."

*She rolls her eyes in disbelief.*

A. "Why? Because 'Psych-101 for Dummies' said so?"

Q. "Is there anyone in your life who you feel does not view you as ...."

A. "Shit?"

*Kristyn pulls both legs in and gives herself a hug. She whispers a quiet reply.*

A. *"Not anymore."*

# chapter two

Q. "What about letting someone in?"

*Kristyn shudders at the thought.*

A. "No way."

Q. "But you have let people in before, right?"

*'When most people reflect on past relationships, they see a Norman Rockwell painting. Not me. My encounters tend to favor the brush strokes of Salvador Dali – mostly distorted and very confusing.'*

*She sneers.*

A. "We all make mistakes."

Q. "Are you afraid to let someone in now?"

*'Every time I let someone in, I get headfucked. It's just not worth it.'*

Q. "Does getting close to someone scare you?"

A. "N-no."

*She crosses her arms tightly.*

*'LIE.'*

Q. "Your protective body language tells me people have caused you great pain."

*'What does your Magic 8 Ball say? I'm guessing, 'Signs point to, yes'.'*

*She quickly snaps back.*

A. "Life has caused me pain."

Q. "We all experience pain in life."

A. "Doesn't make it right, especially when it's done on purpose."

Q. "The mistrust you feel towards others will not disappear until you are willing to trust someone again."

*'Perhaps when hell freezes over then I'll give trust some consideration.'*

Q. "Will you think about what I said?"

*She becomes agitated.*

A. "I just want to be left alone. Fuck's sake!"

Q. "Have you ever tried setting boundaries to protect yourself from getting hurt?"

*She half-laughs.*

A. "Should I draw a chalk line that no one dare try and cross like back in Primary School?"

Q. "You have a metaphoric chalk line drawn already."

A. "Is that so?"

Q. "But I do not believe it to be an actual boundary."

A. "What is it then?"

Q. "A wall."

A. "A wall?"

Q. "I think you try and keep people away because you have a fear of getting hurt again."

A. *"Bugger."*

Q. "Boundaries are not a dreadful thing, Kristyn."

*'Easy for you to say because you're not standing in my shoes.'*

Q. "Boundaries let people know what you will and will not tolerate."

A. "How do I set a boundary for life then? Can you answer me that? Because I can't stand anything 'bout it anymore."

Dear Life,
You suck! I quit!

Piss off!

# chapter three

*Kristyn's cell phone beeps and a vinegary expression appears on her face.*

*'Oh, we're quite the crafty rhymer, aren't we?'*

*The posting: Kristyn Kutter is a SLUT-DUR!*

*She rereads the nasty comment in silence.*

*'So, not only am I slut. But a dumb one, too. Nice.'*

A.  "*Ugh*! It never stops."

Q.  "What never stops?"

*She remains fixated on her phone.*

A.  "Rumors."

*'I need to put this dozy cow in her place. Come on, Kristyn. Pull your head out of your bum and think, girl. Think!'*

*No smart retort comes to mind.*

*'Maybe she's right. Maybe you are a dumb slut.'*

Q.  "Who is treating you ..."

*She cuts in.*

A.  "I'm 'bout to find out."

*Kristyn soon learns who is hiding behind the unoriginal screenname,
FearlessQueenofMean.*

A.  "That *bitch* doesn't even go to my school."

*'I really want to curl up in a ball right now and cry. I'm so bloody tired of
fighting. But I can't quit. I just can't. Not, yet anyway.'*

Q.  "Have you tried blocking people who troll you online?"

*Her attention remains on her phone.*

A.  "Useless."

Q.  "Why is it useless?"

A.  "*They* just come back 'round with a new fake account."

Q.  "Do you enjoy the negative attention you get on social
     media?"

*She looks up.*

A.  "What? No!"

Q.  "Does it make you feel included since you feel ignored by
     your peers?"

*She looks up again with a stunned expression upon her face.*

A. "No!"

Q. "Why are you not pickier about who you allow onto your social media pages?"

A. "If I get a friend request from someone, it's hard to reject it."

Q. "Why is it hard for you to refuse a friend request, especially from someone you either do not know or suspect is a troll?"

A. "Because the number of followers on your page matters. It's like a popularity thing. You wouldn't understand."

*She resumes looking at her phone.*

Q. "So, for you it is about quantity not quality."

*She replies without looking up.*

A. "*Everyone* else, too."

Q. "Why do you think you have difficulty setting boundaries to keep people from mistreating you?"

*'You don't understand. It's hard to crave acceptance and get none. You have no choice but to convince yourself you prefer being alone to keep the pain away. But it's a lie. Nobody likes to be alone — not all the time, anyway. Anyone who says otherwise is full of shit.'*

A. "Maybe I'm just stupid."

Q. "You are not stupid, Kristyn."

*'Lie.'*

A. "People *love* to spread crap 'bout me, true or not."

Q. "Why do you suppose that is?"

*Kristyn holds up her cell phone.*

A. "I guess the bigger the jerk you are, the more popularity you gain. It's really fucked up, right?"

Q. "Have you considered deleting your social media accounts to avoid being trolled?"

*'No. Apparently I'm a masochist.'*

A. "I have to be in the know, even if I'm getting socially slammed by *everyone*."

Q. "Does being trolled online make you feel included?"

*She scoffs.*

A. "I told you already. I prefer being alone."

*'You are so full of it, Kristyn. You do not prefer being alone — especially since 'he whose name you cannot utter without losing your shit in tears and gorging down a dozen donuts' left. Hence the now endless parade of nameless, faceless blokes in and out of your bed, as you attempt to use your fanny to try and detract from the pain inside your broken heart.'*

Q. "Do you really believe that?"

*She does not answer.*

Q. "Kristyn?"

A. "What?"

Q. "You did not answer my question."

*She plays coy.*

A. "What was your question, again?"

Q. "Do you like being alone?"

*Kristyn deliberately ignores the question, again. She picks her phone up and finally replies to FearlessQueenofMean's cruel posting.*

*'STFU!!!!!!'*

*She releases a sigh of displeasure, before setting the phone back down.*

*'Total vanilla response. I suck.'*

*Kristyn crosses her right leg over her left and begins moving her right foot in small, counterclockwise circles. Tension is beginning to grow.*

A. "You know, my Grandpa told me when a baby chick 's born with a spot on its head, the other chicks attack it because it's different. All it takes 's one bird to start pecking at it, and then the rest join in not knowing why they are attacking it, too."

Q. "Do you see yourself as a spotted baby bird?"

*She nods her head once.*

Q. "Are you basing this opinion of yourself on what others think of you? Or is this how you feel about yourself without any outside influence?"

*That's like saying Potato vs Poe-ta-toe. Or Tomato vs. Toe-ma-toe. It's the same damn thing. Just depends on how you look at it.'*

A. "I don't know. Maybe both."

Q. "Why do you choose to believe the hateful things spoken about you, especially if you know they are not true?"

*Her phone alerts. A quick look and she sees FearlessQueenofMean fired back a response to her reply.*

Q. "Please put your phone away."

*She reluctantly complies.*

Q. "Back to my question."

*She mutters like a pissed off brat.*

A. *"Of course."*

Q. "Why do you choose to believe the hateful things spoken about you, especially if you know they are not true?"
A. "I just do."

Q. "I think you can give a better answer than that."

*'Nothing I say is going to be a good enough answer for you is it?'*

*She tries again, anyway.*

A.  "I'm a failure at everything I try and do in life."

*She then flashes a smile devoid of humor.*

A.  "Good enough answer for you?"

Q.  "This is not a test."

*'Maybe not, but you're making me testy.'*

A.  "If you say so."

Q.  "Why do you see yourself as a failure?"

*'How do I not see myself as a failure, I think, is the better question. I mean, don't you listen? Don't feel bad if you don't. Nobody else listens to me either.'*

A.  "I just don't fit in."

*'I don't care to, either.'*

*Another lie she tells herself to help lessen the sting of social rejection.*

A.  "*The Posh Miss Perfects'* can piss off far as I'm concerned!"

*'Always with their noses in the air, constantly posting duck lip – boob flaunting photos on social media. Total stuck-up wannabe models.'*

Q.  "Are the *The Posh Miss Perfects'* a band at your school?"

*Kristyn laughs.*

*'Hardly!'*

A. "Only if a nail file constitutes as a musical instrument."

Q. "I see."

A. "*They're* a popular clique of girls who go to my school. Perfect hair. Perfect teeth. Perfect clothes. Perfect boyfriends. Perfect family. Perfect friends. Perfect life."

*She ends with a snide remark.*

A. "Perfect *twats.*"

Q. "Those girls you believe to be perfect are probably going through a lot of the same issues you are."

*Kristyn rolls her eyes.*

*'Just stop right there.'*

Q. "No one is perfect, Kristyn."

A. "*They* think *they* are. I think perhaps *they're* right."

*'Wow! Maybe the hatred for myself is something The Posh Miss Perfects and I have in common. I wonder if they would invite me to sit with them at their reserved cafeteria table. I could wow them with my vast knowledge of acetone vs non-acetone nail polish remover.'*

*She replays the thought.*

*'Okay, Kristyn. I think you've sniffed too much nail polish remover if you think that is ever going to happen. Why would you want it to happen? Are you that desperate for friendship, you'd be willing to suck up to the Posh Miss Perfects?'*

*She ponders.*

*'No way! It's better if I keep to myself. Besides, I think I may have screwed around with a few of their boyfriends out of spite. Shhh!'*

Q. "The way you think appears to be a bit skewed, Kristyn."

*She bows up in the chair like an angry cat whose fur got rubbed backwards.*

A. "So now I'm not allowed to have an opinion?"

Q. "Of course, you can have an opinion."

A. "But you just said it was messed up."

Q. "I said your *thinking* was skewed."

A. "What does that mean?"

Q. "Mislead."

A. "Huh?"

*'Congratulations, Kristyn! You're now a dumb slut who avoids and is mislead. Three out of three. Cheers!'*

Q. "I would like for you to consider changing how you see things."

A. "I see things how they are."

Q. "Why not try and see things in a more positive light verses a negative one, *hmm*?"

A. "You want me to think like *everyone* else. 'S that what you're saying?"

Q "I want you to be yourself, but with eyes of positivity."

A. "If I do that, then I won't be myself."

Q. "Does change frighten you?"

*'Hell, YES it does!'*

A. "No."

*And the lies just keep coming.*

Q. "It is never too late to change."

A. "But what if it is?"

# chapter four

*Kristyn plops down in the chair. She is feeling completely withdrawn.*

Q. "What do you want to talk about today?"

*She lights up a cigarette, takes a deep drag and exhales.*

A. "Nothing."

*She puts her earbuds in and pulls up the band, The Prodigy/Breathe on her IPod:*

> Psychosomatic, addict, insane
> Breathe the pressure...

*'I wish I could say I am lost in my own private thoughts. But the truth is, I woke up today feeling nothing. Nothing. I just want to bask in the nothingness for a while. Is that wrong? It feels so empty and yet, it's offering me comfort, too. No anger. No sadness. Nothing.'*

*The digital recorder continues recording in case Kristyn decides to speak. For now, there is only the faint sound of music blaring from her earbuds, the soft sound of her lips parting while blowing smoke rings and an occasional serenade from the cricket still hiding in the floor vent.*

# chapter five

Q. "Tell me what a day in the life of Kristyn Kutter is like at school."

*Kristyn's eyes repetitively dart from the window to the door like windshield wipers.*

*'I could shirk this scene right now. I mean, come on. I don't really feel like recounting another shitty day of my life. But I know you won't let up until I answer. Just remember...you asked for it.'*

A. "I get called names."

Q. "Such as?"

A. "Slut, whore, skank and bitch."

Q. "Anything else?"

*'Oh, come on. Isn't that enough titillation for you?'*

A. "I get shoved and slapped 'bout sometimes."

Q. "Anything else?"

*'Do you get pleasure out of hearing 'bout my misery?'*

A. "Guys."

Q. "Guys?"

A. "Yeah. They only care 'bout getting off. They don't want my heart, just my fanny."

Q. "How does that make you feel?"

A. "Depressed. Dirty. Lonely."

*She then whispers.*

A. *"Humiliated."*

*And yet, despite feeling depressed, dirty, lonely and worst of all, humiliated, she woke-up in bed today next to a random hook-up she scored MDMA off the night before at a local club. She had to practically drag him out of her bed by his long blonde locks and shove him, with pants, shirt and shoes in hand, out her bedroom window and onto the roof before her mum came in to wake her up for school.*

*Hours later, she's still struggling to remember the night before.*

*'What the fuck was his name? Tanner? Tank? Tim? Tosser? Oh, well. Guess the shag wasn't memorable, but the MDMA he sold sure was. Hope I see him again – at least for the score.'*

# chapter six

Q. "Are your parents aware of what you have been going through?"

A. "No."

Q. "Why not?"

A. "Haven't told them."

Q. "Any particular reason why not?"

A. "They wouldn't understand."

*Kristyn looks downward at her newly decorated white trainers. Instead of band names and harsh words – this time – she covered the shoes in black ink question marks.*

*'I question everything 'bout life. Why I'm here? Why mean people exist? Will it ever get better? Am I doomed to be a loser my whole life? I wonder why, after all the shit I've been through. After all the shit they've put me through... why am I still here? What's the point?'*

A. "They don't get what it's like to be a loser."

*She puts her hand over her mouth, pretending to be shocked.*

A. "*Oops*, I mean, a teen, today."

Q. "Do you feel unworthy of being loved by your parents?"

*She turns the tables.*

A. "Do you feel unworthy of being loved by *your* parents?"

Q. "Let's keep the focus on you."

*She leans forward and replies in a rather catty tone.*

A. "*You* don't, do *you?*"

Q. "Are you going to answer my question?"

*Kristyn pulls the sleeves down on her shirt enough to cover her hands. It is a mild attempt on her part of hide herself from the world.*

'*I feel unworthy to be loved by a fucking earthworm. What does that tell you?'*

A. "'S hard to live up to their expectations, you know?"

Q. "Do your parents put demands on you?"

*She takes a drink of soda.*

A. "Like what?"

Q. "Do they expect you to get straight A's?"

A. "They never really hassle me 'bout anything."

*Kristyn shrugs her shoulders and begins pulling her hair.*

Q.  "Are you feeling anxious?"

A.  "Why?"

Q.  "I notice you are pulling on your hair."

*Kristyn suddenly drops her hand down onto her lap.*

A.  *"Sorry."*

Q.  "It was just an observation. No need to apologize. Getting back to…"

*Kristyn suddenly shouts out.*

A.  *"Argh!"*

Q.  "What is wrong?"

*'Haven't you ever felt like screaming for no reason?'*

A.  "Nothing."

Q.  "It is obviously something otherwise you would not have shouted out."

*'Getting me to confess 'bout it will be like pulling chewing gum out of my hair. Tedious and painful.'*

A.  "It's just…"

*She hesitates.*

A.  "It's just that…"

*'Oh, cut the crap, Kristyn. Say what you mean, girl, before I knock the words out of you with a smack to the back of the head.'*

*She thinks on the painful release a hit to the head might provide. Or, at the very least, deliver a brief distraction from the extreme pressure she is currently experiencing.*

*'Oh, God! I can't fucking breathe!'*

A.  "It's just that the more I share 'bout myself in these, whatever you call them…"

Q.  "Sessions."

A.  "The more I share, the crazier I feel I am."

Q.  "No more than most."

A.  "Is your comment supposed to help me feel better?"

Q.  "The more you share about yourself, Kristyn, the more you will discover about yourself."

*Kristyn wears a tentative smile.*

A.  *"Great."*

Q.  "Self-discovery can be an adventure."

A.  "Well in my world, you'll likely stumble upon a snake or two."

Q. "Do snakes frighten you?"

*Kristyn releases a sarcastic laugh.*

A. "No. But, I've shagged a few. *Unfortunately.*"

# chapter seven

*Kristyn enters the room in a huff. She slams her purse down on the table, and pops open a can of soda. Fizz from the soda spills over the side of the can and onto her jeans. She reaches for some Kleenex to wipe up the mess while mumbling to herself.*

*'Fucking hell! You, stupid cow! Can't do anything right, can you?'*

*She then swallows a few gulps of the sticky drink before setting the can down beside her purse.*

Q. "I see you wrote something new on your shoe."

*Kristyn raises her right leg and moves her foot side to side, proudly admiring her new artwork. She has once again written the word, 'Slag' in bold lettering.*

A. "It's cool, right?"

*'It's so not, you simpleton, and you know it.'*

Q. "Why did you vandalize your shoe, again?"

*Kristyn shrugs her shoulders.*

A. "Felt like it, I guess."

Q. "You guess? Or, you know?"

*Kristyn runs her hand through her tangled brown hair.*

A. "Maybe something had me feeling a bit tizzy at the time I wrote it."

Q. "What upset you?"

*'The fact that I woke up today. Isn't that enough of a reason?'*

A. "I don't want to talk 'bout it."

Q. "Why the word *slag?*"

*Kristyn glances at the spider plant. Only two green leaves remain on it. The rest are dry and brown.*

*'Once those leaves vanish, so too will the plant. It will be as if it never existed.'*

A. "*Lucky plant.*"

Q. "Why the word, *slag*, Kristyn?"

A. "Why not *slag?*"

Q. "Remind me again what a *slag* is?"

A. "A slut."

Q. "Why did you write it on your shoe again?"

*Kristyn says nothing.*

Q. "No one forced you to write *slag* on your shoe, right?"

*Kristyn's body grows rigid, as anger illuminates from her voice.*

A. "*They* did."

Q. "Who are *they?*"

*She sarcastically replies.*

A. "Tossers, wankers and trolls. *Oh, my!*"

Q. "Sorry. Who?"

A. "Kids at school and online."

*'Asses. Every one of them.'*

Q. "How did *they* force you to write *slag* on your sneaker?"

*Kristyn rolls her eyes and shakes her head side to side in disbelief.*

*'Don't be such a git. You know what I mean.'*

Q. "How do you justify blaming others for something you chose to do?"

*Kristyn draws her bottom lip in and nips it hard enough to invoke pain followed by slight relief. She is struggling to accept responsibility for what she knows down inside she chose to do. To avoid taking it – as is her way - she tries justifying her behavior by placing the blame, instead of owning it.*
*'If they didn't harass me 24/7 maybe I would have drawn a cheery flower or something.'*

A.  "I never fancied myself to be a *slag* until *they* said so."

*'So, I became one. Whether it's to fill a void of loneliness, barter for MDMA, boredom, spite, revenge, to forget...or I'm just feeling horny. Whatever. I do what I want. I do who I want. I don't care. It's just easier to be what they think I am. Least for me it is, anyway.'*

*More lies.*

Q.  "Regardless of *their* opinion of you, *you* are still the one who chose to vandalize her own shoe."

*'Don't you think I know that? Fucking hell!'*

*She tucks the sneaker under her left thigh.*

A.  *"Whatever."*

Q.  "What did you think of yourself before the *slag* campaign against you began?"

*She puts her face in her hands and moans.*

*'Oh, for fuck's sake! Let it go already.'*

*She looks up with a faint expression of disgust.*

A.  "I thought I was connecting."

Q.  "You mean relationships?"

*Her foot is beginning to fall asleep. She removes it from underneath her thigh and plants it firmly on the floor.*

A. "I didn't realize I was going to be branded sodding, *Hester Prynne* for it."

Q. "Have you ever asked why *they* call you a *slag?*"

*'Some people make mistakes. I, on the other hand, have a knack for royally fucking things up.'*

A. "Once."

*She mumbles.*

A. *"Unfortunately."*

Q. "Who did you ask?"

A. "Ian Rhodes."

Q. "Who is Ian Rhodes?"

A. "A complete wanker. He'll do it with anyone or anything. Even a hydrant stands a chance if you put lacy knickers and a short skirt on it."

*Kristyn sarcastically laughs.*

A. "Ian can put a horny toad to shame."

Q. "You do not think highly of Ian, do you?"

*Her eyes grow wide.*

*'You wouldn't either. Trust me.'*

A.  "He's revolting with his baggy pants, shaggy unkempt dirty-blonde hair, warped teeth and this white gunk that's always piled up in the corners of his eyes. All he does is smoke spliff, skate, shag, and sleep in class. Total loser."

Q.  "Why date Ian if he is so repulsive?"

A.  "I didn't date him."

*'Blech!'*

A.  "It's a pity shag thing. If you can even call it that."

*Kristyn shudders, recalling her regrettable encounter with Ian. Both were completely wasted at a party. Him on larger. Her on MDMA. They bumped into one another in the garage. Three wretched thrusts against the rubbish bins beside his mom's shiny black Mercedes, and it was over. Pants up. Skirt patted back down and off they went in separate directions.*

Q.  "Why sleep with someone you are not attracted to?"

A.  "Low self-esteem, plus loneliness, plus MDMA, equals a very bad decision I wish could be undone."

*'Like I said, I have a knack for royally fucking things up."*

Q.  "What was Ian's answer when you asked him why people call you a *slag?*"

A.  "Nothing."

Q.  "Nothing?"

A.  "Well, he did want a shag in the parking lot between English and History."

*Kristyn makes retching sounds.*

Q.  "Did you shag him?"

A.  "I told him to piss off."

Q.  "Why not shag him this time?"

*Kristyn furrows her brows.*

A.  "Simple. I was sober."

# chapter eight

Q.   "I would like to continue where we left off last session."

*I certainly don't. You're going to talk 'bout that fuckwit Ian Rhodes, again. I can feel it in my bones. I just know I'm right. As if those fifteen seconds in the garage wasn't enough punishment.'*

*Kristyn applies strawberry scented lip gloss. She returns the lip gloss to a small pocket inside her purse before fumbling around inside the bag for her phone. She gives the phone a quick look, before dropping it back into her purse with a look of disappointment upon her face.*

*No missed calls.*

*'I can't say I'm surprised.'*

Q.   "We last discussed you being called a *slag*."

*She imagines Ian's wretched lips coming at her neck like a famished vacuum. Slurrrrp!*

*'Gross!!! Just gross!!! Shut it down, Kristyn. Shut it down!'*

*She decides to take command of the conversation to avoid discussing her unenchanted encounter with Ian anymore.*

A.  "I don't understand why I've got a bad reputation and other girls at my school don't."

*Kristyn kicks off her shoes. To date, slag is still the only word written on the right shoe surrounded by a maze of different sized question marks.*

A.  "I mean, we all do the same stuff. It's so confusing."

Q.  "Not understanding why, you are being singled out is understandably..."

*'It worked! No more talk of knob head Ian.'*

A.  "It seems the more I fight back, the worse it gets."

*Kristyn runs her hand through her thick brown locks. Her index and middle finger become tangled. She pulls down hard. The strands give way and her fingers are released.*

A.  *"Stupid hair."*

Q.  "What about sex?"

*She watches as the broken strands of hair leave her hands and float freely down onto the floor, before turning her attention back to sex talk.*

A.  "What 'bout it?"

Q.  "What makes one encounter you have with someone different from another?"

A.  "I don't know. Lots of things, I suppose."

*She pushes her hair behind her ears.*

Q.  "What would you call your encounter with Ian?"

A.  "A clusterfuck of mass proportions."

Q.  "I *see.*"

A.  "I wish I could *un-see.*"

*She shudders.*

Q.  "Have you considered taking things slower?"

A.  "I'm not dating sloths."

Q.  "I mean, getting to know a person. Maybe date them for a while before engaging in sex."

A.  "No."

Q.  "Why not?"

A.  "I'm 'bout being in the moment."

Q.  "What about love?"

*Kristyn remains silent. Love is a touchy topic. She averts her eyes to the window. A thunderstorm has arrived, slamming giant raindrops against the windowpane. For a moment, she fears the glass might shatter. Much like her heart in the last year.*

Q.  "You are aware loose behavior can put you at a greater risk for STDs?"

A.  "*Eh*, so."

Q.  "Having sex with someone is serious."

*She replies in a nonchalant manner.*

A.  "Spare me the crotch infestation lecture. I've heard."

*Kristyn's cell phone suddenly rings. Her heart flutters as she retrieves the phone from her purse.*

'*Oh, please, oh please let it be…Ugh! Wrong number. Fuck!*'

Q.  "That's a nice tune your phone plays when it rings."

A.  "It's from a song from like 2000 or something."

*Before being asked, Kristyn puts her phone on vibrate and then drops it back into her purse.*

Q.  "What sort of music do you like?"

A.  "Depends on my mood. I like listening to techno when I'm in the mood to dance."

*Code for: drop hits of MDMA to dance and try and forget 'bout my shitty life for a while.*

A.  "But I really like alternative, industrial, goth, grunge and metal. The grittier, the better. I like songs that reach my soul, not just my ears, you know. I want to feel something. I think that's why I listen to bands who are real. I don't care if they're popular. Their music has to speak to my soul."

Q.  "So, you tend to relate to the songs you hear."

A. "Pretty much."

Q. "Do you want a boyfriend?"

A. "*Ah*. Can't we keep talking 'bout music?"

Q. "We can discuss music later. Let's continue working on you. Okay?"

*Kristyn pouts.*

Q. "Are you going to answer my question?"

A. "I told you already. I don't date anymore."

Q. "Why not?"

A. "Ask Jamey Marotto."

*She then coughs and speaks at the same time.*

A. "Stupid tosser."

Q. "We will get to discussing Jamey soon."

A. "How 'bout *never*."

# Jamey 🖤

I'm outside laying on my back in the soft grass right now and staring up at the glittering sky while listening to Mazzy Star, wondering if like the song, 'Let Me Get There' if I ever will find *the groove* again. I'm so fucking lost right now.

I keep listening to the song over and over. The singer's voice hypnotizes my soul while the music brings tears to my eyes. I prefer listening to Mazzy Star - all music for that matter - on vinyl. It just sounds better. At least to me it does. But I can't bring my record player outside. So, I'm listening to it on MP3. Digital always sounds like shit. But what can you do?

I think I might go vinyl shopping this weekend. I've got some money saved up. Okay, that's a lie. I nicked forty-bucks off Ian when he was busy feeling up my bum while giving me a hug. The idiot thought I was feeling him up in return when I was taking the money out of his back pocket. You know what? Screw records. I've had a shit week. I need to dance. I hope I run into that Tanner, Tommy, Tosser - whatever his name is at the club. He'll do me right...and then do me proper. Wink! Wink!

The stars are so bright tonight. Wish I was a star right now. How cool would it be to hang out in the sky twinkling light down on the world? How cool would it be having everyone admire you with kindness? How cool would it be having the worlds eyes on you? How cool would it be to be a part of something like a constellation and feel like you really belong? How cool would it be knowing how bummed people feel when dark clouds hide you from view? Wish I was a star instead of having to wish on one.

Speaking of stars...Mazzy Star "Fade into You" is beginning to play. I think I'll close my eyes and try not to think of Jamey and our countless make outs..... but I know that won't happen. I miss him so much. But then again, FUCK HIM!

# chapter nine

Q.  "What is love to you, Kristyn?"

A.  "Overrated."

Q.  "What do you feel when I say the word, *love?*"

*'Hearing the 'L' word makes me want to puke.'*

*She says nothing out loud.*

Q.  "Do you feel anything?"

*She reluctantly replies.*

A.  "Emptiness."

*'Oh, and revulsion, too.'*

Q.  "Why emptiness?"

*Kristyn releases a sigh and kicks her right foot out before bringing it back.*

*She becomes pithy.*

A.  "Love's a mirage."

Q.   "A mirage, *hmm?*"

A.   "Pretty much."

Q.   "For someone who thinks so little of love, you have some interesting observations about it."

*Kristyn looks out the window.*

A.   "So."

Q.   "Why do think love is a mirage?"

*She turns her attention back.*

A.   "Because it eventually leaves you gutted."

*She then lights up a cigarette and takes a deep drag.*

Q.   "Everyone who loves gets hurt, Kristyn."

*She scoffs.*

A.   "Some more than others."

*She takes another drag and flicks ash into a soda can.*

Q.   "Do you love yourself?"

A.   "I want to crawl out of my own skin."

Q.   "Why do you feel this about yourself?"

*She takes another drag.*

*'If you were me, you'd feel the same way.'*

*She shrugs her shoulders.*

Q. "Would you like to love yourself?"

*'No. Way. In. Hell.'*

A. "I don't see the point, really."

Q. "Why not?"

A. "I just don't."

Q. "What if I told you, you are already showing love for yourself."

*Her eyes narrow, full of suspicion.*

A. "How in the fuck am I doing that?"

Q. "By getting to know who you are in these sessions."

*She sharply replies.*

A. "I already know who I am. *Cheers.*"

Q. "We never truly know who we are or what we can endure until we are put in situations that test us."

A. "Well, I've already failed life's test."

Q. "I want to help you learn to love yourself."

*'Well, I certainly don't want to love myself. Nor do I want that disgusting 'L' Word anywhere in my life for that matter. EVER!'*

A. "Is it true we can think we know someone, but never really know them at all?"

Q. "Sometimes, yes."

A. "Then it's possible I could never really know myself no matter how much…"

*She does air-quotations.*

A. … *'self-discovery'* I do in these sessions."

Q. "That depends."

A. "On what?"

Q. "Your willingness to drop barriers and override any fear."

*She rolls her eyes in disbelief.*

A. "Seriously?"

Q. "You do not give yourself enough credit, Kristyn."

A. "And you, give me *way* too much."

i love him. i hate him. i love him. i hate him. i love him. i hate him. i love him. i hate him. i love him. i hate him. i love him. i hate him. i love him. i hate him. i love him. i hate him. i love him. i hate him. i love him. i hate him. i love him. i hate him. i love him. i hate him. i love him. i hate him. i love him. i hate him. i love him. i hate him. i love him. i hate him. i love him. i hate him. i love him. i hate him. i love him. i hate him. i love him. i hate him. i love him. i hate him. i love him. i hate him. i love him. i hate him. i love him. i hate him. i love him. i hate him. i love him. i hate him. i love him. i hate him. i love him. i hate him. i love him. i hate him. i love him. i hate him. i love him. i hate him. i love him. i hate him. i love him. i hate him. i love him. i hate him. i love him. i hate him. i love him. i hate him. i love him. i hate him. i love him. i hate him. i love him. i hate him. i love him. i hate him. i love him. i hate him. i love him. i hate him. i love him. i hate him. i love him. i hate him. i love him. i hate him. i love him. i hate him. i love him. i hate him. i love him. i hate him. i love him. i hate him. i love him. i hate him. i love him. i hate him. i love him. i hate him. i love him. i hate him. i love him. i hate him. i love him. i hate him. i love him. i hate him. i love him. i hate him. i love him. i hate him. i love him. i i love him. i hate him. i love him. i hate him. i love him. i hate him. i love him. i hate him. i love him. i hate him. i love him. i hate him.

i love him. i hate him. i love him. i hate him. i love him. i hate him. i love him. i hate him. i love him. i hate him. i love him. i hate him. i love him. i hate him. i love him. i hate him. i love him. i hate him. i love him. i hate him. i love him. shit!

# Jamey Marotto

# is a total

# HEADFUCK!!!

*'Jamey had called me last night and then ignored me the following day at school. He acted as if we never spoke 'bout our feelings for each other or nothing. Tosser! I was so pissed 'bout it that I snuck into a loo stall and wrote a warning to other girls. No. Wait. That's bullshit. I did it to help keep girls away from him. I don't think my heart can take it right now. Why is he headfucking me? More importantly…why am I letting him?'*

# chapter ten

Q. "You are stronger than I think you realize."

*Kristyn remains silent and maintains a stoic posture.*

*'You are too easy to fool. Too, easy.'*

Q. "You disagree?"

*She rolls up the right sleeve of her black burned out shirt, exposing numerous cuts.*

A. "Exhibit A happens to disagree with you."

*Kristyn's arm and wrists bear signs of the battle she has been fighting within herself. Her numerous scars are now on display like war wounds unworthy of the valor of a purple heart.*

*'I'm pathetic, not brave.'*

*Sprinkled between the old cuts are a few fresh ones etched as recent as yesterday. She stares down at her scars, remembering how and why each one came to be.*

*'So many not-so-fond- memories to recall. Where do I begin?'*

Q. "Pull your sleeve back down, please."

*Kristyn wears a puzzled expression upon her face.*

A.   "Why? I thought you were going to help me sort out this
     cutting thing I do."

*Kristyn half-heartedly pulls the shirt sleeve back down.*

Q.   "I would like to revisit your old shoes, today."

*'For fuck's sake. Let it go already.'*

A.   "Why?"

Q.   "Because you chose to wear them today and I would like to
     discuss why."

*Kristyn folds her arms in defiance.*

*'Well I don't feel like talking 'bout my shoes.'*

Q.   "Please read some of the words out loud."

*She thrusts her right sneaker forward.*

A.   "Read them yourself."

Q.   "No. You do it."

*She knows which words are meant to be heard, but deliberately reads the
band names out loud instead.*

A.   "Prodigy. The Cure. Incubus. Slipknot. Disturbed.'

Q.   "The words, Kristyn."

*She sighs loudly.*

*'Gawd! You can be so annoying!'*

A. "Fine. Slag, whore, easy, loser, stupid, fat, dumb, lame, dork, geek, pathetic, nobody, nothing, zero and worthless."

Q. "Do you believe those words apply to you?"

A. "Wouldn't have written them otherwise."

Q. "Why did you choose to wear those shoes today?"

A. "Do I need a reason to wear shoes? I mean, besides avoiding bacteria or getting worms."

Q. "For those particular shoes, yes, you do need a reason."

A. "*They* think the words apply to me. I happen to agree."

*'Yesterday was a shit day at school for me. I don't want to talk 'bout it because you'll just dissect the hell out of like a damn frog pickled in formaldehyde.'*

*Here's what happened:*

*'The bullying got so bad; I spent my lunch hour hiding out in the bathroom, cutting on my arm and secretly crying. Fearlessqueenofmean, who doesn't even go to my school, spread a rumor 'bout me shagging some cheerleader's boyfriend. I don't even know the guy. Or the cheerleader. But that didn't matter. Apparently. I personally think she's the one who's been shagging the guy. The cheerleader was 'bout to find out. So, she threw the blame my way to avoid getting her own ass kicked.'*

*'I chose to wear the shoes because I was hoping if I showed I agreed with the names they were calling me, they would leave me alone. Didn't work – unfortunately.'*

Q.  "When you say, *they*, you mean the bullies?"

*She mumbles.*

A.  *"Who else."*

Q.  "How do you feel about getting rid of the shoes?"

*She perks up. Shocked.*

A.  "Have you gone mad?"

*She thrusts both sneakered feet forward for emphasis.*

A.  "*Hello!* Converse. Do you have any idea how much these shoes cost?"

*'You really are clueless, aren't you?'*

Q.  "They cannot be worth much if you wrote on them with a permanent marker."

A.  "I was making a point."

Q.  "Looks more like a cry for help to me."

*She snaps back, emphatically over-annunciating each letter.*

A.  "P.O.I.N.T. Point."

*'I may repeat mistakes but never points.'*

Q. "Do you not think your self-worth is more valuable than a pair of vandalized sneakers?"

*Kristyn sneers.*

A. "I didn't vandalize them."

Q. "Then what do you call what you did to your shoes then?"

A. "Enhancement."

Q. "You can do what you wish with the sneakers."

*Her eyes grow wide.*

A. *"Really?"*

Q. "I recommend throwing them out."

*'Of course, you would recommend the rubbish bin.'*

*She glances down at the shoes.*

A. "But I don't have to toss them if I don't want to, right?"

Q. "Correct."

A. "It's my choice to keep the shoes if I want, right?"

Q. "You seem surprised."

A. "I am. My choices never mattered before now."

Q.  "Your choices have always mattered."

A.  *"Pssh."*

*The only choices of mine that have mattered are the endless string of bad ones I keep making. Shagging Ian Rhodes for example. Bad...very bad choice'*

Q.  "You have had the power of choice all along, Kristyn."

*Her body grows rigid.*

A.  *"Wait.* Are you saying I'm responsible for stuff that's happened to me because of my choices?"

Q.  "Some of it. *Yes.*"

*Kristyn shoots a quick look down at the sneakers.*

Q.  "What do you think will happen if you take a step towards living a more positive life?"

*'Same thing that always happens.'*

A.  "Nothing."

Q.  "Throwing the sneakers away would be a good start."

A.  "What if I toss them and nothing changes. Then what?"

Q.  "What if everything changes and for the better?"

A.  "Fine."

*'You better be right 'bout this. These are Converse I'm putting in the rubbish bin. Converse!'*

*She then gets up from the chair, shuffles over to the trashcan and drops the shoes in, before shuffling back and plopping down into the chair.*

Q.  "Throwing those shoes away was a necessary step for your recovery, Kristyn."

A.  "I'll remember that when I'm walking out of here in my bare feet."

*'I just hope I don't contract strongyloidiasis or some other batshit sounding disease, I can't pronounce proper or hardly spell.'*

# chapter eleven

Q. "You seriously have a tattoo?"

*Kristyn flashes a Cheshire smile.*

A. "*Nope,* but, if I did, it would be a butterfly."

Q. "Why a butterfly?"

A. "Because a caterpillar is this gnarly looking creature. No one wants it around. So, eventually, it locks itself inside darkness. You know, a cocoon, where it is hidden away from the rest of the world for a while."

Q. "Do you relate to the caterpillar?"

A. "Yes. It lives in isolation. Then, when it's ready, it emerges from the darkness, back into the light. Only now, it is a new creature. Something beautiful and acceptable to the world. A butterfly."

Q. "Is that how you feel after reemerging from one of your dark moods?"

A. "Sometimes. But I always become a caterpillar, again."

*Kristyn's eyes brim with tears.*

*'Stop weeping before your mascara runs down to your kneecaps.'*

*She quickly switches the topic.*

A. "I do have some piercings."

Q. "Why piercings and not tattoos?"

A. "Piercings are easier to erase if you get tired of them."

Q. "What about the scars from cutting?"

*Kristyn glances down at her wrists.*

A. "What 'bout them?"

Q. "They are not so easy to erase, yet you continue making new ones."

A. "What the fuck's that got to do with anything? My scars are different than tattoos or piercings."

Q. "How?"

*'You just can't leave it be, can you?'*

A. "They bring me comfort."

Q. "Comfort? Or, conflict?"

A. "There's no conflict. I like having them. I choose to have them."

Q. "Do you like remembering painful events in your life?"

*'I can't deal with the pressure you're putting on me. I just can't.'*

A. "I'm done chatting."

Q. "Okay. But know your choice will delay your progress."

*'Ha! I won!'*

*She spends the evening cutting while at the same time, trying to convince herself today's session was a victory for her because she called the shots and ended it. Truth is, she never felt more like a failure for quitting when things got a little bit tough to handle.*

# chapter twelve

Q. "Are you called any other names besides the ones we have already discussed?"

A. "More than a dictionary can hold."

Q. "Such as?"

*Kristyn clicks her tongue several times while thinking.*

A. "*Oh!* Kutter. *They* love to call me, Kutter."

Q. "Your last name?"

A. "Ironic, isn't it?"

Q. "In what way?"

A. "My mum says, '*you become what you say*'."

Q. "Am I missing something?"

*Kristyn carefully slips her left index finger under the cuff of her shirt and caresses her right wrist. A feeling of pleasure washes over her.*

A. "Don't you get it? I'm a cutter and my last name is Kutter."

Q. "*Oh*, now I understand."

A. "It's a brilliant coincidence, *no?*"

Q. "No."

*She cranes her neck back. Surprised.*

A: "*No?* Why not?"

Q. "I thought no one knew you self-harmed, or did I misunderstand?"

A. "*They* don't. It's why I fancy being called Kutter. It's like I'm putting one over on *them* only *they* don't know it."

*Kristyn puts both legs out in front of her and crosses her right foot over her left and chuckles.*

Q. "I find it rather sad and disappointing."

A. "What? Why?"

Q. "How you see your last name in that way. You have so much potential Kristyn and yet, you continually choose to sluff off serious issues instead of dealing with them."

*'Ugh! Make up your bloody mind, will you.'*

A. "I thought I was dealing. You even said so."

Q. "Because I thought you were. Obviously, I was wrong."

A. "Fucks sake! I don't see anything wrong with what I said."

Q. "Therein lies your problem."

*'My problem? Umm…make it plural, then you've got it right.'*

A. "What problem?"

Q. "You happen to have the last name Kutter, spelled with a 'K' and not a 'C', as you clearly wish it to be."

*She tartly replies.*

A. "And why would I wish that?"

*'As if you don't already know the answer, Kristyn. Come on. Who are you trying to fool?'*

Q. "To justify your secret behavior and avoid taking any responsibility for it."

*Kristyn hisses.*

*'Piss off!'*

A. *"Whatever."*

Q. "Kutter…"

*Kristyn cuts in and does sarcastic air-quotations to emphasize her anger.*

A. *"With a 'K' and not a 'C'."*

Q. "Kutter is your last name. Nothing more."

A. "That's your opinion."

Q. "No. It is a fact."

A. "Wh*aaaa*teve*rrr*."

Q. "'*Whatever*', seems to be your stock reply whenever the truth surfaces."

*Kristyn bites her bottom lip, then snaps back.*

A. "*Wh-aaa-t-ev-errr*!"

Q. "We will get nowhere if you continue replying with '*whatever*.'"

A. "Whatever."

Q. "Okay. Let's try something else."

A. "Whatever."

Q. "Enough, Kristyn."

*Kristyn opens her mouth to speak, before abruptly shutting it. Although she feels compelled to continue the 'whatever' game, she senses it will cost her extra sessions. Something she desperately wants to avoid.*

Q. "Why do you think *they* call you Kutter instead of Kristyn?"

*Kristyn shrugs her shoulders.*

Q. "Are you certain no one knows of your secret behavior?"

A. "If anyone knew, it wouldn't exactly be '*secret behavior*' now would it?"

Q. "I cannot help but think if you were called Kutter in reference with a 'C' and not a 'K' you would somehow feel validated and included by your peers."

*She stands up and places both hands on her hips.*

A. "Validated? Included?"

Q. "Sit back down, please."

*She plops back in the chair like a sack of potatoes.*

Q. "Obviously, you disagree."

A. "If anyone found out I'm a cutter, I would feel violated and mortified, not validated or included."

*'And for the record, I don't give a crap 'bout validation or inclusion, especially when it comes to dealing with those tossers at my school.'*

*Lie! She does care.*

# chapter thirteen

*Kristyn avoids making eye contact. She pulls her right leg up and begins tugging at several loose threads on the bottom of her jeans.*

A. "Oh. You'll be happy to know, I'm still a slag."

Q. "I am not happy to hear you say that about yourself."

*Kristyn pulls hard on one of the threads. It breaks free. She then begins rolling it between her left thumb and index finger until it forms a ball.*

A. "I don't get why when I do certain stuff, things always seem to kick off. It's so maddening. But, *whatever*."

Q. "What sort of stuff do you mean? I think I have an idea but give me your interpretation."

*Kristyn attempts a hint at her meaning, by playfully arching her eyebrows a few times.*

A. "Get it?"

Q. "Just tell me."

*'Why don't I just draw you a picture, instead?'*

A. "Okay. Let's say I hook up with a guy."

Q. "Hook up?"

A. "Yeah. Mess 'round for a bit. Again, nothing other girls in my school aren't doing, too."

*She takes a drink.*

A. "Only difference is their reputations aren't being soiled."

Q. "Unlike yours."

A. "Yeah."

Q. "Just so I can clarify, *'hooking up'* means...?"

A. "Making out, shagging and stuff."

Q. "I see."

*Kristyn becomes a tad defensive at the tone of the statement.*

A. "*Everyone* at my school is doing it. *Everyone*."

Q. "I highly doubt *everyone* is doing it."

*'Did you take a poll to get that particular information?'*

A. "*They* are."

Q. "My guess is you only hear about the ones who actually are or the ones who make up rumors about themselves to feel included. You do not hear about the ones who are not doing it."

A. "Why would someone spread a rumor 'bout themselves doing it? That's just dumb."

Q. "Is that how you justify your loose behavior?"

A. "What do you mean?"

Q. "According to you, *everyone* is doing it."

A. "Right."

Q. "Yet, it has earned you a questionable reputation."

*Kristyn sneers.*

*'Judgmental bitch!'*

A. "Hook-ups are no biggie."

Q. "Hook-ups are a very big deal."

A. "Why? You have fun and move on. I've even seen it on the telly and in movies. You're making it sound bad, when it's not. Loving someone is so much worse."

Q. "Hooking-up is bad, Kristyn. More than I think you realize."

*Kristyn releases a loud sigh.*

*'Here comes the sodding lecture.'*

Q. "Hollywood and real life are not the same thing."

'Well, duh!'

Q. "TV and movies are fantasy, not reality."

*Kristyn rolls her eyes.*

A. "I know."

*She then stares out the window.*

'*Sure, would be nice though if they were. I would find the perfect guy who would love me and never break my heart. Though, with my luck, some jerk-off Hollywood writer would kill the poor bastard off.*'

Q. "Are you promiscuous hoping for peer acceptance?"

*She snaps back.*

A. "I don't need or want anyone's approval."

'*Oh, yes, you do. Stop lying.*'

*She grows agitated at herself.*

'*I'll never admit it out loud!*'

Q. "Why continue hooking up if it brings you so many problems?"

A. "Maybe I like the attention. Maybe…"

*She pauses for emphasis.*

A. "… I like *doing* it."

Q. "Are you being honest?"

*She answers with a defiant tone.*

A. "Yup."

*'Hell, no!'*

Q. "I do not believe you are being honest with yourself."

*She gives a hard glare.*

Q. "Unlike television and movies, real life has real consequences. Sometimes we do not understand the consequences of our actions until it is too late."

*'I'd almost rather be shagging Ian right now than listening to this shit.'*

Q. "I believe your sexual behavior goes beyond trying to fit in with your peers."

*A blank stare washes over Kristyn's face.*

Q. "It is rather obvious your self-hatred runs deep. You abuse yourself with cutting and other forms of self-harm. You also allow others to use you because you do not love yourself."

*Kristyn is starting to suffocate under the weight of the truth presently bearing down on her shoulders.*

*'I need some fucking air – like RIGHT NOW!!!!!!!'*

A. "I'm done talking."

*She abruptly stands up and walks out the door.*

*Session over.*

*Later that night....*

*Kristyn stands before the bathroom mirror. She stares at her reflection in disgust. She then spends the next half-hour writing hateful words over her reflection using; lipstick and eyeliner, until the mirror is practically covered.*

*The next half-hour she spends reading the words over and again, while staring at bits and pieces of her revolting reflection.*

*The next hour she spends scrubbing the mirror clean, so her mum and dad don't find out what she did.*

*The hour after that she spends ordering new lipstick and eyeliner online.*

*'Dad's going go shit bricks when he gets my next credit card bill. Fuck!'*

# chapter fourteen

*Kristyn stares at herself in the bathroom mirror the following day before attending the next session.*

*'Christ, Kristyn! You still look like shit.'*

*She gives her hair a nonchalant toss with her fingers, hoping to restore some form of body. No luck.*

*'Fuck it.'*

*The genie of truth had been released from the bottle during the last session. Since then, stress has been smothering her like an un-welcomed lover's arms.*

*'Ian Rhodes comes to mind! Blech!'*

*She walks over to the toilet and flushes her half-smoked cigarette — but not before taking one final drag.*

*As the butt swirls down the mysterious hole, Kristyn wishes she could jump in and be carried away, too.*

*'I am so dreading today. Let's get it over with you dozy cow.'*

Q. "I would like to continue discussing the topic of promiscuity. It is where we left off last session."

*'Of course. Pervert.'*

A. "Can't we talk 'bout something else?"

Q. "I want you to ask yourself why you are promiscuous?"

*Enter sarcasm.*

A. "Okay. *Why are you such a slut bag, Kristyn?*"

*She then stands up.*

A. "I don't feel like doing this, today."

Q. "Sit down."

*She reluctantly plops back into the chair.*

A. "What do you want from me? *Huh?*"

Q. "I want you to answer my question."

*She says nothing and instead, turns her gaze towards the window where her attention is momentarily distracted by a clump of fluffy clouds floating by in the sky.*

Q. "Kristyn?"

*She turns her attention back.*

A. "I'm not as slutty as you think."

Q. "I am confused. I thought you said you have been…"

*She cuts in.*

A. "I may have fibbed."

*She then holds her right thumb and index finger half an inch apart and whispers.*

A. *"Just a smidge."*

*'You didn't lie 'bout your bedroom antics, bitch. Why are you lying now? Is it because of your pal, shame?'*

Q. "Why would you lie about something like that?"

A. "I don't know."

Q. "You don't know?"

A. "Maybe I don't have a reason. Maybe I just felt like saying it."

*Kristyn holds up a pack of cigarettes.*

A. "'S like if someone smokes people assume, they'll get cancer. But not everyone who smokes gets cancer."

Q. "Are you worried about getting cancer from smoking?"

A. "We're all going to die at some point, right?"

*She snarks.*

A. "I'm just speeding things up a bit is all."

*She snickers and lights up a cigarette.*

Q. "I do not see the humor in your comment, and neither should you."

*'You're such a bore.'*

A. "Oh, don't go getting your knickers twisted."

Q. "Back to my question."

*Kristyn leans forward and speaks in a cunning tone.*

A. *"You're rather curious 'bout my sex life, aren't you?"*

*Kristyn then playfully wags her right index finger.*

A. *"Naughty."*

Q. "Let's stay focused, *hmm*."

A. "So, what do you want to know? How many guys I've shagged? If I've been with a girl? What?"

Q. "Do you ever worry your risky behavior could cause more than unpleasant rumors?"

A. "Like what?"

Q. "STD's? Pregnancy?"

A. "That's what condoms are for, right?"

Q. "You use protection every single time you have sex?"

*'Did I use protection that night in the garage with Ian? I can't remember. I was utterly fucked up. Obviously since I shagged Ian up against the bins. Am I late? Oh, God, I can't remember the last time I bled. Shit!'*

*It's been a good while since Kristyn visited the gynecologist for an exam. The thought of potentially being pregnant by Ian is causing her waves of nausea.*

A. "Boundaries, choices, responsibilities and consequences. Life sucks."

Q. "Where do you think your responsibility lies, Kristyn?"

*'I'm guessing taking too much MDMA that night I had with, Ian. Please show soon, period. If you do, I promise I'll eat a ton of chocolate. I don't care if I get six billion zits. Just show-up. Please. I can't breed the spawn of Ian Rhodes. I just can't.'*

A. "Responsibility with what?"

Q. "Sex."

*She becomes spiteful.*

A. "If you must know, with Seth. Last night."

*'Wow! I almost forgot about Seth. Now, his spawn, I wouldn't mind carrying, but I don't want to be pregnant. I want my period. Yes, I want to feel mind-numbing cramps right 'bout now.'*

Q. "I'm sorry? Who is, Seth?"

A. "An FWB."

Q. "What is an FWB?"

A. "Friend with benefits."

*'More like a FWGB. A friend with great benefits.'*

Q. "Seth sounds more like a guy you allow to use you. And there is nothing friendly about being used."

A. "What if I'm using him? Ever think of that?"

Q. "Either way…"

*Pissed about being judged, she cuts-in.'*

A. "I don't see what the big deal is."

Q. "Remember when we discussed choices?"

*She plays coy.*

A. "Vaguely."

Q. "Choosing to avoid taking responsibility for your part in something is a choice."

*Kristyn parrots back.*

A. *"Choice. Choice. Choice."*

Q. "Is it possible you are a victim in some of your scenarios by choice, Kristyn?"

A. "Why would I be a victim on purpose? That's twisted."

Q. "Because labeling yourself the victim in situations such as FWB's, is sometimes easier than taking responsibility for having made bad choices."

*'For the record, if you saw Seth, you would not say that. Tall, dark and hot as hell.'*

Q. "Your risky, rebellious behavior...."

A. "How is my behavior risky and rebellious?"

Q. "The flaunting of negative words on your shoes."

A. "I threw them out."

Q. "Your participation in random sexual acts."

A. "Not the only one doing it."

Q. "Your need to read garbage written about yourself on social media."

A. "Fucks sake. According to your list, I don't do anything right."

*3 days later...*

# Yes!

# I need a Tampon!

# Period!

# Woo-Hoo!

☾☆

# chapter fifteen

Q.  "We will get nowhere if..."

*Kristyn tartly cuts in.*

A.  "Maybe I want to be nowhere?"

*She then throws a bored glance around the room.*

A.  "Maybe I want to be nowhere with nothing. No friends. No homework. No drama. No feelings. No breath. Nothing."

Q.  "Without breath you would no longer exist."

A.  "Exactly."

Q.  "Do you not want to exist anymore?"

A.  "What's the point."

Q.  "Your life."

A.  "I don't have one."

Q.  "Life is what you make of it."

A.  "No. Life is what others force you to make of it."

Q. "You feel others have forced you to see your life as nothing?"

*Kristyn watches raindrops run down the windowpane.*

A. "It doesn't matter. None of this matters. I don't matter."

Q. "Did something happen? Why are you speaking so negatively, today?"

A. "I'm taking responsibility like you told me to do."

Q. "I think you misunderstood."

A. "How?"

*Kristyn's spine stiffens in the chair.*

Q. "The point of these sessions is for you to discover who you are. I cannot tell you who to be. You have to learn who you are."

*She huffs.*

*'Of course. Why am I not surprised by this information?'*

Q. "I think for you; it is more comfortable to stay with what you know then to step out and change your life."

A. "Piss off!"

Q. "Would you jump off a bridge, if everyone else did?"

A. "That's such a lame question."

Q. "But it makes a valid point. So, would you?"

A. "I know some of my choices are bad. I get it. But I can't help it."

Q. "You can help it. You are a smart girl. You know the difference between right and wrong."

A. "I get confused sometimes. Too many thoughts swirl 'round inside my head all at once."

Q. "What sort of thoughts?"

A. "Why am I here? I mean, what's my purpose in life besides pain and rejection? Why don't I fit in? And, why are Little Debbie Oatmeal pies so bad for you, yet, they taste so *ahh-mazing?*"

# chapter sixteen

Q. "Is there someone you like or perhaps love?"

*Kristyn takes pause. There was...heck, there still is someone she loves. But he broke her heart and continues doing so by headfucking her every chance he gets.*

*'It's my fault it keeps happening. I can't help that I still love him. Fuck it! Happiness and love are illusions meant for the delusional. I don't believe in either anymore thanks to Jamey. Fuck em' both! And fuck him, too! Asshole!'*

*To avoid opening the wound in her heart and putting more cuts on her body, Kristyn makes a choice...and lies.*

A. "No."

# chapter seventeen

Q. "What worries you the most if your parents learn about your self-harming behavior?"

*She whispers.*

A. *"They'll stop loving me."*

Q. "How do you feel keeping it a secret from your parents?"

*She fidgets about in the chair.*

A. "Stressed."

*'Can you please change the subject? I don't want to talk 'bout my parents. It's uncomfortable.'*

Q. "You are trying to protect your parents. Your heart is in the right place, but…"

A. "So, lying to them 's okay? I mean, long as I'm doing it for the right reason."

Q. "The truth is always better."

A. "But you're saying it's okay to lie to my parents because I'm protecting them, right?"

Q. "The truth always finds its way into the light."

*She gives herself a face palm.*

A. "Ugh!"

Q. "You need to consider getting honest, especially with yourself."

A. "What I need is to keep my lies sorted."

Q. "What scares you the most about the truth, Kristyn?"

*She takes pause.*

A. "Everything."

# BLUE :(

The teacher's out sick so we have a sub for English class, today. She's young for a sub. Not like the retired grandma's I usually see. She told us we could choose. To let her teach Ms. Mason's next lesson plan or spend time writing in our journals. Of course, everyone went for the writing assignment. A quick look around the room and I can tell everyone is on social media screwing off. Including the sub. I think I'm the only one journaling. Oh, well. I'm used to being a loner. Whatever.

The only reason I'm writing is because; I don't have anyone to chat with on social media, I'm not in the mood to read negative crap 'bout myself and I currently lack the cash to shop online for more make-up. I think my dad's going to cut up my credit card if he sees another hundred-dollar eyeshadow palette on the bill.

I'm feeling rather shit anyway. It's been raining non-stop since yesterday. Rain makes me feel so fucking depressed. It's like it breathes life into the monster that lives inside of me. The one who makes me do horrible things to myself.

I'm sitting at my desk right now periodically watching lone raindrops hit the windowpane and slide down, out of sight. I wish I could slide out of sight sometimes. I'm sure there are a lot of people who wish the same. Not for themselves. But for me. Yeah, I feel that hated by others. I'm not sure I can really blame them because the truth is, I hate myself. Maybe even more than they hate me. I wonder if I should take a poll and find out? Hmm....

I'm really missing Maddison a lot lately. There's so much I want to tell her. I mean, I do anyway, when I'm alone in my room and stuff or if I visit her at the cemetery. But she can't ever answer me back. So, it's not really the same. Not like it used to be, anyway. It really sucks. Talking to her now...well, I basically come off like a loon chatting to myself. Then again, I'm the only company I keep nowadays since she left. Since Jamey left. My life sucks. Why am I here, God? Why?

I wish I was smart enough to figure out how to handle bad stuff. I wish I didn't cut. But I'm not that smart. That fact got verified this morning when I went to the bathroom and saw my name and the word *loser* resting side by side on the wall inside a stall.

Once I was alone, I took out my black Sharpie pen and did the best I could to block it out. Afterwards I felt so depressed. So incredibly depressed. Once I knew it was safe, I dealt with my hurt feelings.

My left arm stings so bad every time I move it to reach certain letters on the keyboard. I have to keep my shirt sleeve down so no one sees what I did. I didn't want to cut, I really didn't. But I'm so gutted with bad feelings right now, I had to let some of them out. So, I did.

I don't know what else to say. I really have nothing else to say, I suppose. Besides, my arm is really hurting. I think I'll just sit here and watch the raindrops continue hitting the windowpane and disappear. And while I do, I'll pretend each drop is me disappearing over and again... at least until the bell rings.

Shit! 20 more minutes to go.

# chapter eighteen

Q.   "Do you ever call yourself negative names?"

A.   "Thought we covered this already. *Crikey!* I wrote nasty words on my shoes. Remember?"

*'You know, the shoes you made me toss in the rubbish bin. What's funny is that I don't feel any different since throwing them out. How is that possible?'*

Q.   "I meant do you ever *speak* negative things to yourself about yourself?"

*'Constantly.'*

A.   "I feel better after doing it. That's fucked up, isn't it?"

Q.   "Do you think you deserve to speak to yourself like that?"

*Kristyn begins to twirl her necklace.*

A.   'I never say what I don't mean.'

*'Bullshit. You lie so much you don't even know what the truth is anymore.'*

Q.   "What does self-harming do for you?"

A. "It helps release the bad feelings I have 'bout myself. At least, until the blood stops flowing."

Q. "What happens when the blood stops flowing?"

A. "The bad feelings return. Sometimes worse than before."

*She stares down at her scarred-up wrist currently hidden behind a maroon burnout long T shirt featuring an H.R. Pufnstuf caricature she drew and ironed on herself.*

*'It was one of mum's favorite shows growing up.'*

Q. "That's because the bad feelings never left."

*Kristyn begins rubbing the temples of her head.*

A. "I have the worst headache right now."

*She pulls a bottle of aspirin from her purse and swallows two pills.*

Q. "I want you to look in the mirror in front of you, on the table."

*She scrunches up her face.*

Q. "What do you see when you look at yourself in the mirror?"

A. "Disgust."

Q. "Do you ever talk to your reflection?"

*'Mirror Mirror on the wall*
*Who is the biggest slag of them all?*
*Kristyn Amelia Kutter.'*

A.  "Sometimes."

Q.  "Why do you choose to look at your reflection while speaking negative words over yourself?"

*'Self-loathing. I thought you knew that 'bout me already?'*

A.  "I don't want to just see the pain in my eyes. I want to feel it in my soul, too."

Q.  "Does it bring you the same type of relief you achieve when self-harming?"

A.  "Not even close."

Q.  "What makes them different from one another?"

A.  "I don't know. They just are."

Q.  "What do you feel when you speak negative things about yourself while staring at your reflection in the mirror?"

A.  "Alive."

# chapter nineteen

Q. "Have you ever had suicidal thoughts?"

*Kristyn stares out the window. Everything is perfectly still. No wind. No waving tree branches. No rain. No birds. No squirrels. Nothing.*

*She takes a que from nature and remains silent herself.*

Q. "You know, people in your situation..."

*Kristyn turns away from the window, now wearing a skeptical gaze.*

A. "Sorry? My situation?"

Q. "People in deep emotional pain."

*'Like the one sitting before you in the dreaded red chair.'*

Q. "It is not uncommon for people in emotional pain to entertain thoughts of suicide."

*Kristyn attempts to hide her relatable feelings by acting obnoxious.*

A. "I'm shocked."

Q. "Feelings of despair can be overwhelming sometimes."

*'You can't even comprehend how overwhelming when applied to my life.'*

Q.  "But not everyone in a state of despair ends their life. Many choose to get help."

*Kristyn's mind immediately thinks of Maddison and her heart sinks.*

*'But some choose to quit.'*

*Her mood sours.*

A.  *"Whatever."*

Q.  "What does *life* mean to you, Kristyn?"

A.  "Rejection 99.9% of the time out of the roughly 30,000 breaths I take in a day."

Q.  "What about the remaining 1%?"

A.  "Sleep, but not really to rest."

Q.  "Why, then?"

A.  "Because sleeping helps me to forget 'bout my shitty life... until I unfortunately wake up to relive the same hell over and again."

# chapter twenty

*Kristyn is rummaging through her purse.*

A.   *"Shit. Where is it?"*

Q.   "What are you looking for?"

A.   "Nothing."

*She continues searching and growing more agitated by the minute.*

Q.   "I would like to talk about your piercings."

*She looks up with a perplexed expression.*

A.   "Why does that matter?"

*'Finally.'*

*She holds up a blue lighter before tucking it back into a hidden pocket inside her purse.*

Q.   "Given your addiction to self-harm…"

A.   *"Blah! Blah! Blah!"*

Q. "You have an admitted history of deliberately doing things to feel physical pain, *right?*"

A. "So."

Q. "Piercings can cause that level of the pain you seek."

*No reply.*

Q. "How many piercings do you currently have, Kristyn?"

A. "I have five in my left ear, three in the right."

*She then lifts her long-sleeved white Zeppelin concert T shirt, revealing faded scars on her pale stomach, along with a turquoise stoned belly ring resting in her belly button.*

A. "My navel."

*Kristyn opens her mouth and shows a white topped post sticking through her tongue.*

A. "My tongue."

*She points to a small silver hoop sticking out of her left eyebrow.*

A. "My eyebrow. I want more, but my mum won't allow it. She says I've wasted enough money on it as it is."

Q. "Did you enjoy getting pierced?"

A. "I did. I enjoyed the pain I felt."

Q. "I find it rather intriguing."

A. "What?"

Q. "How you desire physical pain to avoid feeling emotional pain."

A. "It's crazy, right?"

# chapter twenty-one

Q. "How do you decide where to self-harm on your body?"

*She shrugs her shoulders.*

A. "I don't. I just do it."

*'Should I share more? Ah, fuck it. May as well. You're just going to drag it out of me... eventually.'*

A. "You know, sometimes I let a cut become a scar, sometimes not."

Q. "Why do you choose to make deeper cuts sometimes?"

A. "It depends on how upset I feel."

Q. "So, for you, self-harming is also about control, not just a way of releasing emotional pain."

*She ponders the newly discovered revelation.*

A. *"Maybe. Hmm..."*

Q. "What happens if you change your mind about a scar? Say, you want to get rid of it."

A.   "I won't change my mind."

Q.   "How can you be so sure? People change their minds all the time about things."

A.   "Because each scar I made exists for reasons I never want to forget."

Q.   "Why do you choose to deliberately remember painful things in your life? Most people want to forget moments like that."

*She plays coy.*

A.   "I'm not most people. Or haven't you figured that out, yet?"

# chapter twenty-two

*Kristyn arrives thirty-minutes late. She was hoping by doing so, the session would be cancelled. Nope. Still enough time to make it happen.*

*She looks a mess, on the outside. And feels every bit of it internally, as well. Last night's make-up is barely clinging to her oily skin. Her clothes reek of stale cigarettes and a faint scent of beer she accidentally spilled on her jeans. Her normally clean, coconut scented hair is heaped upon the crown of her head in a messy bun. She sprayed it with extra hairspray hoping to kill any lingering aromas from her night with Seth.*

*'Yup. I had an FWB moment with Seth last night. Big deal. I was lonely. He was available. I snuck out and met him down the street in his car. Cheap beer, cigarettes, a few thrusts and back home I went. No biggie. I got my needs met...sort of. I mean, at least I'm not feeling lonely anymore. So, mission accomplished. Spent most of the next day in bed eating junk food and watching pointless music videos online.'*

*The statement she just spoke inside her head suddenly becomes unsettling in her soul.*

*'Oh, who the fuck are you trying to fool, Kristyn? Yourself? Last night wasn't fun. It was shit. You know it was. I mean, Seth was fun. But I don't know what you were hoping to feel afterwards. Maybe not as lonely? Did you really think Seth held the key to making you feel better? Seriously? Was it even worth it? Look at you. You look as shitty as you feel, swimming in a sea of utter disgust for what you did. You don't feel*

*great. You don't feel whole. You feel lonelier than before your pathetic romp with Seth. Okay, so maybe pathetic isn't a word that suites Seth. But what happened…yeah, I'm feeling pretty damn pathetic right 'bout now.'*

*She smells her right armpit.*

*'And I really stink. Girl, you need a hot shower and a proper douche, as soon as this 'Blah-Blah Session' ends.'*

*The dreaded red chair immediately hugs her body in the most awkward of ways.*

*'Uncomfortable. Party of one.'*

Q.  "Have you ever considered people treat you poorly out of jealousy and not hatred, as you assume?"

*Kristyn scoffs. She imagines flipping a coin inside her head to determine her mood.*

*Heads: Act sweet*
*Tails: Act sour*

*'Tails! / Act sour it is.'*

A.  "Mind if I light a cigarette first before you start hitting me with your annoying questions?"

Q.  "I'm sorry?"

*Kristyn ignores the acknowledgement at her foul mood and lights a half-smoked cigarette. She did not have the stomach to finish it after last night's event.*

*'I hate beer. Makes me too bloody gassy.'*

*She releases a sigh.*

A. "What was your question again?"

Q. "Do you think people treat you poorly out of jealousy and not hatred, as you assume?"

A. "Jealous of what? Me?"

*She appears outwardly surprised.*

*Internally, she's laughing hysterically at the thought of 'The Posh Ms. Perfects' being jealous of her Thrift Store wardrobe vs. their 'Neiman-mark up' attire.*

*'I could almost wee my pants at such an absurd notion.'*

Q. "Jealousy of you is not an impossibility. You project an image of someone who is strong and unique."

*Kristyn displays a faint expression of confusion.*

A. "Have you looked at me?"

*She re-emphasizes.*

A. "I mean, really *looked* at me?"

Q. "There is more to jealousy than looks, Kristyn."

A. "I know. I meant, have you looked in my eyes? Because if so, you wouldn't say something like that."

*'Strong? Umm-no. Unique? Yeah, I guess I'll give you that.'*

*She takes a final drag off her cigarette and blows a few smoke rings, before extinguishing it out.*

A.  "It helps if you have something people want. Which I don't."

Q.  "You…"

*She interrupts.*

A.  "Wait. I take that back. I do have something the boys want. My fanny. But – *meh*."

Q.  "There you go again thinking with a victim mentality."

*Kristyn rolls her eyes.*

A.  *"Whatever."*

Q.  "Why not choose to see yourself as a survivor instead?"

*She remains quiet.*

*'Seriously? A survivor or what? A night of jack rabbit sex with Ian? If I was strong enough, maybe I might give it a go. But I'm not strong. I'm weak. I'm pathetic. I'm nothing. I know it. I am far from being a survivor. Their words still hurt me every day. The day they don't, then maybe I will see myself as a survivor. If only that day would arrive…could arrive. I wish.'*

Q.  "May I see the scars on your wrists?"

*Kristyn places her wrists up to her chest and holds them tight against her body in a defensive posture.*

A. "I tried to show them to you before and you didn't want to see them. Why do you want to see them now?"

*She holds her wrists up to her chest even tighter.*

Q. "Why are you getting defensive about showing your scars to me, Kristyn?"

*Kristyn slowly lowers her arms back down until they come to a rest in her lap.*

*'I feel so exposed right now. Like I'm naked, in Antarctica, floating alone on a piece of ice having no idea where the hell I'm drifting to. And there's no seal or polar bear in sight to point me in the right direction.'*

A. "I've read stories online 'bout what happens when cutters are found out."

Q. "You are not being found out. Your self-harming behavior is a known problem in this room."

A. "Still."

Q. "Where did you read about self-harmers?"

A. "From other cutters online."

Q. "What did you learn?"

*'If you want to know 'bout it so much, look it up yourself.'*

A. "I already feel like a freak."

Q. "You are not a freak."

A. "Well, for a cutter, being found out makes us feel like even bigger freaks. No one knows 'bout my cutting. Well, except my best mate, Maddison. She knew."

Q. "Anything we discuss here is confidential. No one has to know anything unless you want them to know."

A. "I don't want anyone to know."

*She suddenly finds herself leaving the door of possibility cracked open a bit.*

A. *"Yet."*

Q. "If that is your wish, so be it."

A. "Why do you want to see my scars now?"

Q. "Because I want YOU to see them."

A. "I do. I put them there for fuck's sake."

Q. "I want YOU to really look at each scar and think about why you made the choice to self-harm."

*Kristyn tugs at her right sleeve. She is silent. She shifts her gaze down at the floor.*

A. "I told you. Don't you listen? I cut to release pain."

Q. "Nobody can pull you out of the negative place where you are currently at except you. I can help guide you, but only if you want to be guided."

*Kristyn looks up with a glare in her eye.*

A. "You want to see my badges of no courage? My cries for help? My failed attempts to seek attention, as most would say. Is that what you want to see?"

Q. "No. I want YOU to see it."

*Kristyn rears up in her chair. She then leans forward to emphasize her point and her anger.*

A. "I haven't forgotten for one bloody second how, when or why any of my scars exist. The scars *they* caused."

Q. "But you were the one who actually brought the scars into existence."

*Kristyn folds her arms.*

*'Piss off! You think you know me. You don't know shit! You don't know how I feel. Why I hurt. Who hurt me. Nothing.'*

Q. "YOU chose to manage your pain with self-mutilation. YOU. Not *them*. YOU."

A. "Oh, my, bloody, Gawd! Are you being serious right now?"

Q. "I am."

*Kristyn stares ahead, fighting hard not to break. She is not ready to let go of her "hard" exterior. But she can feel the pillars of her tough foundation beginning to crack under the pressure being put on her.*

A.   "Don't you get it? If THEY hadn't done what THEY did to hurt me, I wouldn't have these wretched memorials etched on my skin as a constant reminder of the hell I've been put through."

Q.   "I think you need to ask yourself why you allow anyone to have that kind of power and control over you and your emotions?"

*Kristyn shakes her head side to side in disagreement.*

*'I am not taking responsibility for this. Oh, no, I'm not!'*

*Overwhelmed, all Kristyn can do is cover her ears and scream.*

A.   *"Arrrrrgh!"*

# chapter twenty-three

*Kristyn plops down in the chair. She runs her hand through her hair and adjusts her 'Sex Pistols' Burnout T-shirt before it falls off her right shoulder completely.*

A.  "I need a cigarette."

*Kristyn reaches for the pack and pulls one out.*

Q.  "You really should consider quitting."

*'You sound like my mum. Just stop. One lecturing bore in my life is enough.'*

*Kristyn smirks, lights a cigarette, takes a long drag and exhales.*

A.  "Not going to happen today. Maybe tomorrow."

*She then snickers.*

*'Pah! I can hardly keep a straight face after saying that.'*

*Kristyn flicks the blue lighter with her thumb, causing a flame to appear, then disappear a few times before growing bored and tossing it onto the table.*

Q.  "Have you tried to avoid crutching when situations become uncomfortable in your life?"

*'Have you tried minding your own business and butting the fuck out of mine?'*

A.  "What are you going on 'bout now?"

*She takes another drag.*

Q.  "Your use of destructive behavior to deal with uncomfortable situations."

*She scowls.*

A.  "It's a cigarette, not spliff for fuck's sake."

Q.  "Do you not see what I am talking about?"

*She takes another spiteful drag and flashes a cunning smile.*

A.  "Nope."

*'I get it. But I'm not 'bout to let you know I do.'*

Q.  "You use self-harming, smoking, sex, drinking and drugs, among other things, to cope with your issues."

A.  "So."

Q.  "You do not manage issues in a healthy manner, allowing yourself to heal and move forward in a positive direction."

A.  "You do realize I'm a teenager, right? I'm supposed to be immature and scattered. It's my rite of passage."

*Kristyn takes another drag from the cigarette.*

Q. "Self-destructive behavior is a choice, Kristyn, not a rite of passage."

'*According to who? You?*'

Q. "You can handle your problems without crutching if you choose to do so."

*She smirks.*

A. "Fine."

*Kristyn takes one more drag and puts the cigarette out.*

*Epic fail...*

*An hour later, Kristyn smoked three cigarettes in a row after reading more nasty stuff about herself online.*

'*At least I tried to quit. That's got to count for something, right? Right?*'

# chapter twenty-four

A.  "When I look at any scar on my body, I instantly go back to the moment it came to exist. Sometimes I'll even make an old scar bleed again."

Q.  "Bleed again? What do you mean?"

A.  "I cut in the same place again. *Duh!*"

Q.  "I meant, what provokes the desire to reopen an old wound?"

A.  "I want to reminisce."

Q.  "What do you get out of opening an old wound?"

A.  "I deserve to hurt and feel that pain again."

Q.  "Why do you feel you deserve to feel this way?"

She shrugs her shoulders.

*'I just do. I don't know why. I was sort of hoping you would volunteer the answer because I'm too prideful to ask you why I feel that way.'*

Q.  "Do you have any good memories in your life to focus on?"

A.   "The bad memories far outweigh one *possible* good one."

*'Notice how I said 'possible'? It's because if I do have one good memory tucked away somewhere – which is unlikely, trust that there is a bad one attached to it somehow. That's just how my life works. Unfortunately.'*

Q.   "You could choose to focus on a good memory when things in your life get rough, instead of a negative one which clearly drives your self-harming behavior."

*'Why bother?'*

A.   *"Meh."*

*Kristyn gives her phone a glance before slamming it back down and releasing a hearty sigh. Several new posts have gone up about her and Ian.*

*'I can't believe that jerk ran his mouth 'bout that night in his garage! Loser! Why would he do that? Oh, maybe he found out I nicked that money off him and bought some MDMA for myself. I needed it more. Fuck him! His blabbering lips just gave me the excuse I need to stop shagging him – not that I needed an excuse to stop. He was what I consider a 'pity-fuck'. A pity he's who I had available to fuck. A pity he even considers me shag worthy.'*

*She shakes her head in disgust. But much to her surprise, the disgust she is feeling is aimed more at herself than at Ian.*

*'Slut. Whore. Skank. Slag. Once again, another noted fuck-up notch to add to your belt. Brilliant, as always, Kristyn.'*

Q.   "It is your choice which option you want to focus on. The negative or the positive."

*'There is no escaping this choice crap, is there? But how do I know which choice to make? How do I know the choice I make is the right one? I mean, I'm the queen of royally fucking my life up. I really wish I had some spliff to mellow my brain out right now.'*

*All she can do is listen with her head cradled in her hands.*

Q.   "Everything in life revolves around choice."

*'Wish I had chosen not to shag Ian. Now that would have been a smart choice. But it's too late.'*

# chapter twenty-five

Q. "I would like to focus on another issue, today."

*'I suppose I don't have a say on the topic, huh?'*

Q. "I would like to discuss your best friend Maddison."

*Kristyn immediately puts her hand up and takes control of the session.*

A. "I'm not ready to talk 'bout Maddison, yet. Pick another topic or I'm leaving."

*She stands up.*

Q. "Okay. We can talk about something else, today. But we are eventually going to discuss what happened to Maddison."

*Kristyn sits back down in silence.*

Q. "Where have you self-harmed on your body?"

*'My body resembles a roadmap to hell. I don't' know where to begin.'*

A. "On the inside of my thighs, both of my upper arms, my stomach and hips. You already know 'bout my wrists."

Q. "Do you feel comfortable sharing how your scars came to exist?"

*'I would rather drive rusty nails up my toenails then share.'*

A.　"Nope."

Q.　"The places you mentioned where you self-harmed; thighs, hips, stomach and upper arms."

A.　*"Uh-huh."*

*Kristyn takes a sip of soda before setting the can back onto the table.*

Q.　"Why those areas?"

A.　"Isn't it obvious?"

Q.　"No. That is why I asked you."

A.　"I don't want to get caught."

*She then smirks.*

A.　"Satisfied?"

Q.　"What about your wrists?"

*Kristyn gazes down at her exposed wrists and once again falls under the spell of denial.*

*'Why am I the one feeling ashamed about my scars? They did this to me. I didn't do this to me. They did it.'*

*She looks up with a blank stare in her eyes.*

Q. "You say you do not want to be caught self-harming, yet, you have scars on your wrists. Those scars on your wrists can easily be seen."

A. "Not if I keep them covered up. Which I do."

*She then shoots a cunning smile.*

Q. "Did you cut on your wrists for attention, Kristyn?"

*Kristyn imitates a game show buzzer.*

A. "*Ehhhh!*"

Q. "Was it a cry for help?"

A. "*Ehhhh!*"

Q. "Were you trying to commit suicide?"

A. "*Ehhhh!* None of the above, but thanks for playing."

Q. "Then, why did you do it?"

A. "I don't know. Why doesn't butter come from butterflies instead of cows? Can you answer me that?"

Q. "Why are you avoiding answering my question?"

*She shrugs her shoulders.*

*'Because it's none of your business.'*

Q. "When are you going to be serious about getting better?"

A.   "I'm here, aren't I?"

Q.   "You are not giving up much."

*She winks.*

A.   "The blokes I've shagged will tell you otherwise."

Q.   "I mean information, not sex. I am beginning to think you enjoy playing games because it gives you some control in your life."

*'I'm done. You want to think I'm playing games, go ahead. I'm also a mime now, too. Watch me not say shit to you for the remaining time.'*

*Kristyn lights up a cigarette and tosses the lighter on top of a book on the table. She gets up and walks over to the window. She sees a black crow sitting on a tree branch. She takes a drag and blows smoke at the window. The smoke blows back in her face. She coughs and waves it away. The motion of her hand frightens the crow. He flies away. She stares at the now empty branch until her cigarette is finished and the session time is up.*

# I Don't Like What I See

Most of the time I'd rather be anyone other than me
When I look at myself in the mirror, I don't like what I see
A stupid worthless loser bitch I never longed to be
Fat thighs, bloated belly, ugly face and knobby knees.

I try so hard to have a life, but bad things continue
to get in my way
I find myself seeking help nightly as I kneel down and
try to pray
But nothing ever changes, my world still remains dark
and grey
Sometimes I wish someone would just put their
arms around me,
and tell me... "It's going to be okay".

# chapter twenty-six

*The sessions were put on hold for a week because Kristyn was stricken with the flu.*

Q. "Feeling better?"

*Kristyn shrugs her shoulders.*

A. "I guess. Having the flu sucks."

*She coughs.*

*The congested sound is a lingering reminder of her week from hell.*

*'At least it got me out of school for a bit. Jamey called a few times. We talked. He said if I wasn't so sick, he would come over after my mum and dad went to sleep. I wanted so much to believe him. But part of me knew, it was more of his headfucking games. Why can't I just put a stop to it? What is wrong with me? I'm kind of glad I was too sick this time to cut. Wow…that's odd.'*

Q. "Do you recall where we left off last session?"

*Kristyn holds up her scarred wrists.*

Q. "That's right. Your wrists. Thank you."

*She then rests her arms on her lap.*

Q. "Why did you choose to self-harm on your wrists?"

A. "Why not?"

Q. "I thought you wanted to keep your self-harming a secret?"

*She remains silent.*

Q. "Are you feeling well enough to do this today? Maybe we should reschedule."

*She looks up.*

*'No! I've lost enough time as it is.'*

A. "I first cut on my wrists because of a wanker. I wasn't thinking clearly at the time when I did it. Not that I ever do."

Q. "Who is this person you are talking about?"

A. "Just a guy I know. Or knew. *Whatever.*"

*Kristyn folds her arms and slouches.*

Q. "Just a guy?"

*Kristyn looks away.*

*'Please don't make me talk 'bout him. If I do, I'll start missing him all over again. I don't want to miss him. I hate him. But I still love him. I think. I don't know. My stupid heart. I wish I could get a heart transplant or a lobotomy for my brain so I could forget 'bout him.'*

*She begins to reluctantly release information about the boy who broke her heart.*

A. "He was my boyfriend. Now ex-boyfriend. I've mentioned his name before."

*Kristyn then rolls her eyes and whispers.*

A. *"Tosser."*

Q. "What is his name?"

*She snaps back.*

A. "Jamey."

*Pain clouds her eyes just hearing her voice speak his name out loud.*

Q. "What happened with Jamey that made you choose to self-harm on your wrists?"

A. "He was a cheat and every word that came out of his mouth was a fucking lie."

Q. "Were you hoping to get his attention by self-harming?"

A. *"Whatever."*

Q. "Is that a 'yes'?"

A. "No. It's a *'whatever'.*"

Q. "I'll take that as a *'yes'.*"

A.   "Take it any way you want. I don't give a shit."

Q.   "Were you trying to end your life because of Jamey?"

*Kristyn is insulted by the suggestion.*

*'No asshole is worth ending my life over! Especially a lying, cheat like him. I hate you Jamey. Every bone and organ in my body hates you – except my heart. I wish I could evict you from it… but I can't. My fucking heart won't let me. Piece of shit!'*

A.   "Look. I'm no bleeding Juliet and he's no sodding Romeo. Our relationship was far from being Shakespearian. He gave me a bracelet on our anniversary and then broke-up with me, like two days later. Nice, *huh?*"

Q.   "The thick loom beaded bracelet I see on your arm?"

*Kristyn grows silent, having drifted off into a moment of happiness when Jamey gave her the bracelet, along with promises of forever. She recalls their endless backseat make-out sessions as 'The Cure' played in the background. The smell of his cologne, as her nose playfully nuzzled his neck. The softness of his shaggy brown hair laced between her fingers. It was a young lover's fantasy. One full of hope and promise. Unlike the reality of what she feels now. Alone. She has since tried recapturing that tummy-flip feeling with nameless, faceless others. But has only found herself falling deeper into loneliness and further away from feelings of love for anyone – especially herself.*

A.   *"Yeah."*

Q.   "The turquoise and purple colors are very pretty."

A.   "Purple's my favorite color. He knew that 'bout me."

Q.  "Why wear the bracelet if you and Jamey are over?"

*'Because I hate him, but I still love him. I want him gone, but I want him nearby. I don't miss him…but I do.'*

Q.  "Do you use the bracelet as a trigger to self-harm?"

*Kristyn shrugs her shoulders.*

*'Maybe.'*

*Kristyn gently strokes the bracelet, tending to the painful emotions hidden inside the scars Jamey gave to her the day he first shattered her heart. Since then, he has continued screwing with her heart, emotions and sometimes, her fanny. She has the scars inside and out to prove it.*

Q.  "Do you miss Jamey?"

*'Everyday.'*

A.  "I wish he never existed."

Q.  "Why?"

*Kristyn points to her heart.*

A.  "Because he's still in here."

Q.  "Most want to remove themselves from reminders of painful situations and from the people who hurt them. But you don't. Why do you suppose that is?"

*Kristyn shrugs her shoulders.*

Q.  "Why did Jamey break-up with you?"

*'Did you miss the part where I said earlier, he was a cheat?'*

A.  "He just said we were done and walked away."

*Kristyn puts her head in her hands and fights the urge to cry.*

*'I hope I can ask this next question without losing it — entirely. I need help. I can't keep feeling this way. It's killing me.'*

*She looks up.*

A.  "How do I get my heart to STFU 'bout him?"

Q.  "Time."

*She mutters.*

A.  *"It's been a long time already."*

Q.  "Why do you still wear the bracelet?"

*'You already know the answer.'*

A.  "To help hide the scars on my wrists."

*Kristyn begins spinning the bracelet slowly around her wrist.*

Q. "Maybe it would be a good idea to stop wearing the bracelet since it is a trigger for you. What are your thoughts about that?"

A. *"Umm…*No!"

Q. "Why not?"

A. "Because it helps hide some of my scars. It's funny."

Q. "What's funny?"

A. "How I use the bracelet Jamey gave me out of *'love'* to hide what he makes me do out of *'pain'*."

Q. "Jamey never made you choose to self-harm. You made that choice."

*Kristyn scoffs.*

Q. "How did you hide your other scars from Jamey during your relationship?

A. "You can hide anything if you want to bad enough."

Q. "Does Jamey know how bad he hurt you?"

A. "Don't know. Don't care to know, either."

*'Liar! Liar! Liar! Okay so maybe I don't know. But I definitely do care.'*

Dear Jamey,

You're such a twatwaffle! I hate you! I wish I had never met you! Go fuck yourself! You're dumped! My fanny is tooooo good for you!

*I left that note in Jamey's locker after he shagged me for a week straight and then ignored me, again! I can't stand his stupid games. Why is he doing this to me? My heart is such a stupid piece of shit for believing anything he says. All he does is talk bollocks. Get it through your head Kristyn! He's a twatwaffle! Remember it!*

*Jamey dropped my note back into my locker with this:*

Dear Kristyn,

Sorry. Wanna meet up tonight?

*Annnnnnd....my idiotic heart overrode my brain. I waited up all night for Jamey to tap on my window. He never showed and he ignored my text messages.*

*'Thanks for headfucking me, AGAIN, Jamey. I wound up spending the evening in my closet with the other monster, instead.'*

639

# chapter twenty-seven

Q. "Did you cut last night?"

*Kristyn pulls her right sleeve down and then attempts to lie.*

A. "N-no."

Q. "I see you have new cuts on your wrist."

*'You weren't supposed to see them.'*

Q. "Did our conversation about Jamey cause you to cut?"

*Tears well up in Kristyn's eyes.*

*'Stop. Please. I can't handle any Jamey talk today.'*

A. "I don't want to talk 'bout, Jamey."

*As a means of distraction, Kristyn slams her freshly cut wrist down onto her thigh hard and winces. Her frown becomes a slight smile, as a rush of endorphins from the painful hit washes over her. A perfect release.*

*'Tears – sorted.'*

Q. "Are the new cuts on your wrist because of Jamey?"

A. "He's not the only reason, you know.

Q.  "What else got you upset enough to self-arm?"

*'Jamey. Jamey. Jamey. Oh, yeah. Jamey.'*

A.  "The fact I still exist."

Q.  "Why is your existence causing you to self-harm?"

A.  "Look at my life. What I've been put through. You'd feel the same way if you were in my shoes."

Q.  "While your response…"

*She cuts in with a tone of displeasure.*

A.  "I'm not a cyborg. I'm a person with real feelings that everyone seems to keep forgetting I have."

*'Unbelievable.'*

Q.  "You need to learn how to better handle issues in your life without harming yourself."

*She gives a nonchalant shoulder shrug.*

A.  "Why mess with a good thing?"

Q.  "Inflicting physical pain to relieve yourself of emotional pain is not healthy behavior."

A.  "That's your opinion."

Q.  "What word comes to mind when you think of yourself, right now, in this moment?"

A.   "Broken."

*'Like a bird with two wrecked wings who will never get off the ground again, forever stuck pecking shit with the chickens.'*

# JAMEY </3

when the mind wants to forget, but the heart won't let go.
Blah!

Stupid! Fucking! Heart!

I wish you and Jamey would both PISS OFF!!!!!

# chapter twenty-eight

Q. "How long have you been self-harming, Kristyn?"

A. "I don't know. I just started doing it one day and never stopped."

Q. "Do you remember your first cut?"

*Kristyn avoids eye contact.*

Q. "I am not trying to pry. I am trying to help you."

*Kristyn quickly snaps back.*

A. "Maybe. I. Don't. Want. Your. Help."

*She then scratches an itch on the back of her right calf.*

Q. "How did you connect self-harming with relieving emotional pain?"

A. "How does anyone connect anything?"

Q. "Please, answer my question."

A. "A friend."

Q. "Who?"

*Kristyn looks down at her feet and mumbles.*

A.   *"Maddison."*

Q.   "Did Maddison show you how to self-harm?"

A.   "Kind of."

Q.   "What do you mean, *'kind of.'*"

A.   "I saw her scars one time, you know, by accident."

Q.   "How did that happen?"

A.   "We were changing into our PJ's during a sleepover. I saw them on her stomach when she lifted her arms up over her head while taking off her shirt."

Q.   "Did Maddison ever tell you about her scars?"

A.   "She said they were from surgeries when she was younger."

Q.   "Did you believe her?"

A.   "I did at the time."

Q.   "Did Maddison eventually tell you the truth about her scars or did you ask her?"

A.   "She told me."

Q.   "What did she tell you?"

A. "She said she cut herself on purpose because it helped her deal with the pain she was feeling on the inside."

Q. "Why do you suppose Maddison told you the truth?"

A. "I don't know. I guess she trusted me to keep her secret."

Q. "How did you feel learning Maddison self-harmed?"

A. "I didn't really know how to feel."

Q. "You never thought about self-harming prior to discovering Maddison's scars?"

A. "No. The sight of blood usually makes me want to vomit. But it doesn't seem to bother me when I cut. Don't know why. Just doesn't. Thankfully."

Q. "What did you say to Maddison after she shared her self-harming secret?"

A. "Nothing. I just listened."

Q. "Did you ask Maddison to teach you how to self-harm?"

*Kristyn averts her eyes and whispers.*

A. *"Yeah."*

Q. "Why?"

A. "I wanted my fucked-up emotions gone, too. Cutting seemed to help Maddison. I wanted the same relief."

Q. "You must have realized at one point that self-harming does not really work. The pain always returns because it never left to begin with."

A. "*Yeah*, I know. But it's hard to quit."

Q. "There are no '*quick fixes*' in bad situations. Only band-aids that eventually fall off, exposing our wounds to the world that will never heal if we do not get to the root of the issue. Self-harming is a band-aid, not a solution."

*Kristyn sighs loudly.*

A. "*Brilliant*. I'm fucking up, yet, again."

Q. "I am not criticizing you or your choices."

A. "Sounds like you are."

Q. "I am trying to help you deal with your issues in a healthier way."

'*According to you, I can't deal. And, I don't learn from my mistakes, either — so...*'

Q. "Were you and Maddison together the first time you cut?"

A. "No. I was alone…*as usual*."

*Kristyn takes a sip of soda.*

A. "Cutting was something Maddison and I did in private. We never really talked 'bout it."

Q. "What happened that pushed you to self-harm for the first time?"

*Kristyn remains silent.*

Q. "Was it your break-up with Jamey?"

*Kristyn's palms begin to sweat. She wipes them on her jeans, to hide her nervousness.*

A. "It's complicated."

Q. "How is it complicated?"

A. "Just is."

Q. "Try and explain it to me."

A. "It was a combination of everything going on in my life at the time. I had just started high school at the time. I felt even more overwhelmed. It's like I had all this self-hate and rejection bottled up inside of me over the years, and I had finally found a way to let it out."

Q. "Where did you cut on yourself for the first time?"

*Kristyn throws a glance down at her right leg and then looks back up.*

A. "My blubbery, inner right thigh."

Q. "Any particular reason why you chose your thigh?"

A. "It's fat and nasty!"

Q. "You are not fat, Kristyn."

*'Whatever!'*

A. "Nobody would see the scar. But I knew it was there."

Q. "How did it feel keeping that secret for the first time?"

A. "Free."

# chapter twenty-nine

*Kristyn stares down at her phone, fighting the urge to cry. Today is Monday. But not just any Monday. It is the third Monday of the month — aka: 'Mocha Monday'. The traditional Monday when her and Maddison would stand in line at the coffee shop for Chocolate Mochas after school. She had stopped and purchased a Mocha Coffee before the session.*

*'Damn!'*

*She struggles to swallow a gulp of coffee she just took. The barista sprinkled on too much cinnamon.*

*'Blech! It's fucking bitter!'*

*She resumes staring down at her phone.*

Q.  "Are you reading more nasty posts about yourself?"

*She doesn't look up.*

A.  "No. I'm looking at a picture of Maddison and me being cheeky."

Q.  "Cheeky, how?"

A.  "We put whipped cream on the tip of our noses after getting our Mochas, then took the pic. We used to get Mocha's every third Monday of the month."

Q.   "May I see the picture?"

*Kristyn turns the phone around for a quick view.*

A.   "I snapped it a week before she died."

Q.   "Tell me about Maddison."

*Kristyn remains fixated on the picture.*

*'I can't. Leave it alone. Please.'*

Q.   "It is time we talk about her, Kristyn."

*Kristyn puts her cell phone down beside her with attitude.*

*'First, Jamey. Now, Maddison. I feel like I'm in the middle of a bad nightmare I can't wake myself out of.'*

A.   "She's gone. What's the point?"

Q.   "The impact her loss has had on your life is huge."

*'I have no one to share my secrets with now. No one who gets me like you did, Maddison. Why did you have to leave me, Maddison? Why? You're such a selfish bitch! And, this Mocha really tastes like shit.'*

Q.   "I do not think you realize how much her death has affected you."

*'Oh, I am very aware of it! I may come off like an idiot with the choices I make, but I'm not an actual idiot. I'm taking college courses while still in high school for fucks sake."*

*Kristyn stares out the window.*

Q. "Do you feel like Maddison abandoned you?"

*Kristyn lights up a cigarette. She takes a deep drag and exhales.*

A. "This topic is annoying me."

*'I'm also annoyed the barista screwed-up my Mocha. I mean, seriously. How hard is it to make a fucking Mocha? It's not like you don't make them all day long for other people. Maybe she did it on purpose. Hmm, I wonder if she goes to my school?*

*Kristyn gets up and walks over to the window. To an outsider, she appears to be looking at the tree. But, in truth, she is staring at her own gloomy reflection in the windowpane staring back at her.*

Q. "What happened to Maddison?"

*She takes another drag off her cigarette.*

A. "You already know."

Q. "Are you afraid to talk about it?"

*She does not respond.*

Q. "Kristyn?"

*She takes another deep drag off her cigarette and returns to the uncomfortable red chair.*

A. "Maddison died because of me."

Q. "Why do you blame yourself for Maddison's death?"

*Kristyn pulls her knees up to her chest as if seeking some form of self-reassurance. She takes another drag off her cigarette.*

A. "Maddison and I were a lot alike, yet we looked nothing alike. We were like those twins…"

*Kristyn struggles to find the right word.*

Q. "Fraternal twins."

A. "Yeah! Only Maddison was taller than me. She had shiny black hair, unlike this dark-brown stringy mess on my head. And her blue-green eyes were like a never-ending ocean. She was so beautiful inside and out."

*Kristen sighs and takes another drag.*

*Kristyn begins to feel more relaxed as her attention is now focusing on remembering positive things about her beloved best friend.*

A. "We both loved horseback riding, writing poetry and designing clothes. Sometimes Maddison's mum took us to Goodwill stores or garage sales where Maddison and I would buy the ugliest clothes and turn them into fun, creative outfits. We used to dream about being on a fashion reality TV show and opening our own clothing boutique."

Q. "So, you both had plans for the future."

A. "I thought we did."

*Kristyn takes another drag.*

A. "One thing 'bout Maddison that really bothered her, were her big boobs."

Q. "She felt more mature than the other girls in your class?"

A. "She despised all the attention her big boobs drew."

Q. "What sort of attention?"

A. "She had guys always asking her to send pictures of her boobs to their phones. You know, sexting."

Q. "Oh."

A. "I guess the girls at school were jealous of the attention she got. Too bad they didn't realize how much she hated it."

Q. "Did Maddison ever sext any of the boys?"

A. "No bloody way."

Q. "What about you?"

*Kristyn stares down at her AA cup breasts and half-smirks.*

A. "Are you seriously asking me that?"

*Kristyn licks her dried lips.*

A. "I blame myself for most of what Maddison went through in the last year of her life."

Q. "Why do you blame yourself?"

*Kristyn half-heartedly shrugs her shoulders.*

A.   "Guilt by association."

Q.   "What do you mean, *'guilt by association'*?"

A.   "Maddison wasn't bullied much, until she stuck up for me against Claire."

Q.   "How did Maddison defend you against, Claire?"

A.   "She told the queen of the *Posh Miss Perfects*, Claire, to *'fuck off'*. After that, her life was hell."

Q.   "You know, Maddison's death was not your fault."

*Kristyn slides the palm of her hand up and down on her right leg. She then takes another drag.*

Q.   "I hope you come to realize that sooner, rather than later."

*She rolls her eyes.*

Q.   "We can't live our lives based on *'would haves, could haves or should haves'*."

A.   "How 'bout *whatevers*? That works for me."

Q.   "Maddison was obviously carrying deep secrets and pain long before you two ever met."

*Kristyn says nothing. All she can do is choke down the truth with the help of a very bitter tasting Mocha Coffee.*

Q. "You only knew the things Maddison wanted you to know about her."

A: "I suppose she could say the same 'bout me. I mean if she were here. *Which*, she's not."

*Kristyn then puts out her cigarette.*

Q. "It is not your fault what happened to Maddison. Her pain started long ago. You need to understand that."

*A feeling of relief washes over Kristyn helping to remove some of the guilt she has been carrying over Maddison's suicide.*

*'I would be lying if I said right now, I did not want to cut after talking 'bout Maddison. A part of me really, really wants to cut. But I am going to do my best not to for Maddison. And maybe a little for me, too.'*

*Three hours and several cuts on the right thigh later:*

*'Dammit I fucked-up, again!'*

# chapter thirty

Q. "Have you ever told your parents about being bullied?"

*She replies sharply.*

A. "No."

Q. "Why not?"

*'Why?'*

A. "They wouldn't understand."

Q. "Do you know if Maddison ever told her parents about being bullied?"

*'How would I know for sure? Huh? I'm just now realizing, Maddison kept things from me. It makes me mad and sad at the same time. I feel like she didn't trust me or something. But then I also feel bad for feeling mad and sad 'bout it because I kept stuff from her, too. I'm such a hypocritical douche!'*

A. "She didn't."

Q. "How do you know?"

A. "Maddison comes...."

*'Sorry I'm spilling some of your secrets, Madd.'*

A. "I mean, came, from a super-strict house. Showing weakness of any kind…"

*She shakes her head side-to-side.*

A. "…unacceptable."

Q. "Did Maddison ever express to you how she felt about living in such a strict environment?"

A. "She hated it. She always felt like she could never be what her parents expected her to be."

Q. "What were their expectations of her?"

*'How should I know? I'm just guessing. I hope you know that.'*

A. "Straight A's. Work. Join every club the school offered. Get accepted early by every top college you apply to."

Q. "How do you think that type of pressure affected Maddison?"

A. "She was miserable. I failed to help her when she needed me."

Q. "How do you feel you failed Maddison?"

A. "I was more focused on trying to sort my own issues. I think we both liked to use distractions to help forget the bad stuff. I know I did."

Q. "Distractions? What do you mean?"

A. "Drinking pints until we vomited. Smoking spliff and then gorging ourselves on sweets. Taking hits of MDMA and dancing our asses off to techno at a club. And boys. Lots of mindless shagging and making out."

Q. "What attracts you to those things?"

*Kristyn giggles.*

A. "It's fun."

Q. "You find sex, drugs, alcohol and random sex with boys' fun?"

A. "Depends on what I see once their trousers drop past their knees."

*She winks.*

A. "Actually, I was remembering something."

Q. "Care to share?"

*Kristyn giggles a bit more, than regains her composure.*

A. "Maddison and I snuck into this party one time and got 'pissed off our faces' on larger."

*She sighs.*

A. "I remember standing up against the wall, sipping on flat beer from a red solo cup, watching these 'popular' drunk knob heads acting stupid. I began questioning why I longed to be 'round such losers.'"

Q. "Did you and Maddison leave the party after your realization?"

*'I wish. I was so bored. And, that flat beer tasted like panther piss. I'm fairly certain, my liver will exact some form of revenge for that night in the future.'*

A. "No, because Maddison was having a jolly time chatting up some guy."

*Kristyn's tone drops an octave.*

A. "Then…Claire happened."

Q. "The girl who bullied you in the past?"

A. "She started demanding Maddison and I leave the party. I think the guy Maddison had been talking to might have been her boyfriend or something."

*Kristyn snickers.*

A. "That dozy cow had the nerve to call us whores. Quite an ironic statement coming from Claire."

Q. "How so?"

A. "Claire shags everyone. She's notorious for it. Yet, she's worshipped by *everyone*."

*She huffs in anger.*

A. "While girls like Maddison and I are treated like slags for doing the same thing."

Q. "You should feel sorry for Claire."

*'Have you lost your fucking mind? Have you not heard one word I've said 'bout that bitch?'*

Q. "Claire is lost like you."

*She becomes terse.*

A. "Fuck, Claire! She put Maddison and I through hell."

*Kristyn crosses her arms.*

A. "Let that cow wander, forever lost in a pasture for all I care."

Q. "To heal, you must forgive, Kristyn."

*Kristyn grunts.*

*'To diet, you must stop eating chocolate cake. I don't see that happening anytime soon.'*

A. "Anyway, back to that night."

Q. "Please, continue."

A. "Claire took a swing at Maddison but missed. Maddison then slapped Claire so hard, she lost her balance and fell with her legs up in the air, putting her white laced knickers on immediate display. Everyone laughed and snapped pictures."

Q. "How did Claire respond to Maddison's attack?"

A. "I don't know because Maddison grabbed my hand and we bolted out of there."

Q. "Did Claire come after you?"

A. "And risk breaking a heel on her *Jimmy-Choo* shoe? *Um*, no."

Q. "What happened at school the following Monday, after the party?"

A. "Pictures of Claire's knickers were all over social media. Oh, and I got a big bruise on my upper arm."

Q. "From whom?"

A. "One of Claire's bitch clones punched me in the cafeteria during lunch hour."

Q. "Who hit you?"

A. "This girl, Amber. She tries so hard to be like Claire. She acts like a minion awaiting her next assignment from the queen bee herself. Amber is obsessed with Claire. It's kind of creepy and pitiful at the same time."

Q. "Why did Amber punch you? Did Claire tell her to?"

A. "Amber said I looked at her funny. I didn't. I was pissed 'bout an algebra test I had just failed. So, when Amber smarted off something to me, I did the same thing back to her. Then, she punched my arm."

Q. "Were you and Amber suspended for fighting?"

A. *"Nah,* when security came over, I lied."

Q. "Why did you lie about being assaulted?"

A. "Telling on Amber would have only made things worse for me."

*'If that's even possible.'*

Q. "What did you tell the security guard?"

A. "I told him we were rehearsing for a school project. Amber followed my lead. He believed us and left."

*She coughs.*

A. "As soon as the security guard turned his back, Amber threw me up against the wall and warned if I ever looked her way again, I was going to get it much worse."

*'I should have punched her back. I'm just not as brave as Maddison when it comes to confrontations. Pussy...party of one.'*

*Kristyn stands up and stretches her arms above her head, revealing scars across her stomach. She quickly pulls her shirt back down.*
*'I think all that talking earlier 'bout the party and drinking flat beer peaked my bladder's interest.'*

A. "Can we take a break now? I need to pee."

Q. "Of course."

# chapter thirty-one

Q. "What sort of things made Maddison happy?"

A. "I thought these sessions were 'bout me."

Q. "They are."

A. "So, why do you keep bringing up, Maddison, then?"

Q. "Maddison's influence and suicide have a lot to do with your self-harming behavior."

*'You forgot to mention Jamey, Claire, Amber, the other Posh Miss Perfects, Ian Rhodes, Seth, other nameless, faceless boys, the planet and everyone on it.'*

*She groans.*

A. "I was cutting and doing other stuff to myself before she died."

Q. "But you were also self-harming while she was alive. And she is the one you learned self-harming from."

*'I am seriously relating to the pressure a pus-filled zit feels right before it bursts.'*

A. *"Fuckin' hell. She taught me how to do one thing. That's it."*

Q. "Whenever I seem to speak a truth about your life, you become upset. Why?"

*Kristyn crosses her arms and glares.*

A. "What truth? My life is based on lies."

*She postures with indignation.*

A. "ALL LIES!"

Q. "What sort of lies? Give me an example of a lie you tell yourself."

*She ponders.*

A. "That cutting will take away my pain."

Q. "Self-harming is not a solution to your problem. Can you not see that?"

*She waxes sarcasm.*

A. "What if it is a solution to me?"

*Kristyn then lifts the right corner of her mouth and sneers.*

A. "It's my choice how I see it. Right?"

Q. "Yes. But that does not mean you are correct."

*Kristyn shakes her head.*

*'I should have known there was a catch to the choice thing. I knew it was*

*too good to be true.'*

A.  "Cutting helps me deal. It's not like I'm hurting anyone."

Q.  "Just yourself. Do you ever think about yourself?"

A.  *"Whatever. It doesn't matter. I don't matter."*

Q.  "Are you saying you do not care about hurting yourself?"

A.  "Why should I? No one else does."

Q.  "That is not true. There are people who care about you."

*Kristyn makes a repetitive circular motion with her right index finger.*

A.  *"Yeah. Yeah. Yeah."*

Q.  "Let's get back to discussing Maddison."

*'Why can't you leave her alone?'*

Q.  "How was she acting weeks before she died?"

*Kristyn crosses her right leg over her left.*

A.  "I remember she became withdrawn from everything, including me."

Q.  "How did her distant behavior make you feel?"

A.  "I don't know. I guess, hurt, alone and a little confused."

*Kristyn then lights up a cigarette.*

A.   "I never thought she'd take things as far as she did."

*Why did you push me away, M.? Why didn't you tell me what was going on inside of that beautiful fucked up head of yours?'*

A.   "Maybe if I had said something, anything…"

*She takes a drag.*

A.   "*Shit.* I don't know."

Q.   "You think if you said something, Maddison would still be here."

*Kristyn sheepishly looks up and whispers.*

A.   *"Maybe."*

Q.  "You cannot continue blaming yourself for what Maddison chose to do, Kristyn."

A.  "'*I choose to.*"

*Having to face the reality about what happened to Maddison in the upcoming sessions has Kristyn feeling more stressed than usual.*

*'The weather is complete shit tonight. Endless thunderstorms. One right after the other. No going out dancing tonight. Figures it would happen when I really need to forget 'bout Maddison for a little while. My mind can't handle the truth 'bout what she did. Nor my incredible feelings of guilt.'*

*Kristyn rummages through her panty drawer and underneath a pair of black laced thong knickers, she finds some leftover MDMA.*

*'I hate this fucking thong. It's like having a piece of string up my ass 24/7. As if I don't have enough things up my ass as it is.'*

*She tosses the panties in the rubbish bin. But not just because they are uncomfortable to wear. They were also worn the last time she shagged Jamey – the guy who has her heart wrapped around his finger and her head completely fucked up.*

*'Tosser!'*

*Kristyn plugs in her cat ear headphones, drops some MDMA and prepares to forget about her life as the Trance mix, she pulled up on her iPod begins to play the first song, 'Smoke Machine'.*

*She dances for a few hours, before finally collapsing in the bed. Too tired to dream. Too tired to think. Too tired to care about anything.*

*'Cheers!'*

# chapter thirty-two

Q. "What is on your mind today, Kristyn?"

*'As if you don't already know. Dozy cow.'*

A.   "Maddison"

Q. "Let's spend this session working on accepting what happened to Maddison and then how to start letting go of the survivor's guilt you are carrying."

A. "Oh, just like that, *huh?*"

*She snaps her fingers.*

A.   "And I'll be over it."

Q.   "That is not what I said."

A.   "*Whatever.*"

*She opens a bottle of water and chugs half of it down.*

Q.   "How did you learn about what happened to Maddison?"

*Kristyn stares down at the floor for a minute and then looks up.*

*'Will this torment ever end?'*

A. "Maddison had rung me up and wanted to come over. She had gone to Goodwill and found some 1980's skirts made of this tacky shiny silver material. She wanted to turn the skirts into a train for a dress we had been working on for Prom."

Q. "How was Maddison's mood that day?"

A. "She was smiling. I hadn't seen her happy in a long time."

*'Dammit, Kristyn. You should have known something was tits up with her right then. Why didn't you see it? Why?'*

A. "A counselor said sometimes when a person decides to end their life, it's not uncommon for them to act happy 'round their mates and family right before they do it."

Q. "Did the counselor explain to you why that type of behavior happens?"

A. "She rattled off something 'bout the person feeling relief. Like they see an end to their pain."

*She waves her hands.*

A. "Something like that."

*Kristyn tugs at her bottom lip, trying to remove a strand of hair stuck to her strawberry flavored lip gloss. She eventually gets it and then wipes her lip gloss-stained fingers on her jeans.*

Q. "What happened after Maddison arrived at your house?"

A. "We worked on the dress for a bit. There was one more piece of material left to be sewed on, but Maddison had to get home. I didn't think anything of it knowing how strict her Dad was."

*She flashes back in her mind, to that last moment with Maddison.*

A. "She hugged me really tight before she left, told me she loved me, gave me a kiss on the cheek and…"

*Kristyn takes a deep breath, lets it out and then whispers.*

A. *"She was gone."*

# Current Mood!

Fuck! Fuck! Fuck! Fuck! Fuck! Fuck! Fuck! Fuck! Fuck! Fuck!
Fuck! Fuck! Fuck! Fuck! Fuck! Fuck! Fuck! Fuck! Fuck! Fuck!
Fuck! Fuck! Fuck! Fuck! Fuck! Fuck! Fuck! Fuck! Fuck! Fuck!
Fuck! Fuck! Fuck! Fuck! Fuck! Fuck! Fuck! Fuck! Fuck! Fuck!
Fuck! Fuck! Fuck! Fuck! Fuck! Fuck! Fuck! Fuck! Fuck! Fuck!
Fuck! Fuck! Fuck! Fuck! Fuck! Fuck! Fuck! Fuck! Fuck! Fuck!
Fuck! Fuck! Fuck! Fuck! Fuck! Fuck! Fuck! Fuck! Fuck! Fuck!
Fuck! Fuck! Fuck! Fuck! Fuck! Fuck! Fuck! Fuck! Fuck! Fuck!
Fuck! Fuck! Fuck! Fuck! Fuck! Fuck! Fuck! Fuck! Fuck! Fuck!
Fuck! Fuck! Fuck! Fuck! Fuck! Fuck! Fuck! Fuck! Fuck! Fuck!
Fuck! Fuck! Fuck! Fuck! Fuck! Fuck! Fuck! Fuck! Fuck! Fuck!
Fuck! Fuck! Fuck! Fuck! Fuck! Fuck! Fuck! Fuck! Fuck! Fuck!
Fuck! Fuck! Fuck! Fuck! Fuck! Fuck! Fuck! Fuck! Fuck! Fuck!
Fuck! Fuck! Fuck! Fuck! Fuck! Fuck! Fuck! Fuck! Fuck! Fuck!
Fuck! Fuck! Fuck! Fuck! Fuck! Fuck! Fuck! Fuck! Fuck! Fuck!
Fuck! Fuck! Fuck! Fuck! Fuck! Fuck! Fuck! Fuck! Fuck! Fuck!
Fuck! Fuck! Fuck! Fuck! Fuck! Fuck! Fuck! Fuck! Fuck! Fuck!
Fuck! Fuck! Fuck! Fuck! Fuck! Fuck! Fuck! Fuck! Fuck! Fuck!
Fuck! Fuck! Fuck! Fuck! Fuck! Fuck! Fuck! Fuck! Fuck! Fuck!
Fuck! Fuck! Fuck! Fuck! Fuck! Fuck! Fuck! Fuck! Fuck! Fuck!
Fuck! Fuck! Fuck! Fuck! Fuck! Fuck! Fuck! Fuck! Fuck! Fuck!

Fuck! Fuck! Fuck! Fuck! Fuck! Fuck! Fuck! Fuck! Fuck! Fuck!
Fuck! Fuck! Fuck! Fuck! Fuck! Fuck! Fuck! Fuck! Fuck! Fuck!
Fuck! Fuck! Fuck! Fuck! Fuck! Fuck! Fuck! Fuck! Fuck! Fuck!
Fuck! Fuck! Fuck! Fuck! Fuck! Fuck! Fuck! Fuck! Fuck! Fuck!
Fuck! Fuck! Fuck! Fuck! Fuck! Fuck! Fuck! Fuck! Fuck! Fuck!
Fuck! Fuck! Fuck! Fuck! Fuck! Fuck! Fuck! Fuck! Fuck! Fuck!
Fuck! Fuck! Fuck! Fuck! Fuck! Fuck! Fuck! Fuck! Fuck! Fuck!
Fuck! Fuck! Fuck! Fuck! Fuck! Fuck! Fuck! Fuck! Fuck! Fuck!
Fuck! Fuck! Fuck! Fuck! Fuck! Fuck! Fuck! Fuck! Fuck! Fuck!
Fuck! Fuck! Fuck! Fuck! Fuck! Fuck! Fuck! Fuck! Fuck! Fuck!
Fuck! Fuck! Fuck! Fuck! Fuck! Fuck! Fuck! Fuck! Fuck! Fuck!
Fuck! Fuck! Fuck! Fuck! Fuck! Fuck! Fuck! Fuck! Fuck! Fuck!
Fuck! Fuck! Fuck! Fuck! Fuck! Fuck! Fuck! Fuck! Fuck! Fuck!
Fuck! Fuck! Fuck! Fuck! Fuck! Fuck! Fuck! Fuck! Fuck! Fuck!
Fuck! Fuck! Fuck! Fuck! Fuck! Fuck! Fuck! Fuck! Fuck! Fuck!
Fuck! Fuck! Fuck! Fuck! Fuck! Fuck! Fuck! Fuck! Fuck! Fuck!
Fuck! Fuck! Fuck! Fuck! Fuck! Fuck! Fuck! Fuck! Fuck! Fuck!
Fuck! Fuck! Fuck! Fuck! Fuck! Fuck! Fuck! Fuck! Fuck! Fuck!
Fuck! Fuck! Fuck! Fuck! Fuck! Fuck! Fuck! Fuck! Fuck! Fuck!

Fuck everything!
Fuck everyone!
Fuck life!
Go fuck yourself, Kristyn!

# chapter thirty-three

Kristyn enters the room wearing her typical scowl.

*'I already told three people to fuck off today. If you're smart, you'll watch what you say to me or be number four.'*

Q. "You seem angry."

*She holds up four fingers.*

*'Fuck off!'*

A. "I am."

*She slams her purse down and digs around inside it for a tissue to blow her nose.*

Q. "Who are you angry at?"

A. "Maddison."

Q. "Is it because we talked about her last session?"

*'Seriously?'*

A. "Ya think?"

Q. "Why are you angry at Maddison?"

A. "I miss her, but I also want to beat the crap out of her. Why did she give up? How could she do something like that to me? To her family? To herself?"

*A tear slips out of Kristyn's right eye, navigates down her sturdy cheekbone and onto her lap, where it blends into her jeans.*

Q. "I'm afraid only Maddison holds the key to the real answer because unfortunately she did not leave a note, right?"

*Kristyn releases a loud sigh.*

A. *"Right."*

*She then blows her nose.*

Q. "What happened the day you learned Maddison died?"

*Kristyn's breathing begins to speed up. She is feeling anxious having to relive that horrible day. She pulls on a few strands of hair as she talks.*

*'God help me! Please! I mean if you're not too busy giving some douche in Hollywood another mansion or something.'*

A. "It was the morning after I last saw Maddison. I was walking down the hall at school between second and third period, heading to my locker. I noticed everyone was staring at me and whispering. By the time I reached my locker, I knew Maddison was gone."

Q. "How did you know?"

A.   "My school counselor and another lady were waiting for me at my locker. They both looked sad. I mean, really sad."

*Kristyn takes a sip of water.*

Q.   "Did your counselor speak to you then?"

*'Why do I have to remember this? I don't want to. I don't like reliving this. I really wish I could get drunk right on lager, even though I hate it.'*

A.   "No one said a word. All I remember is screaming out *"No"* a bunch of times before my knees gave out and I fell to the floor sobbing uncontrollably."

*She fights back more tears.*

A.   "I couldn't breathe."

*Kristyn then begins to lightly hyperventilate.*

Q.   "Slow down your breathing, Kristyn. Exhale. Breathe in through your nose to the count of four. Hold your breath to the count of seven."

*She does as she is told.*

Q.   "Now exhale out of your nose to the count of eight."

*She exhales and her body begins to relax. Her breathing soon returns to normal.*

Q.   "Better?"

*She whispers.*

A. *"I think so."*

Q. "Are you ready to continue?"

*'Not really…but whatever.'*

A. "I remember my counselor and the other lady, who I found out was a grief counselor, pulling me up off the floor and taking me to the office."

Q. "Did they fetch the nurse?"

A. "No. One of them did ask if I wanted my parents."

Q. "Did you?"

A. "No."

Q. "Why did you not want your parents with you during such a traumatic time?"

*'Down inside I suppose I wanted my mum with me. But I just couldn't bring myself to reach out to anyone. The walls were closing in around me. I didn't know what to do. I wanted to run, but I didn't know where to go.'*

A. "I was afraid my parents would find out 'bout what I'd been up to."

Q. "You mean, your self-harming?"

A. "I'm a total selfish bitch for thinking like that, *huh?*"

Q. "Not really."

*'I feel like a jerk'*

Q. "What happened next?"

*'I wish I could just take you back in time to that day like the 'Ghost of Christmas Past', so you could see it for yourself instead of making me talk 'bout it. Again. And again. And again.'*

*She pulls lightly on her hair to avoid unleashing a tirade of profanity laced objections to the line of questioning.*

A. "I was really freaking out 'bout all of it."

Q. "That is understandable."

A. "No, you don't understand."

Q. "What don't I understand?"

A. "I was worried more 'bout me, than 'bout what happened to Maddison. I feared being found out."

*'Wow! I really am a selfish piece of shit.'*

Q. "You were in shock."

A. "*Whatever.* I finally demanded they tell me 'bout what happened to Maddison or I wouldn't answer any more of their questions."

Q. "Did they tell you how she died?"

*Kristyn breaks eye contact and whispers her reply.*

A.   *"Yeah. Her mum found her."*

*Kristyn then begins to cry uncontrollably. The session ends for the day.*

# chapter thirty-four

Q. "Have you spoken to Maddison's family since her death?"

A. "No. I can't. I'm not ready, yet."

Q. "Why not?"

A. "I'm afraid of the questions her mum might ask."

Q. "Have you spoken to your school counselor lately about Maddison?"

*Kristyn quickly shakes her head side to side and waves her right-hand side to side, too.*

A. "Not since the day I told them both to fuck off before I left school."

Q. "Why did you leave school?"

A. "I wanted to be alone. I needed to deal with what happened in my own way."

Q. "In other words, you needed to self-harm."

A. *"Cheers."*

*Kristyn rubs her left hand across her stomach.*

Q. "Does your stomach hurt?"

A. "No."

Q. "Is that where you self-harmed the day you learned Maddison died?"

*Kristyn looks down at her stomach before softly replying.*

A. *"Yeah."*

*'You don't understand the pain I was in at the time. Stop looking at me like the weak, pathetic loser I feel I am. I get enough judgmental looks at school.'*

Q. "Where did you go after you left school that day?"

A. "Home."

Q. "Why home?"

A. "My parents are never there."

Q. "Why are your parents never home?"

*She looks around the room.*

A. "They both work a lot. I think my mum has two jobs right now. I'm not sure."

Q. "Are you upset by their absence?"

A. "Sometimes. But I get it."

*'You gotta do what you gotta do sometimes. Like it or not. For instance, the time I had to shag Ian for some spliff. He was the only one holding. I didn't have any money. I didn't want to do it, but I needed to get stoned to forget. Nothing else was helping me. I tried cutting. I tried purging after eating almost an entire cake by myself. Oh, what a bad day it was. My birthday. Maddison and I always did something special together on our birthdays. It was my first birthday without her. So…'*

A. "It wouldn't have mattered if my parents were home that day or not."

Q. "Why not? It is quite common for children to seek the comfort of a parent when they are sick or hurting."

*She spitefully sneers.*

A. "I didn't want to be comforted by my mummy or daddy."

Q. "What did you want?"

A. "To be alone. I had these fucked-up emotions swirling 'round inside my head. I never felt pain like that before in my life. I just wanted it gone."

*She huffs.*

A. "Grief's the worst feeling in the world. It's like you're suddenly emptied out and all that's left is a big hole that can't be filled no matter how many tears you cry, how much you cut, how much you purge or how many boys you shag. Nothing helps. I hope I never feel pain like that again. Ever!"

Q. "Unfortunately, pain is a part of life."

*She runs her tongue across her teeth.*

*'Well, all I have to say to pain and those who cause it – 'Go fuck yourselves!'*

A.   *"Great, more good news."*

Q.   "You should not have been alone that day, Kristyn."

*'I know. I screwed-up, again. Did it wrong. Cocked it up. Made a mess. Nothing new to see here. Keep moving along.'*

A.   "I knew if I saw my parents, Maddison's death would be real. I mean, *really… real.* And I just couldn't…"

*She turns her attention to the window but is so lost in thoughts about Maddison, she fails to notice a red cardinal perched upon the windowsill.*

Q.   "Did you self-harm once you arrived at home?"

A.   "No, but my overwhelmed emotions made me puke."

Q.   "I am sorry you got sick."

A.   "After I came out of the bathroom, I saw it."

*The horrible feelings she felt that day begin encroaching on her memory like the 'Blob' did in the 1958 movie, when it surrounded the diner. No chance of escaping the inevitable.*

Q.   "What did you see when you came out of the bathroom?"

A.   "The dress Maddison and I had worked on the day before. It was hanging on the closet door where she had left it."

Q.  "How did you feel when you saw it?"

A.  "Angry. I was angry at Maddison for leaving me. And I was angry at myself, too."

Q.  "Why did you feel anger towards yourself?"

A.  "I felt like I had failed my best friend."

*'Because you did fail her. Loser!'*

Q.  "You did not fail Maddison, Kristyn."

*'Oh, yes, I fucking did.'*

A.  "I remember grabbing the dress and cussing out Maddison with each tear I made into the fabric."

*She sniffles.*

A.  "I couldn't understand why she did it. Why didn't she talk to me?"

*Kristyn blows her nose.*

A.  "Then, I realized I was destroying the last memory I had of her."

*Kristyn dabs at her eyes with a tissue.*

Q.  "Did you want to self-harm?"

*Kristyn blows her nose.*

A. "Of course. I was suffocating. I had so much stuff to let out. But I had to wait."

Q. "Why did you have to wait? You were alone in the house, right?"

A. "I was sure the school had called my parents. I knew they would be coming home soon."

Q. "What happened when your parents did come home?"

*Her defenses begin to crumble as she finally begins to open-up for the first time about losing, Maddison.*

A. "I was scared. I wasn't sure what they were going to do."

Q. "What do you mean?"

A. "They had this look in their eyes. I think they were afraid I was going to kill myself, too. I was so afraid my cutting secret would be found out if they chose to admit me to the hospital out of panic."

Q. "How did you handle the situation?"

A. "I told my parents what they wanted to hear."

Q. "What did you say?"

A. "That I was okay. I just wanted to be alone and listen to music and try to process everything."

*Kristyn stretches her lanky body, reaching her arms upward as if trying to touch the ceiling. She notices a water stain in the far corner from a prior roof leak.*

A.  "My emotions were so jumbled. I needed to feel anything other than what I was feeling at the time, you know?"

Q.  "What were you feeling?"

A.  "Anger, then nothing, then anger, again."

Q.  "Anger towards Maddison was understandable."

A.  "I wasn't angry at Maddison. I mean, I was. But I was really angry at God."

Q.  "Why were you angry at God?"

A.  "I blamed Him for taking Maddison away."

Q.  "God did not take Maddison away, Kristyn. Maddison took herself away."

A.  "Well, He didn't exactly give her a reason to stay, now did He?"

Q.  "What do you mean?"

A.  "It's like God didn't have her back. He abandoned her."

Q.  "Did you have personal knowledge of what her relationship with God was?"

*Kristyn glances out the window.*

A. "No."

Q. "Then how do you know God did not try to be there for her?"

A. "Claire and her skank friends put Maddison through hell. I've yet to see God punish them for what they did to her."

Q. "Claire and her friends will eventually reap what they sowed."

*Kristyn rolls her eyes and crosses her arms.*

A. "Yeah, right."

Q. "God will right the wrong. Trust Him to do it."

A. "Oh, so what? I'm supposed to sit here and wait for the *Almighty* to do His thing whenever He feels like it?"

Q. "It is in His timing, not yours. You need to forgive them for what they did to you and to Maddison so you can move on in a healthy direction."

*Kristyn lets out a laugh and nearly chokes on phlegm that runs from her nose down the back of her throat due to the crying. She coughs a few times.*

A. "Are you serious? Forgive those bitches after what *they've* done? To Maddison? To me?"
Q. "Yes."

A. "Should I also bake them brownies, too, while I'm at it?"

Q. "You are acting ridiculous."

A. "So are you. Forgive – *pah!* I'd rather tell them all to piss off!"

Q. "Hate is a terrible burden to carry, Kristyn. It can make you sick. You need to release the anger and forgive those who have hurt you. It is how you heal. When you do not let anger go, you only hurt yourself. It is like making a drink laced with poison, intended for your enemy, yet you are the one who ingests it. Forgive, heal and move on."

A. "But look at what they did to Maddison. To me."

Q. "Maddison chose to kill herself. You chose to get help. They chose to be cruel. Life is about choices."

A. "But Maddison never would have had that choice to make if she hadn't been bullied by those bitches."

Q. "You cannot know that for sure. Maddison kept secrets from you. You kept secrets from her. You need to consider that maybe Maddison's issues went beyond just being bullied. Remember the scars you first saw on her stomach? She was obviously dealing with issues and self-harming long before you came into her life."

*She mumbles.*

A. *"Whatever."*

Q. "You are still here for a reason, Kristyn."

*Kristyn snaps back with sarcasm.*

A. "Don't you mean, by *choice?*"

# chapter thirty-five

Q. "Are you ready to move forward with your life, Kristyn?"

A. "And deal with more disappointments? No thanks."

Q. "We talked about forgiveness the other day."

A. "So, what."

Q. "If you would like to move forward with your life, you are going to have to find a way to forgive those who have done you and Maddison wrong. You also need to find a way to forgive Maddison. And you need to find a way to forgive yourself. Forgiveness is the first step towards healing."

A. "So, I've heard."

Q. "I think it bears repeating."

A. "What the fuck do I have to forgive myself for? What'd I do?"

*'I mean, besides suck up oxygen that could have been used by someone worthy. Sorry 'bout that, cruel world.'*

Q. "You clearly have a lot of anger still locked up inside of you."

A.  "You would, too."

Q.  "Forgiveness is…"

A.  "Bollocks."

Q.  "It is a way to…"

A.  "Well, I can't see myself walking up to Claire saying, *'I forgive you'* and really mean it. I can, however, see myself wrecking her nose job with my fist."

*She then punches her left hand with her right fist.*

Q.  "You forgive with your heart. No words ever need be spoken to the person you are forgiving. If you feel the need, you can also write them a letter, expressing your feelings and then tear it up."

*'Well, I don't have a heart anymore. Thank you, Jamey. Thank you, Maddison. Oh, and fuck both of you! Selfish pricks! Because of you both, my heart's been shattered beyond repair. So, how exactly is this little plan of forgiveness going to work?'*

Q.  "Forgiving Claire, Jamey, Maddison and anyone else who hurt you is for your benefit, Kristyn, not theirs."

A.  "Not. Gonna. Happen."

# Later that night...

Kristyn snuck out of the house and into a club. Well, not really snuck. She knows the bouncer. He ignores the fact she is not legal to get in because she slips him spliff now and then.

Five minutes inside and she spied the hottie she scored some top MDMA from and shagged a while back. The same guy whose name she still can't recall. The same guy she had to shove out of her bedroom window before her mum caught them together.

The music was booming loud. Her heart immediately began beating in time with the bass. The hottie did not disappoint. After dropping some MDMA, Kristyn danced non-stop for hours.

'I felt so free on the dance floor. Like a bird. I was able to spread my wings and let go. Really let go of the pain, Jamey, Maddison. All of it. I never wanted it to stop.'

When the club lights came on, what she had been running from returned. The MDMA was wearing off. She desperately needed another kind of fix.

After leaving the club, she snuck back home and cut in the bathroom. But it felt pointless this time. She did not get the slightest feeling of euphoria or relief. In fact, she felt nothing. It was as if the monster inside was smashed on valium.

'What the fuck is happening to me? Why won't the monster leave, like before?'

She stares down at her thigh and watches a small trail of blood run down it. Still nothing. She chucks the razor blade up into the sink.

'Fuck! I look like I'm ragging."

Suddenly, a light tap is heard on her bedroom windowpane. She cracks the bathroom door and sees it's the MDMA hottie with the shaggy blonde hair. He had climbed up the trellis and onto the roof. She quickly cleans herself up and opens the window so he can climb in.
'May as well have a shag. Nothing else is helping.'

By morning, the MDMA hottie is gone. The shagging was fantastic. However, having to face herself in the mirror becomes an unpleasant task.

'You are a proper whore, indeed. And you still don't remember his name? Brilliant as usual, Kristyn! At least you are consistent with screwing up and making yourself feel worse than the day before. I'll give you that. But only, that.'

# chapter thirty-six

Q. "Did you attend Maddison's funeral?"

A. "No."

Q. "Why not?"

A. "Because if I went, she was really gone. I wasn't ready to accept it at the time."

Q. "And now?"

A. "Every day 's still a struggle for me."

*She takes a sip of water.*

A. "But I visit her grave now and leave purple daffodils."

Q. "Were purple daffodils Maddison's favorite flower?"

*She whispers.*

A. *"Yeah."*

A. "Sometimes I'll bring swatches of material I know she would have enjoyed making an outfit from."

Q. "Do you still sew?"

*'Why do I feel so guilty 'bout wanting to keep doing fashion without you, Maddison? You're the one who quit on me. I failed you, but I never quit on you. Never.'*

A. "A little."

Q. "I think that is good."

*Kristyn shrugs her shoulders and looks around the room.*

A. *"Maybe."*

Q. "Designing clothes gives you something positive to focus on."

*'Maddison was the real designer. She's the one who had the talent. I only know how to thread a needle. Yeah, because that takes talent. Not!'*

A. *"Whatever.* It's not like anything's changed since she died."

Q. "You have changed."

*'Only my knickers. Not my mind. Not my feelings. And definitely not my attitude.'*

A. *"Yeah.* I'm more depressed than before. If that's even possible."

Q. "It's understandable. Traumatic events change a person."

A. "You know, the first month after Maddison died, *everyone* sucked up to me. You should have seen it. *They* acted like *they* had lost *their* best friend."

*She becomes snarky.*

A. "What a bloody joke."

Q. "You have doubts about *their* sincerity?"

A. "*They* never gave a bleeding crap 'bout Maddison. Ever."

Q. "I am sure some must have felt sorry for what happened."

A. "Don't you mean what *they* caused to happen?"

Q. "*They* did not make Maddison kill herself. Maddison killed herself because of issues she had been dealing with long before she ever knew you or *them*."

*'You might be right. But I'm not going to lie. It feels good blaming Claire and her douche friends. I still blame myself for not being a better friend and failing to realize you were in so much pain, Maddison.'*

A. *"Whatever."*

Q. "Sometimes it takes a shocking event to make a person realize they need to change their bad behavior."

*Kristyn plants both feet firmly on the floor and leans forward to emphasize her point.*

A. "Maddison was not a sacrificial lamb sent here for wankers to perform a self-righteous ritual to learn right from wrong. She was a person. My best friend. She didn't deserve to be treated like shit."

Q. "What I said was maybe some of those people who were cruel to her actually feel bad now for how *they* treated her."

*Kristyn crosses her arms.*

A. "Too little, too late."

Q. "What about forgiveness, Kristyn? Remember?"

*Kristyn scoffs.*

A. "How can I forget 'bout it when you keep reminding me every two seconds."

# chapter thirty-seven

Q. "Have things settled down at school since Maddison passed away?"

*'I wish my emotions would piss off. I'm so tired of feeling this way.'*

A. "It's like Maddison never existed."

Q. "She still exists. She is in there."

*Kristyn glances down at her chest.*

A. "In my boobs?"

Q. "No, your heart."

*She blushes.*

A. "Oh."

*'Idiot. Party of one.'*

Q. "It is okay to move on with your life. You have nothing to feel guilty about."

*Kristyn mutters under her breath.*

A. *"For some, maybe it is. But not for me."*

Q. "It does not mean Maddison is not still a part of your life. She is, but in a new way now."

A. "What do you mean by that?"

Q. "A memory."

*'Stick your memory idea right up your...'*

A. "Well, I don't want a sodding memory. I want Maddison. Here. With. Me. Now."

*She takes a deep breath.*

A. "I don't want only the memories we shared. I want to make new ones with her. This isn't fair."

Q. "I know it's not, Kristyn."

A. *"Yeah, right."*

Q. "How are you being treated at school since her passing?"

A. "You mean her suicide?"

Q. "You feel comfortable enough to use that word?"

A. "Not really. But, it's what she did. No point in making what she did sound dainty because it's not."

*She drinks some water.*

Q. "Back to my question."

A. "I'm being treated the same at school. Like crap."

*Kristyn glances over at a black and gold Bible sitting on the edge of the table. The cover is hidden beneath a light coating of dust.*

A. "Do you believe?"

Q. "Do I believe in what?"

*Kristyn motions her head at the Bible.*

A. "The Bible?"

Q. "I'd like to think I do."

A. "That's funny."

Q. "What is funny?"

A. "Based on the dust I see; you haven't opened that Bible in a *long* time."

Q. "Do you believe in the Bible, Kristyn?"

*Kristyn shrugs her shoulders and then looks around the room. She suddenly takes notice of the silence. The cricket she once heard chirping from inside the floor vent has grown quiet.*

*'I wonder if he was able to escape this four-walled prison and he's off somewhere hopping his cares away. Or maybe he died of boredom from listening to tales 'bout my lame ass life.'*

A. "Sometimes."

Q. "Why only sometimes? What shakes your faith?"

A. "Depends on what day you ask me."

Q. "So, you are saying your faith operates like a thermometer, going up and down depending on what is happening in your life at the moment?"

A. "Isn't that what most people do?"

Q. "Did you know Jesus was bullied, too?"

*She waxes sarcasm.*

A. "Well, if the God's son was bullied, I suppose there's no hope for the rest of us minions stuck here on earth, now is there?"

Q. "Does it help knowing God's son was picked on, too?"

*Kristyn shrugs her shoulders, unsure of how to answer the question.*

Q. "What are your feelings about God?"

A. "Anger."

Q. "Why anger?"

A. "What happened with Maddison. The life He gave me. You know, I never asked to be born or created, or whatever."

Q. "You do not think you might bear some responsibility in the unhappiness you feel about your life?"

*A warmth, brought about by her subconscious, is starting to feel like a pit of hell fire being stoked beneath her butt. She fidgets in her chair.*

A.   "I fancy myself more like Saint Augustine."

Q.   "Saint Augustine is an interesting comparison. How so?"

A.   "Kind of good and bad rolled into one. You know."

Q.   "Saint Augustine is a very dangerous combination. Keeping the scales in life balanced towards good in one's life can be rather challenging in the world today."

A.   "I think it makes life not so predictable, despite my scales always tipping more on the bad side than the good."

# chapter thirty-eight

*Kristyn pinches her left side, and a look of disgust comes on her face. She is rail thin but fails to see herself that way.*

A.   "*Ugh!* Shouldn't have eaten that plate of chips. Just look at this disgusting muffin top."

*Kristyn raises up her shirt enough to reveal a flat stomach covered with scars put there over losing Maddison. She suddenly realizes her scars are exposed and quickly pulls her turquoise burnout T shirt back down.*

Q.   "You think you are fat?"

A.   "Show me a teenage girl who doesn't?"

Q.   "Do you ever use food as a form of punishment?"

*'Crap!'*

*She plays coy.*

A.   "What do you mean?"

Q.   "Do you starve yourself? Binge and purge? Or just binge?"

*Kristyn shrugs her shoulders.*

*'Oh, who are you kidding, Kristyn? You've done all three. Hell, you still do one of them. Denial is pointless. May as well come clean.'*

A. "Sometimes."

Q. "Which of the three do you do?"

*'Let's talk 'bout what you do with food, instead.'*

A. "I've done them all. But I only bird-diet now."

Q. "What do you mean by you bird-diet?"

*'I eat frickin' seeds. Geez. What do you think I mean?'*

A. "I go a day or two eating only a handful of food, like crackers or whatever's 'round the house."

Q. "That is not healthy eating."

*She whispers.*

A. *"I know."*

Q. "You need at least 2,000 calories a day."

A. "It's supposed to be punishment."

Q. "How do you see starving yourself as punishment?"

*'I don't. Well, wait. That's not entirely true. I do get some feeling of satisfaction knowing I am hurting myself and possibly getting closer to leaving this shitty spinning marble called, earth.'*

A. "Just do."

Q. "In my opinion..."

*She murmurs.*

A. *"Great."*

Q. "Starving yourself of food sounds more like a means of control than a form of punishment."

A. "Figured that one out all on our own, did you?"

*Kristyn pulls in her bottom lip and scrapes her bottom teeth across it before jutting it back out.*

*'You might be right, but I still see depriving myself of food as punishment more than control.'*

Q. "Do you get a release, like when you cut, by denying your body food?"

A. "I wish."

*'But you should know, I do enjoy making myself squirm, especially when those strong hunger pangs kick in and I'm the one who gets to decide if or when my body gets fed. Yes, I do believe I take some sort of twisted pleasure in it.'*

*She ponders.*
*'Wow! Maybe you're right. Maybe it is 'bout control. But I'm not 'bout to let on you're right.'*

Q. "It almost sounds like you are bullying yourself."

A.   "Maybe I am."

*'Maybe I think I deserve it. Maybe I do a better job at bullying myself than they ever could.'*

Q.   "You mentioned you binge and purge, too."

A.   "I used to. But not anymore."

*Kristyn grabs three small pieces of hair in the front and begins braiding them.*

Q.   "How often did you use to binge and purge?"

A.   "A few times a week. But, like I said, I stopped."

Q.   "What made you stop?"

A.   "I didn't want my teeth to fall out from acid erosion.  I read 'bout it happening to some girls."

*She shudders.*

A.   *"Gross."*

Q.   "Did you ever binge and purge because of body issues? I only ask because you commented earlier about having a muffin top."

A.   "A few times. But I did it mostly for punishment."

Q.   "May I ask what you punish yourself for?"

*She pauses.*

A. "Existing. What else."

# chapter thirty-nine

Q. "I am aware you have been abused physically and emotionally. What about sexual abuse?"

*Kristyn pulls at her eyelashes on the right eye and manages to trap one between her finger and thumb. She stares at it.*

A. "They say if you find an eyelash in your hand, you're supposed to close your eyes, make a wish, then blow and your wish comes true."

*Kristyn closes her eyes.*

*'I wish Maddison were here right now.'*

Q. "Why are you avoiding answering my question?"

A. "Because it's pointless"

Q. "Why?"

A. "Because I haven't been messed with. At least not in the way you think. I have, however, been treated like a sperm jar at a fertility clinic by blokes."

Q. "Why do you allow yourself to be treated in such a disrespectful way?"

*'I like boys. Boys like me. So, that's what you do. You have sex. Lots of sex.'*

A.  "I get confused."

Q.  "How do you mean?"

A.  "It's like I feel good in the moment with whomever I've hooked up with. But then I feel disgusted afterwards. It's like a thousand showers and a million douches can't wash the *'ick'* feeling away. I don't know why my feelings change. They just do."

*'You're such a liar, Kristyn. You know damn well why you feel the way you do after sex. It is because of that tosser ex of yours, Jamey. I mean, he wasn't exactly a fantastic shag. He rather sucked. But your love for him helped you overlook the lack of satisfaction his wee willy ever attempted to give to you. All two minutes of it. Stop being a petty bitch. It was more like five minutes. Whatever! The point is, none of the guys you shag now are him. Even though they do it better. Shh. You still love Jamey. That's the problem. Get honest with yourself. Please. You're driving me batty. Oh, and heart – piss off!'*

*A parade of past sexual encounters begins creeping out from the shadows of her subconscious and straight into her conscience.*

*'Ugh!'*

Q.  "If sex leaves you feeling unfulfilled…"

A.  *"Disgusted."*

*'How could three minutes fulfill any girl? Asking for a friend.'*

711

Q. "If sex leaves you feeling disgusted afterwards, why continue doing it?"

*'How does it go? Oh, yeah. The definition of insanity is doing the same thing over and again, expecting a different result. So, I'm apparently insane. Just add it to the list of other fuckups and such; lame, stupid, whore, etc.'*

A. "Loneliness. Boredom. Self-loathing."

Q. "Have you considered not engaging in sex until you understand why it makes you feel so bad afterwards?"

A. "Nope."

Q. "Why not?"

*'Okay. So, do I lie or finally share some truth 'bout myself? I know if I don't start sharing, I'll never get out of this room. I'm barely existing in as it is. But I'm afraid. What if the person I really am is someone I can't stand and never will? Then what do I do?'*

A. "I'm just a girl who wants to be loved and feel acceptable."

Q. "Yet, sex appears to offer you the exact opposite."

*'Who cares what it offers. I think it's better if I just shag n' go. No risk of becoming emotionally attached that way.'*

A. "Like what?"

Q. "Self-hatred. Self-rejection."

*She gets up from the chair and walks over to the window. There is nothing to see but her own pitiful reflection staring back at her in the windowpane. The squirrels are tucked away inside their nests. No running around the tree trunk on this dreary, rain-fueled day.*

Q. "Sex and love are very different from one another."

*She walks back to the dreaded red chair and sits down.*

A. "If I close my eyes right now, I can see different boys on top of me. I can remember their smell and their sounds. Their breaths coming faster, harder. I can hear the many lies they spoke over, and over again only to get into my knickers. And yet, knowing what I know, I still choose to block it out whenever a cute boy flirts me up. I hate it."

Q. "So, why do you think you continue doing it?"

*Kristyn shrugs her shoulders and takes a drink.*

Q. "A shoulder shrug is not an answer."

A. "It's the only answer I can give you."

Q. "You cannot expect someone to respect, let alone love you, while engaging in sexual behavior in the school parking lot between classes, sexting or sleeping with someone right away. Those types of relationships are certain to end before even beginning because there is no foundation to build something from. There is no respect. By continuing to engage in this type of behavior, you are setting yourself up to be hurt and used. You are only damaging yourself."

A. "I told you. I don't sext."

Q.  "My apologies."

*Kristyn drops her head into her hands and shakes her head side to side.*

A.  "Why am I like this?"

Q.  "You are in the process of finding out."

A.  "I'm not sure I want to know, now."

# chapter forty

Q.  "I would like to resume talking about your self-harming."

*She whines.*

A.  "*Ugh!* Can't we talk 'bout something else?"

Q.  "Self-harming is the main reason you are here."

A.  "But we've talked 'bout other stuff before."

Q.  "Have you noticed how it all ties together?"

*She mutters.*

A.  "*Whatever.*"

Q.  "Does participating in self-harm help give you some control over your life, Kristyn?"

A.  "Well, I get to decide how and where I cut. But not when. I have no choice over that part, and it sucks."

Q.  "What do you mean you have no choice?"

A.  "If I'm suddenly stressed over something, I have to do something right then or explode from the overwhelming bad feelings that overtake me. You know, the monster."

Q. "So, for you, self-harming is the answer to fixing the pain you feel?"

A. "No. Cutting just is."

Q. "What sort of items have you used to harm yourself with?"

*Kristyn digs into her purse and retrieves a razor blade from a small mint tin. She holds it up and half-smiles.*

A. "Obviously my first choice."

Q. "Put that away, please."

*Kristen places the razor into the box and drops it back into her purse.*

*'I wasn't going to use it. Geez. If you paid attention to anything I've said in these sessions, you'd know I don't like an audience when I cut.'*

Q. "What else have you used?"

*Kristyn stares up at the ceiling for a moment. She then begins listing off items, raising a finger into the air with each spoken object.*

*She begins by raisings her index finger.*

A. "Broken glass."
*She raises her middle finger next.*

A. "A knife."

*She raises her ring finger.*

A.	"The edge of the hard-plastic package my headphones came in."

*Her pinky finger is raised last.*

A.	"Stolen blades from the art class."

*She lowers her fingers and hand.*

A.	"Pretty much anything that slices skin. I've even used my fingernails. They don't do much damage though, unless I sharpen them into knife-like points. But even then, it's hard to make myself bleed enough to feel a true release."

Q.	"Why use self-harm to cope with your pain? There are healthier options available."

A.	"Because I deserve to feel the pain."

Q.	"You do not deserve to feel pain."

A.	"I don't have to breathe either but...."

*Kristyn takes in a deep breath and exhales.*

A.	"*Oops*...looks like I just did."

717

# Am I Drowning?
# Sure, feels like it to me.

A fish out of water

or one floating at the top

Both gasping for breath, manslaughter

wishing the pain inside of me would stop.

# chapter forty-one

*Kristyn retrieves a stick of gum from her purse, shoves it into her mouth and begins chewing on the sugary goodness at a feverish pace.*

Q. "How do you see self-harming as a way to heal from emotional pain?"

A. "Because when my flesh spreads apart, my twisted emotions spill out. They're now free."

*Kristyn blows a bubble and then pops it with her teeth.*

Q. "But what you just described is only a temporary feeling, right?"

A. "Yeah."

*She hesitates.*

A. "The fucked-up feelings, the monster inside, always returns."

Q. "Tell me about the monster."

A. "What do you want to know?"

Q. "What does the monster mean to you?"

A. "It's just my continuous fucked-up emotions that are always with me. Nothing more."

*Kristyn runs her hand through her hair.*

Q. "What about the physical pain you cause to yourself while releasing your emotional pain or the monster as you like to call it?"

A. "It's just part of the journey."

Q. "How does the journey make you feel?"

A. "Shame."

Q. "Why shame?"

*Kristyn holds up her wrists.*

A. "I can't deal with my emotions…*obviously*."

*Kristyn pops another bubble with her gum.*

A. "I'm reminded of how weak and pathetic I truly am. It pisses me off."

Q. "Why not just stop doing it?"

A. "Because the bad feelings are always there. They never go away. I never get the control no matter how much I cut."

Q. "And you would like to have control of the monster?"

*She lifts her shirt, showing her stomach, before showing her wrists again.*

A. "Wouldn't you?"

# chapter forty-two

Q. "How are your grades in school?"

*'I'd rather drive rusty nails up my fingernails than go to school. Wish mum and dad could homeschool me instead.'*

A. "Not good."

Q. "Are you failing?"

*'At life? Definitely. School? I'm barely passing right now.'*

A. "It's hard to focus since Maddison..."

Q. "That is understandable. This last year has been very difficult for you in many ways."

*'Jamey. Maddison. Jamey. Maddison. Jamey Maddison. Jamey. Bugger!'*

A. "I'm trying my best to pass because I want to graduate and leave New York."

Q. "Is there a University you would like to attend?"

*'More like, is there a University desperate enough to accept my shitty grades and matching loser disposition?'*

Q. "Do you want to go to a University, Kristyn?"

*Kristyn half-smiles.*

A. "Maddison and I were planning to major in fashion together. It's weird making plans without her now."

Q. "Life goes on whether we want it to or not."

*Kristyn drops her eyes and her voice.*

A. *"I want life to go back before Maddison died."*

*She can feel the tears starting to build-up. She is angry over this moment of weakness and quickly reprimands herself.*

*'Don't you cry now, bitch.'*

# chapter forty-three

A. "My Mum almost found out 'bout my cutting."

Q. "How did that happen?"

A. "She noticed a fresh cut on my upper arm when I was trying on a shirt at *Rack It.* She asked me what happened."

Q. "Did you tell her the truth?"

*Kristyn chuckles.*

Q. "I will assume not."

*'You're such a genius. Did you graduate top of your class or something?'*

A. "Of course, I lied."

Q. "Why not tell her the truth?"

A. "I was afraid."

Q. "What lie did you tell her?"

A. "I blamed it on Maddison's cat, Shayne."

Q. "I see."

A. "I'm not sure which felt worse though."

Q. "What?"

A. "The lie I told her or the fact that she believed me."

Q. "Wait. I am confused. How did your cat lie work? According to one of our past sessions, you said you have not spoken to Maddison's parents since her passing. So, how would you have seen Maddison's cat?"

A. "Maddison's mum 's allergic to cats. Shayne used to live in Maddison's room. After she died, her militant brother gave Shayne to me."

Q. "How do you feel having Shayne?"

A. "It helps me feel close to Maddison."

*Kristyn giggles.*

A. "I talk to Shayne sometimes. She doesn't say much back other than *'meow'*, but I think we understand one another."

Q. "What do you talk to Shayne about?"

A. "Mostly 'bout Maddison. But sometimes I chat her up 'bout catching a spider that's been hiding in my room for a month now. Hate those bloody eight-legged bugs."

Q. "I am sure having Shayne helps fill some of the loneliness you have been feeling since Maddison passed away."

A.   "It does, but I still miss her so much."

Q.   "It is going to take time to heal."

*'Blah! Blah! Blah! Time! I'm so sick of that word, time. It's like serving a prison sentence with no chance for parole.'*

Q.   "Getting back to your mom almost finding out about your self-harming behavior. How did you feel about your secret behavior almost being exposed?"

*'How in the hell do you think I felt? Seriously. And by my mum of all people.'*

A.   "Freaked out. I mean, some people drink. Some people do drugs. Some people smoke cigarettes. Some people vape. Some people graze on junk food. I do a combo of self-destructive things and then choose to lie 'bout it. I'm not proud of what I do. It's just the way it is."

Q.   "How do you plan to fix this problem you have?"

*'I don't.'*

A.   "I was kind of hoping you could tell me."

# chapter forty-four

A. "You think I'm batty because of my scars, don't you?"

Q. "Do you see yourself as batty?"

*'Deflecting my question. Nice.'*

A. "I've read online it's not normal. Those that don't cut see those of us that do cut as batty. Non-cutters treat us like we're barmy or seeking pity."

*'Pity can suck it!'*

A. "Nobody understands a cutter except another cutter."

*She sighs.*

A. "My scars are my private journal, only without words. I can look at each scar and go right back to that very moment when it was done and remember everything."

*'Let's see if this next part shocks you.'*

A. "I've reopened areas where I cut in the past."

Q. "What provokes you to reopen an old wound?"

*'Wow! You don't seem shocked. I'm actually…well, shocked by your lack of shock at what I just admitted to doing.'*

A.   "To edit."

Q.   "I do not follow."

*Kristyn snarls and stomps both feet onto the floor.*

*'Fucks sake! It's like I have to spell everything out 'bout myself so you get it. Dozy cow.'*

A.   "To release existing pain still trapped inside. Stop being so daft. It's annoying."

Q.   "I have a few more questions about Maddison."

*Kristyn rolls her eyes.*

*'The bullies won't let her rest in peace. Neither will you. Unbelievable.'*

A.   "What do you want to know 'bout her now?"

*Kristyn lights up a cigarette and tosses the lighter onto the table.*

Q.   "You stated you and Maddison never participated in self-harming together."

A.   "True"

*Kristyn takes a long drag, holds it, then exhales.*

A.   "You know, it's starting to sink in how we both kept secrets from one another."

*Kristyn takes another drag.*

Q. "Why did you choose to keep secrets from Maddison?"

*She shrugs her shoulders.*

A. "Why do I do any of the stupid shit I do?"

Q. "That is why I am asking."

A. "Because I wouldn't be me if I didn't."

*She waves smoke out of her face.*

A. "I'm really not in the mood to play the shame game."

Q. "I'm sorry. What is the shame game?"

A. "It's this thing a shrink told me."

*Kristyn drops her voice a few octaves, imitating the doctor.*

A. "He said, *'Now Kristyn, with cutting comes shame. And with shame comes secrecy, isolation, alienation, depression and self-hatred.'*"

*She then changes her voice back to normal.*

A. "My reply was one of, *'Shut up fossil. You don't know shit 'bout self-hatred despite your sodding diplomas and textbook talk. Unless you've been in my shoes, piss-off!'*"

Q. "When did you visit with this doctor?"

A. "After Maddison died. My counselor convinced my parents I needed to talk to someone, and she recommended the bloke. I think his name was Dr. Fielding. Dr. Fester. Dr. Fuckhead. *Whatever.* All I remember is his last name began with an 'F'. I saw him a few times, then told my parents I didn't want to see him anymore. It wasn't helping. So, they let me stop going."

*Kristyn releases a chuckle.*

A. "He was so bloody clueless and stuck in the 1970's. You should have seen his kitschy office decor. It was something to marvel at for sure."

*'We're talking macramé owls hanging on the walls. I'm guessing his wife made them. Or, maybe he bought them online. Who knows? Who cares? He had an old brown leather couch. I mean, so old, it cracked like dry skin in wintertime when I sat on it. The walls were wood-paneled. There were stacks of books piled up on the floor, everywhere. I never saw so many books in one room. And the place smelled of stale cigars and mothballs.*

Q. "I was going to ask if you thought the doctor was right in what he said, but you answered my question."

A. "Oh, maybe I'm telepathic. Or maybe I'm psychopathic. Haven't sorted that one out, yet. Thoughts?"

# chapter forty-five

Q. "Is there a certain time of day you prefer to self-harm?"

A. "I cut when I need to. It's that simple, unlike common core math."

*Why was common core math invented anyway? Talk 'bout going 'round a mountain when you could just climb straight over and save half the time.'*

*She mumbles.*

A. *"Hate that bloody class."*

Q. "How does your math theory work regarding cutting?"

A. "Pain plus cutting equals relief."
(pain + cutting = relief)

*'Boom!'*

Q. "How about pain plus dealing equals healing, instead?"
(pain + dealing = healing)

A. "I think I like my theory better. But, *whatever.*"

Q. "Do you have a place where you prefer to self-harm?"

A.   "I told you already."

*Kristyn twitches her mouth side to side for her own personal amusement.*

Q.   "Let me clarify."

A.   "You're in charge."

Q.   "Do you have a safe place where you prefer to self-harm?"

*She has a hint of sarcasm to her voice.*

A.   "Not an-*eee*-more."

Q.   "Do you mind telling me where it was?"

*'Yes, I mind.'*

A.   "My bedroom."

Q.   "Why do you no longer feel safe self-harming in your bedroom?"

A.   "Because t*hey* invaded it, through my laptop on social media."

*'I don't like reading bad shit written 'bout myself, especially when I'm at home. But I can't stop myself from looking. Social media, to me, is now like having a bad case of gangrene. I need to sever it so it doesn't wind up destroying the rest of me...only I can't seem to find the courage to quit it.' No sooner are those words spoken and Kristyn picks up her cell phone and begins reading more lies spread about her on social media. She becomes angered by it and glares hard at the cruel words. She feels like throwing her phone against the wall and letting it shatter into a thousand pieces.*

*But she refrains. Not for fear of losing control. Not for knowing it won't make their cruel words disappear. But because her mum warned her if she trashed one more phone, she would be paying for the next one.*

*'I'm so broke right now. Fucking wankers! I hate them so much!'*

Q. "Suppose you had to pick a new safe place."

*She remains fixated on her phone.*

*Without looking up, she fires back a curse reply.*

A. "Let's not and say I did."

Q. "Where might your new safe place be?"

*She looks up again wearing a faint expression of confusion this time.*

A. "I don't know."

*'I'm probably going to burn in hell for that lie.'*

Q. "I think you do.

*'My closet. Spill it, Kristyn. Brilliant! Looks like my conscience is now getting a conscience.'*

A. "My closet. Happy now?"

*She sneers.*

Q. "Why your closet?"

A. "Because closets keep secrets hidden in the dark where they belong."

# Later that Night...

I'm as addicted to *cutting like* a junkie is to heroin.

I want to stop, I really do.

But I can't. It's all I have now.

No more Maddison. No more Jamey - not really.

Cutting's all I know.

I never wanted to be like this.

But I am.

I'm soooooooooo fucking pathetic.

735

# chapter forty-six

Q. "Do you experience feelings of arousal when self-harming?"

*'What kind of fucked-up question is that? And here I thought I was the twisted one.'*

A. "Never."

*Kristyn takes a sip of Cherry Cola and wipes the corners of her mouth.*

A. "But I do think cutting's kind of romantic."

Q. "I'm a bit intrigued. Romantic how?"

*She snickers while taking another drink causing droplets of carbonation from the Cherry Cola to tickle the inside of her nose.*

A. "Well, I don't see the razor blade as a Prince to come and rescue this damsel in constant distress. I'm talking 'bout the touch."

Q. "The touch?"

*Kristyn smiles cunningly.*

A. "That's what I said."

Q. "Explain, please."

A. "It's 'bout feeling that cool piece of metal resting against my skin as I prepare to release the monster."

*She shivers.*

A. 'I get goosebumps just thinking 'bout the warm rush that washes over me as my blood seeps forth from the wound, carrying with it all the pain I've been holding in. It's like I'm grieving, but at the same time, experiencing the most euphoric pleasure in my life."

Q. "What happens once the euphoria disappears?"

*A sour look comes upon her face.*

A. "The pain or monster returns."

*She whispers.*

A. *"It always does. But I can't seem to stop doing it."*

*'Bugger.'*

# chapter forty-seven

A. "I crave it. You know?"

Q. "Self-harming?"

A. "Yes."

Q. "You can replace a negative behavior with a positive one, if you so choose."

A. "That's what I've been trying to do with all of this soul-bearing crap in these sessions. But it's not helping. I'm still cutting and doing other bad stuff to myself. Why am I like this?"

Q. "It takes time to develop healthier habits."

A. "Cutting is not a habit. It's a way of life. My life. I don't know if I can survive without doing it."

Q. "It will take work and patience on your part. You can overcome it, but you have to want to overcome it."

*The fear of change causes Kristyn to invoke her defensive mechanism. She snaps back rather snidely.*

A. "What if I don't *want* to overcome it."

Q. "Kristyn, just admit it."

A. "Admit what?"

Q. "The self-destructive behavior you do to yourself is no longer working for you."

*She shrugs her shoulders.*

*'I don't know what you expect me to say. I don't know what you want me to say. I don't know what to say.'*

Q. "Let me ask you something."

*'I can hardly wait.'*

A. "What?"

Q. "Do you *really* want to quit self-harming?"

A. Do I have a choice?"

Q. "You always have a choice."

*Kristyn glances out the window.*

A. "I want the pain and self-hatred to stop. I really do. But I don't know how to silence it without silencing me. Do you know what I mean?"

*'Please tell me you understand what I'm saying. Please. Because I'm not so sure I do. I only know that I want the monster to go away and never return. But how do I even try and make that happen without cutting?'*

Q.  "No."

*'Fantastic!'*

Q.  "Are you afraid of making the same choice Maddison did if
    you do not stop self-harming?"

*Kristyn remains silent.*

*Later that night….*

*'I'm such a pathetic pussy, sitting here in the dark, in the closet, cutting
because I can't handle my feelings 'bout Maddison right now. I miss her so
much. It hurts so much. There are so many things I want to tell her, to
ask her, but I know she can't hear me. I want to know why you did it
Maddison. Why did you leave me?'*

*Two more painful cuts and still no answers. Kristyn washes up, gets into
bed and cries herself to sleep while holding onto the pillow — a
representation of Maddison and if she were truthful to herself…Jamey, too.*

# chapter forty-eight

*Kristyn pulls her knees up to her chest and starts rocking back and forth. She stares straight ahead and says nothing with her lips, but everything with her eyes.*

*'I'm so fucking confused right now.'*

Q. "You need to make some major changes in your life, Kristyn. It's time to grow up."

*She becomes defensive – angry.*

A. "My life is fine. I manage. Maddison was the one who couldn't handle it. She's the one who's dead, remember?

*She points at herself for emphasis.*

A. I'm. Still. Here."

*'Unfortunately.'*

Q. "Look at your wrists, Kristyn."

*She does.*

A. "Yeah. So?"

Q. "Do you consider those fresh cuts I see as managing your life?"

*Kristyn pulls both sleeves down over her hands and then sits on them. She cannot face the truth — so she chooses to try and hide it instead.*

Q. "You sit in these sessions wondering why Maddison is no longer here, and yet, you still are? I think you fear change. I think you fear letting go and embracing a new life."

*'Shut-up! Shut-up! Shut-up!'*

Q. "I see you trying, Kristyn."

*She whispers, while staring down at the floor to avoid eye-contact.*

A. "I feel nothing."

Q. "What do you want to do about it?"

A. "Cut. Vomit. Scream. Whatever. I just want to feel anything other than the nothing I'm feeling right now."

This shit I'm dealing

with now is

ALL YOUR FAULT,

Maddison!

I hate you!

No! I take it back!

I love you!

Bitch!

# chapter forty-nine

Q. "What do you think of yourself? First impression. Go!"

A. *"Wait. What?"*

Q. "Do not think about it. Just say whatever comes into your head."

A. "O-okay."

Q. "What do you think of yourself? Go."

A. "A lonely naked mole rat."

Q. "Why a lonely naked mole rat?"

*'Because the resemblance is undeniable. Duh!'*

A. "I'm alone in the dark, hidden from the rest of the world, too ugly to look at or love."

# chapter fifty

*It is a rainy day. And rainy days mean only one thing to Kristyn. Depression. She arrives to the session soaking wet; matted hair, runny make-up and in a dreary mood. She had deliberately left her umbrella behind in her school locker.*

*'I was hoping the rain would wash the icky feelings I have 'bout myself away. Didn't work. I look and feel shittier than before. If that's even possible. Which based on how I'm feeling, apparently is.'*

*She sits down in the red chair and then shakes her hair a few times with her hands hoping it will dry quicker.*

Q.  "You seem bothered more than usual."

A.  "Why do you say that?"

Q.  "Because you came in soaked from the rain and you are wearing a look of misery upon your face."

*She wrings more rain out of her shirt.*

A.  "What the fuck have I got to smile 'bout? *Huh?*"

Q.  "What in particular has you so upset right now?"

*She says nothing.*

Q.   "Okay. Let's try this question. What are you feeling?"

A.   "Disgust."

Q.   "At whom?"

A.   "Myself."

Q.   "Why?"

A.   "I don't like learning the truth 'bout myself since doing these sessions. I'd rather know nothing, be nothing and do nothing. I've gotten pretty good at it."

*Kristyn pulls out an ink pen and begins drawing small frowning faces on the palm of her left hand.*

Q.   "Why are you drawing sad faces on your hand?"

*She doesn't look up. She merely mumbles a reply while drawing an upside-down smile.*

A.   *"I feel sad inside."*

Q.   "Why do you feel sad?"

A.   "You keep making me talk 'bout myself. I hate talking 'bout myself. I told you that the first day."

Q.   "I know you find talking about yourself uncomfortable and I am sorry. But…"

A.   "No, you're not."

Q.   "You will not always feel this way, Kristyn."

*Kristyn draws a giant sad face over the little ones and then holds up her hand. She then tosses the pen onto the table.*

A.   "I don't believe you."

# chapter fifty-one

Q. "When you self-harm..."

A. "I told you everything already."

Q. "Aside from pain release and the occasional euphoria, how else do you feel after self-harming?"

A. "How does a carrot feel after being cut?"

Q. "Be serious, please."

*'Buggering hell. What do you want from me? I've told you what you wanted to hear, mixed in with what I felt like sharing at the time you asked. And, yet, here you are, wanting more. Will any of my answers ever be enough for you? Will you ever be satisfied with anything I say? Ever?'*

A. "Sometimes I feel better. Sometimes I feel worse. Sometimes I feel pissed off. Sometimes I feel shame. Lately though, I've felt...*nothing*."

Q. "What causes you to feel anger after self-harming?"

A. "Sometimes it's the situation."

*That wretched moment with Ian Rhodes in the garage for example. It's amazing what a little MDMA and a moment of low self-esteem can make one feel weak enough to do. Blech!'*

A.  "Sometimes I get mad at myself for being so frail."

*'I want to kick myself in my stale, stank fanny when I get a moment of weakness like that. But I never muster up the nerve to do it. To be honest, I'd probably get off on the pain. Wow! That sounds so sad....and really fucked up. But it's the unfortunate truth – for once.'*

A.  "Sometimes I get mad because it didn't help at all."

*'Contrary to what most non-cutters think, being a cutter really sucks. It's hard living with something inside of you that's capable of making you feel so worthless; you harm yourself on purpose just to feel something other than the shitty, emotional way you are feeling in that moment.'*

Q.  "I am optimistic you will eventually overcome self-harming."

*'Good luck.'*

A.  "You do realize you are speaking to an obvious pessimistic, right?"

# Note to Self...

Yeah, I hate me, too.

# chapter fifty-two

Q. "Are you still seeing your school counselor on a regular basis?"

*Kristyn scratches an itch on her left shoulder.*

A. "I check in with her once a month now."

Q. "Does talking to her help?"

A. "We mostly talk 'bout my shitty grades. I don't want to discuss anything else with her."

Q. "Any particular reason why?"

A. "Anything I say she'll run tell my parents."

Q. "I see."

*'Glad you do…for once.'*

Q. "How have you been feeling lately about what happened with Maddison?"

A. "I still struggle to get out of bed some days because I can't handle the pain of missing her so much and still partly blaming myself for not being a better friend."

*She becomes pithy.*

A.  "Other days I'm really angry at her."

Q.  "You sound a bit angry now."

A.  "I am."

Q.  "Why are you angry?"

*Kristyn crosses her arms.*

A.  "Because if she hadn't decided to check out, I wouldn't be here forced to talk 'bout my own shit."

Q.  "Instead of focusing on the anger…"

A.  "Don't tell me not to be angry. I have every right to be angry at her."

Q.  "I am not negating your feelings, Kristyn. I want you to set your focus on the good that is coming out of such a tragic event."

A.  "What good? Maddison's dead and I'm being forced to talk 'bout myself. Which I hate doing."

Q.  "But you are getting the help you need. The help you want."

She becomes sarcastic.

A.  "Am I?"

Q. "Why do you seem to view getting help as something negative?"

*Kristyn suddenly drops her head and whispers.*

A. *"Because I'm still here and she's not."*

Q. "Maddison made a choice, Kristyn. You did, too."

A. "Choice? *Pah!* It doesn't feel that way."

Q. "How does it feel, then?"

A. "Like I had no choice. That's how."

# chapter fifty-three

Q. "Are you ready to talk to your parents yet about the issues you are dealing with?"

A. "What if I tell them and it makes them stop loving me or never look at me the same way again? Then what?"

Q. "How do you think your parents look at you now?"

*'I'm sure they would be super proud to know their daughter drinks, does drugs, has sex with random boys. Oh, and mutilates her body. There's something to brag 'bout at the next High School Reunion.'*

Q. "Are you afraid your parents love for you will change if they learn the truth?"

A. "I know my parents love me. I do. But I don't know if they could handle it. I know I can't and I'm the one that's doing it to myself."

# chapter fifty-four

Q. "Do you feel alienated, Kristyn?"

*Kristyn lights up a cigarette.*

*'If you were me, you'd feel alienated along with a few other things. Trust me. Oh, wait. On second thought. Don't trust me. Hell, I don't even trust me. I lie to everyone 'bout everything...including myself.'*

A. "Duh."

*She tosses the lighter onto the table.*

Q. "Who makes you feel alienated?"

A. "The entire world."

Q. "That seems a bit extreme, don't you think?"

*She takes a drag before answering.*

A. "Not really."

Q. "Have you seen the entire world, yet?"

*'Surely you must know I was being ironic with my answer.'*

A. "I can't imagine it being any better, unless you know something I don't."

Q. "If that is what you choose to think."

A. "How many times are you going bring up the choice crap?"

Q. "If you want to see making choices as a bad thing then...."

*She moves her right index finger in a circular motion devoid of excitement.*

A. *"Yeah. Yeah.* I know. My choice."

# chapter fifty-five

Q. "Who do you think you are in this world?"

A. "God's perfect little joke."

Q. "Always quick to speak the worst about yourself."

A. "Can you blame me?"

Q. "You are not here by accident. Your life has meaning, Kristyn. It has purpose. Did you ever consider that maybe God is going to help you to help others someday?"

*She wears a skeptical expression upon her face.*

A. "Why me?"

Q. "I think a better question to ask is 'why not you'?"

# chapter fifty-six

No show.
The digital recorder was left on in case Kristyn decided to make an appearance.
She never did.

# Instead she...

Kristyn chose to blow off the session and spend time hiding inside her closet and cutting after seeing a photo on social medial of Jamey and Jinger making out.

"Thank you for breaking my heart and rubbing it in, Jamey. Oh, and FUCK YOU, TOO, YOU TWATWAFFLE!"

Later that night she went to her favorite dance club. After paying off the bouncer with some spliff, she ran into her MDMA hottie.

"Toby? Tanner? Tank? Tosser? Whatever. He always gives me good shit to help erase Jamey from my memory."

Jamey was far off from her memory, as she danced wildly to the bass music pumping, until a familiar pair of hands found their way around her waist from behind. The moment she felt a pair of lips touch her neck, followed by the combined smell of sweat, alcohol and cologne, she knew it was Jamey.

"I should have punched him the dick straight away. But I didn't. My stupid heart was overcome with emotion just being in his arms again. We danced and kissed and danced some more under the flashing lights. It was exhilarating. It felt like old times - like we had never been apart. Jamey. The MDMA. All of it. Until..."

Jamey suddenly pushed Kristyn away and acted as if he did not know her when Jinger walked into the club. He immediately left a very heartbroken and confused Kristyn alone on the dance floor. Through the flashing strobe light, Kristyn saw Jamey and Jinger pressed up against the wall in a mad make-out session.

I screamed "FUCKING TOSSER!" at the top of my lungs, but Jamey didn't hear me. Nobody heard me. The music was too loud. I couldn't believe I let him headfuck me AGAIN! WHY ARE YOU SOOOOO STUPID, KRISTYN????????

A few hours and five shots of Tequila later, found Kristyn and her MDMA hottie getting hot and heavy locked inside a bathroom stall in the men's loo. Too bad she learned rough sex pressed up against a wall peppered with loose girls' phone numbers and tacky limericks, a previous emotional ride with the boy who has your heart, plus several shots of Tequila do not mix well.

"At least Ted? Tom? Ty? Tosser? whatever, didn't bail once I started my sickening 'retch-a-thon'. He stayed and held my hair back like a gentleman while I puked up tequila, along with my feelings for Jamey, for the next thirty-minutes. Nice bloke for sure. Feel like a shit though because I can't remember his name. Seems odd to ask it of him since we've shagged, I don't know how many times now."

The next morning, with a hangover from hell, Kristyn truly wished she were dead for she felt pain like no other not only in her head, but still in her heart.

"Te-killa! Never again!"

# chapter fifty-seven

*Kristyn places an index finger on each corner of her mouth and then pulls them up to form an over-exaggerated smile.*

A. "Look! I'm smiling."

Q. "Let's talk about your anxiety attacks."

*She immediately pulls her smile back into a frown.*

A. "They suck."

*'The end.'*

Q. "Is there a particular trigger that brings on your anxiety attacks?"

*She looks around the room and notices the spider plant is gone.*

*'If you keep talking 'bout my anxiety, my stupid brain is probably going to launch into an attack. You've been warned.'*

A. "Life."

Q. "What do you experience during an anxiety attack?"

A. "I don't know how to explain it."

Q. "Try."

A. "I sweat. I feel like I'm going to puke. My heart pounds so hard it hurts my chest. I wring my hands so tight; I almost break the bones in my fingers. I breathe really fast, too. It's like I want to have control, but my body and mind won't listen. So, I suffer through it until it stops. I pretty much feel helpless to stop anything or control anything happening in my life at all."

# chapter fifty-eight

A. "Yeah, so a while back my school counselor, Mrs. Duvayne started questioning me 'bout Maddison's habits."

Q. "What sort of habits did she want to know about?"

A. "Apparently, Maddison's parents gave her journal to Mrs. Duvayne. I guess they wanted answers for why she did what she did and thought I could help. Maybe they wanted to know if they were to blame somehow. I don't know."

Q. "Do you blame Maddison's parents for Maddison's death?"

A. "No."

*She rubs her sweaty palms on her jeans.*

A. "At first I blamed the bullies for what they did to her and then myself. I mean, I still do, just not as much."

Q. "So, who do you blame now?"

A. "Maddison."

Q. "Really."

A. "Yeah. I'm starting to understand Maddison was going to most likely do what she did regardless. I'm just guessing. I don't really know. I'm not a shrink. I'm just a kid, you know?"

# chapter fifty-nine

A.   "After meeting with Mrs. Duvayne, I learned Maddison not only journaled her cutting, but she also took mini-polaroids of the cuts and then taped them in the same journal. What the fuck was she thinking?"

Q.   "Did you ever journal your own self-harming behavior?"

A.   "I have journaled in the past 'bout cutting, but I never took pictures. Never!"

Q.   "Did you see the pictures of Maddison's cuts?"

A.   "Yes, after getting permission from Maddison's parent's and my parent's, too."

Q.   "How did you feel seeing the pictures of Maddison's self-harming behavior?"

A.   "Sick."

Q.   "Why?"

A.   "I felt like I was looking at myself in a mirror."

Q.   "You saw yourself in Maddison's photos?"

A.   "Yes."

Q. "Did seeing the photos help lessen your desire to self-harm?"

A. "Oddly, it made the urge to want to cut stronger."

Q. "Did you ever provide Maddison's parent's any answers to their questions, especially after seeing the pictures and reading her journal?"

A. "No."

Q. "Why not?"

*'Because after reading her journal, turns out, I didn't really know Maddison at all. It's so messed up. She was my best friend. How could that happen?'*

A. "I didn't want to betray her. I still don't."

# chapter sixty

A.  "Sometimes I get a rush from cutting and it's the best feeling in the world when it happens. But..."

Q.  "But?"

A.  "Coming down can feel even worse."

Q.  "What do you feel coming down from a self-harming high?"

A.  "Unbearable pain."

Q.  "From the wound you caused?"

A.  "That, too."

Q.  "What do you mean, that too?"

A.  "Sometimes there is lingering emotional pain I didn't realize I blocked out that suddenly appears without warning."

Q.  "What do you do when that happens?"

A.  "I cut again. I'm basically seeking more endorphins like a junkie."

Q.  "Does it work?"

A. "Not really."

Q. "So why continue doing it?"

A. "Because my head is all messed up at the time. I'm in physical pain from having to cut deeper. And I'm now feeling emotionally frustrated with the forgotten feelings I uncovered."

# chapter sixty-one

*Kristyn snidely raises her eyebrows and then takes a drag off her cigarette.*

Q. "You do realize you are only hurting yourself with risky behavior like self-harm, drink, drugs and cigarettes, right?"

*'Take your judgmental attitude and shove it.'*

*She takes another drag and blows smoke rings.*

A. "That's the point."

Q. "Have you considered seeking other ways to feel better?"

A. "I tried running once."

Q. "And?"

A. "I got a cramp on my side and felt like shit afterwards. The 'high' felt nothing like the kind I get from cutting."

Q. "Maybe you did not give running a chance. You said you only tried it once."

A. "I hate exercising."

Q. "Exercise is good for your health."

A.   "So are strawberries. But I'm allergic, so not happening."

# About Last Night....

"Stupid, Kristyn! Why are you so fucking dumb and pathetic? Huh? Why do you insist on doing stupid shit that is going to hurt you? Why did you look at Jamey's page? Why? He's happy now with Jinger. Get over it will you! Stop letting him headfuck you! Please! Idiot!!!!!!!"

"Yeah, so after bashing myself verbally for still getting upset over Jamey being with Jinger and feeling no relief, I crawled into my closet. Of course, I had to wait until my parents crashed out to avoid getting caught. So, yeah, I cut. The good news? It wasn't that deep of a cut this time. Maybe that means I'm starting to finally get over Jamey, huh? I hope so."

"What sucked though is I grew bored waiting for the teeny tiny amount of blood to seep out from the cut. So, I made the mistake of looking up. That's when I saw the dress hanging there. You know - the one Maddison and I had been working on before she hung herself in her closet. Yeah, so my mind started fucking with me. The dress became her. I saw her hanging there. Sad and alone in the dark. I freaked out and bolted out of the closet. I could barely

772

catch my breath. I had chills running up and down my arms and legs. It was surreal. I mean, really."

"Seth hit me up. All I could think was, "How did he know I needed a distraction?" I really wasn't in the mood to 'party'. But then again, I was so freaked out over Jamey and seeing Maddison, I hit him back and we hooked up."

"I met Seth at a park nearby. We dropped MDMA and played around on the slides and swings and stuff. Oh, and we did some naughty, but fun stuff, too. I always have a good time with Seth. FWB's is the way to go. That's what I tell myself in the moment. But come morning, I always feel like cheap, used up shit. And yet, the next time I need a distraction or to feel something, I do it again. I'm so fucked up!!!!!!!"

# chapter sixty-two

Q. "Is the physical pain you cause worth the emotional pain you seek to escape from?"

*'Well, duh!'*

A. "I hate that I cut, but like I've said before, I can't quit. Sometimes I'll lay in bed at night staring up at the bedroom ceiling and question myself."

Q. "What do you question about yourself?"

A. "Why do I *really* cut? I mean, aside from the reasons I've already given. How did I *really* get here? Where did I go wrong?"

Q. "The fact that you recognize this issue is a good start towards finding the answer you seek."

A. *"Cheers"*

# Goodbye Old Friend

A month has passed by since Kristyn's last session. Unfortunate circumstances caused her to crawl into a metaphoric cocoon. She simply could not handle life anymore. She also could not handle coming close to learning the answer, the truth behind her desire to self-harm. Since then, she has been unable to see any light ahead. Only a road paved in endless darkness.

Jamey 'the twatwaffle' Marotto did not fail to disappoint once again in the headfucking department. Although he's going out with Jinger, he rang Kristyn up one night out of the blue. He asked to meet her at the park where they used to spend most of their 'private time'. Jamey's the type of bloke who enjoys taking risks - cheating on tests as well as partners.

Jamey told Kristyn he wanted to discuss getting back together for real this time. He said he was not happy with Jinger. She was a bore. And shagging her was like putting his willy into the knot hole on a two by four plank.

Kristyn was so excited. She put on her sexiest top and jeans and fixed her hair. She looked stunning for a girl who had been put through a mountain of shit over the last year by the Jamey and Maddison drama. She was so excited to be getting back together with Jamey, again. It was something she had been wishing for since the day he told her to "Piss off!" without reason.

Hours ticked by as Kristyn sat alone on the swing set, in the cool breeze, making endless excuses inside her head as to why Jamey had not shown up, yet;

"His mum wouldn't let him leave so he had to wait for her to nod off."
"He was finishing up homework and lost track of time."
"One of his mates was in trouble so he had to go help them."

Eventually, the reality Jamey had headfucked her once more finally hit. A storm had blown in by this time. Kristyn walked back to her flat, head down, crying, shoes in hand, getting soaked in the pouring rain. It was hard to differentiate between her tears and raindrops. She prayed lightning would strike her. Unfortunately, God failed to answer that prayer.

By the time she reached home, Kristyn accepted it was finally over. Why Jamey kept messing with her head and her heart all this time, especially when he was the one who first ended things, she did not understand.

"Sick, fucking, twisted, bastard! I'm done stroking his ego and his pathetic wee willy! She can have him!"

The following week, Kristyn learned through a social media posting on Jamey's page that he and Jinger were super serious. More than he ever was with Kristyn. He claimed Jinger to be the 'love of his life'. After reading and re-reading the post twenty times, Kristyn flew into a self-harming frenzy. She quit attending her sessions and shut down emotionally - only leaving her room to go to school.

"Bloody tosser! He knew how much I loved him. He just used me to boost his ego. I hate having to see the two of them making-out in the hallway at school like guppies on dry-land gasping for air. But if I stay home, mum will be up my fanny like a cheap, cardboard coated, petrol station tampon, giving me nothing but grief and being a pain. I can't deal with her shit on top of Jamey's shit, on top of my own shit. So, I have to suck it up and go to prison. Sorry, I mean, school where all I do is count down the minutes until the final bell rings and I am paroled."

Day after day, Kristyn would come home and retreat to her room where she would cry, cut, binge, purge, blast dark-depressing music and sleep. Later, after her parents crashed out, she would sneak out of the house and drop MDMA, go dancing, and sometimes shag Seth or the MDMA hottie.

Morning would always find Kristyn passed out on her bed wearing the same clothes from the night before or naked if she snuck a guy home with her. A trashcan would be close by in case she had to vomit upon waking up. As always, the bright sun would arrive, stinging her eyes something awful through the window.

"Fucking ball of yellow shit", she would often shout out, before pulling the duvet up over her head.

"I mean, what idiot came up with that annoying phrase...'ball of sunshine'. Seriously? What is there to like 'bout the sun. All it means is another day of more depressing crap."

Today, she awoke feeling shitty. No surprise. Last night was rough. First, she saw Jamey and Jinger glued at the lips in the club. Then, Seth ended their FWB's because he had met someone. Kristyn didn't really care, as far as her heart. Seth was just a guy she shagged here and there. But he wasn't going to be available to use as a distraction to forget Jamey when she needed to, anymore. It sent her into a panic. That moment of weakness and despair found Kristyn hooking-up with Ian Rhodes in the backseat of his car.

"What the fuck, Kristyn?" was all she could utter after climbing out and walking home sipping on a fifth of liquor she nicked from underneath the passenger seat in Ian's car.

After getting up, taking a piss and brushing her teeth, she stopped and stared at herself in the mirror.

"I felt like I had hit rock bottom before. But seeing Jamey paw the shit out of Jinger after he talked 'bout getting back together with me, made me feel like rock bottom with ten boulders tossed on top. I mean, how could I have ever been so daft to love someone who never really loved me at all? And, Ian, again. Why?????"

She sticks her tongue out at her reflection. Her rank morning breath could wake the dead.

"Fucking worthless bitch. No wonder he doesn't want you."

She half-combs her hair and runs a line of extra-thick black eyeliner under each eye, before smearing it. The purpose? To hide the redness in her eyes from purging after coming home from the club. She throws a casual glance at the trashcan filled with empty Twinkie wrappers and a crushed-up cereal box.

"Whatever."

She exits the bathroom and wanders over to a pile of dirty clothes. After rifling through them, she decides to wear her black 'Slip Knot' burnout T shirt and a pair of baggy blue jeans.

"Jamey always said I never had much of an ass. Suppose it was because he was the ass in our relationship. If you can even call it that. A trip to see a gyno named Dr. Claw would have been less painful."

Today, for some reason, Kristyn woke-up feeling different. Maybe it was because she feared her teeth might rot and fall out if she purged one more night. Maybe she feared a blood transfusion if she cut and bled anymore. Or maybe she was just sick and tired or feeling sick and tired. She walked back into the bathroom to REALLY face herself in the mirror for the first time and get honest.

"You dozy cow. All you've been doing this past month is hurting yourself. Don't you get it? Jamey doesn't give a shit if you live or die. Maddison, either or she'd still be here. Nor do the Posh Miss Perfects - as if I give a fuck what those twats think 'bout me. But, whatever."

She takes a deep breath and exhales.

"Why are you locked away in your room, crying, binging, purging and cutting yourself to death? For what? Him? Her? Them? Snap the fuck out of it, girl! Seriously! It's not working anymore. None of it."

"Who the fuck is Jamey Marotto anyway? Nothing. A nobody. A zero. A twatwaffle who can't shag worth a damn. Who is Maddison? She was your best friend, but she's gone now. It's time to let her go. And the Posh Miss Perfects can piss off!"

Kristyn decides to make the boldest move of her life. She throws her razor blade in the trash. Yes, the same blade she always carried in her purse. The same blade that had seen her through some pretty fucked up times. The same blade that had been sitting on her sink, with blood still on it, from the night before.

The razor blade lands on top of the numerous plastic crinkled wrappers and a crushed-up cereal box.

"No more cutting. I mean it, girl. No more shagging. No more binging. No more purging. No more burning. No more starving yourself. No more hitting yourself. No more doing anything shitty to yourself."

She watches as the razor blade, her metaphoric teddy bear, helplessly sinks into the sea of empty wrappers. For a moment, she feels the urge to retrieve it. But refrains.

"Don't you even think 'bout pulling it out of the bin you stupid bitch. I mean it."

She stares down at it, still fighting the urge to save it.

"I'm going to quit you. I know I will. I just can't give you that kind of power over my life anymore. I can't give Jamey that kind of power either. He broke my heart once. Twice. Three times. Hell, a million times. I refuse to give him the chance to make it one-million and one. And I refuse to let you, my dear razor, who has always been there for me in my time of need, to be there for me anymore while I heal from Maddison, either. I can't. I have to do this on my own."

And so...Kristyn decided it was time to resume her sessions.

"I can do this. I am going to do this. I know it's the right thing for me to do."

Then, a moment of doubt creeps in.

"Right?"

She stares into the bin once more, hoping for confirmation from her old friend that she is in fact, making the right choice for once in her life. The razor blade appears to answer, as it slowly disappears from her sight, as the plastic wrappers finally give way to the weight of it.

# chapter sixty-three

Q. "How long has it been since you last cut?"

*'Come on, girl. You can do this.'*

*She answers in a meek tone.*

A. "Seven days."

*'Way to proudly own your progress, idiot! Seven days is seven days more than before.'*

Q. "That is great news, Kristyn."

*Kristyn half-smiles.*

A. "You actually believe me?"

Q. "Is there any reason I should doubt you?"

A. "I mean, it's been a month since we talked."

Q. "I know. I have been worried about you."

*She feels ashamed for her recent out-of-control behavior.*

A. "To be honest, I was worried 'bout me, too."

*She stares down at her covered wrists before looking back up.*

A.  "Are you sure you don't want me to like pull up my sleeves or lift my shirt or something and make sure I'm not lying?"

Q.  "I trust you."

*'Okay. Now I'm getting scared because I'm a notorious fuck up. How am I ever going to pull off not fucking up? How?'*

A.  "What if I become weak and cut again? Then I've failed right?"

Q.  "If you happen to self-harm again, do not consider it a failure. Failing is a part of life. Not everyone succeeds the first time they try. The important thing is to try again."

*She ponders the statement while reaching into her purse to seek comfort from her stainless-steel friend, before remembering she threw it away.*

*'I miss you, mate. Why did I toss you in the bin? I'm not sure I did the right thing by letting you go.'*

A.  "I don't know if I can do this."

*There is a sudden knock at the door. The digital audio voice recorder is turned off.*

785

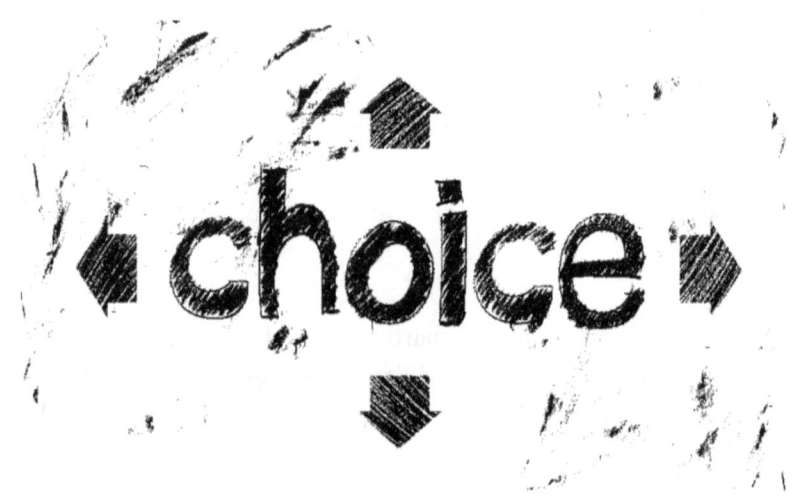

Bugger! what should I do???????
Help!!!!!!

K.  "Come in."

*Kristyn's mum enters Kristyn's bedroom and finds her daughter sitting in a faded-red antique wing armchair placed before a full-length mirror hanging on the wall. She is quick to notice several empty soda cans, a pack of cigarettes, Kristyn's purse and a digital recorder sitting on a small, medium height table next to the mirror.*

M.  "Morning, sweetheart."

*Kristyn lightly mutters a reply.*

K.  *"Hey, mum."*

M.  "Breakfast will be ready soon. I made your favorite. Blueberry pancakes."

*Her mum glances over at a digital clock resting on an end table beside Kristyn's bed.*

M.  "You need to hurry up, sweetie, and get ready for school or you'll be late."

*Kristyn's mum walks over and begins making the bed. Kristyn stands up and grabs the digital audio voice recorder off the table. She takes a deep breath. Her heart and mind are racing at equal pace as an argument begins happening inside her head.*

*'You can do this.'*
*'No, I can't.'*
*'Yes, you can.'*
*'You have to.'*
*'Don't be such a pussy.'*

*Kristyn knows she must make a choice.*

*'It is now or never, bitch!'*

*She looks at herself in the mirror in disgust. Messy hair and dark circles are not helping paint a better picture. Strong waves of emotion wash over her. She feels like throwing-up. Her gut tells her to speak-up. But should she trust it? Can she trust it?*

*'Go on then. Tell her. What are you waiting for? A red carpet to roll out?'*

*She tries to take a step forward, but then hesitates and remains frozen in place. She whispers under her breath.*

*'Chicken shit.'*

*She looks at her wretched reflection in the mirror again for reassurance only to find it staring back at her just as unsure.*

*'Fuck it. You have to do this, or you'll never get better.'*

*Kristyn's mum is busy fluffing a pillow on the bed.*

K.   "Mum?"

*Her mum looks up and immediately notices a look of sadness in her daughter's eyes.*

M.   "What's the matter, darling? Is it Jamey, again?"

K.   "No. Well, yes. I mean, no."

*She hedges before pointing at the bed.*

K. "Can you sit down? Please."

*Her mum sits down on the bed.*

*'No going back now.'*

K. "I need to tell you something, mum. It's something…"

M. "Is everything okay, sweetie?"

*Kristyn then places the digital audio voice recorder with all of her 'sessions' into her mum's hand and then rolls up the sleeves on her shirt, exposing the many cuts and scars on her wrists.*

A. *"No."*

The End

# Note from the Author

Self-harming is not an uncommon occurrence. It is not considered to be a mental illness either, but rather a negative behavior that happens when there is an inability to manage stresses in life.

Mental health illnesses often associated with self-harming are; borderline personality disorder, eating disorders, posttraumatic distress disorder, depression and anxiety. But again, self-harming itself is not a mental illness. It is a negative coping mechanism.

There are crisis centers, doctors and therapists who can help you overcome self-harming behavior. There is no shame in reaching out for help, nor is there shame in being a self-harmer.

Bad stuff happens to us sometimes. It's life. When it does, we all have a way of handling it. But sometimes those ways are not healthy for us. They are damaging; physically, mentally, and emotionally.

Being a self-harmer does not mean you are a weak person who cannot deal with life. You just need some guidance, reassurance and support while learning how to better manage issues in life.

According to Dr. Caroline Leaf, *"75% to 95% of the illnesses that plague us today are a direct result of our thought life."*

How we think and what we think greatly impact us mentally, emotionally, and physically.

We detox our bodies by fasting or eating healthier. But we often forget to detox our brain. The most vital, key element in our body. The brain controls everything in the body. Research has shown a direct connection between negative thoughts and unforgiveness with cancer, diabetes, allergies, etc.

The brain needs to be detoxed from negative thoughts.

So, how does one detox their brain? By changing your thinking. You have control over what you think. You have the power. True, random thoughts can come into your brain. When they do, you have the power of choice. To accept that negative thought or reject it.

For example; *"Nothing goes right for me."*

Do you choose to accept that thought or reject it?

Your choice.

You can change your thinking and change your life. You can overcome being a self-harmer. You've got this…when, you are ready!

# Glossary

**Barmy:**

slightly crazy, very foolish

**Batty:**

insane, crazed

**Bloke:**

guy

**Bloody:**

swear word

**Bloody Hell:**

swear word

**Bollocks:**

nonsense

**Bugger:**

when something goes wrong, jerk

**Buggering Hell:**

swear word

**Bum:**

butt

**Cheeky:**
spunky, sassy

**Cheers:**
thank you, goodbye

**Cocked it up:**
something done wrong or badly

**Crikey:**
an expression of surprise

**Daft:**
stupid, silly

**Dozy Cow:**
stupid, annoying woman

**Duvet:**
bedding cover filled with down, feathers

**Fanny:**
female genitalia

**Flat:**
apartment

**Fuck's sake:**
anger, frustration

## Fuckwit:
clueless, no wits

## FWB:
friends with benefits

## Git:
silly, senile

## Gutted:
unhappy, disappointed

## Headfuck:
someone who knows you love them and strings you
along to mess with your head

## Kick off:
start a fight, argument

## Kitschy:
bad taste (art/thing/person)

## Knickers:
panties

## Knob head:
obnoxious person

## Lager:
beer

## Loo:
toilet

## Masochist:
person who enjoys pain or humiliation

## Mate:
friend

## Mum:
mom

## Nick:
steal, take

## Petrol Station:
gas station

## Piss Off:
leave, go away

## Pissed off our faces:
drunk

## Posh:
classy, fancy, spiffy

**Proper:**
genuine, real

**Rubbish:**
trash, garbage

**Shagging:**
sexual intercourse

**Shirk:**
avoid, neglect

**Slag:**
slut

**Smarted Off:**
to show disrespect verbally

**Sodding:**
damned, fucking, used to emphasize anger or annoyance

**Sorted:**
dealt with

**Spliff:**
marijuana joint

## STFU:
shut the fuck up

## Tits up:
inoperative, broken

## Tosser:
idiot, braggard

## Trainers:
sneakers

## Twat:
obnoxious, stupid

## Twatwaffle:
idiot, dumbass

## Wanker:
jerk, dolt

## Wee Willy:
small penis

## About Normandy D. Piccolo

Hello. I am Normandy D. Piccolo. I am an award-winning author, book reviewer, advertising copywriter and freelance journalist. I have written several books, appeared on TV Talk Shows and in Mom Blogs, written radio scripts for the "Click It or Ticket" national campaign featuring Charlie Daniels and The Chicks (formally known as the Dixie Chicks). I have also written radio/TV scripts for St. Jude Children's Research Hospital. I was also nominated for a D&AD Award for my work on "Operation Lifesaver".

My song, "My Bestfriend Ted," received continuous airplay on Chicago radio. Additionally, I worked on the GodSpeaks Billboard campaign contributing campaign concepts, along with scripts for the televised cartoon, Auto-B-Good. I am a participant of the Hillsborough County Anti-Bullying Advisory Committee.

My latest book, *Bullied: Dying to Fit In* was nominated for the Advocacy / Social Justice Award for the 2019 In the Margins Book Award.

My book *Why is Kristyn A. Kutter?* made the 2021 In the Margins Book Award TOP 10 List for Fiction/Non-Fiction and the Fiction Recommendation List for 2021.

Additional information, including radio, magazine, and TV interviews, can be seen at www.normandydpiccolo.com